Corrina Lawson

above the fold

Trisha & Grayson Mysteries

ABOVE THE FOLD

CORRINA LAWSON

CITY OWL
PRESS

ABOVE THE FOLD
Trisha & Grayson Mysteries, Book 1

CITY OWL PRESS
www.cityowlpress.com

Cover Design by MiblArt. All stock photos licensed appropriately.

Edited by Tee Tate.

For information on subsidiary rights, please contact the publisher at info@cityowlpress.com.

Print Edition ISBN: 978-1-64898-387-0

Digital Edition ISBN: 978-1-64898-388-7

Printed in the United States of America

To Charlie and Kim, who I hope live on in these meager words. Would that you were still here with us.

CHAPTER ONE

TRISHA STAGGERED to her motorcycle just as hangover dizziness hit full force. She dropped to one knee on the slimy blacktop of the narrow alley, clutching the soft leather of the bike's seat for balance. A deep breath brought a whiff of urine and wet rats into her nostrils.

The rising sun peeked over the far corner of the four-story brick monstrosity that held the punk club where she'd spent the night.

Best time to see the sunrise, when I'm ready for bed.

But the beeper in her jacket pocket vibrated. Her fingers fumbled over a wad of tissues, breath mints, quarters, and subway tokens before she finally clutched the beeper.

Her editor's number stared at her from the display.

Damn. Phone. Now. Back inside.

As she turned, the sunlight caught the tank of her restored Indian Chief, making the bike's Indian head logo seem like it was mocking her.

Her sunglasses cut the morning glare enough for her to stumble past the dumpster to the back door of the club from which she'd come. She slapped her hand against the bricks for balance, inadvertently placing her palm right in the middle of the "beware" in the "Beware Out-of-Towners" message spray-painted on the wall.

She pushed past through the creaky, crooked door into the club, where the smell of smoke washed over her. The darkness, such a contrast to the dawn, nearly blinded her. Oh, right. Sunglasses off.

"Dick!' she called.

"Jesus, Red, you don't have to shout," Dick answered from his post behind the bar. "Thought you'd gone. I'm just about to clear out the refuse."

Trisha's eyes adjusted to the light, seeing several people passed out on stage. They'd be in for a rude awakening. Dick wasn't gentle, she knew by experience.

She made the universal gesture for a phone. "Need to make a call. Now." She held up her beeper.

"Aren't we important this morning." But Dick slammed the club's phone on top of the bar.

"Hell, yeah, I'm important. The paper can't run without me," she shot back, sliding onto the stool. She could ask for water, but who knew what was swimming in it. "How about a Coke?"

Dick rolled up his shirtsleeves, dug into the ice, and tossed her the can he'd found. She caught it with one hand. Jolt. Perfect.

"Nice reflexes after all that tequila," Dick said.

"Thanks." She searched her back pants pocket and dropped a five on the bar. It stuck to something. Not her problem. Let Dick peel it off.

She cursed as it took forever to dial the old rotary phone.

"Connell," she announced as someone picked up.

"Trisha, sorry for taking up your day off—"

City Desk Editor Joe Wilson sounded crisp and businesslike and not the least bit sorry. An alcohol-induced migraine, centered just above her left eye, made it hard to focus on his words.

"—but I need you to get to City Hall in the next hour, to cover a press conference about the new zoning regulations."

"*Zoning regulations*?" It sounded worse when she repeated it. "Joe, I'm a crime reporter. Why am I covering zoning regulations? Put a stringer on it."

"Cardoza wants it covered, which means a stringer won't do, and Tony's in court all day. We need someone who can write something catchy, not boring, about this."

"Hell." Cardoza, the publisher of the *New York Herald*. Joe's boss.

Trisha cradled the phone in her ear and pulled out the little notebook and pencil she kept in the inside pocket of the black leather jacket. "Exact time. Which room at City Hall. Anything else you got."

Joe rattled off the information, adding the names of the deputy mayor holding the press conference. Behind her, she heard Dick hauling the remnants of his customers to their feet.

"Got it," she said. "Anything else?"

"Be aware of any undercurrents. Word is that this is just a money grab by developer friend of the deputy mayor. The rest of the reporters will ask polite questions. You won't."

A chance to harass a deputy mayor at City Hall? The assignment was looking up. Some water and aspirin, and she'd be able to focus.

"Oh, and be presentable, Trish. Cardoza is watching this story. He'll hear if you roll up to the press conference looking like a punk."

"He wants me to wear a dress, he can buy me a damn car. He wants me to get there on time, I need to use the Indian."

"Look half-businesslike, at least. Don't show up looking like one of the Ramones."

"The Slits are the female punk band." Trisha took inventory of her clothes. The blue jeans, faded T-shirt, leather jacket, and motorcycle boots weren't even half-businesslike. Not to mention the smell from the whiskey someone had spilled on her.

Dammit, this was supposed to be her day off.

"Sure. No problem."

"Every time you say that, there's a problem. You're not home, are you?" A long pause followed, broken by one of Joe's familiar long-suffering 'what-the-hell-are-you-doing-with-your-life' sighs. "Trisha, have you even been to bed?"

"I'll sleep when I'm dead."

"You know I've got no choice on this."

That was as close as Joe would get to an apology for putting her in a tough spot, "I know," she said. "I'll be there and get what you need."

She hung up, fished a couple aspirin out of her inside pocket, brushed off the lint, and washed them down with the Jolt. She pulled out the Celtic cross she wore around her neck and kissed it, wondering how the hell she'd get presentable in an hour. She'd never make it to Midtown, then crosstown to her place in Hell's Kitchen, and back to City Hall in time for the press conference.

She chugged the rest of the Jolt and dialed another number.

"Hey! Time's up," Dick called.

"Just a sec," she called, putting her back to him. Dick might have grabbed the phone out of her hand, but the kid stumbling out the front door threw up, drawing his attention.

David, be home, she thought. She was only five blocks from David's place near the Village.

He answered. *Score.*

"Hey, I need a favor. I—"

"Hey, Trish, not in position for favors today."

He shouted in Spanish. A horn sounded. Not his apartment. The call must have been forwarded to his car phone.

"What's wrong?" she asked.

"Ah, the damned museum exhibit. It's been a pain in the ass since day one. Now there's some minor deal about the alarm and Grayson's being fussy about it, so I got dragged out of bed to check it out."

"You sure everything's okay?"

Dick slopped a mop at the mess on the floor. She figured she had sixty seconds before he cut off her call.

"It's fine. Like I said, it's probably Grayson overreacting." David shouted again at the other drivers, this time in English. "Look, Trish, what did you want, anyway?"

"I need to get a change of clothes from your place. Is the coast clear?" David's fiancée wasn't her biggest fan.

The sound of squealing tires echoed in the background. "Yep, Darlene's at her mother's place this week, studying. Take whatever you need," he said.

"Thanks. Be careful out there, okay?"

"Always am, unlike you," he said. "Wait, Trish, you're not in trouble, are you?"

"Not yet. But it's early."

"You be careful then, too. Later."

She hung up, yelled thanks to Dick, received a grumble in response, and slipped out the back door again.

This could work. If her memory served, David had a blazer she could borrow that would be suitable over one of his T-shirts. Not strictly businesslike but, hey, *Miami Vice* style jackets with T-shirts were all the rage now.

She might even have time for a shower there.

Waitaminute.

She hadn't concentrated on what David said because she'd been worried about her own problems. But he'd said his boss rousted him out of bed to answer a possible alarm at the museum. David's security firm had installed a sophisticated system to protect a high-profile art exhibit at the Museum of Historic Arts. Several anonymous threats had been made against that exhibit, which contained artwork once lost in World War II. (Presumably, the museum had bought the art from Nazis or their heirs.)

An alarm might mean a break-in and that would equal a big story, especially given the Nazi connection. A story that would beat the hell out of some press conference about mind-numbing zoning regulations, even if the developers were paying off the deputy mayor.

Political corruption equaled business as usual.

Nazis and a museum art theft on the other hand? That was a juicy story. An above-the-fold headline story.

Option one: take the sure thing, file the required story, and get in good with Cardoza.

Option Two: Disobey a direct order on a hunch that, if it fizzled, would get her fired.

Her hand hovered over the scars carved into her midsection. Following the rules had never gained her a damn thing. She jerked the gloves out of her jacket and shoved her hands into them, using her boot heel to push the kickstand up.

A bald guy dressed in skinny black jeans and the remains of a T-shirt stumbled into the alley. His eyes widened.

"Well, hey, sweetheart," he drawled. "You are a damn fine sight this morning."

Skinhead. Thrash metal dude. The club had been full of them last night, even though the band had been pure three-cord punk. But hardcore fought to replace it. Gah. Another great scene lost.

"Buzz off," she said.

He stumbled closer, aiming to cut her off. "Aw, c'mon, I saw you in there, redhead, fooling around. Give us a kiss to celebrate the morning."

With a flick of her wrist, the switchblade appeared in her hand. Another flick, and the blade opened. "Get the fuck out of my way."

"Shit." He scrambled backwards. "Jesus, bitch," he said as he vanished around the corner.

Bitch is right, she thought, as she closed the switchblade and dumped it back into a pocket.

The Indian roared to life, echoing in the alley. Trisha burned rubber as she turned and accelerated onto the street.

———

Grayson slowed down to a brisk walk as he approached the entrance to the *Lost Treasures* exhibit. The click of his wingtips echoed around him, with the shadowed, silent faces in the hanging paintings the only witnesses to his concern.

He turned the corner and blinked at the change from the dim night-lights to the overhead fluorescents illuminating the exhibit's entrance.

Museum Security Chief Conrath stood by the door, his thumbs hooked in his belt and his feet in a wide, belligerent stance.

"I told you, nothing's wrong. You should have stayed home," he said.

If nothing was wrong, why was Conrath so defensive?

"Give me a status report."

"I don't report to you."

A familiar attitude. Conrath had been mulish from the start about working with a private security firm.

"For matters concerning this exhibit, yes, you do report to me," Grayson said.

For a moment, Conrath met his gaze. Then he dropped his stance and jabbed a thumb at the exhibit entrance. "Your alarm's got a glitch. But the door is locked tight. No one's gone in or out. We're secure."

"I'll check inside for myself, thank you," Grayson said.

Conrath stepped in front of him, blocking Grayson from the door. "It's not your problem."

"Exactly what are you afraid I'll find inside?" He kept an eye on

Conrath's gun hand. This could be the man being difficult, as usual. Or it could be something far more sinister.

"Okay, fine, it's an employee problem, and I'd hoped to cover for her. I don't want to fire the girl."

"What did she do?" Grayson asked.

"Abandoned her shift," Conrath admitted. "But that's my problem."

"There's a guard *unaccounted* for?"

"I knew you'd view it that way. But she probably just took off without telling her supervisor. You know how college students are, especially girls."

None of this reassured him. "Which guard?" Grayson asked.

"Adrienne Katz."

"The criminology student?" She'd followed Grayson around, asking exactly the kinds of questions that a person who wanted a career in law enforcement should ask. "It's highly unlikely she'd leave her post voluntarily. For any reason."

"Girls are unpredictable and emotional." Conrath shrugged. "They often think what's a major crisis is only a minor one."

"You checked inside *Lost Treasures* to be sure she wasn't there?"

"I checked to make sure no one went in or out." Conrath glared. "No passcode has been used. I didn't go inside, and it wasn't worth calling the director about."

Entry required two keys plus a passcode to open the door to *Lost Treasures*. Grayson had all three, as did his partner, and his main assistant, David Velasquez. But only the director had all three on the museum side.

"With a guard missing, I should have been alerted instantly, not brought here by an alarm. We need to go inside the exhibit." Grayson suspected Conrath knew, deep down, that the problem was more than a missing guard and wanted to blame Grayson for whatever mess this turned into.

Or else Conrath was involved in something.

Grayson pulled out his keys, though he never took his eyes off Conrath. Most museum robberies were inside jobs.

There were no signs of tampering—either on the entry panel or the locks above and below the door—nor could he see any marks on the heavy metal of the door itself.

"Use your key. They need to be inserted simultaneously," Grayson said. He could do it himself, but then he wouldn't be able to watch the other man.

"Fine," Conrath snapped. "Let's get this over with and then I can get back to doing my job."

Grayson hated the idea of going inside with only Conrath as an unreliable back-up. David would be far better. Where the hell was his second?

As if on cue, David jogged into view around the corner, his sneakers squeaking as he skidded to a halt. A waist holster containing a Glock was strapped crookedly to his belt. Customary stubble decorated his chin, but the lack of a blazer pointed to hurry.

About time.

"Check your outer alarms again, Chief," Grayson said, dismissing the man. "David and I will go into the exhibit."

Conrath glared, deliberately let the key drop to the floor, and stomped off.

"What's his deal?" David pulled out his set of keys.

"The usual griping about outside contractors. At least, I hope that's all it is."

Grayson and David slid their keys in the twin locks and turned them simultaneously. The upper and lower deadbolts disengaged. Grayson punched in the passcode and drew his Beretta out of his shoulder holster, comforted by the familiar weight in his hand. "A guard is missing. The entire area must be secured. Take no chances."

"Yes, sir." David drew his Glock.

Grayson pushed open the door, gun and gaze sweeping from right to left.

On the far wall, the once pristine white paint was covered with black swastikas that resembled malevolent spiders crawling towards the ceiling. The five masterpieces by Cezanne were gone, their frames empty. A crumpled figure in a museum security uniform lay motionless on the floor below. The pieces of a crushed security radio decorated the floor near her.

"Fuck," David breathed out.

Oh, bloody hell, no. His English mother's favorite curse sounded in Grayson's mind.

He tapped David on the shoulder, silently asking for cover. David nodded, his face white. Grayson rushed to the downed guard.

His fingers sought the pulse at her throat, hoping beyond hope. But no breath, no pulse, nothing.

Grayson pushed Katz's hair away from the other side of her head. Half of her skull was smashed in. Pieces of white cranium mixed with bright red blood. A lumpy mess that must be part of her brain had leaked onto the black marble floor.

Bile rose in his throat. He swallowed, the acid burning his tongue.

"We need to secure the rest of the exhibit," he said through clenched teeth.

David glanced at the dead guard, swallowed hard, and nodded.

They moved in silence through the twists and turns of this wing of the museum, searching for anything out of order in the other six rooms. Nothing. The perpetrators were long gone, and oddly, they'd only taken five paintings.

Having secured the scene, they returned to Katz's body.

So young. Katz was only four years older than his own daughter. How had she gotten inside without keys or passcode? Who had relocked the main door? And how had the thieves gotten inside the exhibit without leaving any traces in the rest of the museum?

David holstered his weapon, knelt over the girl, murmured a blessing in Spanish, and made the signs of the cross. Grayson seconded the prayer. He'd made a mistake, somewhere… one that led to this woman's death. Her blood was quite literally on his hands.

He took a deep breath and smelled something odd and out-of-place. "Notice that?"

David sniffed. "Gasoline."

"That or something like it."

The odor originated at the base of the wall where the paintings had been.

"What does that mean?" David asked.

"I'm not sure yet. But we need to leave all this alone until the police arrive to process the crime scene."

"911?" David asked.

"No, you call 911 and it'll go out on the scanner. We'll have a media circus here." He stood. "I'm calling in Dorothy at Major Crimes. I'll use the phone at the front desk. You stay here." He closed his eyes for a second. "Watch over her."

"Of course." David glanced over at Katz and the wall full of the hateful Nazi symbols. "We need to get these assholes."

"Yes."

Not only had Grayson's security failed to protect the exhibit, it'd failed to protect an innocent young woman.

He'd get them, no matter what it took.

CHAPTER TWO

TRISHA PARKED in an alley across from the museum, hiding the Indian Chief from prying eyes. It'd be relatively safe there, especially locked up. She squinted against the sunlight and put her hand over her eyes. No activity at the museum, at least from the outside.

Maybe she'd been wrong. *Fuck.*

She could call Joe, tell him about her lead. He might agree with her but that would risk Cardoza getting pissed at Joe.

If she were wrong, she'd take the fall alone.

She strolled across the street to the museum's parking lot, her hands in her jacket pockets, pretending to be a casual pedestrian taking a shortcut. David's black Chevy Camaro IROC was parked near the end of one row in the lot, next to a gray, late model Mercedes Roadster. She put her hand on the Camaro's hood. Warm. She wasn't far behind him.

She crept to the end of the lot.

A Chevy Nova hatchback with a police sticker, parked sideways, blocked the exit. That car belonged to Lt. Dorothy Gilbert, major crimes unit.

Jackpot.

Dorothy's presence meant this was a robbery or worse. Trisha strolled around the side of the museum to the base of the massive marble steps that led up to the main entrance.

A black and white pulled up and parked in a restricted space. Two uniformed cops opened their trunk and placed orange cones on the sidewalk, blocking off the front of the steps from pedestrians. She'd get nothing from these two if she identified herself as press. Cops were trained to refer reporters to the public information office. She took off her sunglasses, straightened her hair with her fingers, ambled over to the male cop, and smiled at him.

"Excuse me, sir, is something wrong in the museum?"

The cop stiffened, set down his orange cone, and cleared his throat. "I'm not at liberty to say, ma'am."

Gah. He'd called her 'ma'am.' Better than being told to buzz off, however.

"But I have plans to take my daughter later." Trisha said. "She loves Cezanne and the Impressionists. I *promised* her."

The officer shook his head. "No can do, the museum's closed for the time being."

Trisha sighed dramatically. "Crap. My daughter's going to be *so* disappointed. Are you sure it won't be open later?"

"Not likely." His stance was easy and his attitude dismissive. He'd taken her at face value. But she looked like a punk, especially with her Dread at the Controls T-shirt, not like a mom wanting to take a kid to a museum outing.

Then again, this was New York.

"Hey, Lewis, get moving and finish the cones." The second cop, a woman, yelled over at him.

"Gotta go," the rookie mumbled, dropping his head.

"Can you at least tell me why I have to disappoint my daughter?" Trisha asked.

"We got a break-in," he whispered. "By *Nazis*."

"Oh." Trisha widened her eyes. "That's awful," she whispered back.

"Lewis!" The second cop yelled. "Leave the cute redheaded punk alone and get back to work."

"Coming." The rookie went back to blocking off the street. "You have to clear the area, ma'am."

"I will, thanks." She turned and walked away, around the side of the museum again, out of their sight, and pumped her fist.

A break in involving *Nazis?*

Better than she could have imagined. She needed to ditch these cops and get inside, fast, before anyone else heard about the story. Kimba from the *Tribune* especially would pick up cop chatter on the scanner any minute now.

Trisha glanced at the front steps that loomed above the street. Shortest distance between two points was a straight line but she would be in full view of the cops for a minute. Years ago, Trisha had broken into the museum via an abandoned subway tunnel that ran under it. But that had to be at least fifteen years ago, before recent renovations. Odds were long against the tunnel entrance being usable now. And trying it would take her away from the crime scene.

The rookie stood halfway down the street, playing with his cones. His partner was talking on her car radio.

Trisha leapt up the steps, expecting the order to halt at any moment.

She reached the top, ducked behind the marble pillar farthest from the entrance, and sucked in air to slow her thudding heart. She should have slept more last night. She should have had breakfast. Hell, she probably should have gone to that press conference at City Hall.

She crept around the pillar, for a view of the glass doors at the front of the museum. Visible video cameras were clustered over the entrance, but none covered the rest of the exterior. She dared a glance down the steps. Beyond the cones, a curious crowd had started to gather.

Crap. Word of the police presence would spread and there went her exclusive and her job. Hell, Kimba had beaten her out on that triple homicide on the Staten Island ferry just last week.

Trisha sprinted over to the next pillar and closer to that enticing entrance.

One down, three more pillars to go.

Her hand ached for the feel of a cigarette. But, no, she was quitting again, though she'd gotten plenty of second-hand smoke from the club last night. She fingered the gold lighter in her pants pocket to keep her hand occupied. Nicky's lighter. She'd kept it as a remembrance. A widow at twenty-five. No one would believe *that* if she told them. It almost made him seem unreal, as if she'd made him up. But he'd been with her the last time she'd broken into the museum. Seemed right that she took something of his inside today.

She darted to the next pillar. Two to go. She glanced below. The cops were looking in her direction. Trisha scrambled around to the back of the pillar.

Stuck.

Dammit, now what?

———

Grayson stuffed his hands into his pockets, fighting the urge to take over the investigation instead of being relegated to the sidelines. So far, despite their long friendship, Lt. Dorothy Gilbert had ignored him, preferring to examine the crime scene herself and make her own judgments. Yes, she had a crime scene to secure. Yes, he was a civilian now and needed to stay out of the way. Yes, she was following proper procedure. Yes, she always did that.

He'd never felt so useless.

If he were still an FBI special agent in charge, there would be none of this garbage about civilian protocol and all this bloody stupid *waiting*. He re-adjusted his tie. He smoothed back his close-cut hair. He double-checked his cufflinks. All that took ten seconds.

He walked back to the *Lost Treasures* entrance. A crime scene tech glared at him. Grayson glared back, almost a snarl. The tech went back to processing the blood splatters.

To unlock the "why" of this, Grayson first needed the "how."

He could only envision two scenarios. One: The thieves had fooled the exterior security cameras and entered through the exhibit door (duplicate keys? Stolen passcode?). Katz spotted them and tried to intervene but died in the attempt.

Or, two: Katz had been in on it, let the thieves in, covered for them, and then been betrayed by her co-conspirators. He hated the idea, but it had to be considered. Either way, if Katz had been killed inside the exhibit, how had her killer or killers escaped with the paintings?

They would have had to relock the door if they'd gone out that way but there was no evidence of that. Two other guards were stationed at each exit, with a third at the central security office to watch all exit cameras. They'd seen nothing.

None of it made sense.

Unless Conrath was the inside man. He had a key and could have duplicated the second one, he had the alarm code, and he had the access to the security cameras.

"Edmund?" a familiar voice said.

"What?" he growled.

"I brought you some coffee."

His turned toward his ex-wife, who had proffered coffee. Amanda was the assistant to the museum director, and he'd taken the job at her request. The museum had been low on funds for security, she'd said. His firm could do a good job on a shoestring budget, she'd said. He owed her a favor, she'd said.

It had not been his firm's typical job, but he'd wanted to keep the relationship with Amanda cordial for their daughter's sake. Now he'd failed, spectacularly.

He rolled his shoulders, expecting a barrage of anger at his incompetence. But Amanda stared past him to the crime scene, where police were loading Katz into a body bag. Amanda put her hand over her mouth.

His annoyance melted. He took the coffee and shepherded her away from the sight. "Let's get you back from here."

He put a hand on her shoulders. She was trembling. Though she was dressed, as usual, in one of her tailored pastel suits with the shoulder pads that were all the rage, she wore no make-up, and her eyes were red from crying.

He stopped in the outer corridor, away from the exhibit's entrance and the bloody remains. "Better?" he squeezed her hand in support.

"Yes, I should have never looked." Amanda blinked away unshed tears. "She was a very nice kid."

"I know." He released her hand, not knowing how she'd take further comfort from him. But whatever she wanted to say was interrupted by the arrival of her boss, the museum director, Max Windergaard

"You're fired, Grayson," Windergaard poked a finger in his chest.

Grayson swept the finger aside.

For once, Windergaard lacked his aura of WASP imperturbability. The buttons of his shirt were mismatched, his tie was askew, and stubble decorated his narrow face, not for effect, as with David, but out of neglect. The director resembled nothing so much as a scarecrow missing some straw.

"Calm down, Max. We don't know what happened, yet," Amanda said.

"We know exactly what happened," Windergaard said. "He guaranteed his security system, and it failed."

"No security system is foolproof. Even I know that," Amanda said.

Despite her words of support, Grayson knew that disappointed tone in her voice all too well. She was right. He *had* failed Katz. But so had others.

"The murderers needed inside help to do this," Grayson said. "Most likely that help came from one of your own people, Windergaard."

"How do you know it wasn't one of *yours*?"

"I'll be the judge of who's to blame," Dorothy said as she joined them.

Windergaard stepped back. "Excuse me?"

"Lt. Dorothy Gilbert, director." She nodded to him. "Sir, Amanda, if you could please wait with the rest of your staff in the employee offices. I need to talk with Mr. Grayson alone."

"You're going to waste time talking to him instead of searching for my missing Cézannes?" Windergaard asked. "Are you sure you can handle a crime of this magnitude? Perhaps one of your male superiors should be involved?"

An insult to Dorothy as a woman or as an African-American or both. Grayson tensed but held his tongue. Dorothy liked to handle things on her own.

"I'm investigating a murder, Director Windergaard, and every moment you delay me is wasting *my* time," Dorothy said.

Windergaard threw up his hands and stalked away.

"I'm sorry, Dorothy," Amanda said. "I'll see what I can do to calm him down."

Amanda followed in her boss's wake.

Grayson watched her go. He'd disappointed her during the marriage, and he'd failed her now.

"What did you find, Lieutenant?" Grayson asked Dorothy, keeping it professional.

"It's early."

"I need to be more involved," he said.

She shook her head. "Walk with me, English."

She used the college nickname to soothe him, a nickname given because the English accent he'd inherited from his mother still colored his speech sometimes. Grayson clamped down on his frustration as they walked back to the crime scene. Dorothy was one of the best cops he'd ever met. She had to be, to work around the department's ingrained racist, sexist bullshit. And it wasn't confined to the department. There were many of those, like Windergaard, who couldn't see past their damned prejudice.

But, despite Dorothy's competence and his confidence in her, Grayson would rather be the one in charge. Of everything, Amanda would have said. Dorothy might have even agreed.

She clicked the pen she held in her hand, over and over. Like Amanda, she wore a pantsuit, but hers was a severe gray without any of the fashionable shoulder pads. Aside from crow's feet around her eyes and the smile lines barely visible under her dark skin, she still resembled the intense, intelligent girl he'd first met as a sophomore.

Dorothy pulled out her notebook and looked through the open doorway to the swastikas. Paint had dribbled all the way down to the marble floor. She grimaced.

"Give me a quick background," she asked.

"The artwork in this exhibit, thought lost in World War II, is from a private and anonymous collection located last year. The current ownership is in dispute from the heirs of Holocaust victims, though lack of official records is a problem for them. The five Cezannes missing are all of Mount-Sainte-Victoire, from the artist's later period, worth millions, if the current auction prices are any judge."

"The Jewish heirs must be angry that art stolen by the Nazis is here and not in their possession." Dorothy raised an eyebrow, a silent question.

"They are. We've had threats of protests from several Jewish organizations."

"But swastikas don't seem their style," Dorothy said.

"The Jewish organizations wanted publicity and a higher profile for their point of view, not violence. But it's possible the swastikas could be misdirection."

"Possible but not likely," she said. "This feels like a statement. A hateful one."

"Agreed."

"There were double locks on the exhibit entrance and cameras at the exits, but no guards stationed at the entrance to or inside the exhibit. You're always meticulous, Edmund. Why not take that precaution?"

The kid gloves hurt worse than if she'd accused him of incompetence. "I wanted additional guards, but the museum had no funds for them. It's already in the red from extensive renovations finished last year and, as it is, Gray Associates charged them half of what it would cost normally."

"As a favor to Amanda?" she asked.

He nodded.

"How extensive were those renovations? Any chance someone used them to put a hidden backdoor in this place?" Dorothy asked.

"I've rolled that idea around my brain all morning." Grayson rubbed the back of his neck, feeling the sweat that had collected in the collar of his shirt. "The renovations left intact oversize air ducts between a storage closet in this exhibit to another storage closet in the west wing, but it's just a dead end from one side to the other. No exterior access. I checked that when we set up the security system."

"Well, that would have been too easy," Dorothy said. The police radio strapped to her waist crackled. News of the crime scene techs arrival. She gave permission to send them through.

"Who has the keys to this door?"

"My partner, Tony, who designed the locks, and I have full sets, as well as the passcode. So does the museum director, who you've just met. David's set only includes the locks specific to our firm. In the museum, Chief Conrath has the museum key and the passcode, but not the second key."

Dorothy raised an eyebrow. "You and Tony are the only people with keys to the museum and the exhibit in your firm and only *one* person at the museum can get into the exhibit once it's locked?"

"Unless there are duplicate keys, and someone stole the passcode."

She nodded. "Unless that. Such as Katz." Dorothy narrowed her eyes. "What do you know about her?"

"A college student, studying criminology, with a large family that she'd been adopted into, a happy one for how she talked about it," Grayson said. "She asked a lot of questions but then, she planned to apply to the police academy once she graduated college." A pause. "I liked her. She struck me as someone with integrity."

"You're a good judge of people, English," Dorothy said.

"Usually." And yet someone died on his watch.

"Yeah." Dorothy closed her notebook. "Okay, you and David wait in the front office. I assume Tony is on his way?"

"Yes, but—"

"I need the whereabouts of yourself, David, and Tony last night, since you all had access to this exhibit. Standard procedure."

"Of course, but, hold on, Dorothy. I want in on the investigation."

"You're *part* of the investigation, so that's not possible." She crossed her arms over her chest.

Anger rose again. "You remember that federal drug trafficking case you barged into? You had no authority there. But as Special Agent in Charge, I broke procedure because I knew you could help. Solving that case helped you gain your promotion."

"Edmund." She lowered her voice, angry now. "Leave off. I won't play outside the lines. And neither will you, unless you want to be accused."

"I don't give a damn about my reputation. A girl is dead, and it's my fault. I can't sit by."

"That's exactly what you'll do. Have you forgotten everything you've ever known about detective work?"

A final decision. The right decision. He knew it. He hated it. He jammed his hands tight in his pockets, his body practically vibrating with rage.

"Go soak your head and we'll talk again as soon as I have anything," she said.

He nodded, rather than say anything he would later regret, and stalked off toward Amanda's office. Damn procedure.

He'd throw away the rule book in an instant if it would mean catching Katz's murderer.

CHAPTER THREE

TRISHA NEARLY BASHED her head into the pillar in frustration. She had nada. *The Herald* couldn't publish a story based on an off-hand comment by a rookie cop.

Might be time to try the forgotten tunnels, if she could get to the street unseen. She rubbed her thumb against Nicky's gold lighter again. If he were still alive and here with her, he'd be urging her on, as he always had. He'd gotten almost as much a charge hearing about her work as she did. She missed so much about Nicky but when he'd lit up about hearing her nail a story, it'd been special.

People milled about just inside the glass doors. They wore uniforms, but their hats proclaimed them museum security rather than cops. She crept closer. One of them might let slip something about the theft, and that might be enough for confirmation.

Two men walked out the front door, heading in her direction. All she could see clearly at first was their hair—one dark, one slightly gray—and at least one of them wore a double-breasted suit. She tensed. Nowhere to hide. If they walked this way, they'd see her. Maybe she should flip the tables and confront them first.

The footsteps stopped. She strained to catch their words.

"There's *nothing* we can do to solve the murder?"

David. *Excellent*. One reliable source found.

And he'd said "murder."

"Nothing to do but wait." The low, deep voice of the second man sounded seriously pissed. "We," David had said. That meant the second man belonged to David's security firm.

Keep talking, guys.

"Are *we* all suspects?" David asked.

"We have to be considered such, especially with a murder investigation."

She winced. Someone's family would open the door to a grim-faced police officer today. She placed a hand over her Celtic cross necklace and shivered. *No one deserved that knock on the door.*

"Maybe we should search the museum on our own. Dorothy doesn't have enough men to secure the whole place," David said.

The second man grunted. "If we had a good lead, I'd agree. Better to ask forgiveness than permission. But we'd need a place to start."

Her cue.

"I know where to start."

David and the stranger rounded on her.

"Dammit, Trish!" David's voice echoed around the stone columns. "What the fuck are you doing here?"

"My job, same as you."

"We don't need you screwing around with this, not with—"

The second man stepped forward and cut David off. From his voice, she'd pictured him as an older, retired cop but this guy was dressed like an upscale Wall Street trader. Still, classic rugged face and a nice head of hair, though peppered with gray.

His tailored gray double-breasted suit showed off some seriously impressive shoulders. His white shirt was pristine, and he was wearing *cufflinks*, for God's sake. Who the hell used those anymore? His wingtip shoes gleamed.

He'd *sounded* angry and frustrated. But he *looked* calm and collected.

"David. Fill me in. Now," Wingtips said.

David unclenched his hands. "You are so dead, Trish." He sighed. "Edmund Grayson, this is my friend, Trisha Connell. She's the crime reporter for the *New York Herald*. I've mentioned her before, remember?" He shook his head. "Trish, Edmund Grayson."

Grayson? David's boss? This was him? At least her sunglasses hid her shock. Given how David talked about him, she'd imagined Grayson as an uptight, humorless guy. Not some dignified, dynamic, and dangerous man in a suit.

"You brought a *reporter* here?" Grayson said.

"I had nothing to do with it," David muttered.

"Hi." She put out her hand to Grayson.

He ignored the gesture. "You have two seconds to explain what you meant about where to start the search."

Oho. Yep, once a cop, always a cop, even if he had gone private.

She took off her sunglasses and stared at him, holding the eye contact. Nice brown eyes. "I know how someone could break into the museum."

"How?" Grayson crossed his arms over his chest.

"Whatever you've got, spit it out, Trish," David said.

"Get me into the museum and I'll show you."

Grayson glared at her, impassive. "I could always call over the police have you arrested for trespassing."

She shrugged. "You could but then you wouldn't know where the entrance to the hidden subway tunnel is."

Grayson snapped to attention and stepped closer to her, giving her a chance to study his face. His chiseled features would be attractive if his jaw wasn't clenched shut.

Okay, he was attractive despite that.

"Where?"

An order, not a request. "I'll show you," she repeated. "Inside."

He shook his head. "You want to go inside, give me more."

Aha. He'd taken the bait. Now they were just negotiating. "I've done stories on the homeless people who live in the subway tunnels. I learned about the entrance from them." Okay, she'd lied on that one. But the truth of the sneaking in with Nicky wouldn't add to her credibility and neither would the confession that she'd been homeless at the time herself.

Grayson turned to David. "Can we trust her?"

David nodded. "Yeah, she's a pain in the ass while working but she wouldn't lie about something this important."

Grayson grunted. "We did a thorough security check of the museum last month and found no evidence of a hidden entrance."

She forced her hands to stop twitching for a cigarette. "The entrance is covered over by ordinary floor tiles. You'd never spot it if you didn't already know it was there."

"Are you sure?" Grayson said, with no expression at all. A good poker face. She wondered what it would take to make him smile.

"Positive." *Sorta.* It had been a long time.

He let her word hang in the air, appraising her, as if checking off points on a tally sheet in his head. "If you tell me where this tunnel entrance is, I'll come back out and give you the full story of what happened. On the record."

Tempting. But no guarantee Kimba wouldn't scoop her while she waited for Grayson. "I go inside or nothing. And while we negotiate, your murderer has more time to escape."

Grayson stared at her some more, his glare resembling a wolf sizing up his prey. She resisted the urge to growl at him just to see what he'd do.

He glanced back over his shoulder at the main entrance. "The police aren't going to let the three of us past them."

Gotcha! "I bet you know another way to get in."

His lips twitched, as if fighting a smile. "Maybe."

"Easier to apologize than ask permission," she repeated.

Surprisingly, he smiled. "All right. Follow me around this side."

Yes.

Grayson led her and David around the side of the museum. The marble steps tapered off, leaving them standing on a wide ledge. She blinked and realized they were standing next to a metal door that had been painted white to blend in with the marble.

Grayson leaned over the lock and pulled out a set of keys. Master keys, she guessed.

While he worked the lock, she leaned close to David. "Thanks," she whispered.

"If you're wrong, we're all fucked," he whispered back.

"I'm right." *I hope.*

The lock clicked and Grayson pushed open the door. She and David followed him inside.

They were at the end of a long hallway full of glass display cases of clay pots, ancient masks, and little figurines of various gods and goddesses. Damn, she recognized nothing. Where were the suits of armor Nicky had loved?

"What floor are we on?" she asked.

"Early American wing, first floor, west side of the museum, near the back," David said.

"You claimed to know where you were going," Grayson said.

"I do. I just never came in that door. Give me a second to orient myself." Okay, if they were near the exterior wall of the museum, getting out of this hallway should dump her into a larger hallway and then to the main foyer of the west wing, assuming it still existed after the renovations.

She set off at a good pace. "Do I have to worry about running into cops?"

"They were working in the east wing a few moments ago," David said.

"Lt. Gilbert has called in reinforcements," Grayson said. "We have ten minutes at the most before they catch up to us."

"Yeah, I noticed the extra squad cars arriving." That call had gone out over the scanners, alerting every decent reporter in Manhattan to this scene. A knot developed in her stomach. Her fingers twitched for a smoke. She closed them into a fist instead. *Chill. You're fine, Connell.*

They'd really changed the damn place. All the art had been shuffled around and re-arranged. Cleaned it up, too, so it gleamed. A few years back and it had majored in industrial shabby, like much of Manhattan. Everywhere in her city, people wanted to make changes, some good. Some awful.

She could see this ending badly, with Grayson pissed off, with her being arrested for unauthorized entry to a crime scene and, worst of all, being fired.

Enough. Since when did she care about risking her neck? She took a deep breath and strode down the hallway, assuming Grayson and David would follow. Jingling from the zippers on her jacket and boots echoed in the silence. She hoped Grayson was right about his ten minutes because she doubted he'd protect her from the cops.

Last time she'd walked the corridor, the wing had been full of Impressionists, a dreamlike landscape that opened a portal to a strange world of color. She and Nicky had made up stories about the life going on behind those paintings. The early American portraits, realistic men and women, many scowling in disapproval, seemed like a bad omen for today.

She glanced out a side window as she walked past. "The *Lost Treasures* show is in the east wing over there?"

"Yes, it's there. Why?" Grayson snapped.

Patience, Wingtips. "Just wanted to orient myself. It's been a while." Okay, that staircase should be right up—

There.

She stopped in front of a staircase to the basement level. The granite steps were the same dull blue, though more pitted than she remembered. The renovations hadn't extended to this area. The railing had a fresh coat of industrial gray paint.

"There's a closet just around the corner from the steps. The tunnel entrance is inside the closet."

She slung her leg in a high kick and jumped over the velvet rope designed to forbid entry to the lower level. She turned to see if they were following. Grayson unhooked the rope so he and David could pass, then re-attached it.

She turned the corner and there it was, just as she remembered: a dented metal door badly in need of painting. Unfortunately, it was padlocked. *Hey, Grayson had gotten through one door already. Two should be no problem for him.*

"Open it," she told Grayson. "The subway tunnel entrance is inside."

"Give me your gloves," Grayson said, taking out a set of keys from his blazer pocket. "I don't want to leave fingerprints."

She smiled, pleased she'd been right about him being able to unlock it, and handed him her gloves. He used one to hold the padlock as he inserted the key and opened the door.

Grayson flicked on the light switch, again careful to touch it only with the glove.

All four walls of the storage closet were fitted with metal shelves containing various cleaning tools, janitorial supplies, and extra clothing for the maintenance crew. Cans of paint thinner sat on the bottom shelf. When she'd been here, the shelves had been full of old wooden frames and broken statues.

She pushed past Grayson and leaned down to study a ragged throw rug in the far corner. It might have been dark green once, but now black dirt obscured the diamond design. In another life, she had huddled under this rug for warmth.

"What are you doing?" Grayson said.

"Showing you how they got in." She flipped up the rug's corner, revealing several ceramic tiles with a familiar blue and white design. The knot in her stomach unraveled. They hadn't changed this. She *was* right.

"See?"

Grayson knelt next to her.

"If you take out these tiles, you can drop down into an abandoned subway station." She tapped the tiles and was rewarded with scraped knuckles rather than the hollow sound she'd hoped for. *Fuck.*

Grayson ran her glove across the seams in the tiles and brought it to his face for a closer look. The tips came up covered in gray film. He rolled the film between his fingertips, then knelt closer and peered at the underside of the rug. The film smeared that too.

She held her breath. Someone had plugged up this entrance, and they'd done it recently.

"This is new concrete. Redi-mix, maybe." Grayson stood. "Let's assume you are right, Ms. Connell. Someone enters this room from below. How does he or she get across to the east wing to *Lost Treasures*?"

She pointed upward at a screen in the ceiling. "The air duct in this ceiling leads to the maintenance closet on the other side." Her voice started to rise with excitement. "You'd never even have to unlock this closet door to go from the subway to smack in the middle of *Lost Treasures*."

"Which would explain why the exterior guards and cameras spotted nothing." For the first time, Grayson's voice lacked anger.

He tossed her gloves back to her, animated now.

"My alarm wouldn't have gone off if someone entered from underneath. It also accounts for why Katz's body was found near the stairs to the other closet." He paused and frowned. "Though the guard got into the exhibit somehow."

"Someone messed with the alarm?" She resisted the urge to grab her notebook out of her pocket and write this down. No sense reminding him that she was a reporter now that he was spewing all that information.

"Obviously." Grayson's face relaxed. Less wary, more curious.

"So, Katz hears something, decides to investigate, is killed before she can call for help, and her assailants take the paintings and go back the way they came, down through this exit," Grayson said.

The dead guard was a woman named Katz. Dammit, she needed to write this all down. Plus, that name rang a faint bell. Why?

"Except—"

She interrupted him. "If they left this way, somebody stayed behind to put down this new concrete. An inside job, right?"

"Exactly. Tell me again how you knew about this hidden entrance."

She shrugged. "A story on the homeless."

He frowned. "What are you not telling me?"

"Oh, so many things." None of which mattered to any of this.

Grayson snapped back to full attention, the cop once more. "David, is your friend involved in all this?"

David grinned but it faded as he realized his boss was serious. "C'mon. No. Anyway, she has an alibi for last night."

Nice lifeline, Trisha thought.

"Do you?" Grayson asked her.

"Out all night. Punk club. Pretty visible. The bartender could probably vouch for me."

"Interesting," he drawled.

Awfully arrogant, wasn't he? "If I had been involved, why the hell would I lead you here?"

"To remove yourself from suspicion?" Grayson said. "Maybe you wanted to create a headline story."

She laughed. "If I wanted to steal paintings, I'd waltz into the museum in broad daylight with a group of noisy kids. They'd distract the guards while I snatched the paintings. It'd be a damn sight easier and less messy than climbing through dusty air ducts."

The side of his mouth quirked. Another smile?

"I see," Grayson said, but she wondered if he did.

"Now what?" David said. "We bust up that new concrete and open the entrance to the tunnel?"

"Disturb crime scene evidence? No," Grayson said. "We've pushed this as far as we can on our own. We need Dorothy here, fast, and hope she's more interested in following up this lead than punishing me. Us."

Grayson stepped back into the hallway, bleeding enough arrogance for ten people.

"David, find Dorothy and tell her to bring the blueprints for the museum here to see if those provide any clues to this unknown tunnel. She'll be angry, but she'll come, if only to have my hide."

David nodded. "If I'm not back in a few minutes, you can assume Lt. Gilbert killed the messenger."

David rushed off. Trisha leaned against the doorframe of the closet, pulled her notebook from her pocket, and wrote down the mornings' events. She should find a phone, call Joe, but no way would she leave this scene.

"You need to leave now," Grayson said.

Predictable. "Nah," she said. "Things are just getting interesting."

"Lt. Gilbert might arrest you, and I'd hate to see that."

"Makes two of us." She kept scribbling notes but remained keenly aware of his continued scrutiny.

Great, another man who couldn't stop staring at her. Disappointing. She finished her notes, put the pad away, and crossed her arms over her chest.

"Enjoy what you see?" she asked.

He pointed at her boots. "You own a motorcycle?"

"A restored antique, an old Indian Chief. It started life as a bike in a box, and I fixed it up." What a strange question, considering the circumstances, and not at all what she'd expected. "Why do you ask?"

"I thought the leather might be for show."

"I'm not a poser." She shook her head. "What you see is what you get."

"Then what is 'Dread at the Controls' and why is he on your T-shirt?" Grayson leaned against the wall, brushing back a strand of gray hair that had fallen over his eyes.

"Reggae singer. He did some work with the Clash." People outside the scene didn't recognize the album but people usually knew who the Clash were.

"Ah," Grayson replied, giving no sign he recognized the Clash either. "And why the men's jeans?"

"Comfortable plus pockets. Big pockets. Good for holding notebooks and pens." And switchblades.

"Ah," he said again. But after a minute, he nodded. "I'm sorry for accusing you without evidence. It hasn't been a good morning."

Whoa. He was apologizing? "I imagine it's been a lousy morning, especially for the dead guard."

"Yes, a horrible day for Adrienne Katz and her family. I'm glad to know you haven't forgotten that in your eagerness for the story."

Oh, fuck, *Adrienne Katz*? "Adrienne, as in the female version of the name?" *Don't let him say "yes."*

He sighed. "A young woman, a college student. I believe she had plans to enter the police academy."

Trisha made a show of writing the name in her notebook, letting her hair fall in front of her face so Grayson couldn't see her reaction. She fought the urge to toss her cookies. *No, no, no, no.* Adrienne had been adopted. Had a family that loved her now. She had a *future.*

Trisha had last seen her…last spring?… at her home, with her new family. Adrienne had looked good. Happy. Joyous, even.

No more joy for Adrienne. Trisha nearly snapped her pencil in half.

She set her jaw, raised her head, and saw the question in Grayson's face.

"We need to find who killed her."

"I will." He jerked his head at the storage closet. "So, assuming, they used this tunnel to escape, where does it come out?"

Careful, careful. She needed her information as leverage to stay on the story, get justice for Adrienne. Not that justice would do a damn thing for the kid now.

Trisha cleared her throat. "The largest section of the tunnel comes out cross-town, a few miles over, near Gimbels." The entrance she'd been thinking about earlier might be closer, but it could also be blocked off. Better Dorothy took the Gimbels' exit.

"Where exactly near Gimbels?" he asked.

"That would be telling."

"That would be information leading to solving a murder."

Could she trust this guy? According to David, Grayson had passed information to the Feds last Christmas as a favor to him and her. There was humanity under there. Maybe. *Maybe not.*

Boots thudded on the steps above. Company coming. They turned in unison to face them.

Dorothy descended the staircase first, David in tow. Another plain-clothes detective followed them, big and bulky, the source of the thuds. He almost waddled down the steps. His Member's Only jacket, unzipped, swirled around him.

Hell. Newman. When had he shifted from vice to major crimes?

Dorothy ignored her and focused on Grayson. David had the blueprints in hand.

Trisha slipped behind Grayson, using him as a shield as much as she could against Newman. The best thing she could do right now was fade into the woodwork.

"English, you're done here," Dorothy said as she reached the bottom of the steps.

Grayson put up his hands in surrender. "Would you at least look at what we've found? Then you can throw me off the premises."

Dorothy pointed at the open door. "You've already contaminated a possible crime scene."

"I wore gloves," Grayson said.

Dorothy swept past him. Grayson stood to the side of the open doorway to watch, and Trisha lost her cover.

"Well, Connell," Newman formed her name into an insult. "This is going to be fun. I'll be happy to toss you out on your ass."

"The *lady*," Grayson said, "has just supplied us with information that might help solve a murder, Detective."

Trisha bit back the insult to Newman that had formed on the tip of her tongue. It had been a long time since someone called her a "lady." Hell, that *never* happened.

She watched the two men size each other up. Newman was a bulky six foot three, his anger flushing his face to the edges of his military haircut. Grayson was shorter by a couple of inches, lean but well-built, probably older given the gray hair but it wasn't old man gray, more steel gray, *battle-ship* gray.

Grayson stood completely still, projecting cold menace. Damn, she could get to *like* this guy.

Dorothy stepped back out of the closet. Trisha could see film from the Redi-Mix on the edge of her fingertips.

"Stop growling at each other, boys." Dorothy pointed to David. "Spread those blueprints out on the floor."

David flipped to the relevant pages.

"Make your explanation fast and make it good, Trisha, or I'm giving you to Newman," Dorothy said.

Trisha went to her knees and leaned forward on one elbow to study the plans. "Here—you can see the air duct clearly laid out." She traced it with her fingers.

"How large is the opening?" Grayson leaned over her shoulder, retracing the invisible line of her fingers. Almost, but not quite, touching her.

"An average size person could fit through," she said, fighting the urge to flinch. Damn, how had he sneaked up on her?

"You know a person could climb through those ducts because...?" Newman said with contempt.

"I can read blueprints." Thanks to all those incredibly boring municipal planning board meetings she'd been forced to attend in her early days at the paper. She pointed down at the key. "That gives the square footage."

"And the length," Grayson said.

"By the way, shouldn't these blueprints indicate the subway tunnel?" she said.

"Why would you need to do that on blueprints?" Newman asked.

"Well, having a hollow basement isn't good for supporting your structure," Trisha said. "Someone would have to know to make sure the museum's not going—"

"—to have a floor collapse," Grayson finished.

"So why don't these blueprints show the subway tunnel?" Trisha asked.

"That is an excellent question," Grayson said.

"Are you suggesting the blueprints have been altered?" Dorothy asked.

Trisha shrugged and stood up, again resisting the urge to grab her notebook. *Subway tunnels missing in blueprints. Remember that.* "The subway tunnels are there. And they're not on the blueprints. Either the blueprints are wrong, or someone changed them."

Grayson straightened. "We need—"

"You need to do squat," Dorothy snapped.

Could be worse, Trisha thought. At least Dorothy's wrath was split between her and Grayson.

"Newman, I want you to go over to the exhibit and send an evidence tech into the air ducts from the other side," Dorothy ordered.

Newman nodded, wisely not saying anything.

"Then meet me at my car. I'll be over in a second. We're going to check where this supposed tunnel comes out."

"Want me to kick the reporter out first?" Newman said.

"I'll handle it," Dorothy said.

Newman started up the steps, though he turned his head to give Trisha an angry backward glance. She gave him the finger, careful to block it from the others with the rest of her body.

Dorothy cleared her throat. "Tell me where this tunnel exits, Trisha. Now. If you do, I'll let you wander off quietly."

"I'm going with you." Trisha crossed her arms over her chest. No backing down. Not when she'd come so far. Not with catching Adrienne's killers on the line. Trisha remembered the first time she'd seen the skinny kid, undersized, with brown hair that exploded from her head. Adrienne had reported abuse by her foster parents at a group home. The cops had closed it down because of the kid's tip.

That story had been one of Trisha's first. The editors told her it had ended with the arrests of the abusive foster parents. But Trisha had tried to keep track of the kids afterward, particularly Adrienne. She'd been lucky, adopted by a nice Jewish family in New Jersey.

Today her luck had run out.

Dorothy shrugged. "Fine, Trisha. I'll just call up the *Daily News* city desk and give Kimba a tip about what's happening here instead."

Shit.

"Right. I'm thinking the last thing you want outside this museum right now are more reporters," Trisha said.

"The last thing I want right now is a reporter who's withholding information and obstructing justice. I just sent a college student with her skull smashed in two the morgue. You want the people who did that to go free?"

"No more than you do," Trisha said. Skull smashed in. *I hope it was fast, Adrienne.* "You'll call me with what you find, ASAP?'"

"There will be no results if you withhold the information," Dorothy said.

"Dorothy," Grayson said.

"Stay out of this, English," Dorothy said, holding up a hand. "Deal, Trisha?"

Damn, Dorothy knew which button to push. Part of what made her a great cop. "All right, Lieutenant, what do you want to know?"

"Everything." Dorothy slapped her notebook into Trisha's hands. "Write down the exact directions for that tunnel exit and anything else that might be helpful. And none of your dubious sense of humor."

"I get the exclusive if you find something?" She'd know first the whole story of what happened to Adrienne.

Dorothy nodded.

Trisha wrote it down, accurately, mapping the entrance from the old department store's shipping area. She'd been there just last year, when she last dropped off food to some of the die-hard tunnel dwellers.

"This is right next to Gimbels?" Dorothy said.

"Yeah. There's an old delivery entrance that connects to tunnels that were closed up about ten years ago. You just need to hit the bowels of the store's receiving area, near the subway, and go through a maintenance door. I've drawn that part."

Trisha handed the notebook back to Dorothy.

Dorothy read the notes to herself and nodded.

"If this pans out, I might even owe you one. Provided you do things by the book from here on out" she said. "Now, everyone follow me out the *front* entrance. Edmund, I'm going to forget that you just violated one of my orders. Provided you stay outside the museum from now on."

Grayson nodded.

Trisha followed the group to the entrance, wondering how fast she could get to a phone. She had enough of the story to save her job, especially once David and Grayson filled her in on the theft.

But...that wouldn't catch Adrienne's killer.

Going into the tunnels herself would be a longshot. That second entrance had been a mess years ago. Even with a best-case scenario, getting through that door would risk being hit by a train.

But she needed to do it anyway.

Grayson and David were being oddly quiet for being tossed out of the museum. Several times on the way out, a nod passed between them. They were planning something, but she'd bet their idea wasn't as interesting as the one she had.

They passed a crowd at the front entrance hall. A tall, thin man with round glasses tried to intercept Dorothy, but she brushed him off. Once outside, Dorothy turned to Grayson.

"I don't want to see you or hear you or even smell you for the rest of the day. Got it?"

"I don't know what you're talking about," Grayson said.

Dorothy pointed to Trisha. "If you know what's good for you, English, you'll get away from her as fast as possible. She's trouble that you don't need."

Grayson waited until Dorothy moved out of earshot before he spoke. "David, we'll take my car and head to that subway station near Gimbels." He turned to Trisha. "Do you want to come with us?"

They were going to shadow Dorothy.

"Damn, Grayson, you hate being told what to do. I can respect that."

"Do you want a ride or not?"

"No. First, I'm going to check the other tunnel entrance, the one in the subway station around the corner from here." She grinned. "Who's with me?"

CHAPTER FOUR

GRAYSON WAITED until Dorothy pulled away to approach the parking lot. He should send David into the tunnels with the reporter and follow Dorothy himself but then what? Once again, he'd be cooling his heels, waiting, only in a different location.

No. His responsibility. That kid had died on his watch.

David had the patience to stay out of sight, watch, and wait. Grayson sent him to the location where Dorothy had gone and led the reporter to his car. She stood by quietly and patted her pockets, obviously looking for something.

Cigarettes, most likely.

"Those will kill you," he said.

She shrugged. "I doubt I'll live long enough for the smokes to get me."

More bravado? She was full of quips, but that sounded too bleak and world-weary for a joke. She was young, beautiful, and intelligent, with a vibrancy that drew him to her more than any woman since Karen.

She should have the world at her feet, not be busy courting death. But then, her generation had been raised on Watergate and cynicism. If she chose to be a nihilistic punk, not his business.

Grayson unlocked the trunk, removed two flashlights, and offered her one.

"You have two?" she asked.

"My regular flashlight, plus a spare in case the other doesn't work."

"Of course," she said, her mouth twitching.

"If you don't want one...." He turned to put the second one away.

She grabbed the flashlight before he finished. He smiled. This woman usually got what she wanted, especially from men. But he'd never done his thinking from below the belt.

"Thanks, I appreciate it." She peered into his truck. "What the heck else do you have in here? What are the boxes? Is that rope? You have *rope* in your trunk?"

"It's not rope. It's line." He swept her aside with his arm and slammed the trunk shut.

"You could have just told me to back up."

"That was faster." And more effective.

"What's the difference between rope and line?" she asked.

"When rope is used onboard a boat, it becomes line."

"You have a boat?"

"I rent one occasionally. And I'd rather use my own lines than trust someone else's equipment."

"Naturally."

She wanted to get under his skin to have the upper hand. Answering her would only play into that, so he didn't.

She balanced the flashlight in her hand. "Leaded end. You don't mess around, do you?"

"Never. Now, show me that entrance."

"Follow me, Wingtips. And remember, I warned you this could be dangerous."

"I remember." He let the nickname pass because he suspected a non-response would annoy her more than taking offense. She was challenging him to test his limits. She wouldn't win that game.

As they approached the front of the museum, he watched her slip the flashlight under her jacket to avoid notice from the uniforms milling about on the sidewalk. He followed her lead.

Three black and whites were parked in front of the museum, cutting the three-lane road down to two. He counted five uniformed officers directing traffic. Horns blared, tires squealed, and curses filled the air.

He peered down the street, feeling like a tiny ant caught between the massive buildings.

The gift shops across from the museum were still shuttered tight but the convenience store on the corner had a line out the door for coffee already. News vans would show up soon, he guessed.

"One sec, okay?"

Trisha ducked into the store, neatly sidestepping the line of customers, and poured several quarters into the pay phone. He didn't catch much, especially since she talked so fast and low that she barely drew breath.

Finally, she said "Got it? No, not yet. I've got to follow this to the end while I can. Will call back in an hour or so."

She frowned listening to the reply. "Look, you agree I was right on this? Good. Fine. I'll take the hit from Cardoza."

She took a deep breath when she hung up and, again, sidestepped the line on her way out. "Your newspaper?"

"My editor. Had to report in."

"Who's Cardoza and why would you have to take a hit from him?"

"He's the stupid boss and he's not important. Let's go." She pushed past him, striding down the street once more.

Grayson decided this woman probably gave her long-suffering editor heart attacks on a daily basis.

She scanned the street as they crossed to the next block. Despite the crowd gathered at the crosswalk, she maintained personal space with a glare and elbows out. A Manhattan native, he decided, constantly on alert.

As people surged onto the sidewalk, she threw her elbows at a man who came too close. He glared. She glared back. He faded away, apparently deciding arguing with her wasn't worth it.

They reached the crowded steps to the subway platform, and a man dressed in a Mets jacket tried to shove past them. She stepped on his foot with her boot heel. Mets jacket gave way, cursing. She ignored him. Grayson followed a step behind her, impressed. He could use someone this street-savvy on his payroll.

Except for the part where he'd have to be her boss.

A man coming up the steps whistled and made an obscene remark at her. She gave him the finger, carelessly, almost by reflex. Grayson used his shoulder to push past another man stopped on the steps, reading his newspaper and paying no attention to anything around him. *Idiot.*

This is why he drove.

The stench of the subway platform, human sweat combined with stale air and urine, hit him halfway into the station. He swallowed a cough. Another reason to drive.

Remember, you volunteered for this.

Her bright red hair made her easy to track, even several steps behind. Once down on the platform, she sidestepped, let others pass, and waited for him.

"Do you have tokens?" she asked.

He shook his head. "Not a fan of mass transit."

"You have a gun, flashlights, and rope, but no tokens?"

"Line," he corrected.

She smiled. That could be either approval or disdain.

"Stick with me, then."

They stepped into the line for the turnstile. She dropped a token in, went through, reached over, and dropped another in for him. Once on the other side, they let the crowd swarm past them again.

Interesting. She carried no purse. Right. The men's pants because of the pockets. But her cash must be somewhere. Probably in a belt around her waist. That went beyond caution to nearly paranoid. *Who was this woman?*

And why had she had such a strong reaction to hearing of Katz's death? She'd tried to hide it, but that news had shaken her, and it had sent her haring off after a longshot hunch when her editor obviously preferred she come to the newspaper to write up what she had.

Trisha tapped her pockets. No jingle.

"Something wrong?" he said.

"All out of change and tokens." She sighed. "And I'm going to need to phone in again before the day's over."

"I have a phone in my car."

"That would have saved me calling on the pay phone." She raised an eyebrow. "You could have told me that when we were at your car."

"You didn't ask."

She turned left once on the platform. A typical midtown mix of college students, business people, and tourists crowded together near the yellow line. Graffiti decorated the walls and even the turnstiles. He rolled his shoulders to feel the familiar weight of the gun holster on his right side. It had been so easy to bring a gun down here, and they'd both concealed the flashlights. If they could do it, so could anyone else. Hell, he'd been shot at in a subway station only last Christmas.

"This is a crime scene waiting to happen," he said.

"Tell me about it."

But the cost of securing the platform against unauthorized weapons was likely prohibitive. Sometimes it amazed him that people didn't kill each other more often. The opportunities were always there. Too many chances for crime, too few police officers.

Despite her bravado, Trisha also displayed caution. She kept to the wall, always with some of her attention on the crowd. Only two types of people hated to put their backs to a crowd.

The first: military or law-enforcement officers.

The second: those who'd been hurt, perhaps more than once, and learned not to trust.

Most punks were posers who simply listened to the music for the attitude. Not this woman. She might be just as world-weary as her remark about not living long enough for the cigarettes to get her indicated.

Though she'd backed down when Dorothy pressed her on finding justice for Katz. Dorothy had *known* that tactic would be effective. That meant Trisha Connell possessed a heart under all her cynicism, and she possessed a special interest in Katz's murder.

A train roared in. Silver etched with graffiti zipped past them. Trisha put out a hand in front of him. "Wait until it leaves. Then we try it."

The subway doors opened, passengers oozed on and off, shoving and jostling, and the train clattered out of the station.

"Okay," she said, nodding to herself. "This should be safe for a few minutes."

She followed the wall to the edge of the platform and inched her way out onto the tiny ledge that disappeared into the darkness of the subway tunnel. If she lost her balance, she'd fall right onto the tracks.

"You coming?" she called.

He stared down into the dark maw of the tunnel. "What happens if a train arrives while we're out there?"

"We get *real* skinny."

He grunted and followed, gripping the flashlight in one hand, and feeling along the cold tile with the other hand.

"Keep the light off until we're inside," she said.

"I know that," he snapped. "But where is inside?"

"Feel the door yet? I'm on the other side."

He almost said "no" when his hand slipped from the wall to the smooth metal. "Yes."

"Try the doorknob."

His hand closed around it. No give. "It's locked."

"Damn, I was afraid of that."

She turned on her flashlight. He put a hand to shield his eyes from the brightness. The circle of light traced the door. The rumble of an incoming train echoed in the tunnel.

"We need to go back," he said.

"Just a sec." She held the beam on the door hinges. "You see the rusted hinges?"

"Yes." A strong push and, those hinges should give way.

A train whistle blew. "Push. Fast," he said.

He set his back against the door and shoved. She applied her shoulders. Metal scraped against stone. The headlight of the incoming car spotlighted them.

One more shove, and they stumbled inside. Grayson glimpsed the subway cars passing by where they'd just been standing.

So very close.

"Are you *ever* cautious?" he asked.

"No. Are you *ever* unprepared?" she retorted. "But anyway, nice going. Thank you."

"You're welcome." And that was probably all the admission she'd make about being afraid. "Where are we?"

"Technically, a transit employee entrance." She pushed the door back into place to cover their entry. They turned their flashlights inward.

"How did you ever find this place?"

She shrugged. "Reporters know stuff. And this is *my* city."

"It's a big city to know everything about."

She smiled. "That's my job."

"So says your overly large ego."

"Like it's any bigger than yours." She ran a hand through her hair to smooth it down. "You're the one who feels personally responsible for what happened at the museum."

"That failure *is* my responsibility. A woman is dead because I failed to cover all contingencies."

"You should put that blame on the bad guys."

Interesting that she absolved him of responsibility. "I intend to do that as well."

"Good."

Their lights illuminated the yawning black hole in front of them. She pointed. "This turns, goes down under the tracks, parallels them for a while, and climbs again, then veers right and finally opens up right under the museum."

"How far?" he asked.

"As the crow flies, we're just crossing the block to the area underneath the museum storage closet. But this tunnel wasn't designed for flying crows, it's an entrance for transit workers to several stations. Or it used to be. That's why all the twists and turns." She sighed. "The other exit is a nice, straight shot to the area under the museum."

"You gave Lt. Gilbert the better lead."

"Ya got me there. And if we discover someone used this entrance, we should backtrack and tell the cops right away. It's not like I want the killers to get away."

But this descent was still dangerous. His flashlights had a two-foot circular beam, the best high-powered light that he could buy, but it did little to dispel the utter blackness. If someone or something menacing lurked in the shadows, he would have little warning.

I hate this.

The tile wall led to a ceiling about ten feet overhead. Dirty, unrecognizable garbage littered the edges of the floor. Its musty stench made the smell in the station seem like perfume by comparison. In this darkness, once they made a turn, he'd lose his bearings. He tapped the shoulder holster under his jacket, making sure the Beretta was still secure.

"Done casing the place?" she asked.

"I want to be able to find my way back, if needed."

"That's a lost cause. Just stick with me."

"Lead on then." A drop of water from the ceiling hit him in the face. He wiped it away and muttered under his breath.

She snorted. "Ceiling drops will be the least of our problems down here. You could've stayed topside."

"You know why I came."

"I guess I understand well enough."

They headed out at a slow but steady pace. She picked her steps carefully to avoid the piles of trash.

In the beam of his flashlight, her flame-red hair, black motorcycle jacket, and tight-fitting blue jeans seemed to give her a perverse glow.

Bloody hell. He was being led down into the literal underworld by some sort of outlaw goddess.

His career, even his life, depended on this woman he'd just met, an irreverent punk with a dubious past and all the attitude of a cynic.

She did have a nice ass.

"Here's a question for you: who owns the artwork in *Lost Treasures*?" she asked.

She had zeroed in on the exact question that had bothered him from the beginning. He added intelligence to her list of assets.

"A dealer named Dante Sidney, representing an anonymous client, acted as an agent to contract the exhibit. I believe the museum director knows the client's identity, but I'm not in that loop."

"That must bug you."

"Sidney's credentials are impeccable in the art world. I have little reason to suspect him of anything other than protecting his client's identity."

"So where do *you* think the art came from?"

"Likely from a hidden collector, perhaps even a descendant of one of the Nazis who stole them. Sidney has ties in South America, so perhaps Argentina."

"I'll have to talk to this Dante Sidney."

"Good luck with that," he said. Then again, Sidney *had* flirted with Amanda and every other woman with a pulse at the museum. Trisha Connell just might get him to talk.

They reached a curve faster than he'd expected, and he nearly stumbled into the wall. He gritted his teeth. This was a damned tomb. She slowed, head cocked, obviously listening for noise ahead.

He wanted to be in the lead. He was armed. She wasn't. But she knew the territory.

"Okay, sounds clear." She grabbed his blazer lapel. "Stop. Watch where you're stepping."

"Why?"

"Look at the floor."

Glass bottles tied together by string littered one side of the floor. "Why would someone put that there?"

She pointed her flashlight to the left and exposed an entrance about three feet high and two feet wide. An entrance that he'd walked right by, unknowingly. Exactly what he'd been worried about, trouble without warning.

He gripped the flashlight tighter.

"Someone lives or sleeps in there," she said. "These bottles are their warning system."

"Inventive," he said.

"You have to be inventive to survive down here," she said.

"And did you once survive down here?"

She shrugged. "You can take the girl out of the sewer but not the sewer out of the girl."

Her words sounded had the ring of a statement of fact. What could she possibly have lived through to give her this fatalistic outlook? "This is my city," she'd said twice. And the sewer comment added to that. *Who was this woman?*

Focus, Grayson.

They resumed their hike. "How much farther?" he asked.

"Not sure. We have to descend, turn, and ascend again."

He kept the light on her, if only to reassure himself that another human existed near him. Or maybe he enjoyed watching her. No, he definitely enjoyed watching her. She moved like a dancer, all fluid motion.

Focus, Grayson.

He shined his light to the floor of the tunnel again. It slanted down at a thirty-degree angle. That, combined with the grime, created slippery footing. She put a hand out and used the wall for balance.

"Watch. Floor's slicker here," she said.

"I noticed but thanks for the warning." Another drop of water splashed onto his tie. "Damn it."

"I'm still curious, Grayson. David could have followed this up with me, while you shadowed Dorothy. He's used to me, plus Dorothy's more likely to hit pay dirt. So why did you come down here with me?"

Because it had been doing something rather than nothing.

"David has the patience to wait and watch at the other exit," he said.

"And you don't?"

She'd guessed the right answer. He shrugged. "Besides, David might get distracted."

"Distracted?" She glanced over her shoulder. "Ah, you think David wants to get into my pants."

That was far more…forward…than most women he knew. Maybe he didn't know enough women, if he'd missed out on her type.

"It's obvious," he said.

"We're just friends."

"I see."

"Are you jealous?"

He opened his mouth for a scalding retort when he noticed her wavering flashlight beam. The problem wasn't with the light because he kept all his equipment in good working order.

No, the beam shook because the hands holding them also shook.

She was *nervous*. She coped with it by bantering. He was torn between being comforted that she wasn't as nonchalant about danger as she seemed and worried that she might be in over her head after all.

The floor flattened out. She sped up again. Water splashed from the puddles over his shoes. Silence reigned. Damn.

He preferred her teasing to this ominous silence.

"If we are going to exchange sexual innuendo, I think you had better call me Edmund. Or at least, Grayson."

She snorted. "Oddly, Grayson sounds less formal than Edmund. Do you ever go by Ed?"

"Never."

"I'm not surprised."

The tunnel tilted upward and to the right. He put a hand on the wall for balance again and winced at the cold slime under his fingertips.

"I like Edmund," he said.

"It sounds oh-so-dignified. Definitely not suited for tunnel explorations. How you'd end up with the name?"

"Sir Edmund Hilary was a favorite of my mother's," he said.

"Too bad we're in a tunnel, not a mountain."

"But we are ascending."

She snorted. "Definitely."

"You're enjoying this."

"Enjoying? It beats the hell out of a boring press conference at City Hall. It'd be a lot more fun if not for the murder. At least I'm doing something useful."

"You hate waiting," he said.

"Absolutely." A pause. "I also hate murderers."

He shifted his light to the floor, worried about tripping or falling. Time passed, though it was impossible to tell how much in the blackness. He'd forgotten his watch this morning in the rush.

"Did you check this Dante Sidney's background?" she asked.

"Of course. As I said, impeccable credentials with a long history of curating collections. He's a native of Spain but travels all over."

"Which makes it hard to pinpoint where he made the contact that led to the artwork in *Lost Treasures*."

"Yes. He may even be the owner of the collection by now. But those records would be private, as I said." Grayson fought the urge to check his watch. They couldn't go any faster. This would take as much time as it took. He should do the same as her: use this time to gain more information.

"Our arts reporter has contacts and might be able to find more about Sidney," she said.

Grayson doubted the *Herald's* arts reporter would find anything his people couldn't. "Let me know if you eventually discover anything."

The tunnel leveled out once more and widened. The ceiling rose several feet higher and the walls surrounding them became less oppressive. The garbage on the floor petered out.

"Is it usual for this area to be this clean?" he said.

"No." She stopped. "Last time I came into the tunnel, four people were camped out, with their stuff strewn all over the floor. Damn, I hoped some of the homeless would still be here and we could ask them if they saw something. But there's no sign of anyone."

"Yes, there is," Grayson said, "just in a different way. Someone wanted this area cleared. Either your tunnel dwellers have become ambitious—"

"Or the people who broke into the museum were down here."

"Yes."

Small scraping noises echoed from the darkness.

"Rats?" he asked.

"Only a few. There should be more of them. Let's go slower. I don't know what's ahead," she said.

"Agreed."

The darkness ahead of them seemed to alter in shape. Wider. More open, if that was possible. His hand moved toward his Beretta.

She halted again, reached up with the hand holding the flashlight and wiped sweat off her forehead. "We're close." She scanned an archway directly overhead. The white ceramic tiles, decorated with pictures of a train, shone bright in the sudden light.

"Yep, this is it." She pumped her fist. "She shoots, she scores. Excellent."

He smiled. "Are you ever serious?"

"Nah. Life's tragic and sad enough already without my being serious about it."

"Shall I put that on your tombstone?"

"Sure. I've been wanting a reliable volunteer for my funeral arrangements."

He shook his head, glad the darkness hid his smile.

"This is a never-used subway station," she said. "The ceiling just below the museum is on the far side. No, not right. Look left."

He combined his light with hers. Their beams barely reached the wall on the opposite side. This cavern was far bigger than their tunnel.

"How wide is this space?"

"Maybe twenty feet from here to the opposite side. We want the farleft corner."

She moved to step into the cavern.

He put his arm out to stop her. "Wait."

"Why?"

"Because I'm cautious and careful and I want to know what I'm step-ping into. As you said, this is a possible crime scene."

She was silent for a second. "Okay."

He pointed the light up. The ceiling tiles showed little sign of wear or water damage. But in the farleft corner, just below where she said the entrance to the museum storage closet was located, the tile had been replaced by gray cement. Likely, the same ready mix that had been poured in the storage closet.

Yes. He fought the urge to pump his fist as she had.

Focus. The killers were still out there.

He followed the wall down from the Redi-mix with the light. An aban-doned ladder came into view. Musty footprints dotted the floor, disap-pearing into the darkness in the opposite direction. Good, good. Ladder, footprints, Redi-mix. All excellent evidence.

His light glinted off something, and he spotted a can of lighter fluid. That's where the smell had come from in the exhibit.

Paintings and lighter fluid? Bad combination. But if the murderers were going to destroy the paintings, why not do it in the museum, where it would be a public spectacle? Perhaps Katz surprised them, and they'd run out of time.

"What's in the other direction?" he asked.

"It leads right to where I sent Dorothy, to the lower level of Gimbels. If they haven't sealed it off. I'd thought she might be here by now." She sighed and focused her light on the footprints. "Damn. Don't tell anyone, but I'm genuinely surprised this panned out."

"My lips are sealed." He scanned left and right from the ladder. He saw nothing else but heard a small buzz. Odd.

"Do you hear something?" she said. "Sounds a buzz or little clicks?"

He concentrated harder. "Yes."

Clicks? Or ticks? He'd missed something. He slowed his scan and high-lighted a bulky area in the shadows.

The antique brass alarm clock came into his circle of light first. The flashlight beam glinted off the metal casing.

"That clock is ticking, isn't it?" she asked.

"Yes."

Wires ran out the back of the clock. He swallowed hard and re-adjusted the hold on his flashlight. *That better not be what I think it is.*

The bulky object, a square box, came into sharp view at the end of the wires. It was exactly what he feared.

A bomb.

He took a deep breath and involuntarily tapped the Beretta.

Help was at least an hour away. That might be too late. He'd have to evaluate this bomb and defuse it, if necessary. The antique clock must be the detonator. Besides the wires leading to the box, another led out past the clock. He followed the nearly invisible metal wire all the way across the cavern, until it ended at their feet.

A trip wire.

Only by a miracle had they avoided triggering it.

"Score one for your caution," she said.

"Hold off on declaring victory." He took another breath. "Because that's a bomb rigged to blow on a timer."

"Ticking time bombs aren't a myth?" she asked.

"No."

"Fuck."

"Yes."

CHAPTER FIVE

TICK...TICK...TICK...TICK...TICK...TICK...TICK...TICK....

A bomb. Okay, she could handle that part. But the ticking was going to drive her to the loony bin in about ten seconds, maybe less.

Grayson reached out, perhaps to comfort her. She waved away his hand. "I'm okay. Concentrate on the ticking thing." She swallowed and willed her voice steady. She told her knees not to tremble. This was for Adrienne. This had to be done.

He stepped over the tripwire, headed toward the bomb.

Do something useful, Connell.

"I want you to go for help. Grab one of the officers on the scene. Get them to radio Dorothy. It's the fastest way to send for the bomb squad."

"No." If not for her, he'd be safely across town, following Dorothy. First rule of the streets, you pair up with someone, you take care of each other because no one else would. "You stay, I stay. It's my story." And it's Adrienne's story.

Tick...tick...tick...tick...tick...tick...tick...tick....

"Shut up," Grayson snapped.

"I did," she said.

"I was talking to the clock."

"Oh. Too bad it's not listening to you. What's next?"

"I examine the bomb. Follow, if you must."

She followed, literally in his footsteps, and added her beam to his to help illuminate the whole setup. The box holding the bomb looked innocuous enough.

"Are there plastic explosives like C-4 in there?" she asked.

"C-4 is easy to transport and conceal, so that's a good guess. Depending on how much in is that box, this could conceivably destroy the entire museum and kill everyone inside," he said.

"There's a cheerful thought."

Now that they were closer, she spotted a wire that led from the box to the ceiling to a brick-shaped bar of what she assumed was C-4. There was something shaped into a brick mounted up there. More plastic explosives? She'd no idea why anyone would put those on a ceiling. Maybe to lead the explosion upward?

Tick...tick...tick...tick...tick...tick...tick...tick....

Yeah, clock, listen to Grayson and shut the hell up. Her heart pounded in rhythm with the ticking, matching it beat for beat. She curled her free hand over the cross hanging around her neck. Fuck, who was she kidding? She was already damned.

But Grayson deserved to live. He could have turned around and tried to escape the blast, as he'd ordered her to do. He'd stayed to do what he could to save those above, in the museum, who would be killed if the bomb detonated.

She made the sign of the cross and sent a silent plea into the darkness for him.

Grayson focused his light on the clock and nodded to himself.

The darkness in the abandoned platform seemed to grow thicker, more oppressive, magnifying the clock's incessant noise. Hell must be like this.

"Can you defuse it?" she asked.

"Still determining that. The alarm is set to go off on the top of the hour, which is in about seven minutes, give or take some seconds either way."

"It's going to explode in *seven minutes*?" she said. "Fuck."

"We might have as long as ten. Look, I appreciate you wanting to stay but...you need to go. Get out of here. You know the way. You could make it or, at least, escape the blast radius."

"I don't abandon people in dark tunnels with ticking time bombs at their feet."

"You—" He started to point his finger at her but let his hand drop. "We don't have time to argue. Fine."

"Good." She swallowed, trying to moisten her throat. Not the way she wanted to die, in a rat-infested, garbage-strewn subway tunnel. Once, she could've died this way, dirty and alone, and would've been glad to end her misery, especially after she'd lost Nicky.

But now? Adrienne Katz had died protecting that damned museum. Hell, if Trisha would let it be blown up now.

Would a prayer help? Couldn't hurt.

"'Yea, though I walk through the valley of the shadow of death—'"

"If you're going to try prayer, could you make it something less depressing?" he asked.

Crap, she'd babbled the psalm out loud.

"Uh, sorry. Just bubbled to the surface. Too much Catholic school." *Shut up, Connell, you're sticking that foot in your mouth down your throat.* As if it was yesterday, she could hear Father Mike's resonant voice reciting the Bible verses and remembered how safe and warm she'd been in those early years. Catholic priests weren't supposed to have kids. Technically, she'd been just one of many wards of the Church at the orphanage. But he'd been her father in all but name.

She closed her hand around the cross again.

Tick...tick...tick...tick...tick...tick...tick...tick....

If that clock had a soul, she hoped it fried in hell.

Tick...tick...tick...tick...tick...tick...tick...tick....

Her stomach rolled over. Good thing she hadn't eaten. Bad idea to puke all over plastic explosives. Sweat pooled in her palm, making her grip on the flashlight slippery.

Grayson handed his flashlight to her. "Keep them steady so I can work with both hands."

"No problem." She centered one on him so he could see the timer and the other on the bomb itself.

He shrugged out of his suit coat and tossed it aside, into the darkness. He laid flat on the floor and peered at the clock and the wires surrounding it. A stray hair fell in his eyes. He muttered an oath and brushed it away.

She readjusted the lights for maximum illumination on the clock and his hands.

Tick...tick...tick...tick...tick...tick...tick...tick....

When they'd first walked into the tunnel, he'd been appalled at the filth. Now, he was laying in it, stripped down to his shirt.

You're a fascinating bundle of contradictions, Edmund Grayson.

"You've done this before, right?" she asked.

"I've studied how to do it."

Shit. "That's reassuring."

"Either be quiet or go back to prayer. Or maybe some poetry?"

"'I wanna be sedated?'"

"Is that a request?" His voice was low, barely above a whisper, but at least he sounded amused, if that was possible while trying to defuse a bomb.

"It's a line from a song."

"Ah." He grunted. "Angle that second light to the back of the clock, where the wires are coming out. Hmmm...better."

"Better is good."

"The bad news is that the detonator is wired to the alarm, which is now set to go off in five minutes."

Five minutes. Five fucking minutes. "Is there any good news?"

"It's a simple device and it's not booby-trapped."

"I'm jumping with glee."

He peered at the clock, his eyes only an inch from the dial. The corner of his mouth quirked, as if he'd been about to smile.

If he could be calm poking at a bomb, she could ignore the bile in her throat and the panic in her gut. Die smiling. There were worse ways. Far worse ways. She'd almost died at fourteen, cuffed to a bed, the knife coming at her—

She shook her head. Years ago. Nothing to do with today.

Tick...tick...tick...tick...tick...tick...tick...tick....

She studied the clock. Brass, probably, with a fancy font for the numbers, and old-fashioned alarm bells on the top. It belonged in a Road Runner cartoon, not in an abandoned subway tunnel.

Wile E. Coyote sometimes got blown to itty-bitty pieces by bombs. Then the Road Runner would sweep him up into the dustbin, Coyote would be magically recreated, and the chase would be back on. Too bad this wasn't a cartoon. At least if Grayson failed, it would be over fast.

And if he succeeded, the only thing that would die would be that damned clock.

Tick...tick...tick...tick...tick...tick...tick...tick....

Grayson ran his fingers around the edges of the cover of the clock.

"How's it going?"

"I need to bend the hands to break the clock." He could be a newscaster reading off a teleprompter. Must be frozen nitrogen in his veins.

"Sounds easy."

He grunted. "It would be if the cover wasn't locked tight."

"Break the glass?"

"It's thick glass. If I slam it against the cement to break it, the bomb might detonate." He slapped his hand on the floor, frustrated. Terrible sign.

Tick...tick...tick...tick...tick...tick...tick...tick....

He clenched the hand into a fist. "Damn, if I had something to pry open the cover—"

"Is that all?" She laughed and the echo bounced around the cavern, sounding more ominous than the slap of his hand. She stuck a flashlight under her arm, pulled her switchblade from the hidden pocket in her coat and opened it with a flick of the wrist.

He put out his palm. "That'll do."

She slapped the handle of the knife into his hand.

"How strong is the tip of the blade?"

"It won't break," she said.

Tick...tick...tick...tick...tick...tick...tick...tick....

As he settled his hands on the clock, the sweat in her palms slickened her hold on the flashlights. She took a deep breath and closed her hands around them in a death grip.

He ran the knife's edge around the cover. *You're taking too damn long, Grayson!* How long did they have? Minutes? Seconds?

Holding the clock in one hand, he slipped the knifepoint under the latch. He grunted. The tip of the knife came loose and skimmed across the top of the clock's cover. He swore and tried again.

A loud snap echoed in the abandoned station. The clock nearly jumped out of his hands. But the cover was open.

He took a deep breath. "Almost dropped it."

Tick...tick...tick...tick...tick...tick...tick...tick....

He slipped his fingers under the cover, grabbed the big and little hands and pulled.

The whole mechanism holding the hands broke free.

CHAPTER SIX

SHIT!

Trisha jumped back, expecting that to be her last movement on Earth.

No boom?

She readjusted the beams on Grayson and the now-silent clock.

Grayson tossed the broken minute hand aside, slid his fingers under the smaller hour hand and tugged. The hour hand broke in half too.

He froze.

She stopped breathing. It took forever to register that the damned ticking had stopped.

Grayson poked at the clock face with the switchblade.

Nothing happened.

He let out a deep sigh.

"Did you kill it?" she asked.

"I believe so."

His face seemed frozen in a permanent frown. He examined the clock face again and turned it around to study the back. She'd no idea what he concluded, but he disengaged the wires attached to the back of the thing.

"Yes, it's dead." He expertly flicked the switchblade closed. He let his forehead rest to the cold stone floor of the cavern. His chest moved in and out in long, deep breaths.

She stood there, in the darkness, in utter silence, matching him, breath for breath.

"I swear, I am never, ever going to own a ticking clock. It's all digital from here on out." She willed her heart to slow down.

"Agreed."

He raised himself to his elbows, glancing at the bomb.

She sidestepped to the right, away from the plastic explosives. Okay, maybe it was harmless now. No taking chances. "So, no way for it to detonate now? What about the C-4?"

"The best thing about plastic explosives is that they're a relatively inert substance on their own." He got up on one knee, smoothed his hair back down, and stood up. "Thank you for your help."

So formal. "For what? Babbling?" She stepped sideways again and stumbled against the wall. She let it take her weight because without the support, she'd curl up on the floor into a fetal position.

Alive. Not going to Hell. Not today, anyway. *Hope I get old before I die.*

A flashlight slid from her sweaty grasp, clattered to the cement and rolled toward Grayson. He scooped it up with an easy grace.

"You brought me down here, Ms. Connell. If not for you, the bomb would have been undiscovered and gone off. You kept the light steady, and you had the knife. Without it, the bomb would have detonated. You helped prevent a horrible attack on civilians and police officers. And you saved *my* life."

She moved her beam to his face, trying to read his expression. He put up a hand to fend off the light. *Stupid, Connell. No need to blind the guy who'd just saved you from blowing up.*

"Just doing my job like I always do. And the name's Trisha. We should be definitely on a first name basis after this."

"You do your job exceedingly well, then."

So formal again. His way of coping? She decided not to tell him she only carried her knife on off-days, in case she ran into trouble at the clubs, like with the idiot who'd accosted her this morning. Any other day, and she'd have been unarmed.

"If Katz interrupted the thieves, she bought enough time for us to find the bomb. We're alive because of her."

"Yes, I believe that's true," Grayson answered.

He stepped closer to her.

"Do you always carry an illegally concealed weapon?" Pause. "Trisha?"

"It's hard to be a saint in the city."

He snorted and laid a hand lightly on her shoulder. "Ready to leave this place?"

He said it with such quiet concern that she had a fleeting impulse to hug him. No, he was a cop, a cop smart enough to have trained scores of rookies. He was probably just checking on the state of mind of his new partner. But, damn, that resonant voice of his reached inside her, over-turning all her preconceptions about men in tailored suits. Hell, after today, she might develop a fetish for the type. Or, at least, one fascinating man in particular. Not every day a guy saved her life.

She shrugged and his hand slid off her shoulder. "I'm good. This is going to make such a good headline. Above the fold for damned sure." It wasn't enough but a front page was all she could do for Adrienne now. *Sorry, kid.*

He grunted. "Glad to help."

"Don't think I'm not grateful, Grayson. Anything you want, you name it." She meant it. *Anything. He'd defused a ticking bomb.* He deserved what-ever he wanted.

"I'll keep that in mind," he said, his voice dry.

The light from his flashlight wavered. His hand must be shaking. It was reassuring that he had a fully functional set of nerves. He traced the cavern with his light. His beam passed over his discarded suit coat. He retrieved it as deftly as he'd scooped up the flashlight.

"Must be filthy," she said.

"It is. But it's cold down here."

She closed her hands, and the icy tips of her fingers dug into her palm. Huh. The cold hadn't registered until now.

"I wish we had a police radio. Then we could call this in. Nothing to do now but find the police as soon as possible."

"I'm for that. It's likely faster to keep going to the entrance I gave Dorothy than back the way we came."

"Good. Lead the way," he said.

A quiet request, almost somber, but giddiness surged through her. Adrenaline, no doubt.-She swallowed it down.

Focus. Get away from the bomb, get the story. Find who killed Adrienne.

The darkness seemed less oppressive in the new tunnel. The air was lighter and less musty. The footing improved too. No clumps of garbage. That meant she'd likely guessed right, that whoever took the paintings and planted the bomb had gone this way and been careful to clear out their escape route.

"Do you think there are more bombs?" She halted, wishing that had occurred to her sooner.

"God, I hope not." He sighed. "But I'm watching for any sign of them."

"Good." He'd been calm enough to think ahead while she'd still been rattled.

He held the flashlight just above his shoulder, cop style. She stayed at his side, with her flashlight at waist level, so they covered the most area possible with their lights. Her stomach flipped over again. After-shock nerves. She needed a distraction from thinking about blowing up. Or about Adrienne with half her skull crushed in.

"Who are these guys we're after?" she asked.

"All we know for certain is they left a calling card inside the museum. They painted swastikas on the wall after they removed the paintings."

"So Nazis did this for certain?" Nazis reclaiming their property from whomever Sidney had received it from? "But then why would they try to blow up the museum after they had the paintings?"

"It could be someone who wanted us to think it was Nazis," he said. "But there was something odd at the crime scene."

"What?"

"Lighter fluid had been spilled on the floor below the missing paintings. And there was a gallon of it near the ladder back there that could have been the source."

"That's weird." Had the Nazis wanted to burn something? "But why do that if you were going to blow up the museum?"

"Good question. Tell me something," Grayson said.

"What?"

"Is Trisha your full name?"

Huh? "Um, no, it's Patricia Mary Connell. No one uses that, though."

Why would Grayson ask that? "What, you planning on running a back-ground check on me?"

"It's safe to say I know all I really need to know about you already."

"Oooo...ominous."

"No, it means you never have to prove anything to me again." He cleared his throat. "I'd like to call you Patricia. It suits you better."

"I guess if I can call you Grayson, you can call me Patricia. It'll be a first, though. And you'll still run a background check on me anyway. That's who you are."

"What do you mean?"

"You're Mr. Careful, Mr. Prepared. Knowledge helps you plan for the worst. All that preparation saved our lives today." Not just their lives, the lives of everyone inside the museum, including David. "You're a freakin' hero, Grayson."

"I did my job, as you did yours. Had I done it better, I'd have prevented the bomb's existence and Katz would still be alive. You were right about one thing, however."

"Of course." She paused. "Um, about what?"

"The bomb doesn't make much sense, whether it was Nazis or not," he said. "Why destroy the museum if they have what they want? And why the lighter fluid?"

"Maybe they hate museums."

"Or they hate someone employed at the museum. Or they hate Sidney, the owner of the paintings. Or the police, given how many law enforce-ment officers that bomb might have killed." He sighed. "Or it could actu-ally be Nazis, making a statement, warning others about what happens when someone steals from them."

"Not enough evidence to know, is there?" she said. "Can't build bricks without clay."

Another snort. "No, even Sherlock Holmes couldn't do that. Let's hope Dorothy found something at her entrance."

He picked up his pace and almost disappeared into the darkness.

"Hey." She hustled to catch up. "Why the rush?"

"I heard someone ahead."

His cop voice again, flat and authoritative. What now? She wiped sweat from her hand onto her jeans. If they were close to an exit, the voices could be from construction workers or employees in the lower levels of the Gimbel's receiving department.

She concentrated. Male voices, coming closer. The voices sounded strident, angry, but she couldn't make out words over the echo of all the footsteps.

Bad guys, plural?

Grayson motioned her against the wall next to him. He clicked off his flashlight. She followed his lead and cut off her light too, leaving them in total darkness once more.

He wanted to hide rather than attack. *Good.* If these guys were the ones behind the museum job, they'd already killed. Shit, she should've asked Grayson for her knife back. Bad time to pick his pocket, though.

She could hear his breathing, nice and even. They were so close their arms were almost touching. Moisture, wet and cold, dripped from the wall onto her hair. Grayson stretched his right arm in front of her. A finger touched the tip of her breast.

"Uh, watch it," she whispered.

"Sorry," he mumbled.

He moved the hand lower, to her stomach.

He'd just saved her from being blown up. Accidentally copping a feel was forgivable and led her mind down other, more pleasant paths.

Leather creaked as Grayson drew the gun from his shoulder holster. Good cops kept their weapons holstered unless they intended to fire. Possible that Grayson could be overreacting because of nerves frayed when defusing the bomb. But unlikely.

Wasn't being nearly being blown up enough for one day?

Laughter bubbled in her throat, threatening to spew forth. What a fucking ridiculous day.

The footsteps grew louder.

Time to bring in the clowns to today's circus.

Grayson's hand rested easily on her stomach. No trembling, no shaking. Rock steady.

A flashlight beam coming toward them broke the darkness, illuminating a sharp turn in the tunnel. They wouldn't be spotted until the others came around the corner and then only if flashlight beams happened to hit them square on.

She took a deep breath and fought her adrenaline. *Okay, chill, Connell.* Think straight. Rumbles in the pitch black were a stupid idea. The bomb, at least, would have been over fast. Getting beaten or shot was messy.

The footsteps slowed. The voices grew clearer.

"We have to stop!"

"But the cops are right behind us."

"If they knew about one entrance, they'll know about the other. We'll just run into more of them this way. And there's the bomb."

They *were* the museum job guys. Her hand itched for her notebook again, to write down their words exactly. And cops were behind them? Dorothy?

"I'll take my chances. There's another tunnel that branches out from here."

For a second, Trisha almost wished that Grayson hadn't defused the bomb. These guys deserved to get blown up. *They were the ones who'd killed Adrienne.*

Grayson's hand moved from her stomach to her shoulder. He leaned over, closer to her face.

"Patricia. Run."

His voice was so low that she almost missed the words. He squeezed her shoulder once and let go.

Run? She rolled her shoulders. Screw that.

The lights coming at them grew brighter. Muttered curses and heavy breathing grew louder. Four men with guns in their hands came around the corner.

One of them stumbled right into Grayson.

The man froze. Grayson slammed his gun butt into the guy's skull. His attacker flopped to the floor.

She sidestepped down the wall, hoping to remain hidden in the darkness. They had guns, making her a sitting duck if they spotted her. She'd have an advantage unseen.

Grayson stepped left for the cover of dark, but they kept getting the edges of him with their lights. He was in trouble.

She flipped her flashlight to the leaded end and slammed it into the top of the shadow closest to her. The force of the impact reverberated all the way to her shoulder. A body thudded to the floor.

"There's two of them!" Someone shouted.

Ouch, ouch, ouch! Dammit. She shook her hand. That guy must have had one thick skull.

She tightened her grip on the flashlight, looking for another target but everyone was half in shadow, half in light, and unidentifiable.

Grayson. Where are you?

Lights bounced around as their attackers searched for them. She danced ahead of the beams.

"Fuck this," someone said.

Something pinged against the stone. Shit, that wasn't pinging, that was a *gunshot*.

More shots. Small, tinny pops, followed by the louder retort of guns. The beams bounced all over, giving the tunnel the look of a macabre disco. Acrid smoke filled her nose. She stifled a cough, her ears ringing from the noise.

A pained moan that rose above the din abruptly cut off. *Grayson?*

Someone fell against her, slamming her down into the hard, cold stone. Pain stabbed into her chest.

Someone's on top of me.

Her breaths came in short, painful gasps. Her hand jerked, she lost the grip on her flashlight, and it rolled into the darkness. Her thoughts slowed, and her head became heavier.

Shit, she was about to pass out. Grayson had saved her life and now she'd failed him.

A loud scream pulled her back to full consciousness. Grayson? No, not his voice. Someone else. But where the hell was he? Metal struck flesh with a muffled thud to her left. Fuck, what happened?

If she could just get this guy off her, she could move, she could help. Oh, hell, what if the body smushing her was Grayson? She shifted and the weight grew lighter.

Spots appeared in her vision.

I will not pass out.

She slipped her hands under her and pushed up. C'mon, those damn pull-ups every day had to be good for something. She gained a sliver of room, enough for her to take a deep breath. She shifted her shoulders. The man slid off her. Not Grayson. No suitcoat.

She scrambled free, stumbled to her feet, and blinked away the damned spots. She settled her feet into a fighting stance. No room to run or hide.

Fight.

The echo of more footsteps pounded in her ears. Fuckity, fuck, fuck. More of these guys?

"Police! Drop the weapons," said a familiar voice.

Dorothy Gilbert, I could kiss you.

Trisha swayed as pain knifed through her chest with each breath. She groped the air behind her, hoping to find a wall for support.

A hand from out of the darkness grabbed her hair and jerked her sideways. She stumbled, lost balance, and nearly fell. The attacker yanked on her hair again. She stumbled as agony spread through her chest. Her legs trembled. She flexed her knees and staved off the fall.

A hand grabbed her shoulder from the front, keeping her upright.

"No one move or I'll kill her," her captor said.

The cold muzzle of a gun pressed against her temple.

CHAPTER SEVEN

TRISHA FROZE. The hard metal against her skull propelled her back to the last time a gun had been jammed against her head, when she'd been fourteen, and her rapist had used it to terrorize her.

Behave, he'd said, and you'll be just fine. *Sit back and take it and we won't kill you. I bet you'll enjoy it.* She still had the scars from when he'd "played" with her.

"Behave and I won't kill her," her captor said to the others.

Like fucking Hell.

Trisha snapped her arm up and whacked the inside of her captor's wrist, knocking the gun and the hand holding it aside.

A bullet fired. It whizzed past her ear, immediately followed by a near-deafening sound.

Missed me, asshole.

She curled her hand around the man's wrist and kicked out, hoping to hit something, anything. The full force of the steel-jacketed heel of her motorcycle boots connected with his knee.

He screamed loud enough to hear over the ringing in her ears. His gun hand wavered. She twisted the man's thumb until he lost his grip and his gun clattered to the floor.

Lights flooded her corner of the tunnel, and she could see her attacker clearly for the first time. He topped her by about five inches but no bulk, just skinny with a sallow face and a ridiculous soul patch. He swayed, unsteady on the knee that she'd kicked in. He eyed the gun.

"Do not move," Grayson said, his gun now pointed at her attacker. Dorothy and the other uniformed officers also had their weapons drawn.

"Bitch," her attacker said to her.

"Damn straight." She closed her hand into a fist and smashed his jaw with a left cross.

Take that you motherfuckingsonofabitch!

The attacker collapsed to his knees. The older terror consumed her, sending her back to when she'd been cuffed to a bed, with a different man looming over her, a man armed with a gun and an exacto-knife....

Not again! She grabbed her attacker's shirt and let fly another punch. His head lolled back. Blood spurted from his nose.

"That's enough!" Dorothy's order echoed around the cavern.

Enough? Trisha grabbed his shirt again. He covered his nose and cursed incoherently. Oh, hell, no, this wasn't over. He wouldn't hurt her. No one would *ever* hurt her again.

Someone grabbed her from behind. She yelled, flailed her arms out, trying to twist around to face the new threat. No! She'd be handcuffed again, helpless, hurt, sliced, drugged....

"Patricia. Enough." Grayson spoke directly into her ear. "He's down." He lifted her off the ground. "You're safe."

She stilled. Patricia? Why was Grayson calling her Patricia again?

"You're safe," Grayson whispered again. "No one will hurt you now."

Safe? No, not in that room with that filthy bed again. Back to the present. Subway tunnel. Bombs. Bad guys. Fight. Cops. Gun.

Grayson.

Her fingers throbbed. She looked down. Even with only the illumination provided by the cops' flashlights, she spotted the blood covering her knuckles.

She blinked.

Oh, shit. What did I just do?

Grayson set her down and loosened his hold.

"Are you hurt?" he asked, louder this time. His voice was thick and his breathing heavy.

Her throat closed up. She shook her head, reached for the wall, slid down, and put her head between her knees. *Oh, Jesus, Mary, and Joseph, what did I do?* Her breaths came in short sharp gasps, not nearly enough to bring in air.

Can't breathe! I can't breathe!

Spots appeared before her eyes. Air failed to fill her lungs. She felt the shadow of the gun muzzle against her head and again disappeared into memory, into that dirty room, her hands cuffed to the bedposts, her wrists slick with blood, the cold gun muzzle digging into her skull while they laughed. She'd never get away. She'd be stuck there forever, reliving this over and over and over...

"If you don't scream, I'll kill you," said the leering voice above her.

She bit her tongue until it bled, swallowed the blood. A blade slashed across her midsection. Agony erupted.

"Scream, damn you!"

Another slash, she rode with the pain, let it consume her.

"If you won't scream, I'll have to kill you." He slammed the gun against her head, pulled the trigger...

"Patricia." That resonant voice whispered in her ear, those soft hands stroked her shoulder. "Stay with us. Focus on me."

He clasped her hand. Her fingers wound around his. Strong. Steady.

"Slow down, Patricia. Deeper breaths."

I'm not there anymore. I survived. I'm alive. Breathe.

"Okay," she choked out.

Her knuckles throbbed. The bruises on her right side began to erupt into agony. Good, pain helped. It anchored her to here and now. She let it roll over her and squeezed Grayson's hand harder.

She stretched out her legs, raised her head, and let it rest against the back of the wall. She trembled but she stayed with him. Breathe, he kept saying, and she repeated the words inside her head.

Breathe.

Sight returned. The trembling slowed. Fuck, a panic attack. She hadn't had one for years. Couldn't afford it now, either. Back to reality, brain.

Work to do. A story to write. About Adrienne, giving her life attempting to stop the theft.

Don't give in. Don't let anyone see weakness.

Think about anything else but the past.

"You okay?" she asked Grayson.

"I'm fine, thanks to you." Grayson said in a quiet voice. Louder, he said, "You have good timing, Dorothy. Thank you."

How long had Trisha been falling apart?

"You're welcome," Dorothy said.

Combined flashlight beams lit up the entire section of tunnel. The cops pulled Trisha's attacker to his feet. The man whimpered.

Not long, Trisha thought. She hadn't been lost long, thanks to Grayson. Focus. Watch, observe, get the information. *Breathe*. Live. *Survive*.

Adrienne hadn't survived. Unfair.

Grayson brushed hair away from Trisha's face, his fingertips catching the edge of her cheeks. Talented hands, those. Hands that could take down Nazis, defuse a bomb, and still touch with such tenderness.

Did he think her weak now? Dammit, she *cared* if he did.

Trisha counted at least three transit officers plus Newman and Dorothy in the tunnels. Shit. She'd gone berserk and collapsed in front of a crowd. Were they judging her too?

Didn't matter. They'd caught the guys who killed Adrienne.

The cops cuffed two suspects, who were groaning and complaining of aching heads. Detective Newman knelt over a big, beefy man unmoving on the floor.

Trisha's attacker spat blood onto the floor as a cop cuffed him and hauled him up.

"Hah. We'll all be dead soon anyway when the bomb goes off. Boom," he said. "You just watch."

"A bomb?" Dorothy's voice cut through the murmured responses of the officers and the groans of the suspects. "Edmund, what's he talking about?"

Grayson squeezed Trisha's hand. "Relax," he whispered into her ear. "All's well. You're not alone. I'm here."

He rose. "We're safe," he said to Dorothy. "They planted a C-4 bomb under the museum but it's defused. It's in an abandoned station down this tunnel."

"Shit," Dorothy said.

"It's defused," Grayson said again.

Dorothy rattled off orders, first to the cops around her and then into the radio clipped to her shoulder. Trisha tried to keep track of exactly what Dorothy said but the ringing in her ear from the gunshot made it difficult, not to mention the dizziness in her head. Panic attack still? She hoped not. She held a hand out in front of her, determined to stop the trembling.

That's past. I'm fine now. Stop freaking.

Chastising herself didn't work nearly as well as focusing on Grayson's voice had. Oh, hell, he probably thought she was a helpless idiot.

Dorothy called for the bomb squad.

Notebook, now. She needed to write all this down. But her head lolled forward, heavy, overloaded, her hands trembled, and pain came with each breath. *Get up, dammit. Up!*

But her legs wouldn't obey.

"Any chance for him?" Grayson pointed to the body on the floor.

Newman shook his head. "Heart shot," Newman turned him over. "No breathing and no heartbeat. Yours?"

"No, I didn't fire," Grayson answered. "Everyone was too close, and I couldn't see to aim. That had to be a ricochet from one of their guns."

The transit cops had their three prisoners ready to move.

"Get them out of here," Dorothy ordered.

Newman went with them without insulting her, nearly as much a miracle as Grayson defusing the bomb. Dorothy, holding her flashlight at her shoulder, walked over to Trisha and Grayson.

"She's hurt?" Dorothy asked Grayson.

"No." Trisha said. "I'm *fine*. Just got the wind knocked out of me."

"I'm not so sure." Grayson knelt beside her.

Don't fall apart. "Fine," she choked out. "Resting my eyes."

"Dammit, Connell," Dorothy said. "Stop playing it so tough."

"I *am* tough." Ah, hell. If you had to say you were tough, by definition, you weren't tough.

A hand settled on her shoulder. Grayson. "Patricia? I need to check you for injuries. Is that all right?"

The extra lighting revealed his frown. She guessed she looked worse. Great, now he knew the depth of her panic.

"Just got the wind knocked out of me," she repeated. "Breathing's getting better."

"Hold still and let me check. Please, Patricia."

The "please" caught her. "Sure."

He patted her down from the ankles to her hips, brisk yet gentle and, somehow, soothing. She concentrated on his touch, the here, the now, not the past. She concentrated on the fact that they'd caught the guys who killed Adrienne. That she'd broken one of their noses. That one of them was dead.

Her trembling ceased. Her breathing slowed, close to normal. The pain remained. That worked. It kept her in the present, not the past.

"Let me know if you feel any pain," he said.

"Pain? No way. You'd make a killing as a masseuse."

Dorothy snorted.

"Good to know," Grayson said.

His hands moved to her chest. She winced as his fingers glided over the new bruises.

"Sorry. I'm going to have to pat everywhere on your chest to check for entry wounds," he said.

"Is that what they're calling copping a feel these days?" She started to laugh, it hurt, and she stopped.

Grayson's fingers caressed her through the thin T-shirt. She breathed in deeply, even though the movement amped the pain up another notch. No one had touched her like this in years. Everywhere Grayson's fingers reached, they drove away fear and nightmares.

Her body warmed, despite the damp chill. Grayson knew just how much pressure to apply, knew how to caress rather than pat, knew how to bring her alive.

Oh, shit, could he feel the scars on her stomach through the shirt? And if he could, would he start asking questions she never wanted to answer?

He held his flashlight so close to her that she shut her eyes to the brightness. She winced again as he pushed on a tender spot just under her breast.

"Sorry, I had to be sure." He lifted his hand away.

She sighed. Moment over. "Verdict, doc?"

"Given how tender the area is, I believe your entire right side is bruised. You should get X-rays to check for cracked ribs. But there's no blood, and that's good. Can you breathe without pain?"

"Sure. Like I said, just got the wind knocked out of me." In so many ways.

The wrinkle lines in Grayson's face relaxed. Now that she could see again, she noticed his eyes were not just brown but the deepest shade of brown.

"She's clean. No GSW," he said to Dorothy. "She went down under one of them. No doubt she got the wind knocked out of her. That's why she took a moment."

"Good," Dorothy said.

Whoa. Grayson knew she'd been in the midst of a freak out, yet he'd covered for her. Not just with Dorothy but with the rest of the police. Another thing she owed him.

And the pain? She'd had worse hurts from spills on her bike. The breathing issues must have been from the panic, not from any injury. "Help me up, Grayson?"

He held her arm, supporting her while she stood. *Yes.* She could stand.

"If you can walk, Connell, you have to get out right now," Dorothy said.

Trisha blinked. "Why?"

"Your senses really are scrambled. *The bomb.* We're evacuating everyone from here and the museum until the bomb squad gives the all clear."

"We're safe. It won't blow." Trisha pointed a finger at Grayson. "He saved everybody."

"*We* saved everyone," Grayson said.

Dorothy spoke into the radio again. "Yeah, let him pass. He can move the reporter out."

"You're not calling Newman on me, are you?" Trisha asked.

"Not that you don't deserve Newman for the stunt you just pulled but, no. David's in the crowd at the entrance. He's going to get you out of my hair."

"Hey, I helped catch your bad guys. Lieutenant."

"You snuck into the tunnels, against my explicit orders, and it nearly cost you your lives. Twice. You should have told me about the second entrance so I could send trained police officers in." She glared at Grayson. "And what the hell were you doing, messing with an active bomb?"

Grayson slipped an arm around Trisha's waist, steadying her. She could've protested that she could stand on her own now. Hey, maybe *Grayson* needed it. It'd been a helluva day for him too.

"I had no choice," Grayson said. "The bomb was literally ticking. We had no time to find experts." He cleared his throat. "It could've taken out the entire museum and everyone in it."

"Including Amanda?" Dorothy asked.

"Everyone," Grayson said.

"Who's Amanda?" Trisha asked.

"My ex-wife," Grayson said. "My daughter's mother."

"Ah." Divorced? Someone had let this guy who defused bombs, soothed freak outs, and took out armed men without firing a shot *go*? *Dumbass.*

"Dorothy, you don't have to wait for David. I can walk Patricia out," Grayson said.

"Oh, no, you don't. You have to stay here, lead the bomb squad to the device, and show them what you did."

"Seems I missed a party." David walked into view with a uniformed officer at his heels. The officer set up a bank of portable lights that finally illuminated the entire section of tunnel.

Grayson took his arm off Trisha's waist. "Walk her out slowly, David. Her whole side is bruised."

She stifled a protest about leaving him. Truth was, she had to leave. She had to get topside to call Joe with an update about what happened in the tunnels so he could get the whole thing set up to run in the early edition. But she somehow hated to leave Grayson on his own.

David hugged her. "Dammit, you never can stay out of trouble, can you?"

"Not my nature. And careful with the hugging." She winced.

"C'mon. There are already ambulances waiting topside," David said. "I'm having someone check you out."

Hell, no. Being that close to needles and medical smells might trigger another freaky flashback. Her equilibrium was fucked already, and she couldn't afford another collapse.

She turned to Grayson. "Don't let the bomb squad screw up your good work."

He rested his hand on her shoulder. "Thank you. For everything."

One side of his mouth rose into a wry smile. She melted down into her motorcycle boots.

"You're welcome," she said. "Catch you later."

"Count on it."

CHAPTER EIGHT

TRISHA WALKED without David's support, but she kept one hand on the wall of the tunnel, just in case panic struck again. So far, so good. David hovered, illuminating their passage with his flashlight.

"You made a friend," David said as the silence settled in.

"What do you mean?" She quickened her pace. *I am so sick of this damned darkness.*

"Grayson," David said.

"Oh. Yeah, him." The guy who defused bombs, took out three armed attackers in the dark, had magic hands, and covered for her.

Damn, she liked Grayson.

Her side ached worse with every step. Those bruises would be a reminder of this day for a while.

At least she was alive. Unlike Adrienne.

"Easy, Trish." David put his arm around her waist and steered her around a bend in the tunnel.

"Ouch! Careful with your hand."

"I barely touched you. You've probably got cracked ribs."

"I've cracked ribs before. Nothing to be done except endure the pain until they heal."

"Let's try this instead." David hooked his arm around hers. "Better?"

"Yeah."

They started walking again.

"So, what happened to make my boss so friendly?" he asked.

"That was Grayson being friendly?" She shrugged to cover her surprise. Ouch. That hurt.

"Sure. It was even beyond friendly to intense. And he called you Patricia. Twice."

"Ah, we just bonded over everyday stuff like defusing bombs and rumbles in the dark." They'd bonded, right? Unless she'd misjudged Grayson. He'd needed her help, after all. She owed him, he owed her. Even trade.

"You were right when you said he was always prepared. He knows his stuff."

"What the heck happened with the bomb?" David asked.

Answering would help her collect her muddled thoughts for the story. She described the cavern, the box, and that fucking clock. She kept her admiration for Grayson's coolness under fire to herself.

"I held the flashlights while he disconnected the clock. I guess he was happy I held steady."

"Panic's not your style," David said. "Grayson always respects competence."

"And here I was under the impression he liked the red hair and black leather." But she *had* panicked. And, still, he'd covered for her. Why?

"Hah."

The proverbial light at the end of the tunnel finally became literal. She reached up and took the cross out from her shirt. Thank God, fate, and Grayson. She'd escaped this tomb alive.

As she'd remembered, the tunnel exited into Gimbel's back storage closet, one that hadn't been used since the store's heyday, judging by the amount of dust. Empty boxes and broken plastic hangers littered the place. Unattached wires and broken panels hung from the ceilings.

Still, the basement was heaven after the tunnels. She wiped her slimy hand on her jeans. A uniformed officer posted by the door to the exit nodded at them as they walked by. She blinked at the fluorescents, almost blinded by their brilliance.

"You okay?" the officer asked.

She recognized one of the transit cops who'd been in the tunnel. "Peachy," she said. "Any trouble with your suspects?"

He grinned. "The one with the broken nose kept bitching about filing charges of police brutality. He thinks you're a cop."

"God forbid." She laughed. Bad move. It set her ribs aching again. She put a hand around her chest. David steadied her.

"There are stairs to street level behind the door over there, but you might want to take that corridor," the transit cop said. "It slants up to the loading dock and the sidewalk. Easier for you."

"Thanks. Did the bomb squad arrive yet?" she asked.

He shook his head. "Any minute now."

"Are you evacuating the store?"

"Waiting on that. Though once those explosives guys get here, they'll want to evacuate all of midtown." He snorted. "Like New York could ever be hit that hard."

"Trish, c'mon." David pulled at her. "Topside, remember?"

"Thanks," she said to the cop.

He nodded as she passed. His nametag read "Stan Donovan." She needed to remember him. The more friendly cops she knew, the easier her job became. When she'd started working the police beat, she'd still been wary of cops. Now, she knew most were okay. The minority screwed things up for everyone. If only the majority didn't cover for them out of misplaced loyalty.

David led her down the concrete corridor and into the larger receiving area, where bits and pieces of empty cardboard boxes and a few leftover wooden pallets littered the floor. She leaned more on David as the corridor ended and the floor started to slant upward.

Almost there.

Its signal no longer blocked by the tunnels, her beeper started screaming at her

She winced. "I need a phone, ASAP."

"Your editor?"

"Yeah, he's probably pissed because he needs an update. And I ditched another assignment to cover this."

"You probably would have been safer if you hadn't," he said. "But then, half our people would be blown up, so I'm glad you did."

"I need a phone. Now. And I'm out of quarters, dammit. Is your car around? Can I use that phone?"

"Maybe," he said. "I'm going to have you checked out first."

"I'm fine." She tried to relax, breathe in, breathe out. Settle.

They walked into the bright sunshine. Police vehicles, lights flashing, blocked both sides of the street. Yellow tape cordoned off the entrance to Gimbel's and the adjoining subway, and uniformed officers physically blocked the doors.

The smell of car exhaust combined with the aroma wafting from the nearby food carts filled her nose, reminding her that she hadn't eaten breakfast. Hunger pains were a nice change from hyperventilating.

Otherwise, Midtown was the same swirling mosh of car horns, yells, and the rumble of pedestrian crowds as always.

No news vans yet but they'd show soon. And they wouldn't get half the story that she had.

"Trish," David said. "C'mon. We need to get to the ambulance over there."

"No, we don't. Just give me a minute." She held up a finger. "I'm feeling better." Truth.-Plus, getting close to the ambulance might send her right back to a freak out and that damned dirty room again.

David grabbed the sleeve of her jacket. "C'mon."

"Hey, stop being grabby. I told you, I'm fine."

She tried to slip out of David's hold and only succeeded in pulling her arm out of the sleeve of her jacket. Instead of fighting him, she let the entire jacket slide off her shoulders.

"You're going over there if I have to carry you," David said.

The ambulance doors closed, the lights flicked on, and the sirens sounded as the vehicle sped away.

That solved that problem.

David shook his head. "Now I have to have the cops call another one."

"I'm okay, David. I'm fine. I'll even rest for a minute. You've seen me get over worse scrapes, remember?"

He threw up his hands, her coat still tight in his fist. "I guess so."

"And you'll give me a ride and let me use your car phone because I've had a rough morning and you're worried about me, right?" She grinned.

He rolled his eyes. She'd won. Just a second here, and she could call in the story.

She slid down the wall and sat at the base of the bricks, taking inventory of all the aches and pains. Good. No trembling at all this time. Her ribs stopped screaming at her. Her stomach settled. She craned her neck at the clear sky overhead and smiled. It was a beautiful fall day. Perfect for sightseeing in Central Park or strolls in the Village or shopping on Park or even a trip to the Statue of Liberty.

"You know, I feel like the kid in the Dr. Seuss book because I have a story no one can beat."

"That kid made it up, Trish," David said, looming over her.

"That's the thing about this job. You can't make this shit up." Real life hardly ever had happy endings. Look at Adrienne. Look at Nicky. Stupid Non-Hodgins lymphoma.

She held up her hand. "Can you dig aspirin out of my coat? I think there are a couple in the front pocket."

"Sure." He fumbled in her jacket pocket. "Crap!" He held the jacket out from his body.

"Hey, the pockets aren't that dirty."

David raised the right jacket sleeve, exposing a neat little bullet hole at the seam where the arm joined the body of the jacket. One bullet had screamed by her ear, but she'd never had any indication of the one that had gone through her jacket.

"Oh, hell! Do you know how much that will cost to fix?"

Good, Trisha. Complain about the jacket. Then you won't have to think about how close the bullet came.

She tensed, fearing she might freak out but remained calm. She wondered if the same bullet that went through her jacket had killed the man who'd fallen on her. She swallowed hard, her throat dry, and wished she had a drink. Even for her, this was a banner day for dodging death.

"Better the jacket than you," David said, pulling out her Tylenol capsules. "Here."

She swallowed down the capsules without water.

"Why do you have a cigarette lighter in here?" David said, pulling the pack from her other pocket. "You said you quit, Trish."

"I did. I'm down to one a day, sometimes not even that. Anyway, that's

Nicky's lighter. I carry it for good luck. And you never know when you might need luck. Today's a good example of that."

The corner of her notebook peeked out from the jacket. Time to get back to work. Her story would be front page, yeah, but she needed more, especially about Grayson and about how Adrienne had died. She had to memorialize the kid properly.

She rose slowly, using the wall for balance, and put her hand over her bruises at the stab of pain. They'd probably hurt worse tomorrow. She'd have to invest in some ice packs.

David handed her back the jacket. She slid into it with exaggerated care.

"Your hands are messed up," David said. "You hit someone?"

"No big." She flexed her fingers. The blood had dried into her knuckles. The gun to her head freaked her out but, worse, she barely remembered breaking the guy's nose. No hesitation on that either. She'd hoped her worst impulses were under control. Obviously not.

Too much madness in her soul.

She flipped open her notebook, grabbed the pen from the inside pocket. "Tell me how Grayson knew how to defuse a bomb, David. That seems beyond even what a security expert should know."

David stared at her for a minute, then cleared his throat, having apparently decided to stop badgering her about the injuries.

"We had a client with bomb threats a year ago. Grayson made us all learn the basics. He went more in-depth himself. He hates to be unprepared."

She wrote that down. Prepared. Careful. Perfectly Grayson. Yet, it wasn't a full picture. Much more roiled underneath Grayson's placid surface. The man had layers upon layers. "He was an FBI Special Agent in Charge in D.C., right? Isn't that how he could pass on the information I had to a federal witness around the holidays last year?"

"Yeah." David nodded. "He ran an office in the investigative division. Some undercover work, some work that he doesn't talk about. He left the D.C. branch four years ago to go private."

Undercover? "What's with the British accent that comes and goes?"

David smiled. "He's English on his mother's side. She was a war bride. His father is a Marine. A retired colonel, I think."

"That explains a lot." No wonder the guy was a bundle of contradictions. "He mentioned an ex-wife and a daughter." Not needed for the story. But she wanted to know.

"The daughter's sixteen, I think. She's why Grayson came to New York."

"Not for the ex-wife?"

"Who knows? She works at the museum. Assistant Director Amanda Grayson. He took the job because she asked. So it's hard to tell what's going on there," David said. "Why the personal questions about Grayson?"

"I'm curious." Guys who were hung up on their exes were usually bad news, though Grayson had been quick to call her his ex.

"Grayson's too old for you, Trisha," David said.

Oh, please. What a stupid objection. "He's what, maybe late thirties? That's not more than ten years older than me. And he smacked around those Nazis damn good." She shrugged. "Doesn't matter, I guess." She put away her notebook. "Can I get that ride now?"

"Where we headed?"

"Back to the museum, of course. I need to get quotes from the museum officials, if I can."

"I'll give you a ride there on one last condition," David said.

She narrowed her eyes. "What?"

"I want to know how you knew about the tunnels under the museum. And don't tell me it was research on the homeless."

"Why did you support me in front of Grayson when I mentioned them if you thought I was lying?"

"Because you know nearly every back alley in Manhattan. Stop evading and answer my question, Trish."

She stared past the police barricades to Herald Square, at all the residents and tourists who remained blissfully unaware of the life that went on under their noses.

"Nicky and I broke into that museum from the tunnel when we were teens. We were homeless, and it was warm. He liked the suits of armor. I liked the artwork."

"Ouch. I didn't realize how bad it was." David reached for her hand.

"I had Nicky back then. Coulda been worse." It had gotten worse for them, later. "Sleeping in the museum is a good memory." She smiled, remembering how they'd sacked out for the night under a tapestry in the storage room. Not luxury but warm, dry, and they'd had the whole museum to explore too. "We had a great time." They'd always made their own fun.

"Sorry for the rest." David stared at the sidewalk.

"Yeah, me too. Let's get going."

The exertion of the quick walk to the car almost took Trisha's breath away, not that she would show that to David. Still, his leather seats were comfy. Even if the Camaro did smell like a locker room.

David dialed the *Herald* on his car phone and handed her the receiver. Joe answered on the first ring.

"Trisha, I am going to kill you, then dump your body and that bike of yours in the East River. The publisher's on a tear because you missed the press conference."

"The Nazis who robbed the museum set a bomb, Joe."

"What?"

"So far, we've got an art theft, a murder, a bomb, suspects apprehended, and they might be Neo-Nazis."

"A bomb? Nazis for sure? And they've been arrested?"

"Check the police scanners if you don't believe me. They just sent in the bomb squad through an underground Midtown subway entrance. I have an eyewitness account of it being defused."

"What?"

She smiled, pleased that she could still manage to surprise Joe, the editor who'd seen everything. As David pulled into traffic, she filled in details.

She gave Joe the rundown, even with Grayson resting his forehead on the floor after defusing the bomb, and the fight in the tunnels. She kept the fight details vague and instead went with "suspects apprehended in the tunnels due to the efforts of Grayson and Lt. Dorothy Gilbert's team."

Joe's keyboard clicked in the background as he took notes. "This would be much easier if you would just get the hell in here."

"You and I both know I should stay on the scene until it's close to deadline."

He grumbled again but she kept talking and he kept typing.

———

Grayson rested, back against the wall of the tunnel, the morning's images running through his head.

The damned ticking clock, the gun going off an inch from Patricia's head, the lifeless body of the dead man. Hell, the body remained in front of them, a grim reminder.

He'd thought this place foreboding enough to be a tomb. Now it was.

But not *his* tomb. And not Patricia Connell's either, no thanks to him. He should have prevented the man from grabbing her. He'd nearly failed again today, a second death on his watch. He clenched his jaw so tight that his teeth started to scrape against each other. He swallowed to relax.

Danger over. Let it go.

He flexed his fingers and let the memory of running his hands over Patricia's lithe body take over. So much energy in such a thin form. How did one contain such an unstoppable force?

He might have continued to think of her as a goddess rather than a mere mortal if not for her panic in the aftermath of the fight. Instead, she'd proved disarmingly human and even vulnerable. The bomb hadn't phased her at all, so it must have been something specific about the physical assault.

What had she been most afraid of? Showing weakness. At least he'd been able to cover for her momentary lapse.

Calming her had calmed him. More than that. Patting her down had triggered emotions he hadn't felt since the break-up with Karen. Lust had sunk its claws in. And there they remained, ripping his composure to shreds.

He chided himself. Patricia probably chewed men up, spit them out, and laughed about it.

It's just adrenaline. It'll fade.

Dorothy paced the cavern, exploring the crime scene. Mostly, he guessed, moving around to work off nerves.

"Messy crime scene," she said.

Messy day. "Yes, that happens when you fight in the dark."

"Yes." She finally settled on the wall next to him. "I'll get the coroner in here after the bomb squad goes through."

"After the bomb squad goes through, you won't have anything left of your crime scene."

"True." She snorted. "Are you all right, English? You've hardly said a word since the reporter left."

"I'm alive and I shouldn't be, so, yes." An outlaw goddess had saved his life. Twice. Somehow, "all right" failed to cover it.

"Thanks for not protesting when I took your gun for evidence," Dorothy said.

"I want it on the record that I didn't fire." He glanced over at the body. At least this death, unlike Adrienne Katz's murder, wasn't on his conscience.

"How did you show up just in time to help?" he asked.

"I spotted a delivery truck with the logo of a store that's been closed for two months parked in the loading zone near the entrance Connell gave me."

"Good catch," he said. "Where'd you pick up the entourage?"

She sighed. "I only had Newman for back-up, so I called the transit boys over from Penn Station."

"Smart," he said.

"Maybe, maybe not, because the suspects spotted the transit cops and bolted." She tapped the flashlight against her palm. "Right into the tunnels and smack into you."

"We handled it."

"You and Connell shouldn't have been down here in the first place. I'm not sure whether to be pissed you were here or annoyed my delay almost got you killed." She tapped his forearm, a light touch, as if to reassure herself that he was still in one piece. "I'll settle for being glad you're alive."

"That makes two of us." He took a long breath and let it out slowly, reminded of how he'd urged Patricia to do the same. "What did you say about Nazis as the suspects were led out?"

"Connell's attacker had a swastika tattooed on his forearm," she said. "Noticed it when I cuffed him."

So the swastikas painted on the museum walls weren't a diversion. "Did you find the stolen paintings?"

"Oh, sure, in all my free time tromping around the tunnels."

He laughed. "I meant, were they in the van?"

"We haven't found them yet, but if I had hidden million-dollar paintings in a van, I'd have sealed them somewhere inside. We'll tear the vehicle apart. They have to be in there somewhere."

"One would think so." But if they'd planned to blow up the museum, why steal only those five paintings? And where did the lighter fluid fit in?

Patricia had been right. He needed the real story of how Sidney had obtained the paintings.

Dorothy's radio blared.

"Vehicle clear. No explosives in there." That was likely the bomb squad leader.

"Alert impound," Dorothy said.

"Right. Heading to your twenty, Lieutenant."

"I ain't going nowhere."

"About time they started down here," Grayson said when she'd signed off. "It's getting cold."

"Hey, I tried to keep you out of these tunnels," she said. "Which reminds me, just how did you get down here?"

"There's a second entrance at the subway stop across the street from the museum, though we almost were hit by a train getting into it, and the path was roundabout. Patricia gave you the better lead and a more direct route."

"I don't care. You should have told me."

"She only told me about it after you left the museum."

"Uh-huh," Dorothy said. "So you somehow couldn't find a cop who could radio me this information?"

"Do you want to know what happened or not?" he said.

"Oh, by all means, go ahead."

He told her the story, grateful to put it in the clinical language of a police report, which provided much-needed emotional distance.

When he finished, Dorothy tapped his forearm again. "Did the bomb really tick?"

"Not anymore," he said.

For several moments, only the sounds of their breathing filled the tunnel.

"Too close," she finally said.

"Yes." He crossed his arms over his chest, trying to warm his cold fingers.

"You realize that now I owe the damned reporter because her tip panned out?"

He smiled. "She more than earned it."

"You won't say that in a couple of weeks, when she's still pestering you with follow-up questions. You'll never shake her now, not with a story this good."

"Patricia earned it," he said again. Keep that woman at a distance? Good advice, he supposed. But he wanted to know everything about her. How had she become a reporter? What made her so reckless? What caused the panic? He also needed to discover her connection to Katz. She knew the murdered guard, somehow.

Did she have someone waiting for her tonight to help her through the day? A boyfriend? No, he thought. She'd bury herself in her work. As he would.

He tilted his head back to rest against the wall.

"So it's 'Patricia' now?" Dorothy asked.

"It's her name," he said.

"Oh, not you too, English. You, of all people, should have more sense."

"What's that supposed to mean?"

"Half the force wants to smack her upside the head, the other half wants to get her in bed."

That described his initial reaction to Patricia Connell perfectly. "Does she ever date cops?"

"I give her credit, she steers clear of that. She said something once about it being a conflict of interest. Her job is the one thing she takes seriously."

Patricia had ethics, even if they were her own sort of ethics. But he knew that already from the way she'd refused to abandon him at the site of the bomb and the way she'd backed him up when they were attacked. And now that his brain was working, he remembered what David had told him about his friend, the reporter, last Christmas when he'd asked for that favor that dovetailed nicely with a personal case he'd solved.

She'd been in an orphanage as a child. Self-raised then. That fit.

"I see," he said.

"See what? You know, English, you should be past doing your thinking from below the belt."

"It's perfectly normal to be curious about her after what we went through together."

"Uh-huh. So exactly what you were thinking when you groped her a few minutes ago?" Dorothy asked.

"I was checking for bullet wounds." And he had. But he'd wanted to do far more.

"To repeat Connell's words, is that what they call it nowadays?"

"Give me a reason to dislike her, other than she's press."

Dorothy rubbed her hands together for warmth. "The way she went postal on the guy who attacked her. She'd have killed or severely injured him if you hadn't stopped her."

Yes. That.

Patricia had overreacted, fueled by what had to have been pure rage, perhaps even a post-traumatic stress flashback. But, so far, Dorothy remained unaware of the panic attack. Good.

"He threatened to kill her."

"She lost it. You wouldn't have under the same circumstances," Dorothy said.

But neither of them knew the full circumstances of why Patricia had lost control. Bloody hell, he might have lost his temper if the man had hurt her. He'd never wanted to destroy someone so much in his whole life.

"Are you planning on charging Patricia with assault?" he asked. "How could you when it was self-defense?"

"Yeah, I know, it'd be hard to make that charge stick, as a good lawyer would argue what you just did, self-defense. But we both know she lost control, English. It's not the first time I've seen her temper."

Not the first time? Did he want to know those details?

More minutes ticked by.

"Had enough of the subject? Fine, let's talk about you," Dorothy said.

"About me?"

"I'm hoping this close call will jar you out of your isolation," Dorothy said.

"My isolation?" he asked.

She shook her head. "Is there an echo in here? English, it's been three years since you and Karen broke up."

Almost four. And a spectacular break up it had been, right on the heels of his marriage also irrevocably ending. "What's your point?"

"That you've shut down emotionally since then."

"I haven't wanted to date." Desire had been a stranger, an intellectual abstract. Until today, until the moment he'd laid hands on Patricia Connell. An intense longing had exploded, as strong in its way as any bomb.

Adrenaline?

"I'm not talking about a girlfriend. I'm talking about isolation," Dorothy said. "For instance, it's been nearly that long since you've been over to my house for a quiet dinner. It's past time. I could cook."

"No, thank you. Remember what happened last time you cooked?"

"Hey, I wanted to give my husband a break from the kitchen. He does enough cooking at work. Not my fault it turned out so badly."

"Did the dog eat the leftover the next day?" he said.

She laughed. "No."

He laughed and the tension finally left his shoulders.

"Look, if I promise to let James cook, will you come back over for dinner?" she asked.

He frowned. He'd just been neatly outmaneuvered. "I have to check my schedule."

"You always do. You've been busy avoiding everyone but your daughter these last few years."

"I've been building a business."

She backed up a step, as if to study him. "Promise me to think about how you almost got blown to bits and why that should be a wake-up call."

She had a point. Today had been a reminder of how quickly life could end. Time to take a few risks. Did that include Patricia?

"I hear you. But you have to stop reminding me how I, in your words, was almost blown to bits."

That drew a quiet laugh. "Okay. So what about dinner? You can bring my goddaughter. I haven't seen enough of her lately."

"I'll check Eleanor's schedule and get back to you. Promise." Since the divorce, his daughter Eleanor and Dorothy saw each other only rarely. Amanda had never been at ease with police officers.

He cocked his head. "Do you hear voices? I think your bomb squad's here."

"Good," she said. "I'm freezing."

"Yes, next time we have a heart-to-heart, I'm wishing for a couch, a good brandy, a fireplace, and no explosives."

She jabbed a finger into his chest. "Hah. If you had listened to me, you'd have been far away from the explosives."

"No, I'd have probably been caught inside the museum when the bomb went off, as would have many of your cops."

"My cops would have found the bomb. I'd have found it."

"In time?"

She sighed and closed her eyes for a moment. "Maybe not." She walked over and gave him a quick hug.

He returned Dorothy's rare show of public affection. "Careful, James will be jealous."

"Never." She broke the hug. "I think in a few short hours, the reporter's corrupted you, English."

His words came out sadder than intended. "Too late for that."

CHAPTER NINE

"CRAP," Trisha said.

The cops had blocked off all the cross-streets to the museum. No vehicles or pedestrians allowed. One good result: the other news crews, now aware of the story from the scanners and all the activity, had been forced to set up a block away, distant from the action.

Still, she couldn't sneak up the marble steps again. Dammit, she needed those quotes from the museum officials, not some dry public statement written by the NYPD's press office, and she needed more information about Adrienne too, like what her job had been exactly and how she'd been killed.

Trisha slumped in the passenger seat of David's Camaro and pressed a hand over her aching ribs.

"Do you think you could use your credentials as part of the museum security to get me past all that?" she asked David.

"No. But I have another idea."

"What?"

"Trust me."

"Always," she said.

David turned right into one of those dead-end city streets that resembled a lane rather than a proper road. Multi-level brownstones, some covered in ivy, crowded to the edge of the narrow lane. A little rich oasis in the middle of the city's mess.

David pulled his Camaro into a short driveway, edging the nose of the car right up against an antique wrought-iron gate. He pointed past the gate. "There. That small alley on the other side of the gate comes out in the middle of the next street over, right across from the museum."

"That's perfect." She squinted to make it out. The alley couldn't be more than three feet across. "How'd you find this?"

"We cased the entire neighborhood for this job. I spotted the alley. Grayson gave me a commendation for that one. And looks like I found an alley unfamiliar to you, too. Bonus points for me." David unbuckled his seat belt. "If we get to the other side this way, it'll take some time before the cops notice you, depending on how much trouble you cause."

"I mostly need quotes. If I find the officials I need, I could be in and out fast." She stepped out of the car and shut the door. Its bottom nearly scraped the concrete walls of the sunken driveway.

That movement rewarded her with another dose of agony. Nope, she couldn't pass that off as a lingering effect of the panic attack anymore. Cracked ribs, mostly likely. She needed more aspirin.

"Careful with my paint job," David said.

"For finding me a way in, I'll wash and wax your car myself."

"Naked?"

"In your dreams," she said.

"It happens a lot in my dreams."

"That's because it won't happen in real life," she said. David's familiar teasing normalized the day. In truth, he was sickeningly in love with his fiancée. "By the way, won't the homeowners have your car towed?"

"No. They're away this week."

"Let me guess: Grayson had you run background checks on all the residents here."

"Yep," he said. "Damn boring work, too. I hate sifting through reports."

David pushed open the wrought iron gate. It moved squeaked and scraped against the concrete driveway. They had just enough room to slip through, one at a time. She had to take a deep breath in to get past. Bracing for the pain mitigated the agony, at least.

The narrowness of the alley allowed Trisha to use the brick wall for support. Once she got back to the paper, she could fill up a bag with ice and wrap it around the ribs while she typed. She only needed to keep going for an hour or two.

Okay, just one.

As David promised, they came out across the street from the impressive front steps of the museum. Three police cruisers blocked the steps. A line of uniforms prevented anyone from even getting close to the cruisers. Only the occasional squawk of a police radio broke the eerie silence. The cops muttered now and then and the civilians on the sidewalk followed suit.

Trisha wrote her impressions of the scene down, some keywords that would bring it to vivid memory when she typed it up.

"Damn. There's no way to get inside the museum for photos of the crime scene," she said.

She glanced left, toward the bodega on the corner. Past that barricade, the camera crews from the networks were trying to shoot footage but they couldn't be getting much.

Good.

"I can describe it to you," David said.

"That would be great. Thanks. Go ahead." She held the pencil over the notebook.

"Nope, not until you agree to do something for *me*," he said.

"I'm not washing your car naked."

"Hah." He pulled out his notebook and flicked to a page of crime scene drawing while blocking out her view. "I want to drive your bike."

"No one drives my Indian." Her bike was her baby.

"I guess you don't want to know what the crime scene looks like then."

She dug into the inside pocket of the jacket for her keys.

"Fine. You can have it tonight and return it to my place tomorrow morning. I'm probably not in the best shape to drive it anyway." Last time she'd cracked her ribs, steering the bike had been impossible.

Oh. David remembered that. No wonder he wanted to keep her off the bike. She exchanged the keys for his cell phone without further protest.

David gave her a rundown of the crime scene: the missing paintings, the swastikas, and Adrienne, dead, at the foot of the wall.

"Shit," she said as she wrote.

But she knew these details would be part of what made the story.

"You can't use Adrienne Katz's name," David said. "Her next of kin hasn't been notified yet."

"Okay. I'll ask the cops later if notifications have been made." Later tonight, she'd have to call Katz's family. She hated to think what they'd go through today, starting with the police showing up at their door, hat in hand. "Thanks, David."

"I guess since you might have saved my life by discovering the bomb and you're letting me drive the Indian, it's the least I can do."

"Nice that you put saving your life first."

She flipped a page in her notebook and turned her attention to the crowd on the sidewalk.

The civilians stood in a semi-circle, listless, about ten feet away from the alley. Cops ringed them loosely from the front and sides, guarding them. She frowned. Why not just let them go?

"Who are those guys?" She pointed.

David nodded. "Museum employees. Probably Dorothy ordered them kept here to be interviewed. They're all suspects, as far as she's concerned."

Museum employees were exactly the people she needed. "Is the director with them?"

"Windergaard?" David put up a hand against the sunlight and squinted. "Yeah, he's at the edge of the sidewalk. Oh, interesting. He's decided to argue with one of the uniforms."

Trisha walked several steps out of the alley for a better look. A thin, almost emaciated man pointed his finger at a police sergeant, who scowled in response.

She held her notebook behind her back and walked closer to overhear the conversation.

"I must insist you let us pass," Windergaard said. "We have to get to work as soon as possible."

Behind him stood men holding paint thinner and brushes. Maintenance crew? What, the museum director wanted to clean up already? Fat chance with an active crime scene.

"Sorry, crime scene stays secure," the sergeant said.

"Can we at least get back into the museum? I don't understand why we were evacuated," Windergaard asked.

The museum employees hadn't been told about the bomb?

"Can't go in, can't say when you can." The sergeant turned his back to Windergaard.

The museum director threw up his arms.

Trisha stifled a laugh and cleared her throat to cover the noise. But Windergaard must have heard her because he turned.

"Mr. Velasquez?" Windergaard zeroed in on David, who stood several steps behind her. "Do you know what's going on?"

David pointed to her. "She does."

David, you're awesome. Maybe she'd let him have the Indian for several days.

The museum director flicked elegant fingers in her direction and frowned, probably taking in her filthy clothes and dirty fingers. "Who is this person?"

David jumped in. "Mr. Windergaard, this is—"

"Trisha Connell, reporter for the *New York Herald*." She grasped Windergaard's hand, her notebook clasped in the other.

Windergaard made a face. She held her grip longer than necessary and maintained eye contact. "Good to meet you. I understand you're having a rough morning."

She released his hand. Windergaard took out his pocket square from his suit coat and wiped dirt off his fingers.

She smiled, knowing it would add to his discomfort. "The police are worried that you're not safe in the museum."

"Why would they think that?" Windergaard's face lost the pinched expression. He adjusted his glasses.

"If they won't tell you, I shouldn't either. Tell me, do you still plan to open next week, as scheduled?"

"Of course, but—"

"Even if you don't recover the paintings?"

"I fully expect the Cézannes to be recovered. In any case, thieves and murderers don't dictate this museum's schedule."

He held his back ramrod straight, but it only made him resemble a twig that could easily be snapped.

"Do you think Neo-Nazis did this? I understand there were swastikas painted on the museum walls."

"There were, yes. You'll have to ask the police about those." He removed his glasses and wiped them on his pocket square. "But you said the police believe the museum is unsafe. What do you mean by—"

"I understand from David that there is a dispute about who owned the paintings, that Holocaust survivors want to claim part of your exhibit? Is Dante Sidney the owner of all the items in *Lost Treasures*?"

"I sympathize with the Jewish survivors for what they went through, of course, but they have no case, no paper trail, no documentation. We're confident in the provenance supplied by the current owners."

"And by current owners, you're referring to Sidney?"

"He is empowered to act for the owners, yes."

A mystery surrounded Sidney and his paintings. She'd have to get working on that tomorrow.

Windergaard put his glasses back on, fingers twitching.

"What is your theory on who stole the paintings?" she asked.

"Well, it seems clear from the swastikas that it was some radical group. I'm more concerned with the breach in our security system. Mr. Grayson promised me a foolproof system," he said.

Excellent. An opening to another question she wanted to ask, about museum security. "Mr. Grayson actually said 'foolproof?'"

"Well, no, but he assured me the museum was protected," Windergaard said.

"I understand he wanted to post his own people on guard in the exhibit?" she asked.

"We had no budget for that kind of expense and, besides, Mr. Grayson claimed his system would work without additional people, but it did not, obviously. That's why I fired his firm and—"

Trisha's hand stopped in mid-scribble.

What? He'd *fired* Grayson?

"They will be replaced with a better one," Windergaard continued. "Now since you obviously know nothing about what's going on, we're done here."

He started to turn around.

She cut him off. "You *fired* Grayson?"

"Yes, of course. How could I let him continue after today's failure?"

Windergaard tried to step around her but was blocked by one of the maintenance guys holding a can of paint thinner.

"Really, Ms. Connell, it was a simple decision. As you just pointed out, we still don't have the paintings. He failed in his responsibilities."

"Then you fired the man who just defused a bomb, saved your life, and saved the museum from a blast that would have leveled the building. Not to mention his role in apprehending the four suspects."

"A *bomb*?" Windergaard's hands attacked his tie, twitching. "No one has mentioned a bomb. There can't be—I mean, *how*?"

"The Nazis rigged a bomb just under the storage closet. Grayson defused it," David said.

"*That's* why we were pushed out of the museum?" Windergaard's unfeigned horror was rewarding.

She nodded. "Grayson saved your museum."

Windergaard smoothed his tie, removed his glasses again, and wiped them on his shirt. "A *bomb*? Dear Lord." His face drained of color, leaving him so pale that she could see the blue veins under his skin.

"All the artwork, the building, the exhibits—" He took a deep breath.

"The employees and the police inside," Trisha supplied.

"Oh, yes. The people as well," Windergaard said, frowning. "And Grayson saved it all?"

She held up her hand, framing words in the air. "That will make an interesting headline: Director Fires Security Expert Who Saved Museum. What do you think?"

"I, uh, well." Windergaard forced hands to his side. "This does change things, certainly." He turned to David. "Would Mr. Grayson be interested in staying on if—"

"Ask Grayson when he gets here," David said.

"I will." Windergaard bobbed his head up and down. "Excuse me, I must talk to my people." He slunk over to the maintenance crew.

Trisha grinned. David grinned back at her.

"You're awesome, Trish. Would the headline have really said that?"

She shrugged. "Who knows? I don't write headlines. Too bad I'll have to quote him about the museum security failure, though. Ah, well, it'll get lost since it'll be buried below Grayson defusing the bomb and taking down the suspects." She fleshed out the shorthand in her notebook to be sure she had Windergaard's exact words.

David frowned. "You're going to quote Windergaard about blaming us?"

"He's the museum director. I have to quote him. Trust me, Grayson will come across as the hero that he is."

"You were impressed with him too," David said.

"Can you blame me?"

"No." David shook his head.

"Look, I need to talk to the rest of these people, okay?"

"Sure," he said.

She drifted into the crowd of museum employees.

A stocky, overweight man in a museum security uniform stepped in front of her. His nametag identified him as "Conrath." The museum chief of security, if she remembered correctly what David had said.

"Press shouldn't be here," Conrath hooked his thumbs into his belt, belligerent.

If she asked about the murder, she'd get nothing. Leave that subject for now. Her goal was information about Adrienne.

"I understand that one of your co-workers, Adrienne Katz, was killed, sir. I wanted to extend my condolences," she said. "I'm so sorry."

A couple of other museum security officers drifted closer.

"Thank you, that's appreciated, but we have nothing to say beyond she died doing her job," Conrath said. "Anything else has to come through our information director."

"I understand that you're leery of the press and protective of the museum," Trisha said. "But you must realize that all the information director is going to give me is name and a few bland facts about Ms. Katz."

"So?" Conrath said.

"If that happens, her death will be a single paragraph in a story. That's all she'll ever be, a victim, unless you tell people about her."

Everyone crowded closer to her, listening now.

"What do you mean?" Conrath said.

"Katz died during a crime that most readers will find more interesting than her death. She won't even register on their radar. This is the one time she'll appear in a front-page story. Give readers a chance to know her. Give her a legacy." Joe had to agree to give Adrienne a sidebar to herself. The kid deserved that.

Conrath frowned. "Why not talk to her family?"

"Because they'll be too broken up to talk to right now. It's up to you. You worked with her. You all knew her. This is your chance to tell the world about the person you knew." She paused to capture their attention. "Otherwise, the only thing people will remember about her is that she got her skull smashed in." Brutal, but sickeningly true.

"Can this be off the record?" Conrath asked.

"If it's off the record, I can't use it."

"Could you leave out my name?" he asked.

She nodded. "I could, though it would be stronger if her boss went on the record about her."

Conrath finally nodded. "I'll answer what I can. What do you want to know?"

"Anything that you want people to know about her," Trisha said. "What did you enjoy about working with her? What did she talk about? What did she hope to do with her life?"

"She was great," said the guard behind Conrath, a tall, skinny man with a goatee. "Always on time, always took care with her rounds inside the museum."

Trisha nodded for him to go on. That fit with Adrienne, the honor student.

"College kids will sometimes bring homework and only watch the cameras half-heartedly," the guard said. "She always paid close attention."

Adrienne had always had an eye for details. That's how she'd survived the foster care system. "What did she do with all the quiet time on her shift, then?" Trisha asked.

"She asked questions," Conrath said. "I had twenty years on the job before the museum." He paused, choosing the words carefully. "She wanted to know everything I knew about walking a beat."

"Yeah, she was ruthless about learning anything about police procedure," chimed in a third guard. "But you never minded talking to her because she listened so well. And she took notes, too, like you. First time anyone ever took notes when talking to me."

Took notes, like you. Trisha's throat went dry. She'd given Adrienne a notebook last spring. Told her to write down what she wanted to remember.

"Do you know what made her so focused?" Trisha asked, furiously writing.

"She said cops helped her when she was in foster care," Conrath answered. "Said once she got adopted, she wanted to be a cop and do the same. She wanted to apply to the police academy after college."

Yeah, Adrienne had this dream of being a cop. Trisha wanted to rage at the unfairness of it all. But that wouldn't help the kid now.

"Katz didn't have to make the rounds last night, you know," said the man with the goatee. "We'd already had a walk through. But she said better to be careful and double-check."

"We've all been concerned because of the Nazi controversy," Conrath said. "That's why the museum hired Gray Associates. Fat lot of good they did for Katz."

"So Katz wasn't on regular rounds near the exhibit last night?" Trisha asked. Either Adrienne had wanted to be extra careful or her extra rounds indicated something more sinister. Gah, no. Not this kid. But Trisha knew how this would look to the cops. Adrienne would be a suspect in the theft.

"She'd made her rounds once already. She didn't have to do them twice. She died because she showed initiative." Conrath fumbled with a set of keys in his hands. Everyone was silent for a few seconds. "Fucking Nazis."

"You should mention the cookies," a woman dressed in a green pastel suit with shoulder pads chimed in from the back.

"Cookies?" Trisha asked. Adrienne baked?

"Once a week, she brought in homemade cookies for the staff," the woman in pastel said.

"What kind?" Trisha said.

"Oatmeal chocolate chip," the woman said. "She said the oatmeal made them healthy cookies. Well, somewhat healthy."

And that had done her no good in the end. "You'll miss her then, Ms...?"

"Yes, I'll miss her. And the name is Amanda Grayson. You can quote me."

Grayson's ex. She was gorgeous, in a dignified, uptight way, even to her classic hairstyle, different from the poofy style so many women liked now.

"How did you know about the cookies?" Trisha asked.

"One night when I worked late. Ms. Katz brought me a couple of cookies while walking her rounds. After that, she made a point to leave me some. I'd find them on my desk the next day. She was a sweet girl."

Amanda Grayson sounded genuinely shaken by Adrienne's death. Trisha's heart warmed to her. "Thank you," Trisha said. "What's your title at the museum?"

"Assistant museum director," Amanda Grayson said.

"Katz's cookies were excellent." Conrath patted his belly. "It's not going to be the same working without her."

Trisha took the names of the other guards to go with their quotes. Amanda's willingness to be quoted had changed their minds about giving their names. Trisha knew the cookies were going to be the lead in the story about Adrienne. She clenched her pencil tight as she pictured the girl, only twenty, eager to be a cop, eager to help others as she'd been helped, bringing in cookies because it was the nice thing to do.

Had she died because she'd tried to do her job too well?

Life wasn't fair. But it'd be spectacular if fairness won now and then.

Yet her cynical self whispered at her that maybe the cookies and the questions had been a cover to get the rest of the guards to trust her and gain information that could be used to plan the theft of the paintings. The kid could have been in on it. Growing up the way Adrienne had, sometimes that did things to people.

No. Not this kid.

"Chief Conrath, what do you think Katz saw on her last round? How did she get into the special exhibit?"

Conrath laced his thumbs through his belt again, instantly on alert. "I don't know," he said. "I have no comment on that. I think we're done here."

He turned away from her. She let him go. She'd had enough.

She still needed to know whether the paintings had been recovered and she needed background on the Nazis captured in the tunnels. But that would have to come from Dorothy.

Trisha stepped back from the crowd and stumbled over an uneven section of the sidewalk. Someone caught her elbow before she fell.

"Careful, Patricia," Grayson said.

CHAPTER TEN

"BACK ALREADY?" Trisha asked.

"Oh, it's only been an hour or so. Miss me already?" he asked.

She fought a smile.

Grayson shrugged, making the gesture seem elegant. Yes, he and Amanda were a matched set.

"This crime is still my responsibility." Grayson jerked his head at the crowd. "David told me you were pale. He's right. You should have been looked over by the EMTs."

A hospital, with all those smells of the sick and terrified, triggering all those horrific flashbacks. Nope.

"I've dealt with cracked ribs before," she said. "I'm good. Besides, you checked me over."

"I'm not a doctor."

She raised her eyebrow. "I see."

His eyes narrowed. "Did you get anything out of Conrath just now?"

Good, he'd changed the subject. "Mostly information about Adrienne Katz. He gave me the runaround about everything else."

"Katz mattered to you," Grayson said.

Trisha set her jaw. "Yeah."

Dorothy appeared from behind Grayson. "You found a way around my uniforms and into this crime scene, Connell. Figures."

"You promised me access if my tip worked out," Trisha said. "I took you at your word."

Dorothy uncrossed her arms. "We need to talk. Let's go somewhere quieter."

Trisha and Grayson followed as Dorothy walked to the entrance of the alley where Trisha had parked her Indian. She glanced to make sure it was still there, half-hidden by the dumpster.

Dorothy leaned against the brick wall. Now that Trisha wasn't focused on interviews, the agony in her ribs refused to be pushed aside. It came in waves, settling after each breath and cresting when she took in air. Breathing should be automatic. Not today.

"What did you get from your conversations with museum security?" Dorothy asked.

"Katz did an excellent job as a security guard. She paid attention. She baked cookies. And..."

Dorothy sighed. "Go on."

"She was stationed last night in the security office, not the exhibit," Trisha said.

"I was afraid of that." Dorothy took out her own notebook. "Katz either had the lousy luck to stumble onto the crime in progress or she was joining her co-conspirators."

"She wasn't involved! I know her! She was a good kid!" Trisha knew her temper was going. She didn't care.

"Don't shout at me. Facts are facts."

"Look, Lt. Gilbert, I knew this girl. I did a story on her years back when she blew the whistle on her abusive foster parents. She had a good life now. She's not part of this."

Dorothy raised an eyebrow. "You kept track of her?"

Trisha shrugged. "Yeah. Saw her last spring." She should have visited the kid more often.

"I'll keep what you said in mind." Dorothy made a note.

"My judgement is that Katz wasn't part of this," Grayson chimed in.

"I hope you're both right," Dorothy said.

Trisha waited a few seconds to see what else Dorothy wanted and to let her anger about Katz being suspected fade. Dorothy's job meant she had to look at Adrienne as a suspect.

"Has Adrienne's family been notified?" Trisha finally asked.

"Yes."

That meant she could use the kid's name in the story. Give her a eulogy.

"Did you find the paintings?" Trisha asked.

Dorothy shook her head.

"Got anything on the guys in the tunnel?"

Dorothy flipped to another page in her notebook. "Yes. Write this down, Connell, because I'm only going to say it once. Deep background, no quotes from me."

Trisha nodded, pencil ready.

"Neo-Nazi literature and pamphlets were found in the van they were using. We also got a couple of hits on their fingerprints. White supremacists all the way. Minor records for vandalism. One with a record of misdemeanor domestic assault."

All domestic assaults were felonies, so far as Trisha was concerned. Too bad the courts didn't agree. "Names? Ages?" she asked.

"Stephen Warren is the one who attacked you, and he appears to be the ringleader. Age 27. We'll have more later, as the information comes in. Or when we can get a couple of the suspects out of the hospital and talking."

Trisha scribbled in shorthand illegible to anyone but her. "What's their condition?"

"Serious but stable," Dorothy said.

"C'mon, lieutenant, go on record. You'll get some excellent publicity for saving for city from a bomb."

"And I'll get serious shit from my captain that I don't need, which you know," Dorothy said. "I'm not interested in publicity. I'm interested in the job." She sighed. "You want to spotlight someone, use Edmund Grayson. He took care of the bomb."

No use arguing, especially since Dorothy had spilled everything essential.

Dorothy put her notebook away. "That's it for today except for one thing."

Uh-oh. What now?

"If you were a cop, you'd already be on desk duty and Internal Affairs would be opening a file. You went over the line down there when you broke Warren's nose," Dorothy said.

"Are you charging *me* for defending myself?" Trisha wouldn't be able to explain assault charges to the publisher, Cardoza. Dammit, she should have controlled herself better.

But she'd been locked in the past, where the struggle never ended.

"You hit him when he was down." Dorothy sighed. "Go into therapy or something. Get your temper under control."

"The guys I've hit deserve it," Trisha said.

"Let's recap." Dorothy shook her head. "First, you put your elbow in the face of a guy making himself a nuisance at the arson crime scene last year. Second—"

"That guy groped a woman standing at the barricades." Poor woman had been holding a kid, and the guy had still grabbed her ass.

"Second, you beat down the driver who smashed into the storefront six months ago."

"He yelled at the people he'd almost run over. He took a swing at one of them. I made him stand down."

"And third, you broke Warren's nose down there."

"He had a gun to my head."

"Not then, he didn't." Dorothy sighed. "I know you've got this punk defying authority attitude down to a science, Connell, but enough. It will catch up to you and then with my luck, either you'll hurt someone, or someone will hurt you and your case will end up on my desk. It'll be a pain in the ass, either way."

"Thanks for your concern," Trisha said because she had no idea what to do with any of that. Dorothy sounded genuinely worried about her. Weird.

"You've made your point, Dorothy," Grayson said, his voice low.

Dorothy nodded. "If you stuck with him in the tunnels, you're worth saving. Get yourself under control. And one more thing: I need your jacket."

Worth saving? "Why do you need my jacket?"

"It has a bullet hole in it. It's evidence. I need to catalog it. Especially since a bullet hole will go a long way to proving your state of mind when punching Warren, if it comes to that."

The bullet hole supported self-defense if anyone ever tried to charge her for hitting Warren. Despite the lecture, Dorothy wanted to help her.

Trisha slipped off her jacket and handed it over without a word because she had no idea what to say and because the movement set the pain roaring through her chest again.

Dorothy peered at the hole. "That was damn close."

"That's my only jacket, Lieutenant. When can I get it back?" It had been a gift from Nicky.

"He's got a spare you can use," Dorothy pointed at Grayson. "Empty out the pockets and I'll return it as soon as I can."

"I'll get it back intact?"

"Okay."

Dorothy dumped the contents of the pockets– pencils, Nicky's cigarette lighter, and a comb—into Trisha's hands.

Trisha stuffed Nicky's lighter and the rest into her front pockets. When the movement pulled on her chest muscles, she winced and then slipped her hand over the bruises. Those tender spots had to be turning various shades of purple and yellow by now. Dorothy and Grayson stared at her in alarm. Damn.

"You never said if you believed this could be an inside job or not, Lieutenant," she asked.

"You were there in the storage room. You examined the new concrete. What do you think?" Dorothy grimaced.

"So that's official confirmation, then?" Trisha said.

"That's a 'no comment.'" Dorothy waved her hand. "And I have to go. Pester Grayson instead. He seems to enjoy it." She strolled away, issuing orders again on the police radio.

Trisha turned to face Grayson and regretted it as agony sliced through her again.

"Patricia?" Grayson had a blue trench coat over his forearm. "You seem to be in a lot of pain. I can take you to the hospital."

"I need to get to work or everything I did this morning will be for nothing. Besides, it's only pain."

"You seem far too familiar with pain."

"Don't I know it."

"Here, put this on." Grayson draped his coat over her shoulders without asking.

She slid her arms through the sleeves, gripping her notebook and pencil to keep them from snagging the plush lining. The sleeves were too long, and the hem almost touched the sidewalk, but it was warm and sinfully soft against her bare arms. It made her want to find somewhere to curl up and sleep inside it.

Before she could object, Grayson tied the coat shut for her, using the belt as a sash.

"Um, hello. I can tie a belt," she said.

"The smallest movement is causing you agony," he said.

"I'm *fine*," she snapped.

He stared at her, reminding her of his intense once-over while they were waiting outside the storage closet. He missed nothing. He'd seen her lose it. He must believe she needed looking after now. Argh.

"I'm sorry about losing it down there," she whispered and stared at her feet. "I should have held it together. Thanks for the help on that."

"I don't—" He frowned. "Are you referring to what happened after the fight with Warren?"

"Yeah, when I lost it." She met his gaze.

"You backed me up today as well as any partner." Grayson raised an eyebrow. "As for the, ah, attack of nerves after Dorothy arrived, a near-death experience will have that effect on people."

"I should've maintained. You did." What, no lecture?

"I didn't have a gun to my head." He smiled. "You're harder on yourself than you have any right to be."

She cleared her throat. "What about how I lost my temper with Warren?"

"Are you planning on running to the hospital to finish him off?"

"Not while I'm on deadline," she said.

"Then I believe the world is safe from you for the moment."

She stared, not entirely sure what to say. She had comebacks for insults, but his compliments defeated her. "I...I'm not used to people taking my side. Sorry."

"Careful, that's two apologies. Another one and you might use up your yearly quota."

She laughed but ended up wincing and curling her arm around her ribs. Another bout of laughing and she wouldn't be able to breathe at all.

"Hospital," he said.

"Never mind the ride. I'll get a cab. Thanks for the coat. I'll return it." She cleared her throat. "And for the compliments. I appreciate them."

She walked away, though slower than she would have liked. It *hurt*. Spots haunted her eyes. Dammit, every breath brought agony. Still, Adrienne's story remained the priority. She had the quotes. Time to sit at *The Herald's* computer and write.

He caught up to her. "The paper it is, then."

CHAPTER ELEVEN

AS THEY WALKED to the parking lot and Grayson's car, the wind whipped Trisha, but the coat held fast, creating a cocoon of comfort around her aching ribs. She glanced up the street, toward Midtown. The sun's rays were hitting the edge of the Chrysler building's chrome plating. Late afternoon, already?

The lapels of Grayson's suit coat rose and flapped in the stiff breeze, but he seemed unaffected by the chill. She drew in enough breath, she hoped, to talk.

"Sorry that the paintings are still missing," she said.

He grimaced. "We have the murderers, at least. One thing at a time."

He opened the car via remote entry, and they settled inside. She tried to hide her stiffness but suspected Grayson noticed. She checked her watch, noted the time, and frowned.

"What's wrong?"

"You got to the crime scene about five, right?"

He nodded and started the car.

"I got here about thirty minutes later. Then we spent some time talking to Dorothy, getting into the tunnels, and walking until we found the bomb. Then time spent shutting down the stupid ticking clock."

"I remember that part. Vividly." He pulled the car out onto the street, where a uniform waved them past. The news vans crowding the cross street almost took out one of Grayson's mirrors. Trisha slid down in the seat, not wanting any of the television reporters to recognize her.

The smooth ride provided her with a chance to regain her breath. Fuck, this should not be so hard. Stupid anxiety and panic. *Danger's over, brain.*

"Why are you worried about the time?" Grayson asked.

"If the Nazis killed Katz not long before five, what the hell were they doing still sitting in a van outside the other tunnel entrance, at least an hour after they should've been long gone?"

Grayson cut into the traffic easily. "Waiting for the bomb to go off?" he said. But his voice sounded tentative.

"Better to get the heck out of the city before things go boom. Police could easily stop traffic on the bridges and tunnels to search cars."

"As a rule, criminals are idiots, though these—"

"Were smart enough to break into a locked room and put together a bomb." Trisha frowned, the mystery distracting her from the pain. "And the paintings are still missing. How does that jibe with them sitting and waiting? Wouldn't they be somewhere safe with their haul? Then there's the can of lighter fluid we found near the bomb. Why was it there, and why did they abandon it?"

Grayson slid across two lanes of traffic with practiced ease and turned left. A taxi tried to sneak in front of them. He cut it off with a growl. "You raise excellent questions. Do you have answers?"

"Not yet. You?"

"Not yet."

"I wonder why Dorothy didn't think of any of this?" she gasped out. Her breath seemed almost gone. She centered again, thought about the story, and thought about possible headlines. She could do this.

"What makes you think that Dorothy didn't think of this?"

"Ah," Trisha noted the street number. Still about twenty blocks up and six blocks east. "Can I use your phone?"

He lifted the receiver. "Be my guest."

Joe answered again on the first ring. She flipped through her notebook, giving him the quotes from Windergaard, the ones about Adrienne, and the background from Dorothy.

"We're okay to use Katz's name?" Joe asked.

"Yeah, notification has been done." Trisha closed her eyes as the pain sliced through her. Each word seemed harder to say. "Look in the morgue files for the original story I wrote on the foster home being shut down. Adrienne's worth a story all by herself."

"She'll get it." More clicks in the background. "When will you be in? I need you to look over what I've typed up and punch it up."

"Soon. In a car on the way right now."

She closed her eyes again after she hung up, wondering how she'd be able to walk up those steps to the newsroom.

She tried to suck in air through her mouth without Grayson noticing and stared out the window.

"You're gasping words out. We're going to the hospital," he said.

"Can't." She bit her tongue.

"How do you mean?"

"Hospitals. Freak. Me. Out. Like in the tunnels."

She glanced behind them and spotted a tailgating taxi. She might be able to grab that if Grayson kept insisting. Her hand curled around the door handle.

They halted at another light. Grayson turned and gave her another one of those studied looks. God, those brown eyes were deep.

She only half-heard him. She sunk deeper into the soft leather. Sleep beckoned. Spots appeared before her eyes. Getting harder to breath. The pain crested.

Fuck, this could be serious.

Something bubbled in her throat. She fought throwing up all over Grayson's car and his fancy coat. "Stop!" she croaked out.

The car slammed to a halt. She opened the door and spit blood on the coat sleeve and on the street.

Oh. *Not good.* Her weight fell against the door, pushing it open, onto the street, dumping her into the gutter. Through the haze, she saw her beeper fall onto the sewer grate, spin, and vanish.

Joe would kill her for losing that.

Grayson's hand grabbed her shoulder. His mouth moved but his words made no sense to her. Her world narrowed to a pinprick as she struggled to draw a breath, any breath.

Can't breathe.

———

Grayson thought he'd never been as helpless as he had that morning, kneeling over Katz's body. But standing on the sidewalk as the paramedics struggled to stabilize Patricia, he entered a fresh level of a hell.

He knew enough to be horrified by the use of the medical terms "pneumothorax" and "hemothorax." Blood in the lung. Bad. *Life threatening.* He should have taken her straight to the hospital.

But he'd honestly believed her bruises and the other symptoms were caused by a classic panic attack.

He stepped to ride with her, but the paramedic stopped him. "Husband?" she asked.

"No," he admitted.

"She'll be at Mercy."

And with that, doors slammed, and the ambulance sped off, leaving him alone, cold, and afraid. He could go to the ER, but he'd no right as a relative or even a friend to demand information about her. Hell, they'd just met today.

David. He'd know who to call for Patricia. Grayson slid into his car and hoped David was near his car phone.

David answered on the first ring. "Hey, boss, glad you called. They're letting us back inside. I was just about to move my car back to that lot."

Grayson plowed ahead, giving the younger man a quick, clinical report of what happened.

"*Shit*," David said. "I thought she looked too pale. I should have pushed it more with her. Fuck. I'll head to Mercy ER right now."

"Do you know who I should call for her? A relative? Her emergency contact?"

"*I'm* her emergency contact." David sighed. "There was the one time when we…never mind. Anyway, I am, probably because I'm the most reliable of her friends. I'll find out what's what."

It deflated Grayson to leave Patricia in David's hands. But Grayson had only met the woman hours ago, though they'd been among the most memorable hours of his life. "Please keep me informed. I…I'm worried about her." His hand clutched the phone tight.

"Soon as I know something, you'll know."

"Good. Either leave a message on the car's line or call the museum main line. Someone there will find me. And tell Dorothy I'm on my way back there, then, if you see her." He should check in with Amanda. The bomb threat must have terrified her.

At least he could do something useful while waiting, rather than pacing a hospital waiting area. He'd not rest until he knew Patricia Connell would be all right.

———

Finally, Trisha had access to a damn phone. She made the nurse put it on her lap and frantically punched the numbers for the paper.

Her clothes, or what was left of them, were in a bag at the foot of the bed, along with the money belt she'd had on under the jeans, her notebook, the assorted change, the pencils and the notebooks.

She'd been out of touch for…she looked at the clock on the hospital room wall…six hours. *Damn, damn.* Tomorrow's paper had been sent to press already.

She'd missed the deadline. The collapsed lung hadn't killed her. Joe might.

But surely he'd get "coughing up blood, passed out" once she explained.

Trisha winced, trying not to disturb the chest tube as she adjusted the receiver against her ear. She could still flesh the story out if Joe sent over one of those new laptops that *The Herald* has just bought for people in the field. Then she could save the story and messenger the disc back to him.

And she could work the phones for an update.

She practiced her opening line. "So funny thing happened on the way to the paper," but the person who answered Joe's extension wasn't Joe.

"Hey, I need to speak to Joe."

"Is this Trisha Connell?"

An unfamiliar voice. Definitely not one of the other reporters. Weird. "Yeah, but I need to speak to Joe to follow up—"

"This is Mordechai Cardoza. You'll speak to me."

Shit. The publisher. "Sorry for being out of touch, sir, but—"

"There is no 'but' Miss Connell. First, you disobeyed a direct order this morning, then you vanish when the story needs work, and now you call expecting everything to be fine. Well, let me tell you—"

"Look I'm at the—"

"I don't care where you are, there's no damn excuse for this! My bet is you never came in because you were afraid to face being called out for disobeying a direct order in the first place. You have no sense of—"

"*Afraid?*" She sputtered.

"Shut up and listen. You're unreliable. Today just proves that. You're uncouth, undignified, and far too low-class for this paper. We should have never put a woman on the crime beat..." And he continued in that same vein, not giving her another opening.

Unreliable? Un-fucking-believable. Low-class? I'll show you low-class.

She spoke over him. "Fuck off, asshole. That clear enough for you?" And she slammed down the phone, hard.

Fuck you, Cardoza. And it's Ms. Connell, not Miss.

And so ended her job. Shit.

"I take it you're feeling better?" Grayson called from the doorway.

———

Grayson stood, shopping bags in hand, contemplating the woman in the bed.

Patricia blinked twice in response to his words, as if questioning her senses. Her now-pale face highlighted her freckles. A tube jutted out from her right side, presumably something needed to treat the chest injury.

But as she focused on him, she smiled, an action that lit up her whole face, reminding him of how alive she'd felt under his touch. But just as quick, the joy vanished, replaced by wariness.

"Come to say 'I told you so?'" she drawled.

He smiled. So she was down but not out.

"No, I'm wondering what an insane person looks like at rest."

"Certifiable, that's me." She pointed at the tube. "Collapsed lung. Some other technical term. Whatever. So, more than bruised ribs or, um, the panic attack thing."

"Who upset you on the phone?"

She frowned and shook her head. "It's not important. Just another asshole who thinks he's better than me."

Yet this supposed asshole was one she'd called almost immediately after waking up. Interesting. A boyfriend? No, a source, more likely.

"You had me worried," he said. "What's the general prognosis?"

"I'll be fine, eventually. It's bed rest for a while even if I go home, something about being careful not to stress anything, I could collapse the lung again through overwork, etc., etc. It's annoying but that's all."

She sounded calm but her fingers clutched the Celtic cross around her neck, just as when they'd discovered the bomb.

"It's a serious injury," he said. "Listen to the doctors."

"I guess. They keep telling me to rest and then interrupt me every half-hour. That's a hospital for you. At least the pain is muted. But I need to get back to the story."

"David said that you knew Adrienne Katz well," he said.

"Not as well as her family." She closed her eyes, shifted in the bed, winced, and clutched her side. Her movements were stiff, as if her limbs were lead, not flesh.

How could he comfort her? Would she even accept it?

"Sorry for sounding so stream of consciousness," she said. "Still a little woozy from everything. And I'm slow on the uptake. You haven't been to bed yet either, have you? Did you find the paintings? Get a confession from the Nazis?"

He shook his head. "No, we're saving that for when you're well enough to write about it."

She started to laugh and stopped abruptly.

He rushed to the bedside and held her hand tight while she struggled with the surge of agony. Her fingers dug into his hand. People thought he could control his emotions? He had nothing on this woman. What would it take to really know her?

Because that person underneath was well worth knowing, in so many ways.

"Damn. Ouch." She rasped out. After another moment, she released his hand. "Thanks."

"You're welcome." He stared at her for a moment, wishing he knew what to say. "You could ask for some pain medication."

She set her jaw. "No drugs."

He'd no idea what to say to that. Silence stretched out for a long moment. Finally, he displayed the shopping bags. "I brought you presents."

"Presents? Why?" She tilted her head, studying him. "You already gave me your coat. Which I ruined, I think, by puking blood on it. I'll replace it. Sorry."

"The coat is replaceable. You're not."

She blinked again, nonplussed. Not used to receiving praise? Or gifts?

He set the bags on the bed next to her, took a step back and stuffed his hands into his pockets. Any other woman he'd dated would be charmed by a present.

But Patricia Connell wasn't his wife or a girlfriend.

She was…something else, somehow. She'd joked over the discovery of a bomb. She'd fought through panic and pain to do a job that obviously meant everything to her. She'd given Katz a proper eulogy, to judge by what she'd reported over the phone.

"I'm sorry to make you go through trouble for me," she said.

"You have been no trouble today," he said.

"That's a first."

He smiled. "In any case, it's nothing fancy."

She looked over the presents, and her eyes widened. "Is that a Tower Records bag?"

He'd chosen wisely. Very good. "Yes, it is." He handed it to her and watched the joy rise in her smile as she pulled out the Walkman and the two cassettes he'd bought.

"You bought me a new *Walkman*?"

He'd buy her presents every day of her life to preserve that excitement in her face. "It's the latest model. Rechargeable batteries, the clerk said."

She rubbed her thumb over the package, and he wondered what it be like to on the other end of that caress.

"And Springsteen cassettes too?" Her eyes narrowed, suspicious in an instant. "How did you know?"

"You quoted him in the tunnels. 'It's hard to be a saint in the city.'" he pointed out. "I hope you don't have these already. I thought of some punk records, but I'm lost as to which ones are any good."

"The Boss works." She stared at him. "Grayson, this is super-thoughtful."

He shrugged. "I thought you might be bored. I'd have brought you books if I knew what you read." He handed her the white nondescript bag.

She pulled out the contents. "Socks?" She frowned. "Fluffy pink socks?"

He cleared his throat. "My mother spent time in and out of hospitals during her last year fighting cancer. She always complained that her feet were cold. I thought—"

Patricia ripped the socks from the packaging, animated. Yes, that. He wanted more of *that*.

Yet he'd known the woman only a day. She had to be at least a decade younger. They had little in common. His caution ill-matched her impulsivity. He should go skydiving. Buy a Porsche. All less dangerous, he suspected, than being in Patricia Connell's orbit. Next thing he knew, he'd be slam dancing.

But here he was. And here she was, smiling at him.

"Socks are a great idea. I'm going to put them on ASAP. Although pink is not my color." She smiled.

"I know. But there were few color choices at this hour of the morning," he said.

"Ah, you're doing great if you found Tower Records. Next time, stick with me for the rest. You'd be surprised at what you can buy in Manhattan at two a.m. You just have to know where to look."

Skydiving. Yes. Much less dangerous than stalking Manhattan at two a.m. with her. But look what playing safe had gained him—nearly blown to bits today. He shuddered, thinking of what might have happened if Patricia had not led him to the bomb. His daughter could be an orphan.

She tossed off the covers, revealing a hospital gown that left her lower legs exposed. Gorgeous, shapely legs with well-defined calf muscles. Her left ankle had a tattoo of a lightning bolt.

He swallowed hard. Desire roared through him, clawing at his emotions. Not since the first night with Karen had he wanted someone so much. But Karen had been a cop. Solid. Steady. No tattoos.

"Uh, I've found bending is a problem. Would you mind?" She held out the socks.

"Certainly."

He slipped the socks over her feet. Her skin was so soft and her toes more delicate than he expected. The toenails were trimmed nicely but bare of polish. He resisted the urge to linger over the lightning bolt tattoo, caress her ankle, and work his hands up to her thighs...

He was hard and erect despite the fact she lay in a hospital bed, seriously injured. *Grow up, Grayson.*

"Nice tattoo," he said.

"I have another." She closed her eyes.

Another? He finished with the socks and stepped away, clamping down on his internal speculation as to the location of the second tattoo. He thought back to how she'd described spending the night before, partying at a punk club. Not his scene. Not even close.

He could try snake-charming. That would be less dangerous, too.

"These are, uh, well, um, they're great, Grayson. Thank you. I'm thanking you a ton today. I owe you."

"You owe me nothing." He reached into his suit pocket and brought out a Dove chocolate bar. "Almost forgot. This is for you as well."

She snatched it out of his hand with a flourish.

"So far, you've given me a coat, water, a freakin' Walkman, Springsteen, socks, and chocolate." Her face lit up, the fatigue banished. "Careful, I'll ask for a pony next."

I'll give you anything you want. Oh, yes, he had it bad. Tomorrow, though, the adrenaline would fade, and he'd be in control of himself again. "I should go so you can rest."

She sighed. "You should rest too. You're practically swaying on your feet."

"Bed is my next stop."

She patted the side of her bed with a grin. "There's room. I'll even share the chocolate."

He blinked and almost took a step forward to do exactly what she'd said. Curling up with her in his arms would cap this insane day nicely. Stupid. Bantering with him distracted her from the pain, and, possibly, her grief over Katz.

Unless she wanted help, and this way her way of asking. Perhaps the anxiety lurked, threatening to send her into another tailspin.

"Patricia are you…comfortable?"

Her jaw tensed. A defensive reaction.

"Well, I was lying here, staring at the ceiling, feeling sorry for myself, and hating hospitals, but then someone came in and brought me music, warm socks, and chocolate, and I'm feeling *much* better now."

She smiled again and, in that moment, he wished for that smile to be directed at him forever. That smile was life.

"Perhaps more chocolate is in order tomorrow?" he asked.

"More chocolate is good, if they'll let me eat it. I think I can. I forgot to ask. Didn't expect chocolate to be an option." She cleared her throat. "You're always welcome."

"Good." He squeezed her hand and stepped away. "Anything else you need?"

"You're checking on why the Neo-Nazis waited around in the van?" she asked.

"Absolutely."

"And who gave Sidney the artwork?" Her eyes closed. Involuntarily, he suspected.

"Yes."

"Anything new about Adrienne Katz's role in all this?"

"Nothing that clears her," he said. "But nothing that implicates her either."

"That's something. We need to clear her, Grayson."

Those last words had been slurred from exhaustion. "We'll get to work on it when you're well."

"We better."

CHAPTER TWELVE

NEW JERSEY. Trisha sighed. She should be home resting and recovering from the punctured lung, but instead she sat on a bus headed through the Lincoln Tunnel to Montclair, New Jersey, for an interview that couldn't be refused.

Adrienne Katz's parents had agreed to speak to her. Most grieving families kept their silence. This time, the Katzes had called *her*, probably because Adrienne had mentioned her to them.

Adrienne's father had set the time and location.

That's why Trisha sat on a smelly bus passing through the Lincoln Tunnel, her ribs aching in protest. That's why she'd walked into the seventh pit of Hell, aka the Port Authority, to get to the bus. She couldn't blame the homeless, they needed somewhere to rest. But she did blame the drug dealers that she'd spotted in the corner.

At least no one had wolf-whistled at her this time. Probably, she looked too thin, pale, and unattractive. Sad that looking downtrodden kept off the assholes.

The bus climbed out of the tunnel and passed by Hoboken. Ignoring the spectacular view of Manhattan, including the Twin Towers, Trisha turned on the Walkman, put on the headphones, and reviewed her notes to the tune of "The River." That haunting song fit her mood. She shifted, hoping, if not for comfort, a position that kept the pain at bay. A week and a half out from the hospital had dulled the agony but the ache remained, a constant buzz in the back of her mind.

Worse than the ache, though, had been the call from the HR department at the *Herald*. Yep, she'd been officially fired. A ten-year-career down the tubes because she couldn't keep her mouth shut.

Ah, hell, Cardoza had been looking for an excuse, any excuse to fire her. He'd have found one sooner or later. At least she'd gotten to tell him to fuck off first. Still, it hurt to put in all that time and effort and then get tossed out like yesterday's trash.

She hadn't told anyone. It wouldn't come out for a while and then maybe she'd know what to say. That's because "to make things easier for everyone," HR said she'd be put on sick leave and could also use up her weeks of accumulated vacation time before being officially fired. Well, HR hadn't said "fired." They said, "leaving for other opportunities."

Fuck Cardoza.

Firing her hadn't stopped him from using her museum stories, had it? He'd put the main one above the fold, just as she'd hoped. Grayson and Adrienne had made the front page too. At least Adrienne had her moment.

Fuck Cardoza.

Joe, one of the few people with her home number, had called, worried. She told him she'd be fine; she'd look for a new job when she recovered and asked him to clean out her desk. That was asking a ton of him, but he'd done it without complaining.

He felt as bad as she did, which was some consolation

He'd had two boxes delivered by messenger. He'd probably billed them to *The Herald*. Served them right.

Trisha set her jaw. At some point, she'd have to set up a freelance career or look for a new job. But all that could wait. Right now, questions remained in the museum story. The paintings were still missing, and it was a mystery still about how Adrienne had come to be inside the exhibit.

Mr. Katz had made it clear in his phone call that he wanted Trisha to correct misconceptions about their daughter. "Misconceptions," hah. Say, rather, lies and insinuations about Adrienne. While Trisha's story had led with the anecdote about cookies and Katz's dedication to her job, the television news had implied or stated right out that Adrienne could be involved in the crime, asking how else could she have gotten inside that room. So far, Dorothy maintained there was no evidence to implicate Katz. Grayson believed in Adrienne's innocence. Still, television news kept speculating about the kid's "involvement" in the crime.

Fired or not, she'd stay on the story. She could honestly tell the family she'd keep investigating until she cleared Adrienne, even if she had to hand the story, with all her work, over to Kimba at the *Tribune*. That would piss off Cardoza. Good.

The bus pulled into a residential neighborhood made up of nicely landscaped lawns and immaculately kept three- and four-bedroom homes. Trisha navigated her exit from the bus with as much balance as she could muster under the circumstances. Her foot hit the concrete hard, sending waves of fresh pain through her side. She leaned against the stop sign, riding the crest of the agony until it broke and settled back to a dull roar. She could have taken the prescribed painkillers, but one experience with them and the high they produced had been enough.

She'd rather have a figurative knife stuck in her side than be high.

A half-block walk brought her to the Katzs' address, a blue, three-story Victorian with a fenced backyard, complete with a swing set. Two mountain bikes sat on the porch, across from the front door.

A happy place to grow up?

Maybe. Appearances can be deceiving. Despair wasn't limited to run-down homes in the Bronx or inner-city housing projects. Trisha shook her head. *Fuck, you're a cynical bastard, Connell.* Besides, Adrienne had liked her new family.

Trisha smoothed down her blouse, brushed lint off the black slacks, and knocked on the front door.

A medium-size man with the beginnings of a beard opened the door. Jewish custom, she remembered, dictated the growth of a beard while in mourning. She introduced herself but didn't offer her hand, not certain how Orthodox Mr. Katz was and if he would avoid contact with a woman.

"Come in." He gestured and she stepped through the door.

The interior reinforced the family impression given by the swing set and minivan Homework, empty lunchboxes, and various keys lay strewn on the entranceway table. Photos of the Katz children decorated the hallway walls. One with Adrienne in the middle of the brood, everyone all smiles, was displayed front and center. Maybe her adoption day?

"Thank you for coming," he said.

"Thank you for calling me at this difficult time."

"You were her friend," Mr. Katz said.

"Yeah." Trisha nodded, jaw set.

Mr. Katz led her into the living room off the hallway. Photographs sat on the fireplace mantle, including one of Adrienne in her high school graduation gown, and another one with Adrienne and the three younger Katz children. A mirror hung above the fireplace. Trisha spotted a small tuff of black paper in one corner, perhaps left over from the official mourning period.

A woman drifted in from the back of the house, probably the kitchen. Joseph Katz introduced his wife, Louise, and indicated that Trisha should sit on the couch. Trisha crossed her legs as she sat, not yet reaching for her notebook. There was a time to fire questions and a time to let the answers come on their own. This was the latter.

She studied Louise Katz. Dark circles under her eyes matched her husband's. She'd dressed casually, in an oversize sweatshirt and leggings. No makeup to hide the sallow cheeks. Both parents were a mess. Adrienne Katz had been cherished. Finally. At least her last years had been happy.

But there should have been so many more.

Damn you, Nazis. Trisha flexed her hand, remembering how it felt to smack down Stephen Warren, the killer and would-be bomber. She should have killed him. But that wouldn't have brought Adrienne back.

"I'm so sorry for your loss," Trisha said.

Louise nodded. "Thank you. I keep expecting her to bound through the door, you know." She sighed.

Trisha nodded. She knew that feeling all too well. Sometimes, she even thought she heard Nicky's voice in their apartment.

"We wanted to thank you for the article on our daughter," Mr. Katz said.

"I was simply the messenger. Her co-workers spoke so well of her."

"Yes, Mrs. Grayson also sent a lovely note. And Mr. Grayson sent a generous donation to the scholarship fund we've set up in…" she cleared her throat, "…in Adrienne's memory."

That sounded just like Grayson, the man who showed up at two a.m. in her hospital room with a Walkman, chocolate, and pink socks.

Mr. Katz stared at her. "Do you believe our daughter let the Nazis in the museum?"

That was getting right to the point. "There's no evidence of that." At least, not yet. "When I first met Adrienne, she was a ball of righteous fury on behalf of the younger kids in her foster home. I can't believe that righteous, caring kid turned into a thief."

"She talked about you, how you promised to bring the police and shut down that house that day." Mrs. Katz smiled. "And you sent her the Yankees jacket when she turned thirteen, the one with Reggie Jackson's signature."

"I'm sure she outgrew it," Trisha said.

"She kept it in her closet, always," Mrs. Katz said. "Do you want it back?"

Another reminder of loss in her apartment? "No, keep it for her younger sisters. Or for an eventual niece and nephew. I think she'd be pleased with that."

"Yes, she would," Mrs. Katz said.

Dammit, she would not cry here. These people needed her help, her *professional* help.

"Nazis. I thought we were done with them." Mr. Katz spat the word out, stood and wandered over to the fireplace mantle. "Adrienne would never be involved in anything that included their hatred. She heard too many stories from us and her grandparents." He picked up his daughter's graduation photo. "Louise's parents were Holocaust survivors."

Silence for a bit. Trisha's turn to speak.

"Mr. and Mrs. Katz, can I ask what you hope for from me? There's only so much I can do until the police exonerate her."

"I know." Mrs. Katz carefully folded her hands in her lap. "But if you're the person Adrienne said, I suspect you're doing some investigating on your own."

"I am, but..." Trisha took a deep breath so she wouldn't stumble over the words. She hadn't spoken to anyone but Joe about being fired. "But I have to tell you I'm not with the *Herald* any longer. That doesn't mean I'm off the story. I'll find a home for it when it's done. But…I can't promise when or even where it will run."

"Not with the *Herald* anymore?" Louise Katz's voice rose in surprise. "*What happened*?"

She wouldn't lie to these people. "I disobeyed orders to cover the museum story. Then I told off my boss when he called me on the carpet about it."

Silence. Trisha almost stood and left.

"That's appalling, especially given they used your stories on the front page," Mr. Katz said, narrowing his eyes at her.

She shrugged. "This is my story and I'll stay on it, for Adrienne's sake," Trisha replied. "There's more to it than the Nazis who were caught, I'm sure of it."

"So are we." Mr. Katz sat back down and clasped his wife's hands. "That's why we asked you here. We want you to help."

"You didn't have to ask. But you can help me. While I'm working the museum story, I can also do background, so we can tell the world who she truly was," Trisha said.

"How?" he answered.

"If you could provide names of her friends, I could talk to them, add their stories of your daughter to the article, to provide a fuller picture of Adrienne. Anything that either of you feel comfortable telling me would also help."

Mr. Katz nodded and, in halting words at first, described meeting Adrienne for the first time. He spoke of the wary pre-teen she'd been when she first came to their home, her immediate affection for their golden retriever, and how she'd blossomed with care and patience. The words spilled out, and Trisha struggled to keep up with her notes. Adrienne had always been a risk taker, her parents said, always curious, as if there had never been enough time in the day to do everything.

Trisha knew that feeling well. Life could end tomorrow. You had to do the stuff that mattered *today* before your time ran out.

A lump gathered in her throat again. Adrienne should have had more time.

"And she remembered how kind the cops had been when they took her from that awful house," Mrs. Katz continued. "Fifteen and she decided that's what she wanted to do with her life, to serve. We tried to steer her to science, like me, but the most she would do is study forensics in college."

Trisha asked a few more questions, obtained the names of Adrienne's closest friends, and listened until the couple ran out of energy. It was plenty for a follow-up article, perhaps even long enough for a magazine, and by emphasizing what brought Adrienne Katz to that night in the museum, it made for a poignant story. When she cleared Katz, Trisha hoped the article would have a powerful impact, especially on those who doubted her.

The Katzes rose. Interview over.

Mrs. Katz pointed to the cross hanging around Trisha's neck. "Do you have faith, Ms. Connell?"

"I was raised Catholic." The truth, as far as it went. Not the time or place for discussions on faith or her lack thereof.

"Does your faith help you deal with tragedy?" Mrs. Katz asked.

"Not much helps to deal with a loss this bad." Trisha fingered the lighter in the pocket of her blazer. "You just keep moving forward, day to day, and eventually, life happens again. Hemingway had a saying: Life breaks everyone. But sometimes, people are stronger in the broken places." But holes in the soul never closed. You just worked around them.

"That helps." Mr. Katz nodded. "I hope you're right."

"I'm glad Adrienne had you."

Trisha said goodbye, left the house, and spent time at the bus stop reviewing her notes from the interview, already putting them in order. By the time the next bus arrived, tears pooled in her eyes. The Katzes carried their grief with such dignity.

Fuck if she could do that. Some days, she still wanted to punch a wall.

Adrienne's death was damned unfair.

Trisha immersed herself in drafting the interview on the ride back to Manhattan with Springsteen's "The River" album blaring in her ears. She swapped to a local bus at Port Authority. That bumpy ride precluded writing. When the bus let her off on her street in Hell's Kitchen, exhaustion hit as she contemplated the three flights to apartment.

Yeah, the doctors were right. She should still be in bed. A deep sigh only produced another wave of pain, so she gritted her teeth going up the stairwell. She pushed open the door to her floor and blinked.

Grayson stood in her hallway.

———

She resembled a walking shadow, Grayson thought, with pain written all over her face. Wiped out, emotionally and physically. Why the hell did she push herself so hard?

Something about her manner, combined with her somber dress, black slacks and a gray blazer over a gray blouse, stopped him from voicing those complaints. He held up a shopping bag for display. "I brought you some food so you could stay home and rest." He held her gaze. "Too late for that?"

"Nah." She straightened her shoulders and flashed a quick smile. "You have excellent timing, Grayson. Thanks." She unlocked the door and let him inside.

Inferior locks, and the door needed to be stronger. He wondered if she'd allow him to replace both. She tossed the keys on a coffee table full of newspapers. Off came the headphones. She set the Walkman next to it. She'd used his gift. She'd liked it. A warm, fuzzy feeling threatened to engulf him.

"Welcome to the Ritz. Fridge is over there." She crossed behind the far bookcase. "Give me a minute. I have to change. These clothes are strangling me."

"Of course." He crossed the small living space to the kitchen area. Her one-room apartment was neat, if cluttered. Bookshelves built into the wall were stuffed to overflowing, with books stacked on the floor near them. A record player held court in a corner, records shelved around it and stacked near it, and custom speakers were placed to each side of the player.

Her outer "room" had the chair and a couch, non-matching, and sat on what looked like an antique trunk. Two open boxes, full of notebooks, and several Rolodexes, sat next to the couch.

The kitchen had a tiny table with mismatched but solid chairs, with a wide window overlooking a back alley. Only cartons of takeout sat in her bare fridge. A typewriter with a stack of paper sat on the table. A bookcase in front of the bed had blocked it from view when he entered the apartment.

"Where were you?" he ventured while setting the food inside the refrigerator.

"Interviewing Adrienne Katz's parents," she called.

Yes, she would risk her recovery for that. "How are they?"

"Wrecked." She waltzed out from behind the bookcase. He caught the edge of a bed behind her. She'd changed into ripped jeans and a sleeveless "Runaways' T-shirt. Joan Jett's first band, he remembered from his recent research.

"The Katzes spoke well of you and Mrs. Grayson. Though they're under the impression that you and the Mrs. are still a couple."

"It seemed unimportant to correct them at the memorial." Wrecked certainly described the entire family. No matter if Grayson found the paintings or the unknown persons involved, their daughter would still be dead.

Patricia shook her head. "You'd think I'd get used to covering death. And sure, many people do awful stuff that ends in them being dead. But I'm convinced Adrienne did nothing wrong. How do her parents deal not only with her death but the speculation that she was part of the crime? How can they even stand, walk, or, hell, *breathe*?"

Given what he now knew of her personal tragedy from his background check, including a a young husband dead from illness, Patricia's question gained greater depth.

"Some things cannot be fixed," he said. "They can only be carried."

She slipped her hand in the front pocket of her jeans and brought out a battered gold-plated lighter. "Yeah, sounds about right."

The cross around her neck swayed back and forth. He wanted to go to her, comfort her, be there for her, carry half that pain. He'd expected this insane craving to be near her to fade but concluded yesterday that it would not.

Bloody hell. Getting close to her would not be easy.

"Do I smell fresh bagels?"

He held up a bag filled with a dozen poppy seed bagels. "Yes."

"Yum." She padded over in her bare feet and peaked into the other bags. "Whoa. These are Dean and Deluca from SoHo. Those are the *best*. Grayson, you went all out." She stared at him. "Thank you."

"I guessed about your taste in food."

"You did good, though anything hot and fresh about covers it." She studied him, a scrutiny that disconcerted and aroused him at the same time. She'd barreled into his life. Saved it. Rescued his career, even, with that front page story about the bomb. But what did he mean to her?

"Do you mind if I look over your record collection?" It might provide some insight into her.

"Sure, feel free."

He left her to the food and walked to the turntable. EPs, possibly bought at concerts, were stacked on one side. He knelt and flipped through the commercial albums.

The Ramones. The Runaways, with the cover matching her T-shirt. New York Dolls. Plasmatics. Patti Smith. But there were blues albums mixed in as well, as well as some pop and disco.

"You have wide-ranging taste."

"Blues are the origin of everything. Gotta know the blues."

"And disco?"

"A ton of creativity, and it got a bad rap because it was the favorite genre, of well, not straight white America. Plus, you can dance to it." She sighed. "Punk as I remember it is nearly dead. It used to be a cry of rage at the machine. But it's gotten darker and nastier. Maybe Sid Vicious murdering his girlfriend released something uglier. Or maybe the ugly was always there. A question for music scholars."

"You could be one." So much intelligence that she kept hidden under the attitude.

"Nah, then music would be work and not fun. So now that you've satisfied your curiosity about my musical taste, tell me why you showed up at my place." she asked. "What do you want?"

He straightened. "Do you always believe people have ulterior motives?"

"Hell, yes, and usually, I'm right, especially when the gifts are from men." She tilted her head. "In your case, I'm glad to be bribed." She smiled. "What do you want?" she repeated.

You. He placed the last of the food containers in her fridge, fighting lust, hoping the cool air would cool *him* off. Admitting that he wanted toss her down on that bed he'd glimpsed would put him in the same category as all the other men who wanted something from her.

David claimed his friend worked hard and partied harder. No doubt true. But Grayson wouldn't be a notch on her bed. Whatever this attraction between them became, he wanted it to last.

"No ulterior motive besides being worried you'd push yourself too hard." He smiled. "I see I was right."

"Ah."

Still, she watched him.

"And I missed talking to you," he added. "You keep me on my toes."

She stepped closer. Close enough for him to lean down and kiss her. Gorgeous, full-lips. And those clear blue eyes, the soft skin of her face... even the freckles were adorable.

Irresistible.

He leaned over, touched his lips to hers. Her response was an unexpected sigh. They stood there for a second, frozen in time, barely touching. Again, he fought the urge to go further.

"I'm glad to see you, too," she breathed out.

"I see." He cleared his throat. "In what way?"

She stepped back and mischief lit up her face, finally animating her. "If you came looking for sex, you came to the right place."

Direct. Straightforward. He knew she meant it. He could have her. All he had to do pull her against him. He'd feel that lithe body under his hands, curl his hands in her hair, uncover that other tattoo...

He closed the distance between them and took her into his arms. She slid against him as if she'd been made to fit and stared up at him. His hands were locked around her hips. Her breath ghosted against his neck.

Yes, yes, yes.

And she was injured and grieving. No.

He released her. "I didn't come for sex."

"Bummer, because I sure could use some to blow off steam. Or grief. Or whatever you want to call it." She grabbed a bagel and took a bite out of it. "Why not? Still involved with the ex? I could see that. She seems okay. She defended Adrienne."

Trisha devoured the bagel as if she hadn't eaten for days. As he desired to devour her.

"I'm not involved with Amanda." He could have Patricia's body. She'd made that more clear than any woman he'd ever met. But her heart? Not being offered. Too closely guarded.

He took her hand and entwined his fingers with hers.

Her breath quickened again.

"I told you, I came to check on you, not take advantage of you."

"I kinda thought it was the other way around."

He let her go once more and pulled a ticket out of his pocket. "And to give you this."

She frowned, at a loss, and grabbed the ticket. "What's this?"

"A ticket to the grand opening of *Lost Treasures* next week. I had to approve the press requests. I approved the *Herald's* art reporter, but I didn't see your name on the list. I thought you'd like to come."

She turned and set the ticket on the table. "Yeah, I'm technically still out sick. Not allowed assignments yet." There was something in her body language he couldn't read because she turned away. Grief still?

She turned back to him, smiling. "But you saved me from begging David for a ticket."

"I knew you'd want to be there." He kissed her, a soft caress of her cheek, clenching his hands tight so he wouldn't touch her otherwise. "I'd consider it a personal favor if you'd come."

"I'd consider it a personal favor if you'd stay."

He laughed and glided out the door before he could change his mind.

It took all he had not to turn around.

CHAPTER THIRTEEN

TRISHA KNOCKED BACK a flute of champagne and surveyed the opening night crowd of the *Lost Treasures* exhibit, indulging in her favorite pastime of people-watching. Lots of dresses had currently fashionable shoulder pads and were decorated with far too many glittery things for her taste. But there were those who'd also dressed down, in deliberately torn jeans and shirts and blouses that looked like they'd been bought at the local thrift shop but were probably part of the latest designer collection.

Punk was really dead if high society was busy churning out expensive clothes that aped the stuff she'd worn out of desperation years ago. She supposed there might be an article in that, but she couldn't find the energy. That trip to Montclair had taken far too much out of her.

Instead, she lurked on the edges of the crowd, while taking slow, careful steps that kept her pain-free.

If this had been a less prominent crime scene, the whole thing would still have been closed to the public. But somehow Windergaard had received permission to have his opening on schedule.

Opening night seemed to be a hit judging by the size of the crowd, the paparazzi on the red carpet outside, and the number of celebrities in attendance, despite the still-missing Cézannes. In fact, the empty frames with the spray-painted swastikas inside were the most popular segment of *Lost*

Treasures. Everyone wanted to make an anti-terrorism statement, at least when they were completely safe.

City Hall had issued a statement about not letting terrorists win. Hah. More likely, Windergaard, the museum board of directors, or a rich patron had some deputy mayor in their pocket. Trisha admitted the performance art inherent in leaving the swastikas on the wall was a good "fuck you" to Nazis past and present.

And she had a front row seat because of Grayson. Technically, she'd misled him about still being employed at the *Herald*. He didn't need to know, not yet. The Herald's arts reporter, Annie, was there, as expected, with her camera. Trisha had spotted her early and stayed out of her sight.

Trisha glided closer to the swastikas and the storage closet that Stephen Warren's crew had used to get inside the exhibit. The closet seemed unguarded, and she couldn't tag any of the undercover guards that must be in the crowd.

Grayson's people were good.

She shifted closer to the restricted stairway that led to the storage closet. She'd never seen it from this end. Adrienne had died here, but the polished floor contained no reminders of her violent death. Trisha didn't believe in ghosts, but it seemed wrong that Adrienne had been so thoroughly erased from this place.

"Oh, Trish…" David called.

He looked like a dark angel in a tuxedo with his perfectly combed dark hair. He stepped up next to her and handed her a small walkie-talkie.

"What the heck is this?" she asked.

"Boss's orders," he said, giving nothing away.

He pulled out his earplug and put it in her ear. Grayson's voice came through loud and clear.

"Good evening, Patricia."

"Hey, Grayson. Thanks again for the ticket."

"That ticket didn't include unrestricted access."

His deep voice resonated far more than it should have, even through the crackle of the radio. They hadn't talked since his visit to her home. She was still trying to interpret that. She should have done more than kiss him. That would've told her all she needed to know.

I give up. She'd hadn't figured him out yet and she wouldn't tonight.

"Please back away from the stairway," he said.

"What stairway?"

"The one you're standing nearby. I'm watching you on-screen right now."

So there were video cameras in here. Somewhere. "Are you staring at me?" Good, she decided.

"Yes, and I'm glad to see you looking so well. The black dress suits you. But move away from the stairway."

She glanced around again and still couldn't see the damn cameras. "Where are they?" she whispered to David.

He grinned. "I'll never tell."

"You wouldn't throw me out," she said to both of them.

"Do you want to test that?" Grayson asked.

She shook her head. "No, I suppose not."

"Good. Later, Patricia."

"Fine." She backed off from the stairwell and handed David the earpiece and walkie-talkie. "Well, he's a pain in the ass."

"You'll get no argument from me. But stay away from that stairwell, okay? And please stay out of trouble tonight?"

"No promises."

"I knew your recovery had a downside." David shook his head as he walked away.

Fine, fine. No creeping around the crime scene. It wasn't helping anyway, as Adrienne's ghost wasn't about to whisper the identity of the murderer into her ear.

Instead, Trisha wandered around the exhibit, watching the people more than the art. God, this whole big hair trend was too much. Thank God she'd cut hers. Who had the time to mess with teasing it out to such extremes? She eavesdropped on conversations, hoping to learn something to do with the missing paintings. But there were only personal dramas and discussions on the history of the exhibit items.

She finally focused on the paintings that she'd almost died for. The ones Adrienne had died to protect. Were they worth it?

So odd that people would value objects, even masterpieces, over living people, as Windergaard obviously did. The money from selling off all this art could feed the entire homeless population of Manhattan for a year. Hell, it might build them new homes too.

Still, staring at the gorgeous art reminded her of reading a great newspaper story, one that jumped off the page, but in visuals instead of words. The Impressionists and Manet each had a separate room and she lost herself in them for a while. Wait, wasn't Manet also an Impressionist? She'd have to ask Annie. Scratch that. She was avoiding Annie.

There was value in art, as there was value in stories. People could be as hungry for imagination as they were for food. Nicky had liked the museum because he could escape real life in it and believe in something bigger than the world they'd been trapped in. At least he'd had that.

She returned to the hallway, stopped in front of a Picasso, and tilted her head. Did that figure have three nipples or five? Hard to tell. But easy to note Picasso disliked women because he'd painted this one in such harsh colors.

Next, a Toulouse-Lautrec portrait, also of a woman. The shades of black and red made the canvas stark and almost plain. Yet it spoke to her better than the beautiful colors of the Impressionists.

Sad. Intense. But hopeful.

Too bad the figures inside the paintings couldn't tell her who killed Adrienne and where the Cézannes had been taken.

She walked back to the main room and grabbed an hors d'oeuvre from a passing tray. Aha. She bet that some of Grayson's people were working as waitstaff, a good way to hide security. She should've figured that out sooner. Out of the corner of her eye, she finally spotted a camera hidden in the shadow of a sculpture mounted on the wall.

"Gotcha," she whispered.

"Ah, a beautiful lady who defies convention," said a voice from the side. "That puts you at least one step ahead of many of those here."

Oh, please. She turned, thinking that Grayson had sent someone else to pester her and instead came face to face with Dante Sidney, the collector of the artwork in the exhibit. The man who'd been ducking her phone calls.

Well, hello gorgeous.

"Thank you," she said.

Sidney handed her another flute of champagne. His hair and eyebrows were dark, but his features didn't quite seem Latino. According to

Grayson, Sidney was of indeterminate origin, with homes in several countries. An international bon vivant, maybe.

"You're welcome." Sidney clinked flutes with her. "Tonight is my triumph. I must celebrate it with the most unique woman in the room."

His face lit up with a warm smile. Not what she'd expected. A polished charmer, not an oily one, even though she knew he lied. There were plenty of beautiful women in gorgeous gowns floating around, society girls with perfect hair and bodies sculpted by plastic surgery. Not to mention the *Sports Illustrated* models and movie stars vamping for the paparazzi gathered outside.

There would be photos in the society columns tomorrow.

Grayson had given her a ticket. Technically, she was not working, so she'd worn what she'd wanted, which included a black dress, black lace boots up past her knees, and a neon purple jacket. She'd bought that at the thrift shop, not from some designer collection. It did make her stick out. Good. Besides, it'd attracted Sidney.

"And what triumph are we celebrating?" she asked.

He raised his flute to her. "For the first time in decades, my artwork is being enjoyed by the public."

"*Your* artwork?" Bite the lure. *Talk to me.*

"I'm Dante Sidney. I'm the one responsible for bringing the exhibit here."

Oh, no ego there. At all. "Congratulations." She sipped the champagne. "I've heard so many stories about how you came to own these paintings, Mr. Sidney. Which one is true?"

"All of them?" He ventured. "I wanted to right a wrong, correct an injustice, bring this beautiful work into the open, showcase it, much as that dress showcases you."

Quite a pick-up line. "You somehow pried this art from the evil Nazis who stole them from their original owners?" She smiled, trying to sound approving.

He stepped closer, more intent. "You make me sound like another Robin Hood. I take that as a compliment."

She leaned in closer to him, her voice almost a whisper. "Robin Hood robbed from the rich and gave to the poor and mistreated. Why not give these back to the original owners or their heirs if you want to right a wrong?"

He stepped back.

"You're not just a pretty face."

"Most women aren't, you know." She smiled, just a little. "Why didn't you search for the original owners of the paintings?"

"Sadly, all ownership records have vanished. The right thing, the only thing that can be done, is for the art to belong to everyone. Would you rather have them hidden away?" His gaze swept the crowd. "Yes, tonight is for the rich and powerful. But soon, the public will see them. We have given out free tickets to school and civic organizations. I want this experience available to everyone, no matter their status."

This was more than the party line about this exhibit. This was conviction. "I hadn't heard about the free tickets for schools."

"Mrs. Grayson developed the school and civic discount tickets program. We've kept it quiet, to prevent from being inundated from those who might take advantage of our generosity." He smiled. "This is for show. The real legacy of the exhibit will be the children."

That might please Adrienne.

Yet the huge chunk of change the museum reaped from the exhibit, especially now that the exhibit's profile had been heightened by the murder, was another legacy.

"That's admirable of Mrs. Grayson." Trisha touched his arm. "But aren't you concerned that there will be another attempt to steal them?"

He shrugged, elegantly. "When I started this, I knew it would be dangerous." He frowned. "You're not impressed by any of this. How does one impress you, miss...?"

She hesitated for a second, debating a lie. But she'd have to fess up sooner or later. "Trisha Connell." She put out her hand.

"You!" He smiled widely, showing off his perfect white teeth. He took her hand, brought it to his lips, kissed it, and let go with a flourish.

Okay, so not the reaction she expected.

"This is your celebration too. You saved the exhibit. You have made this all possible." He bowed to her. "Thank you."

"Uh, you're welcome." Damn, would people stop *thanking* her? First

Grayson, then David, now Sidney. Hell, even the cops were thanking her! Though not Dorothy. Trisha had been after the story. She was in no way, shape or form, a hero. Adrienne was the hero. And that just needed to be proved.

"If you'd answered my phone calls, you could have thanked me sooner," Trisha said.

"It's been far too busy. Besides, isn't it better to be thanked in person?"

Oh, he was good.

"How about dinner to celebrate and become better acquainted?" he asked. "I must know more about the person who saved the museum. There is a little Spanish restaurant in SoHo that would be perfect. It's informal but the food is amazing."

"Does the food there remind you of your home country?" His Latin accent seemed to have a few different flavors. Or it could be fake. Usually, she could tell Central American from Caribbean from South American, but he seemed all over the place.

"Ah, Americans add their own touch, always," he said. "That's the beauty of New York."

Go to his turf while she was still not at one hundred percent? A public place, though. And she could take a cab and meet him there. "That sounds interesting. When did you have in mind?"

"Tonight. After the opening. It'll be the perfect ending to a triumph that belongs to both of us." He smiled again. "The kitchen stays open late."

What a perfect chance to pursue the story. "I accept."

"I only wish I could do more for you than a dinner."

Now, he seemed sincere, but he had to have ulterior motives. "More? Indulge me, then. If you could take me anywhere in the world to celebrate, where would it be?"

"Another fabulous question. To my beach, of course." He pointed to a seascape on the far wall. "It's been too long since I've been there. White sand, nearly untouched by human hands."

"Why so long since you've been there?" she asked.

"Business, sadly, but it would be a lovely place to take you. I have a house with a private walk to the beach. At night, we could drive into town, eat well, drink well, and dance until the sun rises."

Right offer. Wrong guy. Oh, hell. She wanted to do all those things with *Grayson*.

No, forget it. They had zero in common. He was high class, and she was, well, she was the girl who'd crawled out of the sewer. Exactly what Cardoza had called her. Low class.

"How far away is this place of yours, Dante? Do I have to fly?"

"Fly south like the birds, yes," he said.

Get into one of those planes and be locked inside with no control for hours? Ick. "How far south? You know, I've never been out of the United States. I don't even have a passport."

"Then you should get one soon, Ms. Connell, because now that the idea is in my head, I will not let it go. I wish to see you dance."

"Isn't that what we're doing now?" she asked. "Verbally speaking?"

A smile with perfect teeth behind it. "Yes."

Two women in designer ball gowns approached Sidney, accompanied by an older man in a tuxedo. Patrons of the museum, she guessed.

"Excuse me, Dante," the man said. "I promised my wife and daughter that you'd give them a personal tour."

Sidney nodded. "Of course." He half-bowed to her. "A pleasure meeting you, Ms. Connell. I'll find you later to give you the address of the restaurant."

"Trisha," she said.

"Trisha. I will see you again, quite soon."

She nodded as he left. Interrogating him at dinner would make coming to the opening worth it. Sidney had turned down all other interviews. She knew because she'd been reading all the papers since being fired. Their "date" would be an exclusive and her best chance to uncover what really happened to Adrienne.

Trisha walked back to the Picasso but stopped around a corner to pull her notebook from her clutch purse. She needed to write down what Sidney said. Writing it down always reinforced the memory. Hell, in juvie, she'd sometimes written on the walls.

The World Jewish Reclamation Project had filed suit challenging Sidney's possession of the artwork in court, but that lawsuit had problems, as Sidney had mentioned. No paperwork trail, especially with the Holocaust. Tonight, perhaps Sidney would give some hint about how he'd come into their possession.

A familiar voice caught her attention. She peered around the corner.

Grayson and Amanda were talking quietly, their backs to her, studying the Toulouse-Lautrec. Amanda wore a knee-length, midnight blue dress that went well with her blonde hair. No shoulder pads, only elegance in a classic Grace Kelly style.

Amanda Grayson's whole shape screamed "beautiful and dignified." Nice legs, Trisha thought, and her sculpted shoulders showed that Mrs. Grayson worked out too. Hard to blame Grayson if he still found her attractive. They looked good together. Cary Grant and Grace Kelly, right? They had everything in common, including a teenage daughter. Family should stick together. No need to be jealous.

But she was.

Windergaard walked up to them, his gaze on the painting. Trisha slipped behind a clutch of people admiring the Picasso. Hopefully, she could hear what Windergaard said over their murmurs.

"What a triumph." Windergaard said.

"For now," Grayson said. "But until we know exactly how Warren and his people broke into the museum, I would hold off on declaring it a triumph."

Windergaard tsk-tsked Grayson. Oh, that would not go over well, Trisha thought.

"I hope you're not still laboring under the mistaken impression that one of my people was involved with the theft, Mr. Grayson," Windergaard drawled.

"That remains a distinct possibility," Grayson replied.

"If they had help—and that's an 'if'—you and your people are suspect too," Windergaard said.

Did Windergaard want to anger Grayson? That made no sense. Maybe Windergaard hated to admit that he'd been wrong in trying to fire Grayson.

"Max!" Amanda snapped, "That's uncalled for. Edmund *saved* the museum."

Trisha raised her eyebrows. Good for Amanda.

Windergaard made a show of observing the crowd. Trisha took a step to the side, behind someone tall.

"I suppose there's no reason to argue, especially with tonight so successful." Windergaard sighed. "There's one other thing I wanted to speak to you about, Mr. Grayson."

"Yes?" Grayson said.

"Are you going to let your reporter friend walk around here, asking questions, doing whatever she wants?"

Windergaard hadn't returned her phone calls either. Apparently saving his museum won no points for her or Grayson.

"Patricia Connell had proper credentials," Grayson said. "She's caused no disruptions."

Proper credentials. Interesting way of putting his gift of a ticket.

"She's after some story or scandal. It's only a matter of time before she causes trouble or makes something up," Windergaard said. "You know, common people don't understand things like this museum."

Argh. She tried to ignore the hurt. An insult from Windergaard was practically a compliment.

Grayson crossed his arms over his chest. "Without her, this opening would not have been possible."

"She had a front page story from it," Windergaard sneered. "Her actions were hardly altruistic. Your head's been turned by her looks, Mr. Grayson."

Not that much, Trisha thought, or we would have had wild sex already.

"Patricia Connell impressed me with her *actions.*" Grayson dropped his arms to his sides. Battle-mode.

Aw, Grayson was defending her.

Windergaard clasped and unclasped his hands. He waved to someone in the crowd. "Oh, I really must go. Excuse me."

What a coward.

Trisha walked to the other side of the crowd, to avoid Windergaard as he left the room. If the museum director had wanted the publicity for the museum, maybe he could be the inside man. But that would make this an episode of *Scooby Doo.* Couldn't be. Grayson could never be as incompetent as Fred.

A girlish laugh brought her attention back to Grayson and Amanda. They had their heads close together, almost whispering.

If they started making out, Trisha would throw up.

"If it helps, Max is suffering from an attack of nerves. Your reporter is a convenient target, Edmund," Amanda said. "And that screaming purple jacket made it easy for Max to spot her."

"Apparently, I'm also a convenient target for him," Grayson said.

He rocked the tuxedo he wore tonight. Someone should put the guy on the cover of GQ. He could've passed for a rich museum patron, save for that edge of danger that seemed to surround him, the aura that would always twig him as a cop, no matter that he was technically a civilian now.

"That's only because Max thinks that reporter has you wrapped around her finger," Amanda said. "I think she has a crush on you. The story she wrote portrayed you as the dashing hero of the day."

Trisha choked on her champagne. That noise alerted Grayson, but not Amanda, to her presence. He raised an eyebrow at Trisha in acknowledgment of her presence.

Amanda put her arm around his waist. "Will you be free after the opening? I'm taking Eleanor out to celebrate. This opening caps almost a year of work."

Eleanor, their daughter. They were a family, still.

"No, I'm sorry, I'll have to debrief my staff. But tell Eleanor I'll be at her basketball game as planned."

"I'm not asking for the moon, Edmund. You can have someone else debrief the staff. I hoped you might enjoy celebrating a mutual triumph over dinner."

The ex wanted him back. Bad way to do it, Trisha thought. Grayson would not want his work challenged.

"I'm sorry. There's still a great deal of work to do," he said.

"You've always had a great deal of work to do."

And Amanda walked away, swaying her hips. Attractive woman. Nice legs. But nagging Grayson would make him run away, not stay. Trisha began to understand why they'd gotten divorced. Still, they seemed friendly enough now.

Trisha walked up to Grayson, who was still watching Amanda leave.

"You a leg man, Grayson?" Trisha said.

"Depends on the person." He put his full attention on her. "I noticed you talking to Dante Sidney."

A hint of jealousy? Interesting. "Sure. Gotta cover all the bases for sources. I think Sidney came to me because of the boots. Men have a thing for the boots. But I'm not in your wife's league."

"Ex-wife," he said. "And you stand out well in this crowd, Patricia. That's a fine sense of style."

"Yeah, it's called 'what's clean in my closet today.'"

"Still, you've the looks for broadcast news, if you wanted."

She scowled. "All on-air talent has to do is smile and read copy. Besides, I could never adhere to their dress code. And the producers do all the work and get no credit. Television news is all show. Writing is about the *story*." She tapped her clutch purse against her hip. "And I like seeing my byline on the front page."

"Your ego doesn't need pumping up," he said with a smile.

"Hah." She flipped pages through her notebook. "Tell me, have you found out about how Sidney gathered his collection?"

He put his hands in his pockets again. "That's confidential."

"You can tell me that you found nothing. I won't hold it against you."

"What did Sidney say tonight that has you so curious?"

"He told me a few things that might interest you."

Grayson shifted, moving away from the people in the room. She followed him. Now she had his full attention. About work, of course. Friends? No, work colleagues, at least so far. Except, they both remembered his kiss in her apartment.

Dammit, she'd wished again that he'd taken her up on sex in her apartment. Then she could have moved on. Got him out of her system.

"What did Sidney tell you?" he asked.

"Sidney said he loves white sand beaches that require a long flight south and claims to own a townhouse in a town with nightlife. Plus, he hasn't been able to visit that place for some time because of 'business.' Does that narrow anything down for you?"

Grayson raised his eyebrows. "It opens some possibilities. What were his exact words?"

She rattled them off.

"You have an excellent memory," he said.

"Practice. Plus, I haven't always been in a position to write things down." When even pen and paper had been beyond her meager budget, memory had to work.

"Is that why the scribbling in your notebook is so cryptic?" he asked.

She tilted her head. "Just when did you read my notebook?"

"I caught a glimpse of several pages when you were in my car, before you collapsed. You had them open when talking to your editor."

"I'd forgotten about that." She nodded. "My notes make sense to me. The words trigger the memory of the whole conversation. That way, if I lose my notebook, no one else can make sense of my research and quotes. Keeps them private." Enough about her. "What do you think about the place Sidney described?"

Grayson frowned in concentration. "It's a place to start."

"I'll get more over dinner with him tonight."

"Is that wise? You're still injured, and he could be dangerous."

Grayson stepped closer, almost looming over her.

Disconcerting to have him so close. "I'm cleared for activity starting tomorrow, and I've been trying to interview him for days."

"And you're up to it?"

"Sure." Except when she moved suddenly. Or turned without thinking. Or walked too fast. Or went down steps. Or tried to hold something heavy. Or breathed too hard.

"Up to it in every way?"

Why would he remind her of the panic attack *now*? She narrowed her eyes at him. "That other part is none of your business. Contrary to what you've seen, I hardly ever panic."

"That's not what I meant. That one incident seems to bother you far more than it does me." He sighed. "I'm worried that you're not physically up to it if Sidney pulls something. Be careful, Patricia. Stay in a public place. Don't get into a car with him."

"I've been on my own since I was thirteen, Grayson. I'm still here."

He stared at her for a second, and she cursed herself. He'd seen her fall apart under pressure. He knew it could happen again.

"Still here, yes," he said. "But you run at trouble."

"That's where the fun is."

"Understood." He reached into the pocket of his tuxedo and pulled out a pen and business card. He flipped the card over, wrote a number on the back, and offered it to her. "This is my private line. Call me and tell me what you find."

"And I'll be part of investigating whatever lead I find instead of you giving me a line about confidential client information?"

He slipped the business card into her purse. "Call me. About anything."

He'd wanted her to come as a personal favor, watched her, but then only talked about the investigation. He'd kissed her in her apartment but turned her down.

Grayson certainly ran hot and cold.

———

"Trisha, I do believe you know nearly everything about me. What about you?" Sidney said.

She sipped water. She wanted wine or, better, a beer, but she needed her full wits tonight. Telling Sidney about the painkillers for her injury provided a good explanation for abstaining.

"Maybe I'm fascinated by you and your artwork," she said.

Sidney finished his glass of red. So far, he'd downed an entire bottle yet showed no sign of being drunk. But maybe it would kick in and he'd become careless.

"For instance, how did you transport your collection to New York?" she asked. "It's not the kind of thing you can put in baggage claim."

He smiled and shrugged. "Guess."

Not dismissive. An invitation to play with him.

"Private plane?"

"Too visible," he said.

"Commercial cargo flight," she said.

"Not private enough."

What was left? "Boat, then."

"Ship," he corrected. "A private ship, as it happens." He grinned, showing all those nice white teeth again. "I rented it myself. I wished now that I'd bought it because I do love the sea." He sighed.

"What's to stop you from buying it?" she asked.

"Nothing." He leaned closer. "I'm going to look at a yacht to purchase tomorrow. Do you want to come see it with me?"

Trisha debated an answer. More time with Sidney would be more time to pick up something about him. But she might be alone with him at some point, and that might be too dangerous considering she wasn't fully healed. Be careful, Grayson had said. Good advice, at least for now.

Their waitress arrived, cutting off conversation. Sidney had been dead right about this place. The storefront, a nondescript brown wood door, was easy to pass by, especially on a slightly seedy street. The interior space held about twenty-five diners, with the décor done in soothing browns and earth colors. The dim lighting added to the ambiance.

Their food had arrived in courses, served a-la-carte. She'd sampled most of it: soup, sausages that were served hanging on a rack, chicken in tomato sauce, and elegantly sliced vegetables. Now they were working their way toward dessert. She asked for coffee. Sidney ordered a dessert sampler.

"Did you have security on your ship? Did you have any specific threats against the paintings?" she asked.

He raised an eyebrow. Few men could raise eyebrows and pull it off. Mostly, they resembled idiotic imitations of Spock. But it worked for Dante Sidney. Not as well as it worked for Grayson, however.

"We may be off the record, but I don't think we're that off the record. Besides, enough about me. What about you?"

"I'm not that interesting."

"You are," he said. "I suspect you could keep me entertained with tales of your work for the newspaper but..." He waved a hand, dismissively. "It's what you do in your off time that interests me."

Drinking, music, and sex. Day trips on her Indian. Reading when she stayed home. None of which she wanted to share with Sidney. "I don't have much off time."

"You must have hobbies."

"Hobbies. What a weird sounding word. It conjures an image of someone sitting in a garage, building model trains," she said. "I keep busy with a few things."

"With what?"

What would be safe to tell him? "My Indian motorcycle. It's vintage."

"Aha. Now we are getting somewhere."

He leaned forward. Either he was genuinely interested, or he was damn good at pretending.

"It's a 1950 Indian Chief, originally made in Springfield, Massachusetts. I got it as a collection of parts in a box with a lot of the vital pieces missing." Her mechanic had said she'd never find enough pieces to put it together. "I scoured swap meets all over the East Coast, biker bars, legal and off-the-books, and I drove out to Springfield to interview an engineer who used to design the bikes. He taught me how to jury-rig replacement parts when the originals weren't available."

"How did you find him?"

"Pounding on doors in the right neighborhood." One paranoid old biker had pulled a gun when she knocked at the door. But he'd turned around pretty fast. And he'd had excellent homemade beer.

"How long did you spend rebuilding the bike in the box?" Sidney asked.

"Four years. Well, I had a working model in three. But every time I tested the engine, something would fritz out. It took another year before it was reliable."

"Four years." He straightened. "You spent *four years* putting a motorcycle together."

"You spent more than that putting together *Lost Treasures*, I bet," she said. "Just how did you go about obtaining the pieces to *your* collection?"

"Very, very carefully," he said. "Persuading those who kept them hidden took longer than four years."

Sidney wasn't much older than she was. Those paintings must represent his life's work. She wondered if Grayson could track his travel over the last decade. That might not be much help since Sidney had done legitimate work until now.

Sidney excused himself to go to the restroom, perhaps wanting to halt her questions.

She sipped her coffee and watched him walk to the back of the restaurant. He sure moved elegantly. And smart too, too smart for her interrogation to be successful. Anyone with the patience to gather that collection over a period of years had learned to deflect questions.

When Sidney was out of sight, she searched in her purse for her aspirin. Where had she put those pills?

What the hell is that?

She pulled out a long metal thing about the size of a pencil. Not hers.

She held the thing closer to the candle for a better look. A microphone, maybe a bug? Who could have—

Grayson.

He must have slipped it into the purse along with his business card. Instead of trusting her, he was *spying* on her.

Motherfucking sonofabitch.

She'd trusted him and he rewarded her with *this*?

She almost dropped the bug into her water glass. But, no. Grayson didn't know that she knew about the bug. She could use that. She slipped the bug back into her purse. Grayson valued her, yes, but now she knew why. For the information she could provide about the case. He'd charmed her with his concern, and she'd bought it. *No ulterior motives, my ass.*

Sidney returned just as the dessert sampler arrived. Several types of cheesecake, puff pastries, a fruit tart, and chocolate cake tempted her and distracted her from her anger at Grayson. The waitress also bought her the Spanish version of hot chocolate, a bitter rather than sweet drink, but *good*.

It almost made up for not having beer.

She sipped and wondered what she could say that would piss of Grayson the most. She wanted to hit him where it really hurt. Fuck her, he'd gotten under her skin. And then he turned around and spied on her.

"You had good security on the ship to arrive safely and with your collection intact," she said to Sidney. "Do you wish the same people were protecting your collection now?"

Sidney frowned. "What do you mean?"

"Security was breached, obviously. Someone is dead and you're still missing five paintings, despite the arrest of the Neo-Nazis. Gray Associates is a *small* agency with not much experience in this type of job." *Suck on it, Grayson.* "Why not hire one of the bigger, more well-known firms to protect your life's work?"

Sidney made a show out of taking a bite of the cheesecake. A stalling tactic.

"Mr. Windergaard interviewed the security firms who applied for the job, not me," he said.

"Ah, so the museum director wanted Gray Associates?"

Sidney shook his head. "No. He favored another agency of about the same size. I vetoed it. I liked Gray Associates' credentials better. All my contacts in the city spoke well of them, especially their alarm systems."

She hoped Grayson's ears were burning. "Do you regret your decision?"

Sidney frowned. "Perhaps. Perhaps not." He pointed with his fork to the puff pastry. "Humor me. Try this."

She reached across the table and took a bite. "*Mmmm...*" She moaned. "That's so good."

The crust melted into nothingness, and the tart flavor practically exploded in her mouth. Sidney smiled at her. She smiled back.

"Do *you* think Gray Associates is incompetent?" he asked.

I think somebody at the museum is screwing with Grayson. So does he. It probably wasn't Sidney. Why would he sabotage the exhibit he'd worked so hard for?

"Grayson saved the museum from the bomb." She almost left it at that. But Grayson had violated her trust. "But he obviously missed something."

I hope that one went deep, you bastard.

Sidney winced. "You're a tough audience, considering he saved your life in the tunnels."

"He's good under pressure, yes." Cold as ice, all the way through.

Sidney nodded. "That is my impression. I suspect the problem lies with the museum staff, either through incompetence or involvement in this mess."

"Any idea who?"

"I have no evidence. Conrath strikes me as not intelligent enough to be chief of security, but I can't find a fault other than that." Sidney shook his head. "The only thing I'm sure of right now is you've circled the subject back to business."

She shrugged, smiled, and sipped more of the hot chocolate, wondering where Grayson was fuming. Probably listening in a car close by, depending on the range of the bug. Pounding the dashboard and cursing by now, she hoped. He'd wanted to listen. Though maybe she'd gone too far. Adrienne's death wasn't his fault.

The waitress brought the check. Sidney pulled out a credit card.

"You have to let me pick up half," she said.

"Never."

"Letting you pay violates my newspaper's ethics code about accepting gifts," she said. Not that it mattered anymore. Still, ethics were ethics.

"This is a date, not business."

She sighed. "All right." But only because she wanted him to set the card down where she could see it.

He did, with a flourish. She sipped her water, staring at the card bearing the logo of a company called "Queen Anne's Revenge." Sidney left it out long enough for her to memorize the multi-digit number and expiration date. She repeated the number several times over in her mind and took out her notebook.

"I just want to write down the address of this restaurant, because it's excellent," she said. And she scribbled that down too, along with the credit card number. She flipped the notebook closed before Sidney would see what she'd done.

Yeah, sometimes she and Nicky would rub the numbers from credit cards and used those to order take-out when they were starving. She'd kept in practice memorizing groups of numbers ever since. Oh, not to buy anything. Amazing what you could uncover if you had someone's credit card number.

"So glad you enjoyed this meal. Perhaps you'd like to come again?" Sidney said. "Perhaps with me?"

"We'll see," she said.

She excused herself to the bathroom and popped a couple of aspirin for the ache in her side. When she returned, Sidney had signed the check. He stood and offered her his arm. "Let me show you out."

Almost without thinking, she took his arm and walked outside with him. The street was deserted save for Sidney's Beemer. But she bet Grayson lurked in the shadows on the next street over. "Can I give you a ride home? Or to somewhere else?" Sidney offered.

"Not tonight."

He sighed. "Tell me, if the museum investigation were over, would your answer be different?"

"Probably not. You're part of the story. Dinner is as far as I can go."

"Then I won't feel as if I've completely lost my charm," Sidney said with a smile. "Let me at least call you a car service. It's not particularly safe this time of night, and I don't see cabs around."

"No worries. I know someone around here." One hundred percent true. She just needed a way to smoke Grayson out.

"All right. I know 'no' when I hear it. Thank you for a lovely evening." Sidney kissed her lightly on the cheek, bowed—which should have seemed silly but came off as charming—and walked to his car. She stood in front of the restaurant and watched him pull away before she started walking.

The poorly lit one-way street, more the size of a big alley, could barely fit one car. They weren't far from the Bowery. Sidney had called it unsafe. Probably. But she walked her city's streets without fear. With caution, yes. Afraid, no.

Besides, she wouldn't be alone long.

She walked to the cross street, where the streetlights provided illumination past some of the empty warehouses. Some had signs promising upcoming apartment construction. The city always smashed away the old for the new.

Gentrification rolled on. It was a damn tragedy. The city she knew was disappearing, as the punk scene was morphing into hardcore.

She didn't spot Grayson's Mercedes or a surveillance van. But he wouldn't be so obvious. She racked her brain for the next move as she strolled to the next block.

She'd been in this neighborhood for an after-work party not long ago. But where? She passed a twenty-four-hour Laundromat and the memory clicked.

This was the street with the hidden punk club. Borelli, the court reporter, had dragged half the office down here one night. Nothing fancy and the band had been terrible, no Ramones or Erasure, just bad three cord punk. But the drinks had been cheap and the company good.

She wondered where Borelli and the rest of *Herald* staff were doing tonight. She wondered who'd been assigned *her* job. And she wondered if she'd ever have an answer to how Adrienne had gotten into the locked exhibit.

She entered the Laundromat and headed for the small office at the back.

There were no signs for the club. To get in, you had to supply a password through a peephole at the back door of the Laundromat. She had the wrong password, but they let her in anyway. Gotta be the boots. The downside was that men expected a reward for it. She sidestepped the bouncer, though, and headed into the smoky interior.

Damn, she missed smoking.

The sound of a blues slide guitar enveloped her, a pleasant surprise.

The crowded, smoky room meant two people deep at the bar. The noise level approached deafening. It had to be close to closing time but, hey, illegal meant ignoring the rules.

She took two steps sideways, found an opening on the wall, leaned back and let the beginning of the next number wash over her. The electronic blues riff sunk into her body until she could feel herself vibrating.

Tired.

Once the guitarist finished the set, she pushed her way through the crowd to the back room. Someone elbowed their way past and she took one right in her still-healing ribs.

Argh.

She hissed and nearly doubled over, but the press of people held her up. She needed space, fast. She straightened, sidestepped to the bathroom corridor, and jimmied open the door to the back alley. It had started raining, but the closeness of the buildings kept the alley dry. She leaned against the brick wall and tried to breathe easier. The deep breath brought in the garbage and urine smells lingering in the alley's corners.

Fuck the pain. The doctors said this would go away, with time. Nothing else to do but wait for bones to knit back together.

After a minute, the agony ebbed to discomfort.

She peered into the darkness. Silence, save for the drip of rain. The only thing dangerous out here were the rats lingering under the garbage dumpster. A perfect place to turn the tables on Grayson.

She let a moan escape. Let him overhear and sort that out. She pulled the bug out of the purse and held it in her hand.

"Hey, you don't want to do that," she said to the empty air. Her voice was still shaky. Good. That would add to the effect.

She counted three seconds in her head.

"Hey, buddy, no need for the knife."

She took a step backward and silently counted five more seconds. "I don't *have* any money but here, you can have the purse." She let her voice go shaky again. "Just back off, okay?"

Another five seconds. "Fuck!"

She started counting in her head. *One, two, three, four, five, six, seven, eight....*

She'd reached thirty when Grayson burst through the door to the alley, a gun in his hand.

Gotcha!

She crossed her arms over her chest and leaned back against the wall again.

"A half a minute? I could be gutted by now. You've got to work on your response time, Grayson."

He was an incongruous figure in the dirty, dank alley, still dressed in the tux from the opening. He glared at her, glanced down the alley, and realization dawned.

He holstered his handgun in his shoulder rig.

She threw the bug at him.

Pain lanced through her chest. *Argh.* She doubled over and almost missed Grayson snatching his bug out of midair. She should've smashed it.

He slipped it into his pocket and came closer. "Patricia, are you—"

"You take one step closer and I'll break *your* nose, you son of a bitch!" She straightened. Damn, she'd forgotten how many muscles were involved in throwing. "You *spied* on me."

"You needed backup," he said.

"Trusted back-up would have let me know they were helping, rather than slipping a bug into my purse, listening in on my dinner, and following me around. I *trusted* you!"

They glared at each other.

"It was for your own good," he said.

"For my own good?" She closed the distance between them. "You *stalked* me."

"It was—"

"What? Stupid? Out of line? A mistake?"

"Necessary. Obviously. Look at you."

"Yeah, look at me. I got info out of Sidney that you couldn't get, and I led you around by the nose. Yeah, I'm practically helpless and worthless."

"I'm worried—"

"Know what I've figured out? That people—especially *men*—who do stuff behind my back to protect me don't give a damn about me. It's their way of having the upper hand, of being in control. That's what this is about. You're all about control. You wanted control of whatever I found out. You *used* me."

It's what men like him usually did. She shouldn't be so surprised.

He put up his hands in surrender. "You're right. I'm sorry."

"You're just sorry you got caught, you arrogant bastard."

"You're not the first to call me that."

"No doubt." She took a deep breath. He'd admitted fault. Unexpected.

"I'm sorry I betrayed your trust, Patricia."

"That one's on me. People always have ulterior motives. I forgot that with you. I won't again. But now, you owe me one."

"I don't—"

"Are you going to deny you wanted to listen to the conversation with Sidney?"

He frowned and shook his head. "I never meant to hurt you."

"I'm not *hurt*. I'm pissed."

"All right." He crossed his arms over his chest. "What do you want?"

"You recorded my dinner conversation."

"Yes," he said.

"You're going to give me a copy of that tape so I can review it."

He nodded. "I would have, in any case. Once I sorted out a way to tell you I had it."

"You're lying." She sighed, her anger devolving to disappointment. She'd thought he was different. He'd almost had her with that soft sell of his. "You're also going to let me read all your firm's research on the museum and the *Lost Treasures* exhibit."

"As much as I want to apologize, Patricia, while I can provide some of that, confidential client files must remain confidential."

Push harder. "If you don't, I'll file a wiretapping complaint with the cops. And I'll get Sidney to sign it with me."

"Do what you have to do." He shook his head. "As you already have."

"What does that mean?"

"You had no problem throwing my firm under the bus when talking to Sidney."

"If you hadn't planted a bug, you wouldn't have heard any of that.

Serves you right, especially since you were also spying on your client." She should explain, but, no, he'd *bugged* her. Let him stew.

"The museum hired me, not Sidney, and I have to answer to them."

"I could trade you something else for access to your case files. For instance, Sidney's credit card information," she said.

"I've already checked out all his credit cards."

"This one is from a company called 'Queen Anne's Revenge.' Do you have that?"

"No." A pause. "How did you find out he had this card?"

"I memorized the card numbers when he paid for dinner."

"How the bloody hell can you do that?"

"It's one of my survival skills. I need them, given even people that I trust plant bugs on me."

She stepped back to wait on his decision. Rats rustled behind her in the alley, their claws scouring the garbage bins. A car drove down the street. The nearest streetlight flickered. Rain splattered around them. Just another night in the city.

She hugged herself, chilled.

He finally nodded. "I may be able to share some of the information in exchange for this Queen Anne's Revenge information. It's the best I can do. And it can't be in any article in your paper."

Fine, since she didn't have a paper anymore. Good, she'd gained some advantage from this mess. From now on, she'd treat him as someone to bargain with. For the best, right? They would never have worked.

But she still felt sick to her stomach. "That's acceptable."

"Are we even now?" he asked.

"I'll let you know when we are."

Dammit, Grayson. She hadn't wanted to negotiate with him, like any other source. At least Sidney had been honest about what he wanted from her.

"In the meantime, can I offer you a ride home?" Grayson asked.

She walked out of the alley, letting him follow. He'd parked his Mercedes sideways, with the rear end sticking out into the street. He hadn't wasted any time trying to rescue her from the imaginary danger.

Comforting, in a way.

"Drop me at the nearest subway station," she said.

"I'll drive you," he said.

"Because you so conveniently know where I live." She sighed and it finally clicked. He'd shown up at her building. Her home address wasn't public. "Damn."

She turned around to face him.

His mouth twitched.

"You ran a background check on me, right? That's how you found out where I live, even though my address is a P.O. Box." She should've realized that when he dropped off the food. She'd been distracted that day.

"Yes, I ran a check. I'm cautious that way."

Then he *knew*. But would he ask her about what he'd found or hold it over her head?

They crossed to his car.

"I'm sure you investigated me after what happened in the tunnels," he said.

"I'm just a lowly reporter with haphazard sources. You're the one with the former NSA guy on staff." Who apparently produced some excellent bugs.

"Tony's my partner, not staff, and I'm sure you have excellent sources. Remind me not to flash my credit card around you." He stopped at the car.

How much did he know? About Nicky, for sure. Her juvie record would still be sealed. But about her being fired? Maybe, maybe not. She still had two more weeks before that became official.

"Tell me, if our positions had been reversed, would you have planted the bug on me?" he asked.

Hmmm... "I would have asked you first. Because otherwise, the conversation would be off the record, and I wouldn't be able to use it in a story."

"You have ethics about the most interesting things," he said.

"Just because they're not your type of ethics, doesn't mean they're not valid. Us low-class people have our own way of doing things."

"Low-class? Windergaard's insult. You should know not to give it any consideration." He stuffed his hands in his pockets. "I should have asked. Again, I'm sorry."

That might be a real apology. "Why the hell did you do it?"

"It was a spur of the moment decision. I worried for you and I find myself uncertain how to handle you."

There was a catch in his voice.

"Handle me about what? Is this about the panic attack?" She braced for the answer. "You're waiting for me to fall apart? I won't. I'd gone years without a freak out until the tunnels."

"I've said it before, Patricia, but your breakdown was a human reaction, not a character flaw." A pause. "You take unnecessary risks. Even if you don't value yourself, I do."

"So you're my self-appointed knight in shining armor? I'm not some damsel in distress. I don't get you. You turn down sex but protect me in dark alleys," she said. "Still, I guess I'm impressed you rushed to help me. But I wouldn't have done the same for you."

"Oh, no?" He leaned against his Mercedes. "Why not?"

"You're a big boy, you've got a gun, you can handle it. Maybe if I was feeling charitable, I'd call the cops for you."

"You lie." He opened the Mercedes's passenger door for her. "You'd help me."

"No way." She settled on the seat covered with that wonderful, soft leather.

"Liar." He closed the door and got in the driver's seat. "In the tunnels, you had two chances to run. You stayed with me."

"That was work," she said.

"Liar." He started the car.

He saw through her. *I hate that.* "So, what did you find out in my background check?"

"Not much. There's a gap in your records from age fifteen to age eighteen."

Her time in juvie. But no mention of her being fired. Good.

"Want to talk about it?" he asked.

"Not in this lifetime." Thank God for sealed juvenile records.

"I found out you were a scholarship student at Columbia, and you started as an intern at the *New York Herald*."

"All public record," she said. "That it?"

"I discovered that you're a widow."

Dammit. Now he'd make all sorts of sympathetic noises, and she'd have to think about Nicky dying. She curled her hand tight around the armrest. "You have no right to throw that at me."

"I'm not throwing that at you. The public records are clear. Not something I could avoid. I practically tripped over it." He turned right, heading uptown. "I'm sorry—"

"Save your pity for someone who needs it."

She concentrated on the dull ache in her ribs, trying to think about anything else but Nicky. She followed the sound of the windshield wipers back and forth, back and forth, back and forth.

"Patricia."

"Now what? Find all my parking tickets too?"

"I mentioned my mother had cancer. She died several years ago. In pain." He shifted the car into a lower gear as they were caught behind several taxis. "It was..." He cut off one of the taxis. "It was hard."

His voice had grown deeper, thicker.

"That sucks," she said.

"Yes. But my mother lived a good life," Grayson said. "Losing someone so young is different." His hands tightened into a death grip on the steering wheel. He cleared his throat. "Your husband was just twenty-six—"

"I know his age," she snapped.

They stopped at a light. "You two deserved better."

"Yeah, we did. But nobody gets what they deserve. Look at what happened to Adrienne Katz." She looked out the window at the rain splashing on the streets, remembering Nicky, thinking of all the times they'd walked the city streets together.

Their best day had been her eighteenth birthday, the day she'd gotten out of juvenile lock-up for good. Clean slate. A new start, a new life. Together.

She'd spotted Nicky the moment she stepped off the bus, trying to look cool in his sunglasses, but his goofy grin ruined that attempt. He'd opened his arms wide for a hug. She'd disappeared into those arms, not wanting to ever let go.

She sighed and turned away from the window.

Nicky smiled every time he looked at me.

"I expected a follow-up question about why we got married so young," she said.

"I assume you loved each other."

"We did." She smiled. She should remember that part more. But most of the time, how much she missed him overwhelmed her. Especially lately, with so much damn time to think. "Want to know our favorite date?"

He nodded for her to continue.

"We used to walk lower Manhattan and picture what it looked like one hundred years ago. I'd do the research, and he had a knack for spotting the signs still left on the streets or the buildings. We had to do it in the early morning, around sunrise, or else it would be too crowded." That's how they'd originally found the old Gimbel's entrance to the subway tunnels.

"Whenever you walk the city streets, he still walks them with you," Grayson said.

"It's nice to think so." A lot of ghosts walked the streets. She'd felt them. She shook her head. "Tell me something."

"Yes?"

"Why are you really here tonight? You could have assigned David to trail me and be warm and dry, having dinner with your family, like your ex wanted. Having a life outside work is important. Or so I've been told."

He hit the accelerator just a little too hard when the light turned.

"I said I didn't know how to handle you. That was a lie."

"Go on," she gritted out.

"The truth is that I feel something for you, and I don't know how to handle that."

"You sure as hell don't." She closed her eyes. "So I'm good enough to protect but not good enough for sex? Not that sex is happening after tonight."

His voice thickened. "Patricia, I want to be around you too much for a fling."

"How does *that* work?" she snapped. "What does that even mean?"

"It means I want a relationship, not a one-night stand."

A *relationship*? "You mean dating and all that?"

"That's usually part of it. I want to spend time with you. I want to know you better." A pause. "Always assuming you don't blame me for what happened to Adrienne Katz, as you claimed to Sidney."

Oh, hell, now she regretted the angry words about him missing something. "I said your firm missed something, not that I blamed you."

"It's the same."

She refused to look at him, to see that vulnerability on his face. "I was only trying to prod Sidney to say something. You'd know that if you could work past your guilt."

"What?"

She winced inwardly. "As I see it, Adrienne went above and beyond to check on the exhibit. She saw something or someone inside that she considered no threat. That's how they got the drop on her from behind. That's who's responsible for her death."

Grayson said nothing.

She briefly squeezed his forearm. He kept his eyes on the street ahead.

"And still, you blame yourself, despite all evidence to the contrary. You know it had to be someone in that museum who set up you and killed Adrienne. It's not your fault."

He exhaled as they turned onto her street. "You see me, more than most. And yet you refuse to even try a relationship."

"Because I know myself." She snorted. "I'm lousy relationship material, Grayson. Look at tonight. We've had two fights already. And I don't trust people who plant a bug on me."

"I'm being honest with you now."

She grunted. He'd obviously done some serious thinking about her. And if a relationship is what Grayson craved, it explained why he'd turned her down in her apartment. He wouldn't get involved physically if she wouldn't get involved emotionally.

Most men would grab at the sex and deal with the rest later. Not him.

A relationship? What the hell would they have in common? Would he enjoy hitting the clubs and dive bars with her? Would she enjoy what he liked, opera or something?

He drove a Mercedes sedan. She drove an Indian motorcycle. He loved his suits. She loved her jeans.

He was a cop. She was a former criminal.

High class. Low class.

Yet here he was, wheel gripped tight in his hand, waiting for her answer with a patience few men possessed.

For the first time in a long time, she wished things could be different.

Dammit, Grayson. "I'll think about it," she said.

His shoulders relaxed. "Good."

CHAPTER FOURTEEN

GRAYSON WALKED toward Amanda's office at the Museum of Historic Arts, dreading this encounter.

One unfortunate side effect of Patricia's story was that Eleanor knew her father defused the bomb with only seconds left. His daughter was proud of him but also terrified by the close call, so he'd spent as much time as possible with her.

But his ex-wife had taken his being solicitous as a sign *they* might get back together. Alarming and confusing at the same time.

Amanda had left her office door open. Grayson walked inside only to find the room empty. Her Wang computer was still on, and she had correspondence on her desk. Perhaps she'd been called to another part of the museum unexpectedly. He'd wait.

A new Matisse print hung on the wall behind her desk, cradled in a beautiful frame of natural wood.

He turned at the low murmur of voices filtering through the closed connecting door to Windergaard's office. He walked to the door as the voices grew louder and angrier. He recognized Windergaard's nasal tone first, then Dante Sidney's deeper voice.

Amanda cut Sidney off. "Yelling at each other isn't going to help. We all need to calm down."

"I'm not changing anything because of new so-called threats, and you shouldn't either," Windergaard said.

Grayson put his ear to the door.

"You have no idea how ruthless these people can be, Windergaard," Sidney said. "I want to shut the exhibit down and take what's left of *my* paintings."

Sidney had sounded content and confident when having dinner with Patricia last week. Something had changed.

"You have a contract with the museum for nine months," Windergaard said. "You cannot remove those paintings until then."

"Who will stop me? You?"

"I'll get a court injunction and then law enforcement will stop you," Windergaard said.

"Max, for God's sake, we can work this out without going that far," Amanda said.

"I'm not shutting down, and I'm not letting you shut *my* exhibit down," Windergaard said.

"Dante, think about this," Amanda said. "You've put in so much time and effort with this exhibit. You were as excited as everyone else when it finally opened. Do you want to give that up?"

"If the paintings aren't safe, yes," Sidney said. "You haven't convinced me they are."

"We have a much-improved security arrangement now," Amanda said. "I trust Edmund to keep things safe."

Thank you, Amanda.

"And you think that your ex-husband's arrangements will make a difference?"

Sidney said "ex-husband" with a sneer.

"We have a new backup system for our alarm and additional cameras in that storage closet and the opening to the cavern below," Amanda said, her voice cold. "Edmund's going to give you a tour just as soon as your schedule frees up, Max. Clearly, we may need to reevaluate the security in light of these new threats, but we need experts for that, don't we? Or we could just keep arguing about it amongst ourselves."

She'd defended him nicely. He owed her.

"The paintings are *mine*," Sidney said.

"Not until this is over," Windergaard said. "That was our deal. Sealed in writing."

What did Windergaard have to do with turning over ownership to Sidney?

A chair squeaked as someone sat down. Someone else paced, their footsteps making soft thuds on the carpets.

"Excuse me, I need to check something from my office," Amanda said.

Grayson stepped back from the door as she opened it. She smiled to see him there. "Edmund," she said in a voice loud enough for Windergaard and Sidney to overhear, "how nice to see you. Your timing is perfect."

"Thank you." Obviously, Amanda had wanted to tell him about this. Unwilling to go over her boss's head, she'd outmaneuvered Windergaard instead. A familiar tactic from their marriage. He appreciated it more when not aimed at him

They walked into Windergaard's office.

Sidney, dressed in jeans and a dress shirt, nodded. Windergaard sat in his desk chair, hands steepled in front of him, his double-breasted suit still buttoned. The sparseness of the black desk, combined with the white walls, made the director the center of attention.

"Tell me about the new threats," Grayson said.

Windergaard shook his head, dismissive. "They're vague. Not much to tell."

Sidney paced closer to the desk. "It's serious. I received a phone message today that threatened another bomb."

"Tell me the exact words," Grayson said.

"'Close the exhibit and return the paintings to their rightful owners or we'll reduce them to ashes,'" Sidney said.

"Was it recorded on your answering machine?" Grayson asked.

"No, it was to my hotel phone. I hung up on them."

A hotel that must receive thousands of calls a day. There would be little way to trace that number, unless he had access to the hotel's system and, even then, not easy.

"You received only one call?" Grayson asked.

"One is enough, I should think!" Sidney said.

"One is too many," Grayson agreed. "We need to inform Chief Conrath and the regular security staff and call Lt. Gilbert. She will likely bring in the FBI."

Windergaard scowled. "Unacceptable. That means too many people will know. Word will get out. The press, including your *friend* the reporter, will publish it, and we'll scare our audience away. No one will want to come to a museum under such a threat."

Grayson clenched his jaw, counting to ten before replying. Windergaard wanted to goad him into an outburst. "The press is the least of your problems here."

"He's right," Sidney said. "Warren and the others are under arrest but the person who covered up that hole in the storage closet is still out there. For all we know, it could be one of the museum employees still here. That's the danger, not a reporter. That's another reason why I need to take my paintings and go."

Windergaard slapped his hands on his desk and stood up. "We can't give in to terrorists. I won't let anyone control decisions for *my* museum."

"Threats need to be taken seriously, especially in light of what's already happened," Grayson said. "This must be investigated, not ignored."

He thought of the recent wave of terrorism, including the killing on the Achille Lauro cruise ship. Those had been left-wing terrorists, but right-wing terrorists were just as deadly.

Sidney stuffed his hands in his pocket. "How long will the investigation of the phone call take? I'm not willing to risk my paintings while this goes on for months."

"*One* prank call isn't a risk," Windergaard said.

Sidney pounded a fist on the desk. "So I've imagined that five of my paintings are still missing? And that the person who helped set up the theft from inside the museum is still at large?"

"No one from this museum helped those Nazis." Windergaard crossed his arms over his chest.

"Gentlemen," Grayson snapped. "It's impossible to evaluate how serious this is without the police."

Windergaard placed long fingers on his desk. "There have been no problems since the initial theft."

"Murder," Grayson corrected.

Sidney flushed. Windergaard made a show of sitting back down.

"What do we do in the meantime?" Sidney said. "Shut down the exhibit?"

Grayson leaned against Windergaard's desk, knowing it would annoy the director. "Amanda already summarized our additional security measures. We even drilled a hole in the bottom of the storage closet to place a miniature camera in the tunnel entrance. My people are already on high alert. That should be enough to keep the museum open as we assess this call if—"

"If what?" Windergaard asked.

"If my people are also here, standing guard."

"And thus, increasing your fee?" Windergaard said with a smirk.

Grayson glared. "If you'd paid for my people to be here in the first place, one of your guards would still be alive." He straightened his cufflinks to buy time to calm down. "But, no, this won't change our agreed-on fee." He'd be burning money. But he must catch the killer. When she'd had dinner with Sidney, Patricia had said his firm had missed something. She'd been trying to needle him, but it'd been a direct hit. The fact remained that Adrienne Katz had died because of his mistakes.

"Good. See, we can stay open, Sidney," Windergaard said.

"And what if this threat is found valid?" Sidney asked. "We shut down, yes?"

"Of course," Grayson said. "It's too big a risk to the public."

"A shutdown, even over a few days will kill the museum," Amanda breathed out. "Please say that won't happen, Edmund."

"Better a financial death than another human one," Grayson said.

Amanda sighed. "You're scaring me."

"I'm trying to *protect* you."

In the back of his mind, he heard another of Patricia's biting comments, about people who claimed to be protecting her wanting to control her.

This was different, he told himself. He knew security far better than Amanda.

Windergaard fiddled with the buttons of his suit. "I won't shut down and give some Nazi terrorist the satisfaction, no matter what you say."

"If you stay open in opposition to expert advice and there's an incident, your museum will be liable and could be bankrupted by lawsuits anyway." Grayson shrugged. "That is, if there's anything left of it but rubble."

Windergaard set his mouth. "You're responsible for making sure that doesn't happen."

"I'm responsible for doing what it takes to protect people and property," Grayson said. "If that's unacceptable, then I quit."

"Quit?" Windergaard rose again, his fingertips pushing off his polished desk. "You have a contract too. I'll sue—"

"If you think you can replace my firm on such short notice, think again. After I pull my people out, I'll give an interview to the press, saying you're ignoring bomb threats. No reputable firm will take your contract after that. And your ticket holders will demand refunds in droves."

Windergaard collapsed in his chair for the second time. "You wouldn't. Your firm would go down, too."

It might. But better to let his business die than risk his people for no reason. "Try me."

The silence was deafening as Windergaard adjusted his glasses again, took them off, cleaned the lenses with a tissue from his desk, and put them back on.

Grayson met Amanda's gaze. She was silently pleading him about something. To shut down the museum after all? Or the opposite, to agree with her boss?

Grayson almost wished he'd never agreed to take the job back after being fired that day. Then he remembered Katz's blood and brains spilled all over the marble floor.

Patricia would understand. She'd certainly had his number the other night, when she pretended to be under attack.

Windergaard leaned back in his chair. "What are the odds we have to shutdown?"

"My goal would be to keep the museum open and running," Grayson said. "That's my goal for every client, to provide enough security so they can continue to do business."

Windergaard steepled his long, lean fingers again. "Fine. Mr. Sidney and I will call Lieutenant Gilbert right now. If I could have my office back?"

Grayson accepted the dismissal. Let Windergaard feel superior. As long as they called Dorothy.

He and Amanda stepped back to her office. She closed the door behind them and fell back against it.

"Whew," she said.

"That about covers it," he said.

She frowned. "Would you really have quit and left us in the lurch?"

"Not if the threat had any validity," he said.

"I'm glad to know you were bluffing."

He said nothing because he never did have the right words for Amanda. Despite over a decade of marriage, he never could read her. He had no idea if she agreed with Sidney or her boss's side in this dispute.

Yet he'd been able to read Patricia Connell clearly after only a day. And she'd read him just as well.

"Are we still on for dinner tonight?" Amanda turned off the Wang and straightened her desk.

"I can't, not now. Your boss gave me permission to add guards from Gray Associates. I'm going to have to go over employee schedules to get that in place ASAP."

"Predictable." She shook her head. "Will you take a walk with me first?"

What did she want now? "Yes."

They walked out the front entrance of the museum to the top of the large marble steps. Amanda stopped at the same pillar that Patricia had been standing next to the morning of the murder.

"Where did you get the new Matisse in your office?" Small talk might soothe Amanda's nerves.

"A gift from Max, for the success of the opening," she said with a smile.

"Thoughtful of him."

"Yes. He's a good boss most of the time."

Amanda looked up at the full moon in the clear sky.

"I love New York. It's crazy and scary and wonderful and full of life. You can find just about anything here," she said. "But some days the city makes it difficult."

She was scared. "I'll do everything possible to protect you and the museum."

She sat down on the top step, elbows on her knees. "I know that."

He sat down next to her. She leaned against his shoulder.

"I only wish Max had followed your recommendations in the first place," she said.

"So do I."

She shook her head. "I've never interacted with you while you're working, Edmund. Are you always this unflappable about death threats and murder?"

"I'm not sure how to answer that," he said. "All I know is how to do is my job."

"You nearly died. Twice, according to the story in the *Herald*," she said. "The idea of you being so close to death terrified me. I've no idea if it terrified you."

He'd been too focused that day to be terrified. Later, however, was another story. "I thought of our daughter as the bomb ticked down to zero."

"Edmund, I wasn't just scared for her sake. I was scared for *mine*." Amanda took his hand.

"It's over now." But he'd been a mess until after he visited Patricia in the hospital and assured himself of her recovery. Then he'd been fine.

But Amanda was working up to something. He wanted to be wrong about what it was.

"Our marriage ended badly, Edmund. I know a good portion of that was my fault," she said.

"Our fault. We never did know how to communicate," he said. "We were young, immature, and froze each other out instead of fighting through it. At least, I did."

She'd kicked him out of the bedroom to the couch for a month to get him to listen to her complaints. But after a month, he'd dug in his heels and left, and they'd stayed furious with each other for a long time. He knew he'd let his work consume him. But her demand that he simply quit was unacceptable.

Classic Amanda. Force him into to a corner and leave him with no option but to agree to everything she wanted or walk away completely.

"We should have tried counseling before the separation," she said.

"Yes." That might have avoided the bitterness of the divorce and spared Eleanor from the spillover.

"What happened to her? The woman you dated for a while?" Amanda asked.

"It didn't work out." He'd not been ready. And then Karen had gotten a job in another city. "Amanda, why are we rehashing all this?"

She looked at the sky again. "I had this dream. Live in the big city, have a great job, have a great family. I have the great job. I have a great place to live. I have a wonderful daughter. But I don't have you."

Bloody hell. Now she'd done it.

Three years ago, two years ago, perhaps even last month, he might have responded to her plea and tried again. The bond built by their daughter and their years of marriage exerted a heavy pull. But as Dorothy had pointed out, nearly being blown to bits altered one's perspective. He craved more than the quiet companionship that he and Amanda had shared at the best of times.

He wanted more. He wanted what Dorothy and her husband James still had. He wanted what his parents had had. He wanted fire and intensity and passion and quiet companionship, too.

He wanted Patricia. And she'd given him a sliver of hope that she wanted him.

"I'll never regret being married to you. But…" There was no right way to tell someone you didn't love them like that anymore. "I'm sorry, Amanda."

They sat in silence on the marble steps as the cold seeped into his legs.

"What do you want out of life, Edmund?" she asked.

More.

"For a long time, I thought I only wanted my career at the FBI. I neglected you and Eleanor for it. I'm sorry. I can never make up for that, to you or to her."

"You could if you came back," she whispered.

"You've changed. I've changed. We're different people now."

Amanda stared down at the steps. When she spoke again, her voice shook. "I should have known you'd turn me down. I'm an idiot."

"You're anything but." He squeezed her shoulder. "But I hope you find the person who can give you what you want."

"If you say, 'the right person will come along for you,' I'm going to punch you."

He smiled. "Never."

She sighed. "Do you have any idea how hard it is to find a good man in this city?"

"No, but then, I've never had the occasion to try."

She laughed. "Ah, well. Walk me back inside, please."

He offered to help her up from the steps. She waved him off. He followed her inside.

The door closed and automatically locked behind them.

CHAPTER FIFTEEN

TRISHA LEANED back from her newly acquired secondhand desk, acquired after she'd left the Herald. Even shoved against one of her bookshelves, it barely fit her small apartment. She rubbed the bridge of her nose and cursed as the police scanner squawked about a runaway car near the World Trade Center and a fight near the Fulton Fish Market.

Vendors must be arguing about space again.

She should be out there. She should be working the phones, talking to neighborhood watch groups, talking to the cops who gave her tips, and the people in the bars, and the kids who still hung out on the stoops. She could do that.

But where would she go with that information?

She clenched her fist and resisted the urge to slam it on the rickety desk. Best she could do secondhand. Once she pulled in some freelance work or found a full-time job, she could upgrade.

She hated the quiet. She might have a desk, scanner, a typewriter, and her rolodexes, but her apartment wasn't a newsroom.

I miss it.

She missed the banter with other reporters, she missed the clatter of typewriters and keyboards, and she even missed Joe's nasty editing notes.

She missed the excitement as the stories came in. She missed the hum of the presses that vibrated the walls.

If she'd let Cardoza lecture her, the truth would have come out and he'd have had to apologize to *her*.

He'd screwed her over. She'd have called him out on it, but as soon as everyone knew she'd been fired, her sources would dry up and it'd be harder to find out what happened to Adrienne. Time was ticking on finding answers at the museum. She knew the bleaks stats about solving cold cases.

She had leads. David had agreed to let her into Gray Associates later today to examine the files Grayson had promised, though he made sure to tell her that Grayson gave his permission too.

There would be something in the files that would give her a solid lead again, something someone had missed.

The phone on the kitchen wall rang. Could be a source who wouldn't leave a message. Could be Joe again and she'd have to deal with him being understanding again. She sighed and answered.

"Your order's ready, Miss Connell," the shopkeeper said in his distinct nasal tone.

"It's 'Ms.' Connell and thanks. Look, are you sure that he's going to know what this is?"

The shopkeeper laughed. "Lady, if your guy carries his own rope for line in his trunk, then he's going to love this. Trust me. I know sailors."

He's not my guy. And he's lucky to get anything after planting that bug.

"Good enough. I'll pick it up before your close of day today."

Grayson had apologized, and he'd also seemed to understand what he'd done wrong. She'd see him anyway, working this story, so she decided to give a peace offering. It also might keep him from looking at her job status.

Besides, they were friends, right?

Now she just had to do more digging on Sidney's credit card number. She'd tried a few tactics, but none had yielded results. That meant her last resort, which was slightly illegal. She'd try that tonight, after going over Grayson's records for more info.

She downed a McSorley's beer, sat at her desk, typed up her notes on the Queen Anne's Revenge research, and then did what she'd been avoiding: typing up her interviews with Adrienne's friends. Oh, it was good stuff for a story. Adrienne had picked great friends. Yet all that lost promise closed Trisha's throat, fueling her grief.

It pissed her off that she couldn't clear the kid's name. That no one had found the paintings yet. And that no one had a good explanation of how Adrienne, if it had been her, had opened the locked door to *Lost Treasures*.

The phone rang again. Dammit. She needed a desk phone. A nice solid one so she could slam down the receiver.

She answered. "Trisha Connell."

The caller, whose voice sounded young, identified himself as an editor with a non-fiction book publishing company.

Unexpected. She bit down on a sarcastic remark. She needed work. "Why are you calling me?"

He cleared his throat. "Well, Ms. Connell, after the museum stories, particularly the one about Adrienne Katz, I looked up your body of work. I noticed you've done a number of stories on children in distress. There must be at least twenty of these types of stories about lost kids. Foster kids, victims of domestic abuse, those without homes, those in the country illegally—"

He'd done his research. "Twenty-two kids," she cut in. "I've done stories on twenty-two kids who've never been given a chance."

"You keep track of them?"

Always. "If I can. Sometimes I can't, with privacy concerns by the court and the foster system and all that."

"How are they doing?"

"Why do you want to know?" What the hell did he want?

"Ms. Connell, I realize you don't know me, but I just spent a day researching your work, so please humor me. How are these children doing?"

Play along. Find out his angle. "Some of them made it out of bad situations and some are still struggling." She ground her teeth. "Some are lost for good." Adrienne had made it out. Then she hadn't. "Okay, now, what's all this to you?"

"I think your stories have the makings of a book," he said.

"A book?" *What?*

"Yes, a book. And if you've been tracking these kids all along, it'll save research for the conclusion."

Her voice rose. "You want to use *my* research and stories for *your* book on these kids? Are you fucking kidding me?"

"No, no, Ms. Connell," he sputtered. "You misunderstood me! I want you to work on a book. You would write it. It would be *your* book."

"What? Why?" What's the catch? There was always a catch.

More sputtering. "I…um…really…I didn't expect…" He took a deep breath. "This is an excellent subject for a book. You are obviously well-qualified to write it. And because it's a story that needs to be told."

"Ah." She stalled to assimilate what he said. "I told those stories to give those kids a voice when no one could hear them."

"Newspaper stories disappear in a day or two. A book would give that voice a larger platform. I envision it as something similar to Gay Talese's stories of the working class."

"I'm not disagreeing with you. But this is out of the blue, and I don't know you." At all.

"We need to meet, of course, and discuss this."

A scam or a convoluted come-on? "A meeting at your office?" So she could check him out and do her research before believing a single word he said.

"Not my office. I'll be attending a publishing dinner next week. I hope you'll come."

Alarm bells sounded. "Why a dinner and not a meeting at your office?"

The kid cleared his throat. "There are people you need to meet so they can get behind the book. Um…the publisher of the *Herald* is my uncle and I…want to assure my senior editor that you and your book are worth the investment."

He knew she'd been fired and why. She bit down on her tongue, summoning every professional bone in her body to sound calm. "It's the children whose stories are being shared. If there is a book, they're the ones worth the investment."

Those kids, the ones she kept in touch with, like she did Adrienne, could use the money.

"Having read your articles, that's the sentiment I expected you to have. But, still, we must be able to trust you to deliver a book on time."

Did she get a cookie for not losing her temper? Why not. She reached into her cabinet for an Oreo.

"So I'm to be on display to prove I don't chew out my publisher on a regular basis?"

He sighed. "Yes, that's the concern. I'm going to bat for you. I believe the stories of these children are important. We're on the same side, Ms. Connell."

She doubted that. No editor approached a writer about a book unless they thought they could make money or advance their career. But, if the kids got what they needed, then he could get what he wanted too.

"Give me the date and the details about this dinner."

She wrote it down as he rattled them off.

"Oh, and you may bring a plus one," he added.

Perhaps he wanted to prove he wasn't hitting on her. That would be a refreshing change from ninety percent of straight men. Still, it might be good to have David around because he'd stop her from smacking this editor upside the head if hit on her.

"Put me down for that plus one," she said.

"Very good! Thank you, Ms. Connell, you won't regret it. In the meantime, please see if you can put together an outline of the book. That way we can get started right away after you sign a contract."

"In the meantime, maybe you can send over this proposed contract?"

"Of course."

This time, she rattled off her P.O. box. If he sent the contract, it would give her another means to investigate him and his publishing company.

They each made polite good-byes and hung up. She contemplated calling David right now but then remembered that he didn't know she'd been fired yet.

She'd told no one, save Mr. and Mrs. Katz. Obviously, Cardoza hadn't been so tight-lipped, the son of a bitch.

Everyone would know soon, which only made her interview with Windergaard at the museum more urgent. Time for the library again and more research on the history of the Museum of Historic Arts.

———

Lt. Dorothy Gilbert's blue Chevy Nova sat outside her apartment building, complete with the Lieutenant, dressed in her trademark pale red pantsuit, leaning against the passenger door.

Now what? Trisha rolled her shoulders and set her jaw, ready for battle.

"Checking up on my recovery, Lieutenant?" Trisha put her hand over her heart. "I'm touched."

Dorothy snorted. "I bet you are. Tell me, you recovered enough to interview Stephen Warren?"

Trisha immediately snapped to attention. "Mr. Neo-Nazi? The guy who put a gun to my head? *Hell, yes.*" That would be a coup. "Damn right. What are you up to?"

Dorothy sighed. "I'm working on something."

"You're working on something that helps *me* out?" Dorothy must need her, or the officer wouldn't be outside her building.

"Let's just say what helps you, helps me," Dorothy said.

Trisha leaned against the Nova, looking up at her third-floor apartment. "I'm listening."

"I want Warren to talk. I want to find the missing paintings. I want to know how Katz walked through a locked door to the exhibit." She shook her head. "But the Feds have decided Warren might have ties to terrorists overseas, and they're threatening to whisk him away at any moment."

"And you think *I* can get him to talk?"

Dorothy snarled. "Warren asked for you to interview him. And I'm nearly out of time to uncover the truth of Adrienne Katz's involvement in this."

"Then what you want is what I want, Lieutenant. How do I do this? Visit him at Riker's?"

"I pulled strings to set up a private interview that officially will never have happened."

Trisha raised an eyebrow. "Is the rule-bound lieutenant about to break some rules?"

"You want to do this or not?" Dorothy snapped.

"First, tell me why Warren asked for me. I need to know his angle."

"If I knew, I'd tell you. Could be as simple as he wants a chance to yell at you for the broken nose. You in or not?"

Any other cop, and Trisha would suspect an elaborate prank. Not Dorothy Gilbert. She did not joke about this stuff. "Sure."

"Good." Dorothy walked around to the driver's side door. "Let's go."

"Now?"

"Oh, the reporter who barged into my case a few weeks ago suddenly wants time to think about it?" Dorothy started the car. "You coming or not?"

Trisha practically fell into the car. "Let's go."

CHAPTER SIXTEEN

THE DOOR to the corridor slammed shut behind Trisha, metal clanging against metal. She huddled deeper into her thin coat. Prison. The formal title wasn't important. The purpose never changed.

She walked with Dorothy inside the main entrance to Riker's. In the distance, guards yelled at inmates who tossed insults back, the words carrying in the enclosed space. Yep, it sounded like prison. Fuck, it smelled like prison, disinfectant mixed with sweat and the acrid smell that equaled "fear."

I'm not staying.

Anxiety lurked at the edges of her mind, threatening to grab hold. No, not today, not again.

"What the hell is wrong with you, Connell?" Dorothy said.

"Nothing's wrong," Trisha answered. "Okay, I'm a little claustrophobic."

"You weren't claustrophobic in the subway tunnels," Dorothy said.

"They didn't have locks." Trisha shrugged. Acid churned in her stomach. She concentrated on breathing. Think about work. Think about how to approach Warren. Breathe.

Dorothy studied her. "Been here before?"

"When I'm working," Trisha said.

"Lucky you."

As a rule, Dorothy was sarcastic but not mean. Nerves must be getting to her as well. They both had a lot riding on this interview.

"I'll get all the info I can from Warren, Lieutenant."

"That's not what worries me the most. He either talks or he doesn't. But there are a lot of ways this could go sour. He'll be dangerous, Connell."

"So am I."

"I've noticed." Dorothy frowned and looked down the gray hallway to the closed door at the end of the corridor. "This area is technically closed for repairs. I get the feeling sometimes prisoners considered extremely dangerous are brought here for isolation."

"This is completely off book, then." Not the time to point out that off-the-books isolation violated prisoner rights. Not when Dorothy had broken her own rules.

"I pulled favors from the correctional officers." A pause. "The Black guards are pretty pissed that Warren has attracted a Nazi fan club inside. I'm concerned he could be armed."

"You think Warren called me here to get rid of me?"

"It's possible. Easy enough to slip him a knife, plastic or otherwise, and hide it from a pat down. And since it's off-book, the guards can't stay."

"He had a gun last time. Didn't do him much good," Trisha said. "You must hate this guy, Lieutenant."

"I hate what he stands for. I hate that he's worshipped in here and Katz still hasn't been cleared because every gut instinct I have tells me the kid is innocent. These people tried to blow up police officers and civilians. I want more than Warren. I want *everyone* involved in it."

"For vengeance?"

"For justice," Dorothy said. "Why are *you* here? The thrill? The story?"

Trisha shook her head. "I'm here for Adrienne."

"So here we are, taking a mutual risk, for a kid you liked who's being smeared while the guilty party goes free." Dorothy studied her. "Some-times you surprise me, Connell."

Trisha whistled a Slits song about sisterhood as she pushed open the unlocked door to the prison interview room. She turned around, surveying it. Not much to work with. The lovely shade of puke green painted on the walls was too damned familiar for comfort.

She swallowed hard and told her stomach to stop protesting, stop remembering juvie and stop worrying about being stuck here. If she gave into fear in front of Warren, not only would she not get information, she'd let Adrienne down.

Focus. Her panic attack in the tunnels had ebbed when she started concentrating on her story. The same should be true here, especially since her ribs seemed mostly healed. She went over the crime again in her mind and made a mental note to ask about the lighter fluid.

The clang of chains signaled Warren's arrival and jarred her back to the here and now. Boots thumped on the concrete floor along with more jangling of chains.

She fought an automatic impulse to run.

No chains for me. Not anymore, not ever.

Her head believed it. But the rest of her still needed convincing.

"Company's here," Dorothy said from the doorway of the room.

Trisha nodded.

Warren entered, pushed along by a Black corrections officer. Warren was clad in the oh-so-fashionable orange jumpsuit of the prison population. A chain around his waist locked in his wrists, and another chain led to cuffs on his ankles. He limped. A faded bruise decorated his eyes.

"I'm not talking unless these come off," Warren tapped the chains.

"No," said Dorothy and the CO who had tight hold on Warren's arm.

"I'm not talking otherwise," Warren repeated.

Trisha leaned against the wall. Yep, he definitely wanted a piece of her. Adrenaline surged. Anxiety faded. Good.

"Take 'em off," she said. "We're just gonna chat. Art thefts, nose jobs, the history of the New York subway system. No worries."

Her wisecrack earned a quick smile from the CO and a scowl from Warren. Dorothy glared at her. Trisha shrugged.

"Look, you want to do this or not, Lieutenant?" Trisha asked.

Dorothy nodded at the officer. "Unlock Warren." She held Warren's gaze. "I made this happen. I can also make you disappear. Permanently."

Harsh for Dorothy. Likely a bluff. But the lieutenant sounded damn convincing.

"This is the fucking problem with America. Too many of *you people* in charge," Warren said.

The CO shoved Warren into the chair at the metal table.

The CO unlocked the cuffs and stood up. "We're your lifeline, Warren. The reporter gets hurt, you vanish."

He walked out. Dorothy followed him, and the door clanged shut behind them.

Trisha sat down in the chair across from Warren, letting the silence build. Better for him to make the first move. After all, he invited her. Let him say what he wanted.

His nose looked crooked. He stared, unblinking. Brown eyes, same color as Grayson's but devoid of inner warmth. Physically, he wasn't impressive. She'd long ago stopped expecting people to outwardly look evil, but he looked so ordinary for a Nazi fanatic, never mind their leader. With his goatee shaved, he looked even more nondescript.

She placed her notebook on the table, careful to keep her pencil in hand.

More silence.

Warren finally sighed. "You broke my nose and nearly broke my kneecap. Put me in the hospital." He laced his fingers together. "In bright light, up close, I expected someone more formidable."

His gaze flicked over her, dismissive.

"Sorry. I left the big stompy boots at home."

He leaned back in the chair. "A wisecracking Irishwoman. How common."

She shrugged. Despite his deliberate speech, she detected traces of German in his accent. "An insulting evil genius. How common. Where's the maniacal laugh?"

He ran a hand over his close-cropped brown hair. "I'm told you accurately report what is said during interviews. Is this true?"

She forced her mouth shut until the wisecrack on the tip of her tongue died. "I'm good at my job." Not that Cardoza believed that.

She flipped open her notebook. "Why did you want to see me?" she asked.

He placed his hands on the table and leaned over, closer to her. "I want people to know. We are not thieves. I was reclaiming my *legacy*." He punctuated the last word by jabbing his thumb against his chest.

His breath—surprisingly clean—wafted over her. She met his gaze, much as Dorothy had.

"The paintings belong to Dante Sidney. You and your crew took them."

"We took no paintings." He clenched his jaw tight, finally making his ordinary face look dangerous.

"Who stole them, then?"

Warren stood up and loomed over her, an intimidation tactic. As if that would work.

"No comment," he said.

"Did someone inside the museum double-cross you?"

He placed his hands flat on the table and loomed over her.

She yawned and flipped her notebook shut. "Either talk to me or I'm gone."

He backed off. "I'm in control of this conversation. You're here because I asked you to be."

"And I can leave when I want. Have fun talking to yourself," she said.

"I could put out a kill order on you."

"You and half of New York. So what?" She leaned back in her chair and yawned again for effect.

He sat back down.

"I want information," he said. "If you tell me how Grayson knew to find the bomb in the tunnels, I'll give you my story of the museum break-in."

The story she'd given Joe that night before she collapsed had focused on Grayson and the police. It contained zilch about her own role. If she hadn't been fired, she'd have written an eyewitness follow-up story with the full details. As it was, her first story stood as the definitive one, one that Warren, at least, had never questioned.

"Why do you need to know how Grayson discovered the tunnels?"

"I was told if we used them, we wouldn't be discovered. I was betrayed. I must know who it was."

"You need to know who snitched on you?"

"We were already betrayed once by being labeled thieves. I want to know if the same person is responsible for our arrest as well."

"Tell me who aided your break in," she said. "Then I'll tell you who knew about the tunnels."

"No," he said.

"Fine. Later." She stood to leave. He wanted something for nothing. And he'd probably never believe the truth, that she'd been the one to lead Grayson into the tunnels.

"Wait. I will talk." Warren held up a hand and pointed at her chair.

She contemplated it for a second and decided she'd get more information by staying. She sat back down.

And now he had proof that she wanted something from him. They were even.

"We handle our own problems," he said. "When the time comes, this person will pay for soiling the legacy of our forefathers."

"I see," she said. The Nazi legacy?

Warren frowned, looked around the room, sighed, and reached under his handcuff for something.

She flipped her pencil around, point first, in case he reached for a weapon. But he revealed a crumpled piece of paper. "I want you to publish this. This is our statement. Listen and learn." He cleared his throat and began reading.

"We represent those wronged after World War II, patriots who fought valiantly for their country and, after they lost, were vilified and, in some cases, murdered. Their memories must be preserved with honor."

"You mean they were Nazis tried and convicted of war crimes," Trisha said.

Warren ignored her. "But the patriots remembered. They kept the real history alive. And they kept their rightfully obtained plunder from their enemies."

Translation: the Nazis stole from the Jews, murdered them, and kept their now blood-soaked stolen possessions. Did Warren know where the paintings came from?

"What does that have to do with you?" she asked. "That's at least a generation ago."

"Listen." His voice was almost a hiss. He looked the fanatic now. His nostrils flared and his unblinking eyes focused on her.

"Our heritage was stolen by an agent of the mud people."

"Sidney stole the artwork in *Lost Treasures* from descendants of Nazis? How do you know that?"

Warren banged the table with his fist. "Quiet. Did you write down my statement?"

"Sure." She had. His own words revealed his twisted self better than she ever could. And she could parse them for more clues.

"Then along came one who betrayed his blood. He put our inheritance on display where everyone could see it. Jews, mud people, and others not worthy of such a gift."

"Sucks for you," she said.

"So we sent the word forth, calling for those brave enough to punish our betrayer."

"You recruited the others?" she asked.

"I did. And I honor the one who fell in the line of duty. He will be remembered."

"As a murderer," she said.

"As a savior of the white race." Warren put his paper down on the table and carefully pressed it flat with his palm. "So. The museum. A public example had to be set, an example that would resonate in this city."

The bomb. "But the bomb would have destroyed the artwork too. Isn't that your legacy?"

"The ruined building would have stood as our statement. It is all the legacy I need." He grimaced. "Yet I would have done more if…" He shook his head.

The lighter fluid, she thought. "You were going to *burn* the paintings in the museum,"

He nodded. "You're the first to discern that."

Burn priceless works of art? Almost as sickening as murder. "If you lit them on fire, the fire alarms would have gone off. Brought first responders…" Oh, hell. He had wanted to up the body count from the bomb. "That's why you put the bomb on a timer. You wanted the museum to be full when it went off."

"Exactly," he nodded.

Warren…damn…he admitted to planning mass murder so calmly. But then, only allies and enemies existed in his world.

"But you didn't burn the paintings. Why not?"

He remained silent. Damn, Adrienne still needed to be cleared.

"A museum guard interrupted you," she prodded.

"That girl? A Jew." He flicked his fingers, casually, as if Katz was a fly to him. "Of no consequence. Of course, she had to die. She put her nose where it doesn't belong. Now the world has one less Jew."

"No consequence? Say that to her parents, you fucking asshole."

Trisha clenched her hand tight around her pencil. *Keep it calm.*

"You had no time to burn the paintings because of Katz."

"If you say so." He shrugged. "She still died. The paintings would have been destroyed anyway when the bomb went off. We waited and guarded the tunnel exit, to ensure no one went inside and discovered our bomb." He clenched his jaw again. "But, still, you and this Grayson found the bomb. I want to know how."

She shrugged. "Trade secret."

He leaned forward, animated by hatred. *Back at you, Warren.* But the information chilled her. If she hadn't shown up at the museum, if she hadn't disobeyed Cardoza, if she hadn't enticed Grayson into the tunnels, Warren would have gotten *everything* he craved: the paintings and the destruction of the museum with the people inside it.

Including Grayson.

"We had a deal," Warren spat out the words. "Tell me. Who knew about the tunnels."

She yearned to wipe that smug grin from his face.

"*I* told Grayson about the tunnels."

He pounded the table again. "You lie."

She pushed her chair back. He'd go ballistic in a second. But it felt freakin' good to toss it in his face.

"This is *my* city. I know all about shit like abandoned tunnels. Lt. Gilbert found you at the other exit because of my info. *I* showed Grayson another way in, that's how he defused your bomb. *I* stopped you, asshole."

Warren snapped to his feet. She jumped out of her chair, keeping the table between them.

She needed to keep him talking. People said all sorts of interesting things when they were pissed off.

"Who's the inside member of your gang?" she asked. "Who did you think betrayed you?"

"Someone who is certain to die. As you'll die for your part in this."

"Ooo…now I'm shaking in my stompy boots."

Warren flipped his chair aside with the back of his hand. She caught the flash of something sharp in his left hand.

Shiv.

"Lieutenant!" she yelled.

Warren rushed her. Trisha tossed her chair at him to slow him down. He sidestepped. She kept the table between them and watched his chest and wrist, waiting for him to commit to a move. He had three inches on her and rage fueling his attack. But she knew knife fights.

C'mon. Come get me.

He lunged at her, the shiv inside his fist.

She rolled over the top of the table to the other side, her eyes never leaving the weapon. He closed on her, jabbed the sharp edge at her midsection. She dodged without effort, though she felt a tug in her still-healing chest. Gah, not now.

She allowed him to come closer, shuffled left, and smashed his elbow with her fist. He yelled and swiped at her. His effort went wide, and she kicked out at his leg. She missed the knee but hit the shin.

He flailed, fell and hit the floor hard on his shoulder. But he still clutched the shiv.

Warren scrambled to his feet, his face red with rage. She'd have to get closer, risk getting stabbed, in order to disarm him. *Fuck.* She grabbed a chair and held it up in front of her. It should keep him at arm's length for a few seconds.

Again, he hesitated. He'd hesitated in the tunnels too. "You're a damned coward," she said.

The cell door opened. Warren turned, distracted.

Trisha threw the chair at him.

He dodged and lunged at her. She backpedaled but hit the wall. She was stuck in the corner. Trapped.

Dorothy grabbed Warren from behind, her elbow around his throat. With her other hand, she pepper-sprayed him.

Warren collapsed to his knees, howling, tearing at his eyes. Trisha grabbed his wrist, tore his thumb from the shiv and twisted. The weapon fell to the floor. She kicked it to the corner.

Warren hardly noticed being disarmed, instead whimpering about being blinded.

The CO re-shackled a writhing Warren and pulled him to his feet.

"To the docs for you and it's more than you deserve," the CO said to Warren. "You both okay?" he asked her and Dorothy.

"Sure." Trisha grabbed her notebook off the table and flipped it shut, suppressing the wince from the pain emanating from her chest. Moderate level, at least. Not agony anymore. The CO pushed Warren out the door. "Next time, listen and keep the cuffs on, Lieutenant."

Trisha took a deep breath. "Thanks, Lieutenant."

"You were doing okay on your own." Dorothy rubbed her arm and slid her little bottle of pepper spray back into her pocket. "I overheard. You got him to talk about Katz."

"Yeah, he did, didn't he? But it didn't completely clear her. He just insulted her."

Dorothy put her hands on her knees, breathing hard. "Still, it's a help. I didn't expect him to say as much as he did." She wiped her face with the back of her hand. "Dammit, Connell, you taunted him to get him to talk. That's a dangerous tactic. And aren't reporters supposed to be objective?"

"My objective judgment is that he's a murdering racist asshole."

"Yeah." Dorothy agreed. "C'mon, let's get out of here." As they exited into Riker's parking lot, the afternoon sun warmed Trisha's face. Her stomach settled. No panic attack. The anxiety had vanished.

Free.

But as they settled into Dorothy's car and went past the security checkpoint, Trisha finally spoke the truth about being fired, bracing for Dorothy's reaction.

"Interesting," was all the Lieutenant said.

CHAPTER SEVENTEEN

GRAYSON LEANED against the doorway to the conference room at Gray Associates. The clock read two a.m. but, still, Patricia was on the phone with someone, the receiver curled between her shoulder and her ear, furiously taking notes in a reporter's notebook.

Her voice too low for him to hear specific words.

She lifted a hand in acknowledgment of his presence but otherwise ignored him.

"I appreciate your help in this delicate matter...I'm so pleased there are no signs of misuse so far...wait, could you give me the location of that last charge again?"

She sounded polite and carefully professional.

She sat on the floor among the museum files, everything from copies of the museum blueprints to his report of the murder and theft, and the history of the paintings. Her flats lay under the table, leaving her feet bare. Her customary ripped jeans exposed the lightning bolt tattoo on her ankle. Her T-shirt of the day featured *Sesame Street's* Cookie Monster.

More polite statements to the person on other end of the phone. More scribbling in the notebook with a pencil.

"Good. Can I have your direct number for more questions? And, again, I appreciate your discretion," she said.

He noticed one other thing: she'd picked a corner of the conference room with a clear view of the door.

She'd quipped in the tunnels about not being able to take the sewer out of the girl, an interesting comment from someone who'd graduated with honors from Columbia. Nothing average about her, even as a student. He wondered if she'd been involved in any student protests? Nothing had shown on his background checks.

Lousy at relationships, she'd said. But she maintained her friendship with David well. And she obviously still mourned her husband.

Patricia ended her call.

"You're here later than I expected," he said.

"Early. It's technically morning," she said without raising her head, finishing off her notes. "I'll put everything back the right way. Swear."

She slipped the notebook into a nondescript backpack, and smiled, and finally giving him her full attention. The fiery hair, the bright eyes, the energy that crackled around her and that lithe body that he had no doubt would be as flexible as he imagined, all perfect. Vibrant. *Alive.*

"You're up late, too," she said.

"I took a night shift at the museum."

"Why?"

"I have a theory," he said.

She scrambled to her feet. "You think the paintings are still in the museum."

What? How did she know that? "Just how did you come to the same conclusion?"

She held up her hand and began ticking off points. "Three places the paintings could be. One, Warren's crew could have handed them off to someone, in which case they're gone, and we're screwed. Two, they could be destroyed, but there's no evidence of that. That leaves number three; they're in the museum still, and you worked late at the museum so—"

"Your conclusion is that I must have been looking for them."

"Were you?"

"Yes." It felt good not to have to explain this, to have his thoughts understood quickly.

"I've also been pondering the presence of the lighter fluid at the scene. It's a loose end."

"The lighter fluid is key." She sat on the table, her legs dangling from it. "Go on."

"All right." He took off his jacket and tossed it over one of the chairs. "I'm Steven Warren, a dedicated Neo-Nazi. I have nothing but contempt for the museum. I plan a break-in, not to steal, but to showcase my anger at the existence of *Lost Treasures*, especially since a part of the exhibit is about how these paintings were once stolen and propagate what I, Warren, believe are lies about the Nazis who stole them. I, Warren, rip down the paintings and my team paints the swastikas. I open the lighter fluid because I'm going to turn the paintings to ash to showcase my contempt. Plus, the uproar about the fire destroying such precious things brings more people in the museum and my body count from the bomb goes up."

She jumped off the table, gesturing, and took up his theory.

"And then my inside guy, the one who helped me get in, realizes I'm about to *destroy* the art, rather than steal it, and tries to stop me. Maybe this inside guy had a black-market buyer lined up, or maybe he hates to see paintings destroyed. But whichever it is, they argue. It gets loud."

Grayson crossed to the door. "And then Katz overhears the commotion, notices the alarm is disabled, and walks right into the middle of it."

Patricia swung an imaginary crowbar at him. "And Warren kills her." She set her jaw. "The fucker."

"Then Warren worries he's running out of time. Someone will come to look for Katz. So he leaves the way he came in without burning the paintings."

She nodded. "He's willing to leave the paintings intact because knows the bomb will blow up the museum anyway. Why worry if the inside guy keeps the paintings? It'll be a Neo-Nazi victory anyway."

"Exactly," Grayson said. "That leaves the inside guy with a murdered guard and paintings torn from their frames. Now what does he do?"

She caught his gaze again. "He has to hide those paintings, and fast, because if Katz found them, someone else might come along any minute."

"Leaving the only hiding place somewhere in the museum and he could do that without being seen because he already knew how to disable the alarms. Plus, the cameras were down at that moment."

"It's a great theory." She grinned. "I can corroborate some of it."

"How?"

She took a deep breath and detailed a trip with Dorothy to Riker's Island to interview Warren. Anger settled over him, anger he controlled, until he heard it to the end.

"So Warren confirmed your theory about the plan to burn the paintings. That means the rest of it must track too," Patricia concluded.

"You interviewed Warren. You got him to clear Katz. Dorothy Gilbert set it up." Ice laced his voice. Dorothy had kept him away from the case, but she brought in a reporter?

"I got him to insult Katz. He didn't go far as to formally clear her." Patricia tilted her head as if sensing his rage. "Dorothy didn't have much choice about setting this up. Warren would only talk to me."

"I see."

She put her hands on her hips. "You look the opposite of someone who just had his theory confirmed."

He shook his head, shoved his ego aside. "Do you realize the risk Dorothy took for this? Do you realize when you run this story, *her job* will be in jeopardy?"

"Dorothy can make her own decisions about jeopardizing her job," Patricia snapped. "And what makes you think I'm going to run the story, never mind run it with her name?" Patricia twiddled her pencil in her fingers. "You're making a lot of assumptions."

"You're a reporter. It's a good story. Of course, you'll run it."

"*If* I run it—which I might not because it gives publicity to a murdering Nazi. Breslin ran into a ton of trouble for running Son of Sam's letter to him, you know." She sighed and something sad passed through her face. "Right now, I'm saving it for deep background for a follow-up article. And nothing will run yet without Lt. Gilbert's say-so because that's the way it works with sources for reporters."

He said nothing for a long moment. He'd assumed. He'd let his ego get in the way of good work. Dorothy would be the first to tell him she could take care of herself. And he'd managed to anger Patricia again and for good reason because, again, he hadn't fully trusted her.

"You're right," he said softly. "I was wrong. I'm sorry."

"Stop judging me."

"I'll stop making erroneous assumptions."

She stared at him, her brows furrowed in concentration, as if he'd done something unusual and unexpected. "Okay," she finally said. "Thanks."

"All right. So what's next?" He asked her to restore the equilibrium to the conversation.

"The best thing for the story and the best thing for the case is to find those paintings. Find them and I bet we find the inside guy. Just how many places are there to hide paintings in that museum?" she asked.

"Thousands," he said. "Starting with behind other paintings or displays. In storage too, mixed in with other similar paintings. I looked there last night but, dead end."

"Why not take the displays apart and look?"

"Too damaging to do so on a hunch."

She frowned, clearly intrigued by his idea. Having their thoughts in sync again intoxicated him more than an entire bottle of Scotch. He wondered if she felt it as much as he did.

"Does your ex have any ideas? She's in a position to notice anything unusual," she asked.

"No, I don't think so. She would have mentioned it."

"But David said you took the job because she asked. Why did you do that? You hadn't taken on a job this big before."

Was Trisha accusing Amanda? That had been a passing thought but, ex-wife or not, he knew the woman would never be a killer.

"We had a nasty divorce, Patricia. We've only recently become human with each other again. When she asked for help, I wanted to do what I could to preserve that, for the sake of our daughter."

"Ah. You are good with thinking past anger."

"Thank you." Apology fully accepted, he thought. "What was your phone call about earlier? The one I caught the end of?"

"Another piece of the puzzle." She grabbed the backpack and consulted her notes. "I talked to the bank that issued the credit card Sidney used when he took me to dinner. They gave me a list of charges from the last two months."

"You used illegal means to get that information."

"Sure. I had the number and expiration date. I told them I was looking for possible fraudulent charges."

He smiled. "Of course you did."

"Anyway, you looked into the card too, right?" She grinned at him again, full of mischief. "I'll show you mine if you show me yours."

"I couldn't get into the exact charges. But I discovered Queen Anne's Revenge is a shell company," he said. "The day the contract for the *Lost Treasures* exhibit was signed, an untraceable deposit was posted to that account."

"From the museum?"

"No, the museum money for the exhibit is accounted for," Grayson said. "Sidney is likely using the shell company to hide income, probably in concert with the person who originally owned the paintings in Germany. Where did he use the credit card?"

"That's the interesting part." She held out her notebook. Her hand-writing was busy and sloppy but readable. Once he read the first page, she flipped to the second. He squinted and, finally, one address stood out to him.

"This is in Munich." He tapped the notebook. "Interesting."

"Why?"

This address was located near the one in Munich where they'd traced the origin of Sidney's threatening phone call, the one his client had ordered him not to mention to the press. "This is an area of interest for me that I can't explain due to reasons of client confidentiality."

"Okay." She had one leg dangling from the table and one knee pulled up to her chin. She stared at him over it. "And so?"

"This means now I have a specific search area for Sidney's movements and for where the paintings might have been originally hidden," he said. "You've saved me days of research."

"This is what I do." A pause. "Along with interviewing anyone I can."

A dig. He let her have it. "You do it well. How much does the news-paper pay you, Patricia?"

She frowned. No, almost froze. A weird reaction. But perhaps she hated discussing her salary. Many people did.

"Why do you ask?" she finally asked.

"Because you'd be an asset to this firm."

Although hiring someone he wanted as badly as he wanted her was a lousy idea. Ah, but the buzz he'd get from working together.

She laughed, amused. "You'd want to strangle me inside of a week for disobeying orders."

He leaned over and gripped the back of one of the empty conference room chairs. "What makes you think I'm so inflexible? The work pays well." He named a figure a few thousand more than David's original salary. She had more experience than David.

The laughter ended immediately, and her eyes widened. "Holy Blessed Mother of God, that's a lot of money. No wonder David could afford a Camaro and a parking space for it."

"I mostly employ people with law enforcement experience. You're used to working around rules or pretending they don't exist. It's a valuable perspective from my standpoint, and I'm willing to pay for it."

"Damn." She rubbed the bridge of her nose. "I'm tempted because... damn, I'm tempted." She shook her head, as if shaking off something. "I understand it's a compliment too, because you are careful who you hire. But I can't. No. It's not what I'm meant to do."

Her work was her calling. He nodded. "I understand. But you would be an asset. There are other security firms, if you ever change your mind. I'd recommend you."

"Oh, don't stick your neck out on that. I'm a lousy employee," she said but she smiled. "Look, I have a question for you, Grayson, and you have to promise not to get all growly on me."

"What?" he snapped.

She tilted her head again.

"Go on, ask," he said.

"There has to be more to taking this job than doing a favor for your ex."

"Are we on the record or off?"

"Off. This is just for me. I'm curious."

"Art fascinateds me."

She pushed the hair away from her face again. "You have a particular interest in art?"

"My mother was an artist, a good one. She'd approve of me protecting a museum."

"Ok. Thanks. I appreciate the answer. I just wondered." She reached into her backpack. "And since we've cleared the air here, here's *my* peace offering. I figured I owed you for the socks and Walkman but, mostly, for those socks. I love them. I'd have given it to you sooner except for the stupid stuff about the bug."

"You bought *me* something?" She'd thought of him?

"Don't act so shocked." She pulled a thin box, about the length of his hand, from the backpack. "I thought about wrapping it but, well, it's a bit early for Christmas, it's not your birthday, at least according to your office manager, and Happy Upcoming Halloween didn't seem to cut it."

She handed him the box. She had bought something for *him*?

He opened the box. "Patricia, this is—"

A boatswain's pipe! He held the silver pipe up to the light, catching his initials, E.M.G., on the handle. "You had it engraved. How did you know?"

"I got your middle initial from your office manager, after I told her what I needed it for," she said. "What's the 'M' stand for?"

"Marshall. But that's not what I meant. How did you know about boatswain pipes?" He turned it over again in his palm.

She shrugged. "I remembered the line in your trunk and what you said about going sailing when you could."

"You remembered a chance remark I made and came up with *this*?"

She shrugged. "Research is what I do, remember? Can you get it to make noise? I tried but got zilch. I wondered if it was a dud."

He raised the pipe to his lips and arranged his palm carefully around the bulb at the end of it. He took a breath and blew into the end of the pipe.

One long piercing note echoed around the room, and he began to play one of the few songs that he knew. The distant memory of his father teaching him the pipe surfaced, sending him back to those innocent days. What a beautiful gift.

He faltered, overwhelmed. She'd cut him to his heart. When she gave, she gave so much. Only she never wanted to show how much she cared.

Too late. He knew.

He lowered the pipe. "I'm out of practice. Sorry."

"Sounded good to me," she said. "Very martial."

"It's 'Reveille,'" he said. "Wake up call."

"Is that how they used it on ships?"

"Yes. The pipes can be heard over the sound of the sea and other shipboard noises."

Patricia, I love this.

He put the pipe reverently back in the box. "I've rarely received a more thoughtful gift."

She waved that compliment away. "Hey, it was just a thing."

The way to read Patricia would always be through actions. Her standing with him over the bomb; her backing him up in the fight; the browbeating of Windergaard that had gotten his firm rehired; the story she'd offered about dates with her late husband; and the gift of the pipe. He'd worried about being a notch in her bed. About them having so little in common. But she understood him. Did he understand her?

He put his fingers on her chin and raised her head. "Just a thing?" he whispered.

"Yeah." She flushed.

He leaned in closer, until their lips were almost touching.

"You had it engraved."

"Yeah," she whispered.

"This is more than lust." He enclosed her face in his hands.

"Let's see."

Soft skin, so warm. She leaned in. He kissed her.

Her lips were warm, inviting, and they parted after a brief second, allowing him to deepen the kiss. She shuddered. He could feel himself falling, falling down into a hole that he'd never be able to climb out of. Freefall. No parachute.

"I want you, Patricia."

"Cool," she breathed.

He wrapped his arms around her waist. She smelled of pencil shavings, combined with something floral and sweet. He trailed kisses along her face and down to her neck. Her back arched, just the way he'd imagined. She moaned.

She pushed on his chest, a clear signal to halt.

He stopped. *Damn.*

She rested her head just below his shoulder, breathing heavily. "Dammit, Grayson."

"Is that a complaint?"

She raised her head. "No." She wrapped her arms around his neck. "No promises."

"I expected none." Promises were just words, after all.

She kissed him. Yes, *now*. He pushed her down on the table. She unbuckled his belt. He swallowed hard. He was hard and ready for her already. But he wanted to make love to her, in every sense of the word.

He enclosed her wrists, brought her hands over her head and broke the kiss. Now she was sprawled under him. Their faces were an inch apart. They'd have sex on his conference room table.

This is insane.

But he was tired of being sane, of being careful. He'd wanted her since he put hands on her in the tunnel. Perhaps from the moment she'd appeared beside the pillar.

Patricia stared, breathing heavily. She flexed her wrists against his hold.

"Getting a little kink on, Grayson?"

Yes. "Is that a problem?"

"Not if you let go when I say so."

"Absolutely."

Gripping her small wrists with one hand, he slipped the other hand under the Cookie Monster's eyes and unhooked her bra.

"Nimble fingers," she mumbled.

Soft skin, hard muscles underneath.

He slid his hand around to her stomach, toward her breasts, and froze at the feel of cuts under his fingertips.

"Um, Grayson?" she asked.

He let go of her wrists, caressed her flat stomach and touched the ridges there again. He looked down, expecting to see recent scars because of the rib injury. They were there but...

He caught his breath. More scars. Ugly razor blade scars that covered her from breast to hip.

"My God, Patricia," he said. "Who *hurt* you?"

She took his face in her hands and pulled his attention away from the scars. "You're fifteen years too late to play Galahad. Now, where were we?"

Fifteen years? She'd been assaulted as a *child*. He stood up. No wonder she kept people at bay.

"Oh, for God's sake." She reached under her T-shirt, seeking to hook the bra shut. "Every now and then, someone gets freaked by the scars. I'd have never pegged you as one of them, Grayson. Fine. Later."

She pushed him aside.

"Wait, no, Patricia, that's not it." Repulsed by scars? Never. How did he salvage this?

"Oh, so then you feel bad for me." She put her back to him and her nimble fingers hooked the bra. "You know, pity's a real turnoff."

Why did his being concerned about her make her *angry*?

"You're the least pitiful person that I've ever met."

She rounded on him. "Then why the hell did you *stop*? What is this about?"

"Pardon me for taking a moment to absorb the fact that someone I care about was badly hurt."

"It happened to me, not you, and a long time ago. You're a fucking piece of work, you know that?" She gathered up the boxes on the floor and slammed them together. "Put them back in your storage room yourself. I'm done."

He put a hand on her shoulder. Lightly. No, she couldn't leave. Not now. "Wait. Please. Just give me a chance to catch up, here."

She shoved his hand off. "Look, it's late and I'm tired and this thing was a ridiculous idea anyway. We both know that. I'm your walk on the wild side and you're my...hell, I don't know. But it won't work."

Sympathy would drive her away. "Fine. At the least, you could clear up something before you stomp out of here."

"What?" She put her hands on her hips, belligerent.

"How can someone who quotes rock lyrics and make jokes when defusing a bomb and taking on four armed men be terrified of a conversation with a man who cares about her?"

She glared at him. But she remained in the room.

"Patricia, please. Stay. *Talk to me*."

CHAPTER EIGHTEEN

SHE SHOULD WALK AWAY. But Grayson waited for her answer with that innate stillness of his, and all her good intentions went out the window. He wanted her to stay, did he? Let's see how much.

"Screw talking."

She grabbed his shirt, pulled him to her, and kissed him.

He wasted no time in kissing her back. She pulled off his shirt and T-shirt and finally put her hands on bare skin.

A hard body, strong muscles. Nice. His chest hair was in short, black curls that collected in a thin line that led down his flat stomach, giving her fingers a trail to follow. She smelled something musky, aftershave and sweat.

His erection pressed against her stomach. *Okay.* The scars definitely hadn't turned him off. Good.

She tilted her head back as he kissed her neck again and shuddered when he hit that sweet spot between neck and shoulder. He grasped her hips and pushed her against the wall. The upraised wallpaper and the chair rail pressed against her back. If she wanted to stop, it had to be now.

What the hell? It wasn't the dumbest thing she'd ever done.

She grabbed his belt, tugged it off, and tossed it across the room. He pulled the T-shirt over her head. Her bra went flying in the same direction as his belt.

He knelt in front of her. *Oh, yes.* She buried her hands in his hair, anticipating what would come next. His breath warmed her skin. But instead of sliding down her pants, he kissed her stomach, in the middle of the longest scar. A feathery light caress that drove her out of her mind.

He kissed the scars, stroking her hips with the same soft touch he'd used on her in the tunnels. Her throat closed up. She shivered. Too close, too intense, too *intimate*.

She tilted her head back against the wall. He trailed the tip of his tongue over the scar that ran under her breasts. He stood and rested his forehead against hers. He stared at her, as if he could warm her with his eyes alone.

"You're beautiful," he whispered.

She swallowed. It ached to look at him, ached deep down where she hadn't been awake in years. *Grayson.* She kissed him with all the intensity he'd aroused, full of all the words she couldn't say, all the words she'd deny existed.

He pressed against her, the bulge in his pants jutting out. She unbuttoned and unzipped his pants, sliding them down from his hips with her feet.

"Now what?" She murmured against his cheek.

"Pants are stuck on the shoes," he said.

"I got it." She leaned down, lifted his foot, and pulled the polished wingtips off. She tossed one to one end of the room and one to the other end.

She stood. "Shoes off."

He pushed her against the wall again and pulled her jeans off, throwing them and her underwear aside as quickly as she'd gotten rid of his shoes.

"I want to make love to you," he said.

Oh, hell, it probably would be inappropriate to fall at his feet, wouldn't it? Instead, she got rid of his boxers and pushed him toward the table. Revealed for the first time, he was as attractive out of the suit as in it, in shape, all in proportion, and all hard for her. His arms went around her hips, but before he could do anything else, she hooked a foot around his ankle, half-tripping him, and used the leverage to push him flat on the table.

She straddled him. The smooth surface of the table was cold on her knees, but the rest of her was on fire. White hot.

He looked startled but only for a second and then filled his hands with her breasts. She moaned and reached down to grasp his erection. She was wet and ready for him. Right this second.

I want a long, crazy ride. Now.

"Hell," she said.

He frowned. "What?"

She leaned down close enough for their lips to touch. "I don't have condoms with me." She supposed they could do a bunch of other things instead, but there went her ride.

He ran the back of his hand over her cheek. "Inside left pocket of my suit coat," he said.

"You *are* prepared for anything."

"Semper Paratus."

"What's that? Some Boy Scout motto or something?" She rolled to the side, snagged his blazer off the chair with her foot and brought it close enough to fish the condom out of the pocket. "Because I don't believe you were ever a Boy Scout."

"It's Latin for 'always ready.'" Grayson took the package from her and opened it. "And guilty on not being a Boy Scout."

"I knew it." She took the condom from him. "Allow me."

She rolled it over his hardness with one hand, snaking the other hand around the back of his neck while she kissed him, and swallowed his groan as she stroked him. Make love, eh? Whatever he wanted to call it. She lowered herself onto him, sliding in easily. He let out a long moan and grasped her hips with a grip so tight it almost hurt. *So good.* She threw her head back.

"Hold on," she said, and went crazy.

She arched her back and rocked back and forth. He caught her rhythm perfectly. Their moans melded together and echoed in the conference room. He took one hand from her hip and caressed between her legs, where her clit was already wet and warm. She shuddered, groaned, and kept riding, faster and faster, harder and harder, and her breathing grew more ragged. Her vision blurred, and she threw back her head, letting out a scream as the orgasm shook her. His hips bucked, and she felt him pulse inside him as he followed her over.

She wasn't sure how much time passed before she stopped rocking and lowered herself until they were face to face. His arms came around her, solid, holding her tight.

"So," she said into his ear. "How many more condoms do you have in that coat pocket?"

"It depends on how much more you can take."

"Let's see what you got."

He flipped them over, so he was on top.

"Patricia, when I'm finished, you won't be able to see at all."

"Prove it."

———

Trisha zipped up her pants and picked up her T-shirt. Cookie Monster. *Num. Num.*

"Where's my bra?" she asked.

Grayson pointed left. "On the seat of that chair over there, though it seems a shame to cover over the tattoo on your shoulder."

"You like my Phoenix?" Yeah, he had a few kinks. Cool.

"I need a longer look to be sure."

"It's late. Maybe another time." She grabbed the bra from the chair, glancing sideway at his bare chest. Whew. He looked good naked, though that was nothing next to how he moved naked.

"I'll hold you to that." He pulled his T-shirt on. "My socks?"

She pointed right. "Over there in the corner, I think."

After she hooked the bra, she tilted her head to study him.

"What?" he said.

"The black boxers. Would've picked you for a tightey-whitey type."

"And now?"

"I know better."

She watched him dress, watched the suit cover up all that intense energy. They said still waters ran deep. Grayson sure as hell proved that.

When he let loose, he held back nothing. She was going to have bruises on her hips, her back muscles were going to be stiff and, well, at one point, she had lost her sight. Her mind too.

She wanted this again. She wanted to spend more time with him.

Damn, Grayson.

He let his tie hang loosely around his collar as he put on his blazer. That was freakin' hot.

"Breakfast? There's a place I know that's open all night." Somewhere public where she could think clearly. She should tell him everything. The being fired for sure. But he'd be pissed when she told him. Maybe he'd be mellow after breakfast. Maybe she wouldn't tell him at all.

"Breakfast sounds perfect," he said. "I could cook for you."

His place? Big mistake. She didn't fancy being tossed out. "Nah, this will save you the trouble of cooking."

He hesitated before agreeing. "All right."

"Don't push your luck, Grayson," she said. "I live day to day. Sometimes hour to hour. I don't know another way. Great sex doesn't lead always to great relationships."

"We understand each other." He slid his finger under the chain of the Celtic cross she always wore. "You hide that you care, but you do. Why else do you wear this?"

"It belonged to my foster father. It's all the legacy I have left of him. Call it a memento."

She glanced at the door. She could leave. Grayson wouldn't stop her.

"You are a risk-taker. Take this one." Grayson brushed her cheek with his thumb. "Patricia, give this a chance."

She should never have bought him the damn pipe. Or fucked him on his conference table. She'd had enough heartbreak. Her time in juvie. Her husband. Her job.

How had Grayson become so important to be on that list?

She turned away, hiding whatever he'd see on her face. "Warning you, my breakfast place is a basic greasy spoon. But they have great sausage patties."

He set a hand on her shoulder. "Let's go."

———

He drove to her breakfast place. Patricia relaxed in his passenger seat. Her greasy spoon was in midtown, near the Lincoln Tunnel entrance, in the Hell's Kitchen area. The hole-in-the-wall, as she'd warned, held only five booths, all full but one, and a long counter, also full. No menus. Everyone seemed to know what to order. Several cops sat in one booth. A man huddled in a threadbare raincoat at the counter, sipping a cup of coffee.

The place was pure Manhattan and pure Patricia.

An older man in a greasy fry cook's apron took their orders. Patricia ordered the works. Grayson did the same, with hash instead of French fries.

The food arrived in minutes, warm and steaming. He took a deep breath, and his mouth watered. He cut into the sausage patties, still sizzling, and decided she was right. These were excellent.

She smiled. "Told ya."

He lifted a forkful of the hash. "Want some?"

She blinked. "Yeah. Sure."

He reached over and fed her the forkful. She took it in one gulp and smiled. "Thanks."

"My turn." He reached over to steal a French fry. Her arm came down in front of the plate so quickly that she almost squashed his fingers.

Her face flushed red, embarrassed, as she withdrew the hand. "Sorry. Force of habit." She lifted a fry and handed it to him. "Here you go."

He ate the fry and pondered her again. Protecting food was a learned reflex. At some point in her life, she'd had to fight for her supper. That indicated time spent in juvenile prison—he'd have found an adult record— or perhaps fighting on the streets when she'd been homeless.

It was going to take a long time to solve the puzzle that was Patricia Connell. He looked forward to it. Despite life treating her so harshly, she had a generous heart. She simply hid it from most people by kicking up dust around her. She'd slipped the man at the counter sipping coffee a ten when she thought he wasn't looking.

"So where'd you grow up, Grayson?" she asked.

"All over the world," he said. "I'm a military brat. My father's a Marine. He met my mother when stationed in England during World War II. Their romance caused a scandal with her noble family."

"A war bride," she nodded. "But it worked?"

"I think so." He'd been sure his parents were the best-suited couple on the planet, at least until the mess at her funeral. He'd never understood how his father could be with another woman so soon after his wife of thirty years died. He hadn't spoken to the man since that day.

Maybe it was time to change that. Life, as last month's events made clear, was short.

"So you lived in England?" she asked.

"I summered there quite a bit, once my mother's family got used to her idea of a husband," he said. "And we lived there while he fought in Korea."

"That explains the English accent," she said. "Though I notice it comes and goes, depending in whether you need it or not."

He smiled. "It sounds more authoritative. People respond to it faster."

"Remind me to have you use it to read poetry to me."

"Anytime," he answered. That sounded promising. "What about you? Have you ever lived anyplace but New York City?"

"Nah. All Manhattan. Well, okay, I lived in a foster home in Queens for a month or two. But that hardly counts."

"But you only have traces of an accent, and sometimes, no accent at all."

"I do when I need it. Lot of people won't talk to me unless they know I'm one of them."

"You also know a lot of the history of the city."

She shrugged. "I got curious." She launched into a history of the city boroughs. He listened, intent. This was as interesting as her talk about walking the city streets with her late husband. Under that tough exterior lurked a scholar. No wonder she'd graduated from Columbia with honors.

"So after Nicky and I found the tunnels years back, I remembered and researched the original stations, which leads us back to how we met." She wolfed down her last French fry. "Hah, you should've seen Warren's face when he realized I messed up his plan."

"I can only imagine. Careful, that could put a target on you." He would have expressed more concern except she would hate it. Let that resentment go.

She shrugged. "Warren can get in line. She swallowed the last of her coffee. "Hell, he can get in line behind my former publisher who..."

She trailed off in mid-sentence and blushed.

"Your *former* publisher?" He tensed again. "What does that mean?"

"Crap." She pushed aside her empty plate, looked away for a moment, and met his gaze.

"I got fired."

"*What?*" His voice was so sharp that every eye in the diner turned to him.

"Jesus, Grayson, chill. It's my life, not yours. Anyway, I'll find a new job soon as we find the paintings."

Had she lied to him to stay on the story? Used him? Even tonight? He turned to ice again. "When were you fired?"

She stared out the grimy window. "The first night in the hospital. The publisher lectured me about not calling in. Called me irresponsible and low-class. So I called him a fucking asshole and hung up."

He'd heard the tail end of that. She'd brushed it off. She'd brushed off every mention of her job. He remembered the boxes of stuff from her office in her apartment. She'd lied then too.

"When were you going to tell me?" he growled. "When you had what you wanted for your story?"

The cook leaned over the counter. "This is a peaceful place, buddy. Out."

Patricia slapped two twenties on the table to pay for their dinner, about double their check. "It's okay, Chef. We were just leaving."

She walked, no stormed, out of the diner and kept going once they reached the street. He followed, hard-pressed to keep up.

"This conversation is not over."

She wheeled, hair flying. "I never lied to you. *Not once.*"

"A lie of omission. You cut me out." Cold rage settled in. She could make love to him and still hide keep this from him. For the story. "I offered you a job. You could have told me then."

She crossed her arms over her chest. Her breath hung in the morning mist. "Oh, and you've told me everything you know about the case?"

He grimaced.

"You're still sitting on stuff." She drew closer. "I shared my information with you. That's what I promised." She drew her coat tighter around her as it started to rain. "I kept my word."

"You weren't going to mention it at *all*." Fury filled him again. "Why the hell not?"

"When should I have told you about it? After sex against the wall? Or maybe I should've said it during the blow job. 'Hope this feels good, oh, by the way, Cardoza fired my ass.'"

"Enough." He cut the air with his hand. "You're being facetious. You had plenty of opportunities to tell me. You kept it from me so you could get the story."

She paced around. "That wasn't my job, that was my *life*, Grayson! I didn't want to talk about it yet. Fuck." She faced him. "Dammit, I'm *trying* here."

"You call this angry diatribe *trying*?"

She froze, wiped the rain away from her eyes with the sleeve of her coat. "I agreed to breakfast, I listened to you, I..." She shook her head. "You don't believe me. You think I fucked you for the story."

The long seconds he took to formulate an answer gave him away.

"You're mental." She whistled for an oncoming cab. "Screw this whole damned thing."

She flung the door to the cab open before it had fully stopped.

Fear replaced fury. Oh, bloody hell, what he had done? He curled his hand around her arm. "You're giving up because of this?"

"You gave up on me first, Grayson."

She brushed him off, slammed the door of the cab, and left him standing in the rain like some stupid movie cliché.

He crossed the street to his car, and drove home, eyes on the road, mind occupied on the argument. She'd come to him, trusted him when he asked, made insane love to him, agreed to breakfast and then…

She should have told me in the hospital.

She liked having the upper hand, gloried in knowing more than everyone else. She loved getting the story before anything and anyone.

Bloody hell, he was the wronged party here, and she walked away from him?

He arrived at his condo in a foul mood, hung his wet coat on the hook just inside the entranceway, and checked his kitchen for dirty dishes. He pre-loaded the coffee machine with grounds. This morning would come far too fast.

His daughter had left him a note on the counter.

"Thanks, Dad, for letting us use the place for homework. Jenn and I drank the soda, but the glasses are in the dishwasher. And thanks for leaving out the chips and sandwiches. See you at my game next Sunday. You are coming, right? Love, Eleanor."

He crumpled the note. His daughter had followed his directions to the letter about cleaning up. What was *wrong* with him? why did he care about that? Eleanor felt comfortable bringing her friends to his home. That was the important part.

In his bedroom, he hung the suit in the side of the closet reserved for items needing to go to the dry cleaner but stopped when he found the boatswain pipe, still in the box, in the pocket. Furious, he tossed the rest of his dirty clothes into his hampers, one for darks and one for whites.

He sunk down on the bed, the pipe in his hand.

Patricia had reached out to him. Trusted him. And instead of being furious at her boss—how dare the man fire her!—he'd yelled at her for keeping it from him.

Accused her of using him.

He rolled the pipe around in his hand and wondered if he should play "Taps."

CHAPTER NINETEEN

BY THE AFTERNOON, Grayson thought he'd sorted his emotions. He resisted the urge to show up at Patricia's door. In their short acquaintance, he'd already apologized to the woman twice. He doubted she'd believe him.

Her emotions were too raw. Apologizing would not fix it, not when he'd made such an error. Not a good sign for a good relationship in their future either.

Grayson did what he always did when stuck personally: he went back to work.

He needed to review the museum's new security system that Tony Alfonsi, his partner and the firm's tech expert, had spent countless hours installing since the murder. Now he waited with Tony in the museum lobby for a tour with Chief Conrath.

His partner hadn't shaved in at least a day, and his pants were covered in dust. Several museum visitors glanced warily at Tony as they walked past, focusing on the Sig Sauer he wore openly in a waist holster. Tony grinned at a few of them. People liked David. People seemed to give Grayson himself instant respect. But Tony? People often mistook Tony for muscle or the stereotypical Italian mobster. He liked being underestimated.

"You looked tired, Edmund," Tony said. "Busy last night?"

Grayson almost flinched at the implication. But Tony knew nothing of last night in the conference room. "I'm fine."

"No doubt," Tony said.

Conrath walked up to them, hands on his belt, as was his habit. The security chief had been wary of them since the murder, but some of his attitude had been beaten out of him by the repeated questioning from Dorothy and other detectives. Still, they'd found no evidence of Conrath's involvement in the crime.

"Chief," Tony said. "Ready?"

Conrath nodded, curt. "But this new system is a like locking the barn after the horse has been stolen, isn't it?"

Edmund bit back a remark.

"We'll see," was all Tony said.

Tony led them away from *Lost Treasures* to the museum's east wing. Grayson glanced at the passing exhibits, remembering that Amanda had told him how this section set the events of Eastern and Western history side by side, according to their timeline.

"Same time, different places. It provides perspective," she'd said.

He noted the Chinese artifact directly across from a Greek statue. They stopped at the staircase, the same one that led down to the storage closet where the tunnel entrance had been hidden. Images of Patricia jumping the rope across that staircase swam into his vision.

Enough, he thought.

Conrath actually smiled as they walked further into the west wing.

"You two don't know what a mess this used to be." He waved a hand. "Exhibits all in the wrong order or so old as to be outdated. I know he can be fussy but Windergaard brought this place back to relevance."

Amanda had said the same. "Over five hundred items were in storage, yes?" Grayson asked.

"That's right." Conrath stopped at the open doorway to the new European medieval wing. "I'm proud of what the old place has become." He narrowed his eyes. "Now, show me why we're on this side, Mr. Alfonsi."

Tony ignored Conrath's imperious tone and pointed to where the ceiling and wall edges met. "Our original alarm could only be tripped inside *Lost Treasures*. These wires connect to an alarm at the front desk that will trip at any unauthorized activity in all sectors." Tony kept his voice low and mild, but it still echoed in the nice acoustics of the hallway.

Conrath's eyes widened. "That tiny wire can do that?"

"Oh, sure," Tony said. "And the alarm will ring in your security office instantly."

Grayson remained silent because he recognized those wires as also capable of carrying a video feed, a feed Tony had not mentioned to Conrath. Tony was up to something.

"Let's move on," Tony said.

They continued into the medieval wing. The recent renovations had turned this wing into a full-scale mock-up of a real tournament. Colorful murals on the walls depicted the watching crowd, several real-looking mannequins posed as squires, and full-sized armored knights on armored horses forever prepared to charge in the center of the main floor.

The high-pitched laughter of kids dressed in medieval costumes, chasing each other, playing with Nerf swords and other weapons, echoed from the vaulted ceilings. Grayson sidestepped to avoid a child bearing a sword and shield. The girl turned around to face a group of attackers with pikes. He smiled as the girl charged them, scattering the boys.

Conrath scoped up a plastic pike on the floor and handed it to the boy who'd dropped it. The boy bowed to him. "Thank you, good sir!" he said before he scampered off.

"I've never seen it so busy in here," Grayson said.

"My kids would love it," Tony said.

A young girl who barely came up to Conrath's waist tugged at his belt. Grayson judged her at seven or eight years old. Eleanor had seemed that age only yesterday.

"What can I do for you, young lady?" Conrath asked.

"How come none of these knights are ladies?" The girl waved her hand at the life-size mannequins, her dark hair falling in front of her face.

"Women weren't usually taught to fight back then, but they could rule." He pointed to the stands constructed against the wall. "The queen sitting there is Queen Eleanor of Aquitaine. She acted sometimes as regent for her husband and son. Aquitaine was her land, not theirs."

The girl frowned. "Could she use a sword?"

"I don't know," Conrath said. "But she did control a lot of knights who used swords."

The girl smiled. "Okay. Good." She turned and rushed back to a crowd near one of the life-size model horses.

"You have kids?" Tony asked Conrath.

Conrath's two children were grown and married. Tony knew that from the Gray Associates background check. His partner was making small talk for some reason.

"Yeah, two kids, but they're grown now. I'm practicing for the grand-kids," Conrath said. "You should be sure to report to Mr. Windergaard how much the kids enjoy it. He loves hearing about that. He said it's what he imagined for this place as a child."

Grayson raised an eyebrow. "He used to visit the museum often as a child?"

"His father used to work here," Conrath said. "He used to scamper all over the museum while his father worked. I'm surprised you didn't know that, Mr. Grayson. I guess that proves you're not infallible after all."

Ouch. Grayson fought a wince. "None of us is infallible, Chief." He exchanged a glance at Tony. Yes, they should have known that. Grayson pointed to several smaller rooms to the side. "Tony, do we have alarms in the rooms the children are getting the costumes from?" he asked to change the subject.

The kids went in looking normal and came out with not just with the Nerf weapons but plastic armor and other costumes, including dresses for the girls and more formless clothing for peasants.

"No, those are a dead end, and kids get into everything anyway. They'd be tripping them all the time," Tony drawled. "It's the entrances and exits I'm concerned about, all over the museum."

Grayson gestured to the main display of medieval knights, frozen in various combat poses. That was, at least, cordoned off from the children. "Chief, shouldn't the museum be concerned about those weapons being so close to the children?"

"They're wooden and too high for the kids. The idea is that it gives the adults something to look at while the kids play." Conrath wiped a smudge off one of the locked display cases, one that held authentic axes. "You wire these cases too?"

Tony shrugged. "Yes, as should have been done in the first place. We can't protect what's in *Lost Treasures* without also protecting the entire museum."

Grayson hid a frown. Tony had lied about something other than the purpose of the wires to Conrath. His partner trusted the man as little as Grayson did.

"That's shortsighted!" Conrath objected.

Tony launched into a technical explanation consisting of part technical jargon, part bullshit. Amused, Grayson wandered away to refresh his memory of the room. He stopped in front of the tournament display with the life-size knights and read the display, which had a key to the names of the knights involved.

Originally, tournaments were a melee, with the strongest competitor awarded the winner. It was a way for landless knights to learn war and attract the attention of potential patrons. Knights were often killed. Geoffrey, Duke of Brittany and son of Henry II of England, died in one of them. It likely changed the course of English history.

The tournament we've re-created is in Normandy, during the time of Henry II. The knight at the front of the charge is William Marshal, later the English Earl of Pembroke and Regent of England. He never lost in tournament. He was known as the greatest knight of his age. Even at age sixty, no one would face him in single combat.

Grayson knew all about William Marshal. His mother's family claimed some sort of descent from him but then, so far back, probably half of England could claim descent from the old warrior's daughters. In any case, that family tradition had resulted in "Marshall" as his middle name.

Grayson craned his neck up at the tall figure underneath the replica armor, the artificial fingers curled around a wooden lance, the other arm around a shield. Not all the knights in the display were white, either, a historically accurate touch but one usually forgotten. Amanda's work, most likely.

He smiled again at the children running around. Eleanor would have loved this at the same age. Amanda insisted that the controversy over *Lost Treasures* was worth it because the museum would thrive once its coffers were full. She believed museums did important work, educated the young, and provided institutional memory.

Windergaard was of the same mind as his ex-wife. Get the man going on the value of museums and he never shut up.

I need to find out about his father's employment at this museum. How did I miss that?

Finally, Tony led them across the open courtyard, the one with a fountain of dancing dolphins to the east wing and *Lost Treasures*. Grayson, clad only in his suit, shivered a bit. He needed to replace the coat that had been ruined when he lent it to Patricia.

He thought of that night in the hospital and Patricia apologizing for ruining the coat. He rewound the memory back further, to what he now knew had been her boss screaming at her for missing a deadline, not caring that she'd nearly died for his newspaper.

She must have been devastated. She'd put on a helluva brave face.

Even to herself?

Damn. Despite his best efforts, Patricia snuck into his thoughts again.

They stopped outside the entrance to *Lost Treasures*, where a line about twenty people deep snaked from the entrance. "Did you add new security here?" Conrath asked.

"I've changed the passcode and the locks," Tony said.

"That's all? Despite the fact Adrienne Katz must have walked through an open door?" Conrath asked.

"No one is getting that door open again by themselves," Tony said. "And that's a fact."

Conrath hooked his fingers in his belt again. "If you say so."

"I've installed hidden infrared cameras above the door as well. Those cameras operate on a battery," Tony said, pointing upward. "Even if the power goes out, they'll catch anyone going through that door, at any time."

Conrath only said "hmm…"

Finally, Tony concluded the tour at the security office, located behind the admissions desk. Conrath proclaimed to be pleased with his new camera displays. Grayson remained silent, wondering what Tony hadn't told Conrath.

When they finished, Tony led Grayson out to the information desk located off to the right of the admissions desk.

"What haven't you told him?" Grayson asked.

"That I've made the world safe for us and set a trap for him or whoever of his people fucked up security." Tony flipped open a cabinet under the information desk. Underneath the counter, various wires were attached to several computer banks. He glanced at the guide stationed at the desk, but customers occupied her attention.

"I told Conrath this was the brains of the new security system," Tony whispered.

He made a few more taps on a keyboard connected to a tiny display next to the desktops. "Aha. That's set up. Good. Follow me again."

"You could tell me without dragging me around the museum."

"Nah. It'll be easier to show you. Patience, Edmund. Not everything can be under your control."

"I've been remarkably patient this whole time." But Grayson followed Tony back down the hallway toward *Lost Treasures*, they stopped near the door. "So?"

"Take some time. I bet you can see it."

Grayson slipped his hands into his pockets and scanned the hallway. It took over a minute, but he finally spotted more thin wires concealed in the cracks between the ceilings and the walls, the same as the ones in the west wing. It took him longer to spot the new, strategically placed, miniature cameras. Top of the line tech.

He returned to Tony. "I have a feeling that not all these feeds go to the museum's security center."

"None of them." Tony smiled. "I read the FBI's assessment of Sidney's threats as inconclusive."

"The worse possible result," Grayson said.

"Yeah, I hated that too," Tony said.

They were stuck in limbo.

"But I refuse to allow our people to operate here without a better system." Tony led him back to the front desk, flipped open the cabinet once more, and patted something that resembled a radio receiver.

Grayson finally recognized it.

"You're sending this feed to a remote site."

"A van outside, as a matter of fact, manned 24/7." Tony straightened. "Their security can watch the museum. We will watch the watchers."

"You're spying on them. Excellent."

Tony nodded. "Whoever the inside man is, assuming he exists, he won't fool my feed because he won't know it's there and can't counter it," Tony said

"Why not tell me in advance?"

"You were busy with the logistics of personnel, juggling the police investigation interviews, and dealing with Windergaard. Besides, it's time I started pulling my weight on this job."

"Yes, I'm still bitter you took that particular day off to attend your son's college tournament. You should have known that would be the same day Nazis broke into the museum." Grayson said. "You're slipping, Tony. NSA agents, even former ones, should be more prescient."

Tony grinned at the sarcasm. "We're still working on the secret formula for foreknowledge. Algorithms can be so damned complicated sometimes." He tapped his brain. "The best instrument is still in here."

"I see one problem," Grayson moved them away to a quieter section of the hallway. "Tony, eventually they're going to need a reliable system for the museum."

"They have what they paid for already, for now. When we're done with the job, I'll hand this one over to them as well."

"Perfect," Grayson said.

Tony grimaced. "There are no perfect systems. But this is close. I should've followed my instincts up front and damn what Windergaard wanted. But now, if you're right about the stolen paintings still being in the museum, the inside man will not be aware of the extra cameras or our private feed."

"I'm right," Grayson nodded. "Nothing else fits. Anything else I should know?"

Tony cleared his throat. "There is the little matter of another set of cameras, the ones in our office conference room. I believe, in your, ah, activities last night, you forgot the hidden switch for them."

"*What?*" Grayson stepped back. *Cameras. In the conference room.* Placed there because he was paranoid and wanted a record of what might happen in a security meeting.

Heat warmed his face. He was *blushing*. Lovely.

"*Now* you remember," Tony said, with the trace of a laugh in his voice.

"What do you know?" Grayson snapped.

"Turns out that if you slam a chair against the switch hard enough, the cameras start recording and continue recording until someone turns them off." Tony stroked his beard. "I arrived at the office this morning and found an eye-opening bit of video. You're lucky the feed comes right to my office. Though, the video is grainy, and the sound needs work. I'm going to have to adjust those in the future."

Grayson clenched his teeth. Exactly when had he and Trisha pushed aside the chair? Hell, he couldn't even remember which chair. They'd knocked them all aside.

Tony clapped him on the back. "Just wanted you to know, so it doesn't happen again. Also, I made sure our cleaning service paid special attention to the table today."

"Tony...where is the tape now?" Had Tony *watched*?

"Gone. I cut it to shreds. For what it's worth, I think she's perfect for you."

"Good." Grayson narrowed his eyes. "Why is she perfect for me?" How much of this tape had Tony watched?

"You steamroll people if you can, Edmund. You enjoy it when people stand up to you, like she did. Though there was a little less standing and a little more horizontal going on last night"

Tony walked away, whistling.

CHAPTER TWENTY

IN NO MOOD for company after *that* revelation, Grayson disappeared into the temperature- controlled vaults in the basement at the museum. Amanda guided him to the appropriate area when he said he wanted to research more of the museum's history, to get a better feel for anyone who might have a grudge against it.

His ex-wife had called it "grasping at straws," but she'd done with minimal grumbling and no nasty asides about their conversation the other night.

Windergaard's background check had shown his father had been an adjunct professor at a city university. If Windergaard's father had worked at the museum, it had been scrubbed from his employment record. But this vault contained files and photos that went back over fifty years. If there were a record of Windergaard's father's employment, it would be here.

A folder with laminated photos of museum staff from thirty to forty years ago sat on the table in front of him, representing the time periods when Windergaard would have been five to fifteen, which should have been when his father worked there.

Grayson opened the top folder of images. He owed a thank you to whoever had archived, laminated, and labeled them. He glanced at several color photographs of the museum staff posing in front of the dolphin fountain that still occupied the inner courtyard. Nothing, nothing.

He continued the search, using a magnifying glass to study faces of the sometimes grainy images. An hour later, with watery eyes and a creaky back, he wondered if he were truly grasping at straws. Patricia, he thought, would have liked doing this.

He thought back to that night at the hospital and the sound of her voice when she cursed at her publisher. Righteous anger, he thought. He thought about her voice last night when he accused her of lying.

Hurt.

Could she have kept it from him because she couldn't look at it clearly herself? Likely. He knew she cared not just about the story but about clearing Adrienne Katz. And Patricia already had what she'd wanted from him: information and access to his files before they slept together.

A sinking feeling grew in the pit of stomach.

He ignored it and turned back to the latest photo. A man who looked eerily like Windergaard stood in the middle of a photo of the staff in front of the dolphin fountain, on the first anniversary of its dedication. Unfortunately, only first names were below the individuals.

The man was labeled "Henry," which was the first name of Windergaard's father. But there were a number of Henrys in the world and resemblances could lie.

He needed more. He kept sorting through the photos. Another hour. More bleary eyes. He looked at the clock. Past nine p.m. Almost time to quit. One more folder.

There, he hit pay dirt.

He studied a candid photo of a man and child standing together near the old information desk. The photo was labeled *Max Warren & Max Windergaard, the curator's son.*

Warren?

Grayson flipped the photograph over and discovered a half-size image stuck to the back of it. He used his Swiss Army knife to gently pry the smaller photo away from the larger one.

Two smiling men stared at him from the photo. They were identified as "Henry Windergaard, European exhibit curator" and "Max Warren, his assistant, in charge of the post-World War II items."

The men could have been twins. But the background check of Max Windergaard stated that his father, Henry, had been an only child.

Grayson put it side by side with the photo in front of the dolphin fountain. Henry Windergaard appeared only in these two photos. Max Warren only appeared in this one. They'd both been purged from the official museum records, save for these two forgotten images.

A Warren and Windergaard, obviously related, stared at him, opening up so many possibilities.

Stephen Warren, murderer, and Max Windergaard, the museum director were connected by blood. Closely connected.

Grayson's portable radio, resting on the chair next to him, crackled with David's voice.

"Problem, boss. Need you at the *Lost Treasures* exhibit. The van crew just radioed in. They said Sidney just tried to open the door to *Lost Treasures.*"

"And failed because Tony's new system won't open after hours, save for emergencies," Grayson finished.

"Yep. But Sidney's not giving up. He's stalking around the hallway. He doesn't know he's on Candid Camera."

"I'll deal with him. You remain on duty at the security desk."

When Grayson arrived, Sidney had company. Windergaard. The two men were shouting and close to blows.

Windergaard jabbed a finger into Sidney's chest. Sidney pushed him away and focused his attention on Grayson's arrival.

"What the hell do you think you're doing, Grayson, locking me away from *my* artwork?" Sidney snarled.

"My job."

"I've had enough of this. I'm going back to my office and calling our lawyers," Windergaard said, pushing past them and into the museum.

Sidney followed, perhaps to continue the argument. Grayson grabbed his arm. "We need to talk."

"Do you think you can stop me because you have a gun, and I don't?" Sidney sneered. The man had charmed Patricia, but his manner held only fear tonight.

Grayson released him. "You're afraid for yourself and for these paintings. Tell me why. Tell me what you know about Stephen Warren and his connection to the museum director."

"That's none of your business!"

Sidney telegraphed his punch. *Idiot.* Grayson ducked, sidestepped, and Sidney lost his balance and flailed to stay upright.

Something pinged off the wall.

Gunshot.

Sidney fell, a face-plant. Grayson covered Sidney, drew his weapon, and fired three quick bursts in the direction of the shots.

He thought he heard a moan near the men's rest room, down the hallway. But he could not be certain. He was out in the open, exposed, with an injured man.

"Boss!" David's voice rang out from the connecting hallway.

"Stay there!" Grayson ordered. "Cover me."

He dragged an inert Sidney by the collar toward David, expecting to feel a punch from a bullet any second. Not another man down on his watch. Not another close call with death, after all their precautions.

Overhead lights bathed the darkened hallway, exposing a figure in a security uniform down near the men's restroom.

His shots had found their target. Luck, pure luck, Grayson thought.

Relatively safe behind the hallway, Grayson checked Sidney's pulse. Weak. Blood stained the front of the man's shirt. Sidney gurgled, his breathing rough and shallow.

Possibly bleeding out.

More backup arrived in the form of Tony's people who'd been stationed in the van outside. They tended to Sidney and called 911 while Grayson and David, weapons drawn, stalked the hallway to the man down.

It was Chief Conrath. The man had a chest wound, similar to Sidney's. Conrath's breath rattled, signaling life. His service revolver, still warm, lay inches from his fingertips.

He'd fired the shots.

Grayson tore off his coat and applied pressure to the wound, praying the man would survive.

Why the bloody hell had Conrath attacked them?

———

Police officers rushed into the museum. The paramedics arrived seconds later, shooing Grayson and his people away from the injured. Grayson heard the sound of sirens blaring from outside.

He braced himself against the wall, watching and waiting for his heart rate to return to normal. He looked down at the blood soaked into his hands, and the blood stains on his shirt and suit coat. The tie his daughter had given him was ruined.

"You okay, boss?" David asked.

"Not injured," Grayson said. "Take charge and call Tony. See what his cameras picked up from this confrontation. The police will need those. Then head to the hospital. Get an update on the victims."

"What about you?"

"I can't leave. The police will want a statement from me, possibly even at the precinct," Grayson said. "And Dorothy will likely be here any moment."

David nodded, awkwardly patted Grayson's shoulder, and left to follow orders. A good man to have around. Solid. The NYPD should never have forced him out.

Windergaard strode down the hallway, crossing paths with David, but he clearly heading to Grayson.

Lovely. Just what Grayson needed.

But Windergaard only watched in silence as the paramedics loaded Sidney and Conrath onto stretchers and whisked them away to the ambulances.

"This is awful," Windergaard said.

"Yes." Grayson had no comforting words tonight. "But your paintings are safe. I hope that makes you happy."

Windergaard made no reply. Grayson's gaze fixated on the blood seeping into the concrete. Detective Newman came up to them. Grayson asked if Lt. Gilbert would be arriving.

"Any moment," Newman said.

"I'll be in the restroom," Grayson pointed to the door near where Conrath had been felled from his bullet.

"I'll let Lt. Gilbert know," the officer said.

"Thank you." Grayson strode down the hallway, hoping to collect himself.

He'd skirted death, once again. And the one person he wanted to talk to it about, Patricia, might never talk to him again.

CHAPTER TWENTY-ONE

TRISHA MADE several calls that afternoon, researching the editor who'd called her the other day, and the supposed dinner/banquet he wanted her to attend. So far, his credentials checked out. And the banquet appeared to be real, according to a friend who worked in the society pages and the venue owner that she'd called.

Attendees included numerous editors and publishers, including her old boss, Cardoza.

She wanted to avoid him. But, no, she would not screw up a possible job because he was an asshole.

After, she went back to the museum story. Something was fishy about how Windergaard had contracted for *Lost Treasures*. Sidney knew something too. Normally, she'd visit the Herald's morgue files, in the basement of the paper's building to pull up old stories on the museum, searching for any clue. But that'd been when she worked there.

Hell with it. She'd brazen it out later, walk through the Herald's front door, and hope building security hadn't gotten the memo about her being fired.

Adrienne was probably clear, given what Warren said. But that needed corroboration. And Trisha still wanted the inside guy, the one who'd gotten Adrienne killed. She wondered if Grayson had new leads, because he wouldn't give up either, but screw calling him. He'd made what he thought about her clear. He'd accused her of exchanging sex for information.

He could go sniff some Carbona or, lacking that, glue, for all she cared. Like Cardoza, Grayson hadn't even bothered to listen to her explanation. Men dressed in tailored suits were all the same.

She glanced at her kitchen and her collection of miniature motorcycles she'd built in the months when Nicky was sick. On his good days, he'd helped her build the bookshelves, including the one that acted as a wall between her bed and the living room.

This place was the home they were supposed to have, the life they were supposed to have.

She was asinine to have even had a passing thought about a future with Grayson. Hell, if he couldn't take learning she'd been fired, what would he say once she revealed the details of her juvie record?

The scanner in the corner crackled to life, reporting shots fired–at the Museum of Historic Arts. She cursed. The code for an ambulance went out and, from the chatter, Trisha could tell at least one person had been seriously injured.

A second later, a description of the injured man came over the scanner. Dark hair, possibly Hispanic, male.

David!

She grabbed her coat. Where? Museum? No, all the other reporters would head there. The victim of the shooting would be headed to the hospital, the same one where she'd been treated. She knew the nurses. They'd seen David with her. They might talk to her.

She'd fucked up with Grayson. She'd lost her job. She couldn't lose David too.

———

Once alone in the bathroom, Grayson stared at the blood on his hands. The same sick feeling he'd had when kneeling over Katz's body overwhelmed him. He swallowed down bile.

Bloody damned hell.

He needed Patricia to make a smart remark that would make him laugh. But she'd kept secrets from him too, the same as everyone else tied to this damned case. Grayson tossed off his suit coat, almost ripped off his shirt and tie, and hung them from a hook on one of the stall doors. A spot of blood had soaked through to his white T-shirt.

He washed his hands clean in the sink.

Out, out damned spot, eh?

The door swung open.

"English, is that blood on your T-shirt?" Dorothy asked.

"I'm not stripping that off. You can have the others if you need them for your crime scene evidence." His voice was almost a growl.

She shook her head. "I worried it might be your blood. Are you all right?"

"No, I'm not. So far, I've got one dead guard, I've nearly been blown up, I've had to fight for my life, had a woman collapse in my car, been lied to by my employer, been shot at, and shot someone who may die. And I'm no damn closer to finding out who's behind it all."

He turned off the water and shook off the droplets.

"But, no, I'm not physically injured," he said.

Dorothy remained still during his tirade. She wore jeans and a sweater tonight, meaning she'd been off duty, probably relaxing at home with her husband and sons.

Dorothy had a life.

"You saved the museum from a bomb, caught the murderers, and possibly just saved Sidney's life by shooting his attacker. And Conrath is still alive, so don't jump off that bridge just yet." She took a deep breath. "Besides which, your firm is providing some very interesting video footage of Conrath stalking down that hallway and aiming, proving he attacked first. You're in the clear. All I need is a quick statement right now." She set a hand on his forearm. "Perfection isn't obtainable, Edmund. Now take a deep breath, run down what happened from your point of view, and we can sort out the rest."

He used the sink for support, stared down at the white porcelain, and gave her a blow-by-blow description of tonight's events, concise and without emotion. He started with finding the photos of the older Windergaard and Warren. As he talked, the vice grip on his chest eased. By the time he finished, he'd calmed down and could think again. He handed

Dorothy the photos he'd found earlier. They'd still been tucked into the pocket of his suit coat, undamaged by tonight's events.

"A Windergaard and a Warren again." Dorothy slipped the photos in her inside jacket pocket. "I'll have a long talk with the director. But why the hell was Conrath shooting at you and Sidney?"

"In Windergaard's employ? If both of them were in on it, that it would explain bypassing the alarm the day of the murder."

"Possible, but there are a great many questions about that. If they wanted the paintings, why wait until the alarms were installed to take them?" Dorothy shook her head. "There's still a tangle here."

"I want to question Windergaard," he growled.

Dorothy was unfazed. "That anger is why you're staying on the sidelines."

"You expect me to do *nothing*?"

"I expect you to make a statement to me, provide all of your video footage to one of my officers, and make your people available to me."

"Fine." Once again, she was right, and he hated it.

"Quit the bitching." Dorothy shook her head. "You've done good work getting these photos. The case will break open soon. The only thing that surprises me is that Trisha Connell wasn't helping you."

"I'm sure she'll be angry to have missed this," Grayson turned his back, imagining Trisha's reaction. At least she hadn't been in danger tonight. That was something.

He paced away from Dorothy, resisting the impulse to punch a stall door, having nowhere to go with his anger and frustration. He grabbed the top of the door and braced himself. Anger had screwed up his relationship with Patricia last night. Anger would not solve the case.

Calm is what he needed.

He took a deep breath, inhaling the smell of antiseptic covering urine. Dorothy laid a hand on his back.

"Let it out for once. Anger won't kill you, English. You bury things too deep."

"What do you mean?"

"Hello, you gave up dating after Karen left. *For three damn years*. Classic overreaction to a rebound romance. And then you go off the deep end for the reporter? Talk about overcompensation."

He turned around. "You're just upset we haven't settled on a date for dinner yet."

"At least you're calm enough to tease me."

He shrugged. His rage has lessened, though the ball of anger remained, ready to strike with the right trigger.

"Is it a mid-life crisis? Because I'd recommend a sports car as a cure for that. It'll be cheaper and less trouble than the reporter."

"Whatever it is with Patricia, it's real. And serious. And a mess right now."

A pause. "God help you, Edmund, you've grabbed onto a stick of dynamite. Be careful, dammit."

She hugged him.

He stiffened in surprise and then hugged her back, hard.

She broke the hug after a long moment. "I don't know if that helps you, but *I* feel better. So tell me something."

"What?"

"Why Trisha Connell?" Dorothy asked. "I mean, I see the obvious, her looks, and that bad girl thing must be sexy as hell for men, plus the adrenaline rush from dealing with the bomb, but basing a decision on those things isn't who you are. Usually."

"It's all and none of those things." Grayson shook his head. "Patricia pisses me off enough to get through to me. Just like you."

Dorothy's mouth twisted, as if she'd just eaten something bitter. "We're not alike. I'm a cop. She spent time in juvie."

Grayson frowned. "How would you know that for certain?"

"She came with me to Riker's."

"I know that. You should've told me about the interview with Warren," he said.

"Once again, I cannot go over the case with someone involved in it. Let's leave it at that. Do you want to hear about your girl or not?"

He nodded. "Go ahead." Yes, he wanted her perspective.

"She turned pale the minute we entered the prison. I've never seen her so freaked. I give her credit, she fought it, but the fear grabbed onto her."

Never seen Patricia so freaked? Dorothy had missed the panic attack in the tunnels.

"Not everyone reforms, and she seems to run her life by a set of rules only she knows." Dorothy shook her head. "Did you know the *Herald* fired her for calling her boss an asshole? Not that she was wrong there."

"She told me, finally. Last night. I didn't take it well. She took my reaction even less well."

Dorothy grinned. "Then things are looking up. Remember. Sports car. Less dangerous."

Her police radio crackled. He caught Sidney's name.

"Is he going to live?" Grayson asked.

"He's alive, going into surgery," Dorothy answered.

"And Conrath?"

"Still alive as well. Now, come with me so I can write down your statement. I'm not taking it in a bathroom."

He followed her, glad to know he'd killed no one. Yet.

CHAPTER TWENTY-TWO

TRISHA CUT through several hidden alleys between buildings on the way to the hospital, nearly running down a rat, which skittered under a dumpster just in time to avoid the front tire of the Indian.

Cars were a pain in the ass in Manhattan. But the Indian could take shortcuts. She winced once as she took a turn, the rib injury reminding her it wasn't fully healed, but it was bearable.

She made good time, pulling into a lot across the street only twenty minutes after getting the scanner. She unbuttoned the denim jacket and shook out her hair. Cold. The denim didn't cut the wind like her leather jacket had, the one still in the police evidence room.

She rushed into the emergency room, sidestepping past a toddler throwing a fit in the waiting room. The wail cut through her. Poor kid. She turned, wondering if she could help, but he'd been scooped up by a woman who held him tight. He sniffled into her shoulder.

The kid had someone to watch over him. He'd be okay.

The air whooshing through the emergency room automatic doors blew away the antiseptic smells, a relief, because the one thing Trisha didn't need right now was another panic attack. She scanned the place, running her hands through her hair, hoping to spot a nurse or an orderly who she knew.

A hand tapped her shoulder.

She spun, fist clenched, only to be confronted by David himself, alive and well.

She threw her arms around him and hugged him tight. She buried her face in his shoulder, holding back the sniffles she didn't want him to see. "You're okay," she whispered.

He kissed the top of her head and ruffled her hair. "Yeah." He held her out at arm's length. "You were worried about me? Why?"

"Description over the scanner said one of the gunshot victims was Hispanic. I thought of you." She cleared her throat, collecting herself.

"Oh. That makes sense, given Sidney was one of the victims." David stared at her. "Wait, you were so concerned about me that you came *here* instead of covering the story at the museum?"

See, that's what happened when you let people know you worried about them. They called you on it. "Yeah." She breathed out. "Besides, I don't have a story to file anyway. Got fired from the paper. The publisher had a fit when I didn't report in that first night. Bitched me out. I called him an asshole. Bam. Fired."

The words came out in a jumble. There. She'd told three people now. She could handle this.

"Trish," David said in a low voice. "Damn."

"It's not important." She gritted her teeth and pulled him over to a corner. "David, what happened at the museum?"

"Good question. Sidney got shot. Grayson fired back—"

Grayson. She grabbed the lapels of David's coat. "Is he okay?"

"He's okay." He squeezed her hand tight. "So there is something going on there, huh?"

She shrugged and backed off. "I don't want to talk about it."

David shrugged back. "Good, because I sure as hell don't want to know about his sex life or whatever. But, hey, it's good to know you thought of me before him." He grinned.

She laughed and playfully hit his shoulder.

"See, you should have told me sooner about being fired. I'd have made you laugh about it."

"I know." She nodded. "But, c'mon, David, what happened at the museum?"

He glanced around, checking to see if they'd be overheard and launched into a quick rundown of the night's events.

"*Conrath* shot Sidney?"

"Yeah, surprised me too. I called Grayson for an update at the museum. He said Dorothy's executing search warrants on Conrath's home right now. Some judge got woken up in the middle of the night. But at least we'll have answers soon."

She nodded. "I hope so." She frowned. "If you're okay, why are you here?"

"I'm stationed here, just in case. Sidney and Conrath are in surgery, but someone shot at Sidney once. They might try again. So here I am. Want to keep me company?"

"That's the best offer I've had in days," she said.

She and David settled down in chairs that gave them a view of the outside doors and the hallway that led into the hospital. David had asked her to stay because he worried about her. She'd been too ashamed to tell him about being fired.

She should've known he'd offer her a shoulder. David wasn't Grayson. He'd never be her boyfriend. It wasn't as if she had many friends, and, damn, she would not lose the one she had.

"So anyway, I do have one job prospect." And she told him about the book editor as they settled in for a long night.

———

The next evening, Trisha stared in the mirror of her bathroom, smoothing out her new, classy but simple black dress. Makeup covered any signs of her lack of sleep. She'd stayed with David until the early hours of the morning. Conrath and Sidney had made it through surgery, but both were still sedated. She'd cut out of the hospital when David left. No sense waiting around when the nurses wouldn't talk to her and, more importantly, she had no story to write.

The dress exposed the tattoo on her back and the lightning bolt on her ankle. Hell, she'd even bought proper black pumps instead of the thigh-high boots she'd worn at the museum opening. This editor would have to be satisfied with her going this far.

Someone knocked on her door. David? Nah, he must be asleep. Probably Mrs. D. from the first floor. She liked to keep track of the coming and goings in the building.

Trisha looked through the peephole. *Grayson*

Shit.

She collapsed against the door. He knocked again. Face things, she thought. Pull it together. She opened the door. He looked immaculate, dressed in one of his tailored gray suits.

"Patricia. Thanks for letting me in."

"Better than arguing in the hallway." She shut the door behind him. "You were the last person I expected to see tonight. You doing okay after the shooting?"

He frowned, as if the question caught him off-balance. "Yes, I'm fine." He put his hands in his pockets and cleared his throat. "First, I wanted to apologize—"

"Not necessary."

"Excuse me?"

She walked to her window, opened it, and lit a cigarette from the pack sitting on the counter because she knew it would make him angry. That would make this easier.

"I was wrong," she said. "I should've told you about being fired. One of the many things I fumbled this past month. Not that it would've made a difference in the end with us."

She flicked cigarette ashes off the window ledge but didn't take a puff.

Silence, save for his breathing. She'd no idea what he was thinking. If only he would say something. Yell, scream, storm around her place. *Anything.*

"You were right," she repeated. "You don't need to apologize." She glanced at the clock on the stove. "Look, I gotta go."

She snuffed out the cigarette in her sink.

"I didn't expect—" He cleared his throat again. "I thought you'd be angry with me."

She shrugged. "Nope. My mistake. You're free and clear here."

"I don't want to be."

She pointed at him. "What is that supposed to mean?"

He focused on her, a shark that had scented blood.

"It means that walking away is not going to solve this. Patricia, I know I overreacted."

"Because you don't trust me," she said. "I get that."

"I'm doing this all wrong again." He rubbed a hand over his brow. "I'm sorry. I overreacted. Worse, I overreacted, the same as your publisher did, and never gave you a chance to explain. I jumped to the wrong conclusion. I know you're staying on the story because you want to clear Adrienne Katz and you already had all the information from me you needed before we had sex." A deep breath. "I'm here because I know apologies aren't enough. I want to come with you tonight to this dinner, be your plus one, do what I can to support you."

"Oh." The silence stretched out while she tried to sort out what he'd said. He'd realized what he'd done wrong without her pointing that out. "That's a damn good apology."

"You had trouble telling me because you were struggling with being fired yourself. It had nothing to do with deceiving me. It wasn't about me."

"That's for damn sure."

He dropped the mask and let her see the frustration in his open expression and the fear in his eyes.

She checked her watch. Still time. She almost wished she had to go. Maybe it was good to get this over with, now. "I'm sorry that you were shot at. I'm sorry you had to shoot someone. That sucks. I'm glad you weren't hurt." She wanted to hug him. Hell, she wanted to drag him off to bed. "But that doesn't change the fact that this thing between us is a mess. It was what, *two hours*, before we started sniping at each other?"

"But I think, ultimately, we understand each other."

Understand each other? Cops and killers. No way they should be together.

She'd been convicted of four counts of manslaughter in juvie court, though it was worse than that. She'd escaped her rapists and been home free. She could have walked away. Instead, she'd picked up the gun and killed her rapists. Not manslaughter. *Premeditated murder.*

Grayson looked over the blue couch and matching chair that faced her TV and stereo, then to the bookshelves that lined the walls, and the red Oriental rug that covered her floor.

"I won't pass a white glove test," she snapped.

"I never asked you to."

Damn you, Grayson. Get out.

She lifted the coffee mug that she'd drained while getting dressed. She rolled it around her hands to still her nervous fingers.

"It still won't work."

"That's it? You're just giving up?" he said. "You fight for everything else in your life but not us?"

"Do you have any idea how *sick* I am of fighting?" she asked, her voice rising. "Every time I think I've made progress, every time I think I'm fine, someone or something steps in the way and blindsides me.

"My foster father, dead. I watched the man I loved waste away before my eyes. My job, which I do better than any other reporter out there, and my publisher fires me because I don't fit his fucking employee profile." Well, that and she'd called him a fucking asshole. Because he was.

She tossed her mug into the sink. It made a nasty clinking sound against the metal. Likely she'd smashed it. So what. "You were right. It'll never be just sex with us, Grayson. It'll be heartbreak."

He shook his head. "You remember every word I'd said to you, don't you?"

Yeah, pretty much.

He took a step forward, she glared at him, and he froze. She put her back to him.

Oh, hell, if he touched her, her resolve would crumble.

He put his hand on her shoulder.

"You care so deeply about people it wounds you, so you hide it," he said. "Bloody hell, Patricia, you had enough for a story before we went into those tunnels. You went there because you were driven to know the truth of what happened to Adrienne Katz. And David, do you even realize what you did for him?"

"What does *David* have to do with this?"

"Dorothy told me David went into a serious free fall after his forced resignation from the NYPD. I agreed to interview him for a job because she asked, but we were both afraid that he was in such a tailspin he wouldn't show."

She frowned. "Yeah, so? What's that got to do with me?"

"The night after the murder, after we discovered you'd been rushed to the hospital, David was distraught. He told me what he owed you, that you'd practically dragged him to my office that day for the interview. He told me that's the kind of friend you are. 'Trisha would walk through hell for me,' he said. 'For any of her friends.'"

"Hah. I would walk through hell just for the hell of it."

"David added: 'And then she'd claim that she did it for another reason.'"

She shrugged and faced him again. "David wanted your job. All I did was give him a swift kick in the ass to jump-start him."

"You made certain he got his life back on track," Grayson said. "And then you rushed to the hospital last night in fear he'd been shot."

"Whatever. Does this lecture have a point?"

"I made my point already. Though it's odd you consider a compliment a lecture."

She had no idea what to say. Telling him to go would wreck him. Reaching out to him terrified her.

He shoved his hands into his pockets. He did that when he was nervous. "Whatever war you're fighting within, Patricia, I'll help you win it." He held out his hand. "You don't have to do this alone."

She reached out, as if in slow motion, as if there were a thousand miles between them, instead of inches. Finally, she clasped what he'd offered. He stroked the back of her hand with his thumb.

She ducked her head because her face felt hot and flushed. "This thing tonight, I hate the idea of being put on display. But I need the work, and it's a good idea to spotlight kids like Adrienne, see if telling their stories will make a difference."

"You helped me with my work. Time for me to support yours."

A firm but quiet voice. Even soft. She took one more deep breath and stared at him. He'd come to her. He'd apologized. No, he'd put actions behind his apology.

"What the hell," she said.

CHAPTER TWENTY-THREE

TRISHA CHECKED her dress one last time in the mirror before they left, conscious of Grayson staring at her.

"You look beautiful," he said.

"It's work. It's a room full of men in suits, including this editor. I know what this is. Maybe they'll want to check my teeth." She showed him her teeth.

"'No one can make you feel inferior without your consent,'" Grayson said.

"Quoting Eleanor Roosevelt? Not bad."

They walked down three flights of steps to the stoop of the brownstone outside. Grayson had parked his Mercedes Roadster at the end of the street. He was lucky to have found a spot so close to her building. Still, a few years ago, the Roadster might have been up on blocks or completely gone in five seconds flat. But Hell's Kitchen was changing—hell, real estate agents called it Clinton now. Plus, Mrs. Donohue, the old lady in her building's first floor apartment, kept a careful eye on her street. Everyone knew she'd spot a theft and probably confront the thieves themselves, if she was feeling especially spry.

The sun was just starting to set. Trisha put on her sunglasses to block the intense, low-level rays. Several teenagers sitting on the stoop across the street wolf whistled at her. She blew a kiss and gave them the finger while walking to the Mercedes.

They laughed.

She glanced over. Grayson's posture had changed to guard mode.

"Take a chill pill," she told him as they climbed into the car. "They're just kids, teasing."

Grayson looked back at them as they pulled out. "You know them?"

"Sure. Neighborhood kids." She settled back into the soft leather of the passenger seat. *I could get used to this pampering.* She didn't belong in this world. Grayson confused her. He moved so easily among the high class despite being a cop. He'd be great at this party. He'd fit in effortlessly.

She was a mess about it. Treat it like a story, then. Think about work. She pulled her notebook from her clutch purse. "So, what went down at the museum last night? From square one."

He drove and talked, not even asking her why she wanted the information. David had given her much the same information, but Grayson had a firsthand account. His voice grew flatter as he reached the shooting.

"Why the hell did Conrath shoot at you and Sidney?" She wanted to ask Grayson if he was okay. But he wasn't. He couldn't be. Still, he'd come to her. Maybe he needed her too. "Conrath had to be desperate."

"Yes, for some reason. But it's Windergaard I suspect now." And Grayson dropped the bomb about Warren and Windergaard who worked for the museum thirty years ago.

"Damn," she said. "*Legacy,* Warren used that word during the interview at the prison. I thought he meant the Nazi legacy. But maybe he meant a family legacy? What's Conrath's role in all this?"

"Maybe the museum connection is how Warren learned about the paintings. Conrath could be in Warren's pay."

"I'm not buying Windergaard is ignorant. He knew enough to be in a photo with Max Warren when he was a kid. And *someone* knew enough to purge the museum's written records," she said. "Why would Conrath need to do that?"

"I have no answers, only speculation." Grayson said.

"If Dorothy executed the search warrant, she might have evidence."

He scowled. "She won't tell us, not unless there's been an arrest. And I couldn't speak to Windergaard at the museum last night. Dorothy had him surrounded by officers."

"I made some calls at home, to my sources. I might hear something tonight."

He raised an eyebrow. "Who?"

"That would be telling." She smiled, feeling more herself. "So where does Sidney fit in, other than as broker?"

"Another question that needs an answer," he said as they reached the Plaza. No, the *Westin* Plaza now, at least until someone else bought it. Grayson skipped the valet parking and instead pulled into the lot under the hotel.

"I have an idea how to find information about Max Warren," she said.

"Another one of your mysterious sources?" he asked.

"Not quite. But you can help, after this, if you want."

"Absolutely," he said.

Grayson parked and walked around to help her out the passenger door, being a gentleman. Because she was wearing heels, she let him. He offered her his arm as they walked towards the parking garage elevator, and she accepted because why the hell not. It brought her close enough to feel the metal of the gun in his shoulder rig.

Her heels echoed on the empty concrete around her. They stepped into the elevator, and the doors closed. She shook her head as they stepped off the elevator into the elegant lobby.

"You know, I'm the one seen as the dangerous wild thing, Grayson. But here you are, the image of a perfect gentleman, and you're packing heat under that suit jacket. So who's the dangerous one?"

"People are seldom what they seem," he said. "It's not always a bad thing."

She swallowed hard, the nerves taking over again. She reflexively closed her hand around the cross. "Look, we walk in there, people will look at you, see the tailored suit, see the way you carry yourself, and give you respect."

"And?"

"And most of the men in the room will look at me and instantly start thinking of ways to get me into bed." She sighed. "Hell, probably this

Sarkozy guy does too. And yet *I* have to jump through their damn hoops. Lust isn't the same thing as respect, and you damn well know it."

"That's disappointing," he said.

"I know."

"I meant that it's disappointing that no one looks at me and thinks of how to get me into bed."

She laughed, despite herself.

They walked in together, her arm tucked in his. Just get through these few hours, she thought. Get her career back on track. She couldn't clear Adrienne if she couldn't afford to eat.

Crystal chandeliers hung from the high ceilings of the ballroom. White linen covered the tables, topped off with floral centerpieces and tall silver candlesticks. Classical music quietly serenaded the guests from unseen speakers.

A typical, stuffy high-class party, except for the banners. Book covers dating from the founding of the publishing house to the present day had been blown up and plastered all over the wall. It was odd seeing a book on the Watergate hearing plastered six feet high, to say nothing of the cover featuring the Son of Sam. What a crying shame nobody but their families and the cops remembered the names of Sam's victims. Dammit.

Was all that tragedy just entertainment to the people here? She'd believed journalists spoke truth to power, but maybe her work had just been a big show to entertain the people in penthouses. She needed a drink.

A young man in a power suit made famous by Wall Street brokers detached himself from a group and made straight for her.

"Ms. Connell?" He asked.

"Yes?"

"Hi, I'm Jim Sarkozy. It's very good to meet you."

The man was tall, on the thin side, and good-looking in a pretty-boy way. His haircut was designed to artfully fall in front of his left eye. He looked about seventeen. *Does your mama know that you're out, kid?*

They shook hands, quickly. Decent grip, she thought.

"Ms. Connell, I'm so glad you came," Sarkozy said. "I look forward to working with you."

"It's just 'Trisha'" she said.

"Then call me Jim."

She turned and introduced Grayson. Sarkozy frowned as the men shook hands. Grayson's face held no expression, and she had no idea if that was his bored party expression or if he'd taken an instant dislike to Sarkozy.

"So now that you've got me here, what did you want to talk about, Jim?" she asked.

He cleared his throat. "You get right to the point."

"It's not the usual place for a meeting with a potential editor to discuss a contract," she said.

"All will be explained," he said. "Come with me, I'll show you to your table."

Trisha knew she was being maneuvered, but her curiosity won. She'd hear him out. Job. Work. Food and rent money. She liked eating. And a roof over her head.

Those were the same reasons she'd put up with this bullshit of being studied for flaws all those years at the paper. That and she loved the work.

"How old is he? *Twelve?*" Grayson whispered into her ear.

"I started as an intern when at nineteen," she said in a low voice, making sure they were several steps behind Sarkozy.

"He's not you," Grayson said.

"Tell me about it."

When they reached the table, she spotted a familiar figure.

"Joe?"

Joe's eyes widened in surprise, and then he grinned, which was even more disconcerting because Joe never grinned. He never wore suits either, though this wrinkled green one hardly qualified. At least his wavy hair looked as disheveled as ever.

"I've said it before, you clean up well, kid."

She ignored the compliment. "What are you doing here?"

"I have to do some of these publisher-style events now and then. I'm standing in for Kent, the managing editor, who begged off."

Trisha looked at Sarkozy, who managed a weak smile. "What's going on?" she asked.

"All will be clear soon. I'll be right back." He put a finger to his lips, conspiratorially. "I think you'll be pleased."

Trisha watched him go. "That's one suspicious exit." She shook her head. "Shit. I shouldn't have come."

"Careful with the language," Joe said, tilting his head at the girl standing in his shadow.

The kid looked about fifteen or sixteen. But–why would Joe bring a teenager...oh.

"*Jenna?*" When did Joe's daughter get so grown up? "It's been a while."

Jenna stood, nearly the same height as her father. "I remember you. You whooshed into my ninth birthday party. You brought the best present." She smiled quietly, composed.

"Thanks." Trisha remembered the birthday party, a cacophony of high-pitched voices, cake, and screeching. God knows how Joe had managed to convince her to deliver Jenna's present in person. Maybe he'd been worried about disappointing his daughter.

Jenna had grown from that little girl to this nearly grown person in an elegant purple dress? The party didn't seem that long ago.

"You haven't introduced your date, Trisha," Joe said.

Date. Yes. She supposed this counted as date, except that it was really a business meeting and she and Grayson had settled nothing.

"Joe, Edmund Grayson. Grayson, this is Joe Wilson, the *Herald's* city desk editor. My editor." She frowned. "Ex editor."

"Grayson." Joe said. "Not the man who disarms bombs with one hand and takes down armed Nazis with the other?"

"Only as a hobby," Grayson said.

Jenna laughed. Joe smirked. Trisha only glared when Joe raised his eyebrow at her. No, she wasn't going to talk about Grayson, especially not here.

Instead, she pointed at the crowd. "What am I doing here at a table with you and Jenna and Sarkozy?" She glanced at the empty seats. "Do you know Sarkozy? And who else is sitting here?"

Joe crossed his arms and rubbed his chin, a contemplative look. "Good question. I thought it was odd for Kent to pass an invite onto me. Something's going on. As for who else is at the table, there's the senior editor at Sarkozy's publishing company." A pause. "His name is Paul Cardoza, brother to the Herald's publisher. I suspect the other seats are for him and our Cardoza."

Trisha bit her tongue to stop the string of curses about to escape. Not in front of Jenna. "This is a setup," she hissed out. "An ambush."

Grayson moved closer to her, whether to stop her from doing something stupid or for support, Trisha didn't know.

"They want something from you," Grayson said.

"Sure seems like it," Joe agreed. "I'm curious as hell about what."

Jenna's eyes grew wide. "This is gonna get messy, right?"

"I don't have to stay here and take this," Trisha said.

Grayson pulled out her chair. "The only way to find out what they want is to stay and let them reveal it."

"Maybe he's going to apologize," Joe said in a low voice.

"Yeah, and maybe I'm Mother Theresa."

But Trisha sat down anyway. She'd been neatly maneuvered into this party. Time to find out why.

She scanned the crowd. "Where are the Cardozas, anyway?"

"Probably watching us from somewhere," Grayson said. "Wondering what you might do. I can do a circuit of the room and look for them." A pause. "And get you a drink at the same time."

"You're on," she said.

Grayson offered to fetch drinks for Joe and his daughter, too, causing Jenna to preen at the attention.

Once he left, she pounced on Joe. "You were setup to be here too."

"I'd agree," Joe said. "I sure hope it's for Cardoza to apologize and rehire you. Borelli is good with the courts, but he's no match for you on the crime beat."

"Who is?" Trisha snorted. "But, c'mon, you think Cardoza will apologize in front of his brother and everyone else at the table? Fat chance."

"Still, Sarkozy invited you for a reason." Joe glanced at the bar in the far corner, where Grayson stood in line. "At least you brought back-up. Good for you."

"He's watching over you," Jenna said, leaning forward past her father. "That's sweet."

Trisha rolled her eyes. "He ain't sweet." But he'd brought her a Walkman. And fluffy socks. Maybe he was.

"Oh, gimme a break," Jenna said.

Smart kid.

Grayson's return cut off that conversation. He handed out the drinks. Trisha sniffed her glass. Smelled like whiskey plus something else.

"What is it?" she asked.

"An old-fashioned," he said. "It's strong. Drink up."

She sipped the drink. He wasn't kidding. Though she'd prefer whiskey, straight up, this thing was seriously deadly. Exactly what she needed.

Argh. Grayson. Stop doing perfect things.

Grayson's gaze swept the room again. She'd instinctively put her back to the wall when choosing seats, and he'd grabbed the chair that afforded him the best view of the room. He never went completely off-duty.

She glanced over to make sure Jenna and Joe weren't watching and took a long swallow. It burned her throat on the way down, chasing away the last of her nerves.

"What present did you get for your ninth birthday?" Grayson asked Jenna.

"Excuse me?" Jenna frowned.

"You said Patricia 'whooshed in your party and brought the best present.' What was it?"

His voice was mild, friendly, and soothing.

"Oh. Yeah." Jenna smiled quietly again. "An autographed baseball. It was great—the entire lineup of the Yankees and Steinbrenner, too. It's on my desk at home, in a protected glass case. How'd you get it, Trisha? I've always wondered."

She shrugged. "It wasn't too hard to find Boss Steinbrenner. He hangs around the stadium a lot during the season. The players took a little bit more work, but you just have to know where to look for them after hours. I'm glad you liked it."

"It was great." Jenna leaned back in her chair, craning her neck. "That tattoo on your back is very cool. Is that a flame bird?"

"It's a phoenix."

"Did it hurt? How much does it cost? How long did it take?" Jenna asked.

"Jenna, just because Trisha chooses to let someone inject her with dye through a sharp needle and deface her body doesn't make it right," Joe said.

"Jenna, yes, it hurt, although the one on my ankle hurt worse because it was over bone. The cost depends on the artist, and it took several hours. The tattoo will be stiff and sore for several weeks, but then it'll heal nicely," Trisha said. "Any reputable tattoo artist will turn you away until you're eighteen. And believe me, you want a good one, so you better wait. Unless you can somehow con your dad into agreeing while you're underage." She looked over at Joe, who was still scowling. "Doesn't seem likely."

"You're corrupting my daughter," Joe said.

"Oh, right. Give the kid some credit."

"Yeah, Dad. Gimme credit."

Father and daughter started bickering, though it seemed too good-natured to be a real fight. Trisha looked away and blinked away a tear in her eye. Lucky Jenna.

Warm breath washed over her back. Grayson, shifting close enough to stare at her phoenix tattoo.

"You're supposed to be watching the room so we have warning when my firing squad shows up," she said.

"I can do two things at once." He lowered his voice. "What do you think they want?"

"Me, and that's not a good thing." She took another long swallow of the old-fashioned.

Joe, finished with the good-natured bickering with his daughter, finally, turned back to Trisha. "So tell me what Sarkozy wants with you, Trisha?"

Joe always had good insight. As she had with Grayson, she gave him the rundown, about how Sarkozy had talked about reading her stories of children caught in the system, or tragedy, or both, and their struggles to make it to adulthood.

"You still track them all?" Joe asked. "I didn't realize."

"When I can. The juvie courts don't make it easy to find a paper trail, and some of these kids want to vanish. The idea is to find someone who's making it, see what worked, and if that can be applied to the other kids in the system. The right social worker, the right school, that kind of thing. There's an informal network to help them, above and beyond what the law requires." And sometimes those people bent the laws too.

"You're a part of that," Joe said.

She shrugged. "Networking—connecting to people who know what they're doing—is what I do. It's what you taught me to do."

"Sounds more like saving kids than networking," Grayson said.

She gritted her teeth. "Not all of them. Sarkozy's book might get them publicity or money, might lead to some changes in the whole system down the line, so I'm for it, if it's done my way. But he brought in the Cardozas, so I doubt it'll be *my* way."

"There is one comforting thought to add," Joe said.

"What's that?" she asked.

"If they maneuvered me into this dinner, like they did you, they wanted someone you're comfortable with around, maybe even an ally," he pointed out. "Whatever they want, it's a good thing for you."

Grayson nodded. "That's my assessment."

A good thing? Fat chance. But before she could voice that doubt, as if on cue, Sarkozy returned, this time with his senior editor, Paul Cardoza. This Cardoza brother was slightly older, grayer, and a little less rumpled than his brother, Mordechai, who ran the *Herald*.

Mordechai Cardoza arrived during his brother's introductions. He merely nodded and took the seat to the other side of Jenna, and barely looked at Trisha. So she stared at him, hoping to bore holes in his tux, thinking evil thoughts, until he broke and spoke to Jenna instead.

When she introduced Grayson, he said something polite and complimented Mordechai Cardoza on having hired the best reporter for the *Herald*'s crime beat. He'd stuck that needle in deep, Trisha thought. Cardoza pursed his lips, uncertain, and Trisha decided he didn't recognize Grayson from the museum story. So much for him paying close attention to the *Herald*'s best stories.

Servers arrived with the first course of salad, cutting off any conversation. Trisha remained silent, remembering her tactic with Stephen Warren. People talked into the silence and revealed themselves. Let these men stew. Trisha's fingers twitched and she fiddled with her now empty glass.

Grayson, sensing her tactic of silence, made small talk with Jenna, the only other person at this table without an agenda. He asked her about school and mentioned the name of his daughter's high school. Jenna knew a few kids who also attended that school. That sent them to talking about the women's basketball team. It seemed Grayson's daughter was a point guard. A good one.

Grayson charmed Jenna by being so gushy about his daughter. It was kind of adorable. Trisha bet he was a good father, given he knew so much about her life, even the names of all her teammates. A lot of men wouldn't like having daughters play sports, even now.

When that thread of conversation ended, Paul Cardoza finally spoke into the quiet that was punctuated by silverware scraping across plates.

"My assistant editor, Jim, is most impressed with you, Ms. Connell."

"He's impressed with my work, you mean." Here we go, she thought.

"*You* and your work," Jim said, glancing at his boss. "I want to move fast on this book, to capitalize on the publicity around the museum articles, especially since Adrienne Katz, as one of the kids you've followed, will be in the book."

"Especially given her mysterious role in the museum robbery," Paul Cardoza interjected. "Speculation about that has been leading articles in all papers for the past week."

Not all the papers. Kimba at the *Tribune* had never pointed the finger at Adrienne.

"Adrienne's role was simple: she tried to stop a theft and ended up dead," Trisha snapped.

Mordechai Cardoza spoke into the silence that followed. "Is that opinion based on any facts, or is that your personal observation yet to be corroborated?"

Oh, hell, yes, they were going to do this. *"Fact."* She glanced at Joe. "Off-the-record."

"But it would make an excellent article," Joe muttered.

"Fact," Grayson added.

"I'd expect your date to agree with you," Cardoza said.

Trisha shrugged, unwilling to show he got to her. "As it happens, the police know the truth, especially Lt. Dorothy Gilbert." She glanced at Joe again. "That is also off-the-record, so you can't give the tip to Borelli to pursue."

"Trisha, you're killing me here," Joe said.

"Ms. Connell," Paul Cardoza said in a sharp tone that refused all eyes on him. "I don't deny that Mr. Sarkozy has a terrific idea for a book, and I can't and won't deny that you can write. You're talented. But if you're going to be the face of a book, we have to know you're responsible and presentable."

Rage flooded her. "Explain," she said.

Sarkozy glanced at his boss. The young editor's face was flushed. Perhaps this wasn't going as he planned.

"It's great you have the information on what happened to Adrienne Katz. That's perfect for the book. Um, as for what's meant by responsible, I'm willing to take Mr. Wilson's word about how conscientious you are."

"I've always been an advocate of Trisha Connell's work." As Joe said that, he stared directly at Mordechai Cardoza.

Thanks, Joe, she thought. The compliments felt good. But he had a family to support. He shouldn't piss off his boss.

"I see that's settled." Jim Sarkozy cleared his throat. "And by presentable, Mr. Cardoza just means that we need you to look good for our publicity campaign. Which," he smiled, "you do. You're perfect for television, Trisha. I can arrange a photo shoot and some interviews with reviewers, and I suspect we might get a magazine story or two, which would give the book the right push—"

"You want the kids as part of the photo shoots and interviews?" She frowned, trying to digest this. "I'm not sure they'd agree to that level of going public."

"Oh, no." Sarkozy waved that away. "It's your book, Trisha. You're the face of it. All this would be for you. The book contract would be a considerable investment, so Mr. Cardoza wanted to meet you in person before signing off, to ensure you had the right look for the campaign."

"And I can see that you will do well in that respect," Paul Cardoza said.

Jim nodded in agreement, his eyes lit with eagerness.

She'd been right. They were examining her for flaws. Worse, Sarkozy had missed the point.

"It's not my book, Jim, it's the *kids'* book," she said. "I'm just the messenger here. I want to tell their stories to help them, expose the systems that screwed them over, and give them a share of the profits in any book."

"Oh. I hadn't…" But he smiled again, quickly back on track.

"Some profits donated to a charity that would benefit the subjects of the book would be a fine marketing angle," Paul Cardoza said, taking up the conversation. "That is an excellent idea, Ms. Connell. May I call you Trisha?"

She narrowed her eyes. "Trisha's fine. But the kids aren't a marketing opportunity. They're the *whole point.*"

"For once, you are downgrading yourself, Ms. Connell," Mordechai Cardoza interjected. "You can write. That I've known for some time. And your passion for your work has never been the problem." He glanced at Grayson. "And perhaps you can change, given your presence tonight, and the company you're keeping. You might be worth the investment after all."

"Excuse me?" Had she heard any of that correctly?

"I gave you a compliment, Ms. Connell," Mordechai Cardoza said. "Take it. And perhaps after this book contract is finalized, we could have a discussion about your role at the *Herald*. I understand there were some mitigating circumstances to your situation, such as you being ill and under the influence of painkillers."

Discussion about her role at the *Herald*. Mitigating circumstances. No apology offered. Using getting the kids and money earmarked for them as a marketing angle.

Fury, pure unmitigated rage filled Trisha.

Sarkozy, unaware, kept talking. "I'll get the book contract to your home by tomorrow, Trisha. I think you'll be happy with the offered advance."

She stood, drawing all their attention.

"No," she said.

Sarkozy blinked. "I don't understand."

"None of you *understand.*" She focused on Paul Cardoza. "These kids that you want to use for marketing have had enough trouble in their lives and shouldn't star in your dog and pony show." She speared Mordechai Cardoza with a glance. "And your mitigating circumstances, Mr. Cardoza, is that I had blood filling my lungs. I almost died getting a story that you put on the front page, *even after you fired me.* And I had to fight like hell with HR to get workman's comp insurance to cover the hospital bills."

Mordechai Cardoza tossed his napkin on his plate. "Careful, Ms. Connell. You have a lot at stake here."

She laughed, gone round the bend now, no longer caring. "I have *nothing* at stake. I can freelance and cover whatever stories I want. But for some reason, *you* wanted me here. Why? To bow down and acknowledge all these gifts you're giving me?" She looked at Sarkozy again. "A book contract." She focused on Paul Cardoza. "A publicity campaign that might make me famous." She met Mordechai Cardoza's gaze again. "My job back." She gripped the back of her chair, her hands clenched into fists. "But only if I grovel for you. Only if I toe the line and make you all look good."

She took a deep breath and met Joe's eyes. Yes, she read understanding there. Good.

"You three can find yourself another girl. Take your book contract and your job offer and shove them up your ass."

With that, she turned and strode to the door, anger and fury fueling every step. Jenna's "whoa" echoed in the silence behind her.

CHAPTER TWENTY-FOUR

GRAYSON FOLLOWED in Patricia's wake. It wasn't until they entered the lobby, away from them, that she turned to face him.

"What the hell do you want?" she growled.

"You," he said simply. "Bravo, Patricia. Well done."

"They wanted to use me without accepting any fucking responsibility. They wanted to use the kids for the same reason. That's not why I do this."

"I know," he agreed.

"That's all you have to say, Han Solo?"

"That says it all nicely, doesn't it?"

Patricia stood there, in the elegant lobby, looking more beautiful in her fury than anyone he'd ever met, and all he wanted to do was seize her and do what he'd done that night at his office.

Trisha would walk through hell for me. David's word rang through is brain again. *And she'd probably get a kick out of it too.*

She would, and had, walked through hell for these kids that she worried and celebrated and mourned, like Katz. She needed the adrenaline rush of chasing stories, yes, but the kind of stories mattered to her. They always would.

"So, what's next?" he asked.

The question seemed to reach her past her anger.

"Let's go."

They retraced their steps, back to the elevator and the parking garage. When they stepped out of the elevator, she elaborated. "That photo of Max Warren you talked about. He worked at the museum, but you couldn't find anything about him in the records, right?"

"Nothing except his job title."

"I bet the museum tried to scrub out his history. We need to know what happened to him."

"Absolutely. Research at the library, perhaps?"

"Better than the library. But we have to hurry before the *Herald* completely locks me out. We need their morgue files, and we need them now."

He stopped at his Mercedes. "The *morgue*?"

"The morgue is what we call the room where the *Herald's* physical files are kept. The morgue holds all the microfiche plus clippings arranged by subject, from papers that haven't been digitized yet. I want to research the years that Max Warren and Henry Windergaard were employed at the museum."

"That's an excellent idea."

"If I hadn't been fired, one of the first things I'd have done the next day as a follow-up would've been to spend time in the morgue files, looking at the museum's history. But Joe didn't have time and obviously no one else thought about it. If I had, we might have found this connection sooner."

Grayson held open the passenger door for her, they settled in again and he pulled out of the parking spot. She closed her eyes. Tired? No, pondering, he decided.

"Do you want to go home and change first?" he asked.

"I just pissed off everyone again, and my last official day is tomorrow, according to HR, so we better go tonight before they have orders to toss me out of the building."

They made good time to Hell's Kitchen and the nondescript squat building that held the newspaper's offices.

"You can drop me at the corner," she said.

"We're working this together. I have as much at stake as you do." He wasn't letting her out of his sight again.

"Okay, sure. It'll be faster with two people looking."

Huh. That was easier than he expected. He found a rare parking spot on the street, and she used her newspaper ID card to gain them entry to the *Herald's* offices.

"Keeping odd hours again, Red?" the guard at the front security desk asked.

"Always, Jerry," she answered. "How's the new kitten?"

"She's moved on from shredding the couch to shredding paper. At least that's easier to replace."

"Awesome," she laughed.

Grayson wasn't surprised she knew the guard's name or that he had a new kitten. She paid attention to people. Always.

He followed her down the flight of steps off the lobby.

"When you said morgue, I wasn't picturing an actual basement." His voice echoed in the cramped stairwell. He had a good view of the phoenix tattoo on her back or would have, if the lighting had been better.

And once again, they were descending below ground together.

"It's something to do with it being easier to maintain an even temperature down here and that helps preserve the clippings," she said. "But we won't encounter anything more dangerous than paper cuts in this underground."

She'd also been thinking about their descent into the subway tunnels. Good. She'd called their fledgling relationship a bad fit earlier, like a cop dating a criminal. She didn't see any of her actions as heroic. But they were. He wouldn't give up on her. And after that scene at dinner, he knew she hadn't given up on herself.

The morgue sat on the far side of a cavernous basement. As with the museum archive, the morgue was air-sealed, and temperature regulated.

Patricia pressed the code into the door lock, and it opened. "Whew. Easy enough to get in. I was worried they'd changed the code."

Gray file cabinets dominated one side of this morgue. Black cabinets marked "microfiche" dominated the other, with microfiche readers in the middle.

"Charming," he said.

"Hence the gloomy name," she said. "Morgue also comes from the fact that the paper keeps files on famous people. Makes it easier to write up the obituaries." She pointed at the file cabinets. "You take W for Warren, I'll take M for museum in a minute. Use that big table next to the copiers in the back to sort them out."

"What are you going to do first?" he asked.

"I'll call from the phone down here to see if my contact knows anything about the search of Conrath's apartment."

She could have used the phone in his car. He wouldn't tell her that. She'd probably forgotten he had one.

He knelt to the W file, watching her out of the corner of his eye. She spoke in a low voice, teasing, friendly, evidently learning something that she scratched into the miniature notebook that she'd stuffed in her clutch purse.

"Nope, not talking about that. You'd got enough from me already," she said.

He opened the drawer as she hung up. "Learn anything important?"

"Kimba, who has my job at the *Tribune*, said $40,000 cash was found stuffed in the mattress of the spare bedroom of Conrath's house." Her eyes gleamed, on the hunt once more. "It's good info. Newman's her contact."

"That makes money his motive," he said. "But where did the money come from?" He frowned. His theory of the paintings still being in the museum was shaky again.

"Conrath sold the paintings?"

"Or someone paid him off. Sidney, wanting to grab some of his paintings? Warren's people? Hell, maybe Windergaard? Let's see if we can find the answer."

She grabbed files from the "M" drawer and sat at the industrial metal table, concentrating. He'd seen her chasing a story, badgering people for quotes, and at crime scenes, noticing everything. But now she reminded him of how she'd poured over the files at his office.

A true scholar lived inside her, hidden under the punk. He wondered if she'd memorized homework at Colombia the same way she memorized credit card numbers.

Yet all that restless intelligence had almost been lost. Rage bubbled as he thought of how she'd been scarred as a child. Fate had been unfair to her. He wanted to be a part of evening that balance.

"Grayson, are you going to just stare at me or get to work?"

Busted. "Sorry."

He took off his coat, rolled up his sleeves, and set to the task at hand. None of the file folders in the W drawer were marked "Warren," and no others related to the information they needed. That left him with the two folders with general "W" clippings. He laid the clippings out flat on the table to flip through them.

Patricia had taken off her strappy high-heeled shoes and already had her end of the table stacked with file folders marked "Museum of Historic Arts."

She glanced up. "Hopefully, we get lucky."

I already have.

He glanced past articles about waterfalls, corruption in the city's water department, and wallpapers. Often two parts of articles clipped from the paper where stapled together, creating irregular shapes, and causing them to overlap. Separating them was slow and painstaking.

Patricia read faster. But she'd done this before.

More time passed. The ancient newsprint left dust on his fingertips.

"Aha! Survey says: Nazi!" She displayed a long, thin article headlined *Museum Curator Resigns Because of Nazi Ties.*

"'Max Warren was asked to leave his post,'" she scanned the article. "...'he is the son of admitted Nazi...there was criticism that his post-war exhibit was too forgiving of the Nazis and there wasn't enough emphasis on the Holocaust...Warren contacted for comment and refused...crap."

"What?"

"That's the end of the first part of the article. It's continued on another page, but that page is missing. Possibly someone forgot to clip it out. It happens often enough."

"Maddening. What now?"

She grinned. "Now that I have a date, I can check the microfiche files for the rest of it."

They dived into the drawers of microfiche, sorted by date. He found it first, gestured to her, and plugged it into one of the machines.

"You know your way around one of these," she said.

"I've learned primary sources are the best sources," he said. "I researched the history of the Museum of Historic Arts back for a decade when I took the job. I should have gone further."

The original Max Warren article had been on page one of the city section and continued to page eight. He zoomed quickly to page eight.

She leaned over his shoulder, her breath on his ear. He blinked, his concentration broken, and refocused.

Warren refused comment when contacted. His cousin, Henry Windergaard, the museum's director, issued a statement that he was appalled at the hate directed at the post-war display and promised to be open to any changes. Windergaaard denied that his father or Warren's father, both natives of Germany, had any Nazi connections and challenged this reporter to prove it.

Despite those denials, several patrons of the museum, speaking on conditions of anonymity, suggested that Windergaard should also resign.

Patricia straightened, her eyes quite literally sparkling. There. That. That was the high voltage energy he needed for the rest of his life.

"The grandfathers of our Warren and Windergaard were German, probably served in the German army in World War II. That collection in *Lost Treasures* had to come from one of them."

"And one or both of our contemporaries found it and used Sidney to front for them." he said.

"We need confirmation of our Warren and Windergaard as cousins. Windergaard's unusual. That helps. But Warren is a common name. There must be something else in here," she said.

More digging through the clippings on the museum. He finally uncovered a follow-up article on Max Warren. "Max Warren died not long after resigning his post at the museum."

"How?"

"Records are unclear," Grayson said. "But the obituary lists a son, Stephen, as a survivor."

"And I found a later story that confirms Henry Windergaard was forced to resign as director about six months later," she said. "And we know our director is his son from the photos you found. I wish we had a copy of those."

"I should have made copies. I was distracted by someone shooting at me."

"Yeah. Sorry."

But he smiled. This was confirmation they needed. Trisha photocopied the articles, after printing another from the microfiche reader.

"No wonder our Windergaard is so dedicated to the museum, to prove they were wrong about his father," she said. "And Stephen Warren must be out for revenge against the museum. That would explain why he wanted to blow up the place."

"Perhaps Windergaard knew of his grandfather's hidden artwork, commissioned Sidney as the middleman, then had him transport the collection in order to raise the profile of the museum," Grayson said.

Patricia picked up the speculation. "And then Warren, who is steeped in Neo-Nazi culture because of *his* father, heard about the exhibit and decided to get his revenge."

"That would fit if Warren wasn't aware of the exhibit until it was publicly announced." Grayson placed the copies in a blank folder. "And Warren paid off Conrath?"

"Maybe? Someone paid him off but Windergaard has to know that Warren is his second cousin and vice versa. Yet neither mentioned that."

"That does not look good for Windergaard," he said.

"He knew all this artwork had been seized from the original Jewish owners. He's taking blood money for the museum."

She leaned against the file cabinets, staring ahead at nothing. Her mind was already whirling seven steps ahead. He decided not to tell her that her dress was riding up almost to her underwear and instead enjoyed the view.

"You already have the lead for that story you're contemplating," he said.

"Naturally." She frowned. "But I'd have to get a comment from Windergaard before it runs or, you know, if it ever runs. And I'll have to ask for that comment in person, since Windergaard's not answering my phone calls. Wish I had those photos. They'd make a great addition to the article."

She smoothed down her dress. Too bad.

"We could talk to Windergaard at the museum tomorrow, er, today." Grayson glanced at his watch. Three a.m. already? "He told me yesterday that he would be at the museum early today, working the phones, hoping the police would let him reopen ASAP."

"Sure."

Grayson grabbed his coat. "Come with me to my office. It's daytime in Germany. I may be able to get that confirmation about the grandfather."

A smile flitted across her face. "Sure you're not thinking of sex in the conference room instead?" She filed the folders and slipped her shoes back on.

"I'll always think of the conference room differently, but my office is on the same side of Manhattan as the museum, and I can work there until it's time to confront Windergaard with the information."

"Perfect. Though if I'm going to be up all day and all night, I should change at some point. Stupid dress feels like a straitjacket."

"I have clothes at the office."

"You have women's clothes at your office?" She locked the morgue door as they left. "Have a lot of women to dress, do you, Grayson?"

"Often, my people need to blend into the crowd," Grayson said. "We have a walk-in closet with clothing appropriate for all types of security details as a result. I found it works better to supply clothes than letting the detail guess the proper attire."

"That. Is. Cool. And this, I gotta see."

They walked to the stairwell. Machines hummed around them, and the pinging of the pipes echoed off the ceiling. She closed her eyes and set her palm flat on the wall. "Those vibrations are the printing presses. You can feel them in the whole building when you're working through the night. All the writing I'd done, rolling off the presses. I'm gonna miss it." She shook her head and removed her hand. "Let's go."

———

They drove cross-town, and Grayson parked in the lot under his office building. Trisha glanced at her watch. *The Herald*'s print run had just started, but the other newspapers could be out already if nothing had pushed up against deadline. "There a newsstand nearby?"

"Out in front. Why?"

"I want to see if any of the papers are out yet and if they've got anything on the museum story. Kimba obviously has the info about Conrath's cash, but I don't know if it'll be in today's story."

"Of course," Grayson said in that elegant way of his.

The newsstand owner informed them the day's newspapers hadn't arrived yet. Grayson gave the man his office number and slipped him a twenty to call when they were delivered

"Thanks," she said because that was thoughtful.

They took another elevator up to the floor that housed his company and rode in silence. Grayson seemed to be good at quiet. She hated quiet but had no idea what to say except about the story.

He unlocked the glass front doors and entered his firm. As they walked down the carpeted hallway, Trisha caught a glimpse of a black leather couch behind his half-open office door. She wondered if he ever got up to shenanigans on that couch.

Or if he wanted some tonight. Or if she did.

Grayson was *serious* about her. Terrifying.

Grayson turned left in the hallway and opened the door to an interior room with no windows and turned on the lights.

"Whoa."

Walk-in closet, ha. This room was almost as big as her apartment. Men's clothing on one side, women's on the other, plus a changing area in the back. Shoes of all kinds were neatly stacked on the wall.

"Damn," she said. "You picked out all the women's clothes?"

"My office manager, Lois, did," he said. "She said it was the best part of the job. She especially liked shoe shopping."

"Next time Lois needs to make a clothing run, have her call me."

"Several of my female agents and one male agent expressed the same sentiment."

"Send them on shopping trips with Lois and they'll love you as a boss forever," she said.

"Good to know."

She skipped past the dresses and evening wear and grabbed jeans, a black T-shirt with a Batman logo from the old TV show, and a pair of black Converse High Tops. Perfect. She held up the sneakers. "Why do you have these?"

"We work certain large events for record companies. Apparently, they're in fashion among their new recording artists."

"High Tops are always in fashion. But they need to look more worn, like the pair I have at home. But these will do." She glanced around, trying to guess where his people would wear the other clothes. "What other kinds of parties do you work?"

"All kinds."

"Not all kinds, or you'd have more black leather and latex in this room."

Grayson pointed to an oversized, locked metal trunk set against the back wall. "In there."

"You're kidding."

He smiled. "Try me."

She laughed and shooed him out of the room before ducking behind a divider to change. The jeans fit except for some extra room in the calf probably to allow room for an ankle holster. Nothing in this room was here by chance.

She settled on a black leather duster for a coat. Nice. Not good for fighting, but she wasn't going to do any fighting today.

She walked out into the hallway. "Grayson?"

"Here in the conference room."

The conference room. *Great.*

The table was just as she remembered, though the chairs were all in their proper places tonight. Grayson spoke to someone quietly on the phone. He'd changed into gray slacks, a collared shirt, ditched the tie, and wore tassel loafers instead of the wingtips.

Yummy, yummy.

"I'm getting something right now from my contact," he said, his hand over the phone.

"Great." When in doubt, fake the nonchalance. She flopped into one of the chairs, put her feet up on the table, and pushed the chair out toward the wall.

He scribbled on a pad, said, "Danke," hung up, and focused on her.

"Careful with the chair."

"Why? The sneaks are white-glove clean," she said. "Besides, we weren't worried about the table getting dirty the last time we were in here."

Oh, crap. She hadn't meant to refer to that.

He blushed. Grayson blushing? What the hell?

"A little late for modesty, don't you think?" she said.

His blush deepened. "Just don't bang that chair against the wall."

He hadn't worried about banging her against the wall the other night, but now he was worried about a chair? She inched back a little more to tap the wall with the back of the chair.

"Don't!" He stalked over to her.

Odd. "What's wrong with you?"

He stuffed his hands into his pockets, a clear sign of nerves.

"I, um, there is a hidden switch to the cameras that bracket this room in the chair rail. I would rather not turn them on tonight."

"Why not just say that in—" Her eyes widened. "Cameras? *You have cameras in here?*" She stood up so fast that she did ram the chair into the wall.

"You sonofabitch. You *filmed* the other night. You went behind my back and—"

"No."

The single word, spoken with conviction, stopped her rant. She took a deep breath. Stop overreacting and listen. "What happened then?"

"We hit the switch that night, though I didn't know it at the time. We recorded the whole thing inadvertently."

She dropped back in the chair. "Fuck." Someone could pull photos from the stills, blow up the scars on her stomach into a close-up. Her worst moment, visible for all to see, on her flesh.

If that video got out, she'd be a laughingstock. No one wanted to work with a woman with a leaked sex tape, dammit.

She pointed at Grayson. "I swear to God, if you don't destroy the video right this second, I—"

"It's done, it's gone, it is officially an ex-tape."

"Oh, *c'mon.* You're a guy. You sure as hell watched." Hmm...she might have too. Hell, why not? But she'd have pulverized the tape afterward.

"I don't have it, I didn't watch it, and I didn't tell you because it's destroyed already."

"If you were unaware that we were being recorded, how did you know to look for a tape?"

He took a deep breath. "Tony came in that morning and found it."

She buried her head in her hands. "Your partner has a *sex video* of us?"

She clenched her hands into fists. Dammit, the scars belonged to her, not the world. "Maybe he made copies."

"I trust my partner. He would never lie to me about destroying it, and he would never make copies. Besides, it's not the kind of publicity we need for the firm."

Yeah, that was true.

Grayson stared at the floor. "My word is all I can give you, Patricia. I'm sorry that this embarrasses you."

"I'm not embarrassed. I'm *angry*. You remember how you reacted to my scars? With pity? Now I have to deal with your partner knowing that about me."

"He still likes you. He said you're perfect for me."

"*Seriously?*"

"He said I couldn't steamroll you." Grayson nodded. "Said I needed that."

"Okay, then." That had been easy. He'd solved a problem before it even started. And his partner liked her. Or approved of her. Or something. "So, what did you learn on the phone?"

Grayson relaxed his shoulders at the change in subject.

"It's the confirmation we needed of the family connection. Henry Windergaard changed his name when he immigrated from German. Max Warren didn't. They're not cousins, as it said in the articles we found. They both list the same father, Jurgen, on their birth certificate. Henry Windergaard and Max Warren were brothers."

"Outstanding."

The phone rang again. Grayson answered. She walked close enough to overhear the conversation. It was the newsstand owner. Grayson offered him another twenty to bring the newspaper up to the office.

They both met him at the door. Trisha tossed the *Herald* aside, saw the *New York Post* headline focused on a murder in Queens and the *Daily Tribune...*

She blinked. What was *her* name doing in their paper?

"*NY Herald* Fires Reporter Who Saved Museum" read the *Tribune's* headline. Kimba Sue had the byline.

"Jesus, Mary, and Joseph," she said.

CHAPTER TWENTY-FIVE

"PATRICIA," Grayson said, while she stared, open-mouthed, at the headline.

"Patricia," he said again.

She finally looked at him.

"This is why Sarkozy and the Cardozas ambushed you at dinner. They knew this headline was coming and wanted to report that you still worked at the paper. They wanted to kill this story."

"Oh, hell, you're right." She picked up the *Tribune*. "Kimba—this is her byline—kept badgering me about the rumor that I'd been fired. I wouldn't confirm it. I didn't want to deal with it. Which is why is says I didn't comment when asked about this." Trisha narrowed her eyes. "Kimba must have called Cardoza for comment about this article. That's how he knew."

"And if you'd accepted their offer, they could have called this Kimba back and reported that you had not been fired and be saved the embarrassment of the headline."

"Those sons of a bitches. They wanted me to bail them out." But she grinned. "And I wouldn't. Good for Kimba. Well. I guess this saves me the trouble of telling everyone I've been fired." She scanned the article. "Wonder how...ah, here it is: 'Multiple sources report that Connell was fired after she called in from the hospital following emergency treatment for her injuries and reacted angrily for being berated at having missed a deadline.'"

"'Reacted angrily' is very diplomatic." Grayson applauded this Kimba for the support. Trisha had more allies than she knew.

"But it's very specific," she said. "Only a few people know that." She glared at him. "Did *you* do it?"

"No. I would never have done it without asking you. And I wouldn't have known who to call with the tip, in any case."

The suspicion written all over her face cleared. "That's true. It had to be somebody who knew Kimba would love the tip. David might know but he wouldn't have done it without clearing it with me."

"Dorothy, possibly," Grayson said. "Injustice infuriates her." His old friend had cringed at the comparison to Patricia, but there were similarities. "Especially since she owed you for help in interviewing Warren."

"Really? I wouldn't have thought so, but you know the lieutenant better than me. It couldn't be Adrienne's parents because I didn't tell them my exact words to Cardoza. Joe might have confirmed it, though, as deep background." She sighed. "I hope this doesn't get him in trouble."

"Firing a respected editor after this bad publicity would only draw more bad publicity," he said.

She frowned, wary again. "Are you sure it wasn't you trying to rescue me again?"

He put up his hands. "No."

"Okay." Trisha tucked the paper under her arm and checked her watch. "Fine. It's out there. Nothing I can do now except be glad I told them to shove it last night. But maybe Kimba will help me out when I have the full museum story. Is it time to go there yet?"

She didn't know how to handle having allies. Or positive attention.

"Close to time. Let me just get something and we'll be on our way."

He returned with a Nikon camera around his neck.

"What's that for?" she asked.

"I want to take photos of the area where Conrath was shot yesterday. It might tell me something."

"Can't hurt," she agreed.

But Patricia seemed to deflate during the drive to the museum, reading the story about firing over and over.

"Jesus, fuck, the whole front cover," she blurted out.

"People care about the unfairness of what happened to you."

"People care about a juicy story, and I guess it is. It's just weird, is all, especially since there's a full rundown of what happened in the tunnels. I never reported my role in the fight. If it wasn't you and it wasn't David, then it had to be Dorothy Gilbert."

He glanced at Trisha during a stop at a red light. She'd propped her elbow against the window rest and stared out in the dawn.

"What?" he asked.

"Pondering lots of things."

"Ah."

He gripped the steering wheel tighter, turned right for the final block to the museum, and clamped down on the hope in his heart. He parked in the museum lot and helped her out of the car, a polite gesture that she accepted with good grace. The black leather duster from his employee closet suited her. He wondered if she would keep it if he offered.

She put on her sunglasses as she stepped out of the car.

"Going Hollywood on me?" he asked.

"It's a look, since I'm getting my fifteen minutes of fame. It's punk enough, between the duster, the Converse sneaks, the T-shirt, though the jeans aren't ripped." She twirled. "What do you think?"

"Twirling would go better with a Wonder Woman costume."

She laughed, grabbed the lapels of his coat, and pulled him into a kiss.

He crushed her against him, taking her mouth, hard and fierce. *Yes.* He slipped his fingers under the coat and around her waist. Who cared why she picked now for this or about the coming confrontation with Windergaard? Actions mattered. Patricia in his arms again mattered.

She broke the kiss. "Whoa, nice, Grayson."

He grabbed her hand and pulled her toward the car.

"What are you doing?" she asked, though she let him pull her.

"We're going to my home, and my bed, and with any luck, we won't come up for air for several days."

She threw back her head and laughed, and it was as if notes of joy sounded in his heart.

"Grayson, you could no more miss poking around the museum and this confrontation with Windergaard than I could."

He pulled her close and brushed hair out of her eyes. "Fine. I'm also tempted to throw you across the hood of my car right this second."

She laughed again and he was so caught in that it took him a second to realize that she'd undone his coat and was halfway to unbuckling his belt. He closed his hand over hers and leaned in close to her ear. "Patricia. That van over there has my people in it, monitoring our own set of cameras."

"Frack," she said and buckled the belt back up. He blinked and wondered what she might have done if he hadn't stopped her. *Focus.*

He took her hand and led her to the front entrance. Better to go in that way than the employee entrance where Windergaard might see them first. She rested her head on his shoulder as they walked. He swallowed hard and decided to ask the question.

"Patricia, what changed your mind?"

She straightened as they went up the steps but kept hold of his hand. They climbed the stone steps in silence.

"You listened," she finally said. "You heard."

He leaned over and kissed her cheek. "Thank you."

"Don't get all slobbery now. This could go south in a day. Or an hour. Hell, maybe it's the lack of sleep and the promise of sex that changed my mind." She shook her head. "What about you? Why did you come after me?"

He smiled because it was pure Patricia for her to turn the question back at him. He took a moment before he answered.

"Well," he said. "I'm just in it for the sex."

She laughed once more. "Fair enough."

He put his arm around her shoulder.

They reached the top of the front steps. He glanced over at the pillar where they'd first met. So did she.

They walked through the entrance with his arm around her shoulder. Tony was waiting for them at the circular front desk. His partner raised his eyebrows at the sight of them.

"You're here early," Tony said.

Grayson raised the camera. "Needed to poke around."

"You're not the only one. Windergaard's in the medieval tournament room," Tony said. "I was in the van when he came in, all twitchy and looking over his shoulder. No wonder because Dorothy had a tail on him.

The unmarked cars are parked at both cross streets. He's not running out on her. But he's alone in the museum now."

"Good. We can surprise him, and we'll get some answers." And Grayson outlined the Warren/Windergaard connection.

Tony nodded. "Yeah, our director's hiding something."

"And you've put us in a position to record what he's doing," Patricia focused on Tony. "Have we met?"

Tony nodded. "Not formally. I've seen you around."

She glared. "I just bet you have."

Patricia held Tony's gaze longer than necessary. Tony's ears actually started to turn red. He cleared his throat.

Message received.

"You're taking this one with you to pester Windergaard?" Tony jabbed his thumb at her.

She stuck out her tongue. Tony laughed.

"If she's with me, she can't cause trouble elsewhere," Grayson pointed out.

Patricia snorted. "Like you stay out of trouble without me."

"Be careful," Tony said. "Desperate men can do desperate things."

Grayson tapped his shoulder holster. "I'll be careful."

"Good."

With Patricia a step behind, Grayson walked the quiet hallways to the tournament room on the East side. Her high-tops made little noise on the waxed floors, but the leather duster creaked as she walked. On the day of the murder, when she'd conned him into sneaking inside this place, her motorcycle jacket had creaked in just the same way.

They passed the stairs to the storage closet that led to the tunnels. She glanced over and halted.

"What's wrong?" he whispered.

"I…" She smoothed back her hair. "What if I have another panic attack when you need me? It's not like I can predict them. And it's been a helluva couple of days."

He knew what it must have cost her to make that confession. *Oh, Patricia.* "You won't."

"You're sure?"

She stared at the floor. Once again, she'd opened herself up to him. A gift far more valuable than any pipe.

"There's no one else I'd rather have with me today."

"Okay." She set her jaw and nodded.

"I want to slip into the room and watch him. Surprise him in the middle of something. That should be revealing." He slipped the camera off his neck and gave it to her. "Hold this. It'll interfere if I have to draw my weapon."

"I doubt Windergaard's a threat. It's Conrath who had the gun." Still, she did as he asked.

They padded silently into the wing, using the tournament display as cover. Windergaard seemed lost in a world of his own.

"Idiot cousin," Windergaard muttered. "Ruined everything."

Grayson crouched behind a knight, silently signaling to Patricia to stay with him. Perhaps Windergaard would keep talking and implicate himself. What a relief it must be for him to get this all out. Most people hated keeping their secrets. They wanted to justify their actions.

Windergaard glanced over his shoulder and walked to the plexi-glass display case detailing the tournament. Grayson tensed. Had he seen them?

But no, the museum director pulled out a screwdriver and began taking the display apart.

The missing Cezannes must be in there. A surge of triumph ran through Grayson. Windergaard worked, ever so slowly, in removing the screws. Grayson's knees began to ache from holding the crouched pose. Windergaard slipped the screws into his pocket and began to pry the top off the display case.

Nothing happened. "Stuck. Of course, this would be stuck." Windergaard cursed and pulled out a putty knife. The putty knife cracked and went flying out of his hands, almost at Grayson's feet.

Windergaard turned, headed in their direction. Grayson picked up the putty knife. Behind his back, he motioned for Patricia to remain in hiding.

Grayson stood, the putty knife in his hand. "Lose something?" he said to Windergaard.

———

Trisha wanted to literally tackle the museum director. Get this done. But Grayson wanted a confession, so she stayed hidden.

"You," Windergaard spat out.

"Me," Grayson agreed. "You've lied to me from the start, Director Windergaard. I'm owed an explanation."

"I owe *you* nothing." Windergaard backed away, toward the tapestry, out of Trisha's view. "I owe the museum *everything*."

"And what did you owe your cousin, Stephen Warren? Access to the museum and the paintings?"

"He's an idiot. He's always been one." Windergaard's voice remained shaky. "Stephen absorbed all of his father's stupid prejudices and all his Nazis views, the ones that got his father and my father fired."

"He must have hated it when you took your grandfather's paintings to put them on display at the same museum that caused his father's suicide," Grayson said.

A long pause. "You seem to know everything," Windergaard whispered.

"Not why you'd keep your relationship with Warren secret. Not why you'd let him into the museum that night." Grayson spoke in that calm, cajoling voice, the one that soothed. A little disconcerting, since he'd used it on her.

"Let him? *You think I let him?* He blackmailed me." Windergaard came closer again and punched his chest. "Stephen said he was rightful co-owner of the art, and if I failed to help him steal at least some of the paintings, he'd take the entire story public."

"And that would have churned up the stories about your father being a Nazi again, to say nothing of admitting your grandfather participated into stealing art from victims of the Holocaust."

"I'm not responsible for my grandfather. I *am* responsible for this museum."

"I see," Grayson said. "The *Lost Treasures* exhibit is the key to the museum's success. You couldn't risk Warren going public. You even paid off your security chief to look the other way that night."

"It should have worked out!" Windergaard was practically screaming now, composure gone. "I told Stephen about the tunnels—I knew about the blueprints. I insisted on being there to prevent damage to the exhibit. But then they wanted to burn the paintings. *Burn them!* But I stopped them."

Silence for a while. Grayson was eating rage, Trisha guessed, because she was doing the same thing.

"Someone died," Grayson finally said.

"That wasn't part of the plan! None of the guards were supposed to be making rounds then. Conrath was supposed to give us quiet." Windergaard's voice weakened "But the door was slightly ajar. Katz heard the argument and walked in. Stephen killed her before I could object. *It wasn't my fault!*"

It was, you asshole, Trisha thought, you left the door ajar. He couldn't even admit that, now.

A pause with a lot of heavy breathing.

"But her death wasn't in vain. She gave me the chance to stop them. She punched the failsafe on the alarm. I turned it off but, by then, they knew someone would discover them soon. They left without burning the paintings."

"But they left a bomb." Quiet fury laced Grayson's words.

"I didn't *know* about the bomb," Windergaard said "I did what I could. And I hid the paintings, so they would never get to them again. Unfortunately, I'll have to quietly sell them now. But the money will be invested in the museum." A rustling. "But for that to work, you can't talk."

"Put down the gun, Director Windergaard," Grayson said, his voice flat.

Shit. Trisha poked her head around the corner. Windergaard had his gun pointed directly at Grayson.

"Sidney knew or figured this out as well? That's why he wanted to take some of the paintings last night and to run away from you before you silenced him."

"Sidney overreacted. Did you know he fabricated those threats so the museum would shut down and he could *steal* my paintings?"

"Conrath, ever the loyal guard, shot him for you."

"And you ruined everything, Grayson. You may have defused the bomb, but you've wrecked all this. And you'll never agree to keep it quiet. You'll probably tell that reporter everything." Windergaard said. "I'm sorry, I am, but this has to be that way."

"You didn't kill Katz," Grayson said. "You didn't shoot at Sidney. You're not a killer."

Anyone could be a killer when they were desperate enough, Trisha thought. She crept around the display, looking for something that might cause a distraction, deliberately not thinking about that gun muzzle, so close.

Grayson was counting on her.

Sweat rolled down Trisha's back. Her breathing sped up. The images before her began to blur. *Fuck.* If she fell apart now, when he needed her, she'd never forgive herself. *Focus on him.*

"Some things are worth killing over," Windergaard said.

"If you kill me, you'll go to jail," Grayson said. "Conrath is awake and has already started talking. The secret's out. But you could mitigate the damage, share your story, blame everything on your cousin. That could be a way out, Windergaard."

Heavy breathing from Windergaard. Grayson was getting through to him. At least for now.

Trisha curled her hand around a fake horse's tail for balance, fearing being seen. But the director stayed focused on Grayson.

Trisha yanked the fake spear out of the knight's hand, snapping off the mannequin's arm.

Windergaard turned and fired. Grayson drew his gun. Shards exploded from the knight directly behind Grayson. The display collapsed, smashing Grayson to the floor.

Shit.

Windergaard aimed the gun point blank at Grayson.

Trisha, yelling like a banshee, rushed Windergaard with her makeshift weapon. The camera bounced against her chest. It hit the healing ribs, but she ignored the jolt of pain.

The deranged director spun to face her. He fired again. Trisha flung the spear. The shaft hit him sideways in the stomach, sending him down to one knee. He clutched his belly, but the gun remained tight in his hand. His face twisted in pain and anger. Trisha scrambled for the spear, curled her hand around the shaft, and slammed it down on his shoulder.

The flimsy wood splintered into a million pieces.

Windergaard screamed. Another shot went off. Trisha pulled what remained of the spear hilt up for another blow, but she somehow lost her footing and fell at Windergaard's feet instead.

Fuck. That's what she got for being vain and wearing a coat that tripped her.

Windergaard stood over her. Gun. *Oh, God.* The world wavered again.

"I should have known," he said. "You've never cared about anything but the story. You never gave a damn for this museum."

Gun. At her head. *Again.* Think.

Fuck, panic attacks weren't voluntary. Cope, then. Distract the brain. Focus on the overall situation. Forget the gun. Watch the man. Windergaard hadn't shot her yet. His hand trembled, hesitating. The muzzle of the gun shook. He couldn't look someone in the eye and kill them.

She wasn't the only one close to panic.

Gun muzzle. Her mouth went dry. Images from fifteen years ago scratched at her memory, about to burst forth once more, as they had in the tunnels.

You're so clever. Think of something to say to keep Windergaard talking, like Grayson had.

"I defused the bomb," she said, voice hoarse.

Windergaard blinked. The gun stabilized.

"You—"

"I broke Stephen Warren's nose." She smiled. Good memory. Yes. Focus on the victory.

"Yes, and that was beautiful but—" Windergaard shook his head.

The muzzle of the gun loomed before her, and all distractions failed. It was a snub nose, maybe a .22 caliber. Not what her rapists had used. *Not the same.* It might not kill her. Oh, fuck, maybe she'd be crippled rather than dead.

"My museum meant nothing to you," he said. "You only wanted the story."

"I wanted to clear Adrienne." She gritted her teeth. "You should have saved her!"

She bunched her hand into a fist. Anger, good. *Fight. Move!*

Grayson, brandishing a wooden shield and sword, smashed into Windergaard.

Windergaard shrieked and stumbled. Grayson smashed the flat edge of the sword down on Windergaard's wrist.

Windergaard's gun clattered to the marble floor. Grayson dropped the sword and plowed his fist into Windergaard's nose.

Blood spurted. The museum director screamed and curled into a fetal position on the floor. Grayson grabbed the .22. He made quite a figure, looming over Windergaard with a shield decorated with a Crusader's cross in one hand, a gun in the other.

Well, hell, look at that. A knight in tassel loafers.

Trisha put the camera to her eye, framed the shot, and clicked. *Perfect.*

"Everyone stay still," Dorothy called from the entrance.

As if Trisha planned to move. Her upper arm throbbed worse with each beat of her heart. She had to force air into her lungs to get rid of the spots before her eyes. Stupid panic attack. *Again!* Damn the flimsy spear, the coat, and clumsiness.

The dizziness threatened her again. She repeated "the gun is gone" silently to herself, over and over. The panic attack receded, though she'd fall on her face if she stood up right now. Floor good. Dorothy walked to Grayson and Windergaard, gun drawn, in that walk that cops used when they were approaching a potentially dangerous suspect. Tony, David, and two uniformed officers followed.

It all turned out okay. Dorothy had Windergaard. Grayson wasn't hurt.

Grayson caught Trisha's gaze. She flashed a thumbs up. *Yep, no meltdowns here. I'm totally fine.* He smiled, took two steps toward her, but Dorothy set her hand on his elbow.

"Expecting the Saracen hordes, English?" Dorothy tapped the shield decorated with a red Crusader's cross.

Grayson looked down, as if surprised he still held the shield. He had to be less calm than he looked. No one had that much ice water in their veins.

He smiled. "No one ever expects the Saracen hordes."

CHAPTER TWENTY-SIX

IT HELPED to focus on Grayson, but the panic threatened to overwhelm Trisha again.

She shoved her head between her legs and took several deep breaths, reminding herself that she'd taken action, that she'd bought Grayson the time to disarm Windergaard. She hadn't let him down.

Good. Okay, staring down a gun barrel repeatedly probably wasn't the way a shrink would recommend getting over the panic but, hey, whatever worked. Maybe familiarity bred contempt, not fear.

And she could still work. Writing this would complete the calm. She needed a newsroom. She needed to call Kimba, offer to share the byline, bully the *Tribune* into paying a freelance rate for her work. What a terrific follow-up this would be to Kimba's story today. And, this time, Adrienne Katz would be at the center.

And Grayson.

Pain stabbed into Trisha's right arm, above the elbow. Argh. You'd think she could get through this story without being hurt again. But, no, she'd been clumsy enough to catch a splinter from that flimsy spear.

Trisha glanced over at the police and, unfortunately, Dorothy finally seemed to focus on her. Trisha contemplated sneaking out of the room, grabbing pencil and paper, and writing the story. But she was still, weirdly, lightheaded. *Fuck panic and post-traumatic stress.*

Grayson and David walked over and knelt in front of her.

"Told you, boss." David shook his head at her.

"What? That I'm trouble?" Trisha asked.

"That you'd walk through hell for people, but even I didn't think you were crazy enough to attack an armed man with a fake spear."

"It was all I had handy at the time." She smiled at Grayson. Hell, she bet it was a stupid, silly grin.

"Gah, you two are making me sick," David said. "I'll let Dorothy know we have footage of all this. Should save her any need for a confession. And hope Tony doesn't break his arm patting himself on the back for hiding these cameras from Windergaard."

"Well," Grayson said as David walked away.

"Guess this is all wrapped up," she said.

"It seems so." He knelt in front of her and brushed the hair out of her eyes.

An ambulance crew arrived on scene and loaded Windergaard onto a stretcher. He moaned and continued to cover his nose.

Good, you sonofabitch.

"Let me help you up." Grayson offered a hand to her.

Trisha almost refused the hand, worried she'd collapse against him. That would be embarrassing with all the cops here. Never mind the endless teasing she'd get from David.

She reached out to clasp Grayson's hand, and pain jolted the length of her arm.

"Crap." She let her arm fall limp against her side.

Grayson grabbed her wrist. "Patricia." He said her name with a low growl.

"What are you so angry about?"

"You lied when you gave me the thumbs up."

"I told the truth," she snapped. "It's nothing. One of those splinters from the spear dug into my arm during the fight. That's all."

"It's not nothing." Grayson held up her hand. Blood dripped down her arm and over her knuckles.

What the hell? "Why am I bleeding?"

"You've been shot."

"Shot?"

Grayson held her hand up to stop the blood flow. "Keep your head down. Breathe deep." and, in a lower voice, he added. "Are you okay?"

Translation: are you about to have another panic attack?

"Shouldn't being shot hurt more?"

"Not necessarily, at least not until the adrenaline wears off."

"Good to know." She focused on the pain. Used it as her anchor. *No, dummy, use Grayson as the anchor.* She rested her head against his chest. Mm...he smelled good. A little bit of a fresh after-shave. Even a little sweaty.

Shot?

Grayson waved at the ambulance crew. "Help. Now."

He didn't yell but his voice cut through the conversation in the room just the same. David followed them over.

Grayson touched the ripped sleeve of the leather duster.

She shifted her arm to get a better look at the rip, and what had been a dull ache roared into intense pain that had her dropping her head between her knees again to stave off the spots in front of her eyes that signaled the beginning of a faint.

That *burned.*

Hey, good news. Not a panic attack. Plain, old-fashioned agony.

Grayson stroked her shoulder. "Easy, Patricia."

I won't cry.

David and the EMT knelt on her right side.

"What is it?" David asked.

"GSW, I think," Grayson said in a low tone.

GSW. Gunshot wound. Hearing it put that way made it sound real. *Fuck.*

The EMT—a short, thin woman—took Trisha's elbow in a tight grip and peered at her upper arm.

"Yep, GSW. I'm going to slide the coat off to get a closer look," the EMT said. "It's gonna hurt, ma'am."

"Yeah, whatever, do what you need to do." She shrugged her good, left arm out of its sleeve. The EMT pulled the other sleeve off.

Trisha hissed.

Grayson held her, and she didn't give a damn if anyone saw her needing support this time, not even David, who kept hovering. She peered at the exposed injury. The blood started just below the sleeve of her T-shirt and streamed down past her elbow to her hand. The mess covered the original entry wound.

"This is why you were clumsy," Grayson said. "You were hit." He stroked her hair.

"A through-and-through," the EMT declared.

"So it's no big deal then?" Trisha blinked and straightened her back. "Patch it up so I can get to work."

"No," Grayson said.

"You need transport to the ER," the EMT said. "A GSW must be looked at right away."

"Bandage it up." *I have work to do.* "I'll hit my doctor later."

"No." Grayson and David said simultaneously.

"You're outvoted," the EMT said. "Let me stem the bleeding before we go."

The EMT grabbed her kit from where Windergaard had been and returned.

Well, fuck.

"You go to great lengths to ruin my coats." Grayson fingered the hole in the right sleeve of the discarded leather duster.

Trisha smiled. "I really liked this one too."

The EMT wrapped the wound. Trisha stifled a few moans. Grayson and David helped her stand after she'd been bandaged.

No getting out of this hospital visit. Dammit. "David, could you call Kimba at the *Tribune*? Tell her I've got her follow-up story. Tell her I can come to her office in a couple of hours. Tell her I want a double byline." She ducked her head and pulled off the camera. "Tell her I've got photos."

David smiled. "Kimba? That's the blonde with all those tight dresses? Sure."

Trisha rolled her eyes. "That blonde will eat you alive."

"Perfect," David said. "Consider it done."

He left at a jog to find a phone. Trisha sighed. Okay, she'd bought time to get treated. In the meantime, she could work. "And I need a notebook and a pencil."

"I have a notepad and a pen in my inside breast pocket," Grayson said.

"Awesome."

Dorothy finally strolled over.

"Hey, Lieutenant, got any updates for me?" Trisha asked.

"You ask that *now*?" Dorothy shook her head. "The good news: Sidney's conscious. He started talking."

"Sidney's conscious? Cool. What'd he say?"

"Get to the ER, and maybe I'll tell you later," Dorothy said.

Trisha flipped her off.

Dorothy grinned. "That won't change my mind. Call me when you're patched up."

Trisha walked with one arm around the EMT to the stretcher that had somehow appeared. Grayson placed a notepad and pencil into her had.

He knew her well.

———

It was hours before Trisha left the ER. She'd managed to reach Kimba, had given a verbal report, and had written down the longer story on Grayson's notebook. Next stop, *the Tribune's* office to type up her rough draft.

The lead would be about how Adrienne Katz, because she'd been conscientious, had interrupted the thieves, set off an alarm (even if temporarily) that had alerted Grayson, and that the early arrival of Grayson and the police had saved the museum and the people inside it from being destroyed.

Adrienne had been a hero, when all those in authority around her had failed or been corrupted. It should have felt great to clear the kid. Except it didn't bring Adrienne back to life. If she'd been one of the Slits "Typical Girls," Adrienne would still be alive.

And I'd be dead, Trisha thought.

As Trisha walked into the waiting area, Grayson grabbed the yellow sheet of treatment instructions from her before she could object.

"Hey!"

"I'd rather trust what this says about your injury than whatever you say," he said.

"Gunshot wound, stitches, antibiotics and painkillers prescribed, gotta go fill those, blah, blah," she said. "Gotta figure out if my insurance coverage is still valid to do that, though."

She headed for the doors, eager to get away from the hospital smells. He followed. Once outside, she took a deep breath. Exhaust fumes hung in the moist air. The scent of peppers and onions wafted from a vendor across the street. *Her city.*

She sat on a metal bench just outside the hospital entrance, needing a second.

"Can you give me a ride to the *Tribune*? I need type up what I have and proof what Kimba's written."

Grayson nodded. "Of course." He smiled. "But no interviews."

"Hah," she said. "You're right, Kimba would pounce on you. Anyway, I don't need interviews. I've got that photo they're developing."

He sighed. "I should've stopped David from delivering the camera and film."

"Accept your heroism." She smiled.

"If you accept yours. You saved my life today. Again."

She took a deep breath again. *My brain hurts. So tired.* Maybe once she sat down to proof the typed story, the adrenaline rush would come back.

Maybe it was the getting shot thing. She'd been beaten, sliced, stabbed, whipped, and even bitten. But this was the first time she'd taken a bullet. The arm throbbed still. It'd probably kill her tomorrow when the local anesthetic wore off.

Clearing Adrienne was worth it. It just didn't seem like enough. Nothing would ever be enough.

"Pete Hamill says that if you circle around a murder long enough, you get to know a city." Trisha sighed. "Look at Adrienne. Her story is the story of a foster kid. She got out, made good for herself, wanted to give back. Then she's back in the city, doing a job, and it gets her murdered. That's New York for you."

"I won't forget what she did. And with your story, neither will anyone else, especially her family."

"Small consolation for a gravestone. It's unfair."

"Yes. Justice sometimes isn't enough." A pause. "We need to talk, Patricia."

"Grayson, we've *never* needed to talk. We do other things so much better."

He put his hand on her knee. She rested her head on his shoulder, a lump in her throat. *Feels so good.*

"Are we okay now?" he said.

"We work well together, and I basically want to jump your bones anytime we're alone, which is fun for me and probably for you. But we're also kinda a mess."

"Does the age difference bother you?" he said.

"What?"

"You're only thirty. I'm the other side of forty. Is that a problem?"

She grinned. "You're hardly ready to sign up for retirement. And if you're having a mid-life crisis, I'm happy to oblige."

"All right," he said. "It's not a mid-life crisis. Call it my second chance."

They sat for a little longer in silence. People on the street passed by. Horns honked. Awnings flapped in the breeze. The sky turned gray, threatening rain. She kept her head on his shoulder. He slipped an arm around her.

"I know there are things you don't want to tell me about your past," he said.

Here we go. She leaned forward with her good elbow on her knee. "Can you live with that? Think about it before you answer."

She'd had a chance to escape her rapists, gone back and murdered them instead, and been in juvie for it. Her record was wiped clean at eighteen. But the memory remained. She felt guilty that she didn't feel guilty. She'd kill them again. Probably.

"I would hope that you would feel comfortable enough to tell me everything, at some point," he said.

"The present matters, not the past," she said.

"Ah," he said. "Then I'll take the present."

"This won't be easy, you know. If you want easy, you should date someone more your style. Maybe a cop."

"I dated a friend of Dorothy's for a while."

Now that was interesting. "And?"

"I broke up with her in a failed attempt to reconcile with Amanda."

"That sucks. How long ago?"

"Almost four years," he said. "I haven't dated since then."

"That's taking a breakup a little harsh, don't you think?" Damn. She'd done the opposite after Nicky died. Wham, bam, boom, when the mood hit. It helped in the moment. Sometimes.

She left her hand on Grayson's knee. Four years. He'd shut down for nearly *four* years. And then he'd gone after her. And caught chaos.

"Patricia, you said you didn't need rescuing."

"I amend that. It seems that I do need rescuing from crazed museum directors." She shook her head. "But not otherwise, no. I choose my life, as messed up at it is. No rescuing required."

"You don't need rescuing," Grayson said. "But *I* do."

Sound disappeared. The world closed in, until it was just her and Grayson, frozen in time on the dirty bench in front of the hospital while the world swirled around them. Something twisted in her gut. She turned to face him. Now that she allowed herself to study him, she could see the stubble on his face and the tiredness signaled by the dark circles under his eyes.

No, not tired. *Sad.*

She took her hand off his knee and raised it to his face. She rubbed his chin stubble with her thumb. Oh, hell. She wanted to kiss it and make it all better for him. She wanted to see him smile and hear one of his dry jokes again.

And, God, she wanted him, wanted him in the same way she'd wanted Nicky.

She let her hand rest on Grayson's cheek.

Her breath caught, everything inside jumbled and messed up. Heat rushed to her face. She suspected if she tried to stand, she might collapse at Grayson's feet.

He cupped her face with his hands. *Oh, God.*

She leaned in and kissed him.

The city disappeared again. She felt his lips against hers and his stubble against her cheek. All she heard was the beating of her own heart. Desire, yes, but comfort mixed in this time, too.

She laid her forehead against Grayson's chest. He wrapped his arms around her.

"So." She cleared her throat. "How about that breakfast you promised to cook for me after I'm done at the *Tribune*?"

––––––––

Trisha woke to the feel of soft cotton sheets against her body, the smell of waffles and the sweet scent of hazelnut coffee in the air. Only the sharp ache in her arm brought her back to reality.

She'd woken up in Grayson's bed. She'd gone home with him after polishing the story, then gone to bed with him, then finally slept with his arms around her. Sleeping with someone's arms around her was something she hadn't done since Nicky died. Gah. She'd have to turn in her punk card.

Or maybe she could drag Grayson to a club. He'd look good in a black leather jacket and jeans.

A piercing whistle cut through her brain. She opened her eyes. He had that silly pipe.

"Stop already! I surrender."

He smiled. "I accept."

He sat next to her. His fingers stroked her bare back, a light, teasing touch that traveled from her shoulder all the way down to her ass. She forgot about the pain in her arm.

"Breakfast is ready," Grayson said.

She rolled over. He wore a black T-shirt with an FBI logo and blue sweatpants. His hair was messy, for a change. "You are so fucking sexy it kills me."

His eyes widened, then he smiled. "Thank you."

"Don't sound so damned smug about it."

"Too late. I can't help it. The most beautiful and exciting woman in the world is in my bed."

"'In the world' is a bit much, don't you think?"

"In the city, then," he said.

"That'll do."

She closed her eyes and wondered how long it would take to get used to this...joy? In his eyes, she wasn't a victim or a murderer. To him, she was a hero.

Grayson pushed several strands of hair off her face. "If you'd rather stay in bed, I'll pour maple syrup over you and have my own version of breakfast."

"Too sticky. Probably wouldn't do the bullet wound any good, either." She sat up. "You're smug now, but I give our thing a month before it implodes."

"A month?" Grayson repeated. "I'll mark that on my calendar. Would that be a month of twenty-eight, twenty-nine, thirty, or thirty-one days?"

She hit him with a pillow. "Grayson, you're an arrogant pain in the ass."

"I know." He pulled her close. "By the way, you could call me by my first name, Patricia. We are fairly well-acquainted now."

She traced kisses from his neck to his shoulder. "Edmund. That's so formal. Could I call you Ed instead?"

"No," he snapped.

"What about Eddie?" she teased. "Like Eddie Munster?"

"You call me that, you're not getting waffles," he said.

"I'm running out of names, then. Let's see, Ned was Nancy Drew's boyfriend. Hmmm...still not right." She studied his face. How many people ever saw him this relaxed? He was such a teddy bear underneath all that dignity.

Perfect.

"I've got it. Ted. No, wait. Teddy. What do you think?"

He brushed her cheek with his fingers. "Teddy? Like a teddy bear?"

She nodded, biting the grin trying to escape.

"I can live with that, Patricia. I can live with that for a very long time."

She kissed Teddy to seal the deal.

———

Thank you for reading! Did you enjoy? Please add your review because nothing helps an author more and encourages readers to take a chance on a book than a review.

And don't miss the next book of the *Trisha & Grayson Mysteries*, BURYING THE LEDE, available now!

Also be sure to sign up for the City Owl Press newsletter to receive notice of all book releases!

SNEAK PEEK OF BURYING THE LEDE

The angelic topper on the Christmas tree leaned precariously to the right, a festive disaster waiting to happen. Great, a dead-on metaphor for her relationship with Grayson.

Trisha Connell stepped back, hands on her hips, to survey the tree in full. Boxes of tinsel, lights, icicles, and a few cheap ornaments sat nearby, waiting to be used. She'd wanted to have it fully decorated as a surprise but now? Not a chance, she decided, and removed the angel, leaving the branches bare again. They could decorate it together. That was supposed to be romantic, so everyone said. Her experiences included a ton of shit, but holiday decorating wasn't on that list.

Tree. Romance. Christmas, blah, blah, blah. Ho, ho, ho!

She retreated to the kitchen and dumped a week's worth of her letters and magazines for sorting on the marble countertop of Grayson's fancy kitchen island.

She flipped through the mail, ignoring the ads, flyers, and magazines, seeking the check that would pay next month's rent. She discovered a Christmas card from Joe, her former editor. There was another from Kimba Sue. How did the woman find the time when buried in her new job as the *Herald*'s crime reporter? Perhaps Trisha should reciprocate. Get into the Christmas spirit, whatever that meant. Maybe she'd purchase a red or green leather jacket to wear instead of her black one.

A postcard caught between junk mail slipped out and floated to the floor. She grabbed it in mid-air.

From Florida.

Grayson.

A sailboat decorated the front. She turned it over. Stamped November 28, 1984. The same day he'd left.

Been sailing & thinking of you. See you soon, Patricia.

Aww…

Oh, damn, now he had her being all mushy. Next, he'd be sending her flowers and chocolates for Valentine's Day, and *she'd like it*. Fuck. Anyway, if he missed her that much, maybe he should have invited her to Florida. No, never mind. Had she really wanted to be cooped up on a family vacation where his ex was also invited?

She finally found the check from that history magazine. As hoped, it was big enough to pay rent. Enclosed with the check was a request from the editor to pitch her again. Who knew a history magazine would pay so well for a feature on the elevated steps in the Bronx?

Finally, all that remained was a single white envelope with no return address. Uh-oh. Another one of *those*. She dug out the other letters from the depths of the backpack. The typewriter font on the new one matched. No return address, but they were stamped by the same post office in Upper Manhattan.

Trisha set the new one aside and tapped her fingers on the marble counter, deciding what to do now. The first three letters had been full of Bible quotes about vengeance. A cut above her usual hate mail yet oddly unsettling. What Biblical call for punishment had the asshole sent this time? She probably should just toss them all and forget about it.

Except she was pissed and wanted to find the person responsible. That meant opening the envelope and hoping to find a clue about the sender.

She slit the flap with her finger.

Hell!

Sudden pain sliced through her hand. Blood poured out of her fingertip and pooled into her palm. Dark red drops splattered onto the envelopes of the Christmas cards and oozed onto Grayson's marble counter. She seized her wrist, raised it over her head, and fumbled for the sink. What the heck had just happened?

She spotted the answer: a blood-covered razor blade peeked out from the half-opened envelope. *Motherfucker.*

Blood dripped from her palm into the stainless steel sink. *Fuck.* She needed to wrap it, but bandages had to be in the bathroom, and she'd be damned if she dripped blood over the expensive carpet between the kitchen and the bathroom.

She closed her eyes, swallowed hard, and counted to ten to avoid thinking about the last time she'd been cut with razor blades. She still carried those scars.

Trisha shoved her injured hand under the water and fumbled for a dish towel. She wrapped the towel tight around it, ignored her dizzy head, and scooted for the bathroom. Once there, she washed the cut in the bathroom sink, poured half a bottle of hydrogen peroxide over it, and wrapped it with a washcloth.

A deep slice, enough for stitches. This was more than just threats now, it was action. That probably meant a police report, if only to create a paper trail if things got worse. Could take hours. Fuck.

———

Trisha called the local precinct from a pay phone in the ER's waiting room. The desk sergeant took her name and said someone would get back to her. She provided her number and Grayson's and told him she'd be at Mercy's ER for the next couple of hours, in the unlikely chance anyone wanted to take her statement there. Fat chance with such a minor injury, especially on a holiday weekend.

Thankfully, it only took an hour to be seen and stitched up. She gingerly slipped her jacket back on over the bandage on the finger. She could run by the precinct in person and have the report filed before Grayson came home tomorrow.

But when Trisha walked back in the ER waiting room, Lieutenant Dorothy Gilbert and Detective Harold Newman of the NYPD's major crimes unit were waiting for her.

"Connell. Heard you had a problem," Dorothy said.

Grayson and Dorothy were friends. Trisha might buy the lieutenant checking up on her because of that. But her partner Newman too? The guy actively disliked her.

"Damn, Lieutenant, how does my sliced finger rate a visit from *two* major crimes detectives?"

Dorothy drew out a notebook. "Do you want to tell me what happened or not?"

Newman simply glared.

"Fine. Be mysterious." Trisha flopped into the hard, featureless chair opposite Dorothy, squinting from the bright overhead lights that were feeding a developing headache. "We doing this here?"

"Unless you'd rather go to the precinct?" Newman suggested.

"No." Trisha grimaced at the idea of being surrounded by so many cops. "Where do you want me to start?"

"I understand you received a letter with a razor blade?" Dorothy asked.

Troubled, Trisha provided a quick and dirty rundown of the injury. She handed over a sealed plastic bag that contained the envelope and the blade, complete with blood splatter.

"Thorough," Dorothy said.

"Almost too thorough," Newman added.

"I know enough about crime scenes to follow procedure," Trisha said.

"You've never followed rules or procedure in my experience," Newman said.

"Look, detective, you want to know what happened or you want to snipe at me?" she asked.

"Tough choice," he said. "More fun to do both."

She'd gotten off on the wrong foot with Newman years ago, on one of her first stories. She'd noticed his mistake. She could have gone to him directly, given him a chance to correct it. But she'd published it instead because he was an ass, an old-school NYPD cop who didn't like being challenged. Newman had never let her forget it.

Now, he stared at her with unveiled hostility. His barrel-chested body, six-foot height, and nasty stare tended to intimidate people. But she was used to him.

"Did you come for a statement or to harass me?" Trisha replied with a sigh.

"Statement," Dorothy said, elbowing her partner, gently. "What happened after you were cut?"

Trisha described the mess and the cab ride to the ER. "I'd have left the whole thing intact in the kitchen, but I figured this would hardly be a crime scene that would rate a visit. It's a minor injury, after all. What are you two doing here again?"

"Working a case," Dorothy answered. "Was this the first letter you've received?"

Trisha narrowed her eyes. "Sounds like you asked that question because you already know the answer."

"Until you answer my questions, I won't know anything," Dorothy said.

Trisha smelled a story, a bigger one than her simple cut. Dorothy, like all major crimes detectives, was overworked, and while Newman was an ass, he didn't waste his time.

"Easier to show you than tell you." Trisha handed over the brown paper bag stuffed with the other letters. "I tossed them together before going to the hospital. Evidence."

Dorothy opened the bag and raised an eyebrow at their crumpled condition. "You saved the earlier ones. Why?"

Trisha shrugged. "The Bible quotes struck me as odd. Usually, my hate mail runs the gamut of 'fuck you' to 'all women are cunts,' to death threats and bravado about kicking my ass."

"You knew you had something unusual and waited to call it in?" Dorothy asked.

"Because there was *nothing* to call in." She pointed at the mail. "Just letters and, like I said, I get hate mail a lot. I tried to bother the cops with it once, back in the day. Got brushed off."

"I bet." Newman narrowed his eyes.

A patient on crutches maneuvered past them. They were in a corner of the ER waiting room, but Trisha wondered if anyone was trying to eavesdrop. Paranoid. She was becoming paranoid.

Dorothy cleared her throat. "We'll send the letters to be dusted for fingerprints, but tell me your thoughts on them, Trisha, since you obviously have some."

Trisha brought her attention back to the detectives but decided to keep track of the man in the suit slumped and slurring over near the nurse's station.

"The letters are Bible passages concerning vengeance, but they're typed, not handwritten. From that, I infer the sender is worried about being caught by someone recognizing their handwriting. And, of course, they know their Bible, or they have one handy to consult. But they also have a grudge they consider personal against me."

"Can't imagine why," Newman said.

"The list of people with grudges against me is a phone book, for sure," Trisha agreed. "But what set the sender off doesn't have to be something I actually did. I've found I get slammed for stuff people think I did or might do."

Dorothy wrote that down in her notes. "Excellent distinction. Yes, it could well be someone with a one-way obsession."

"Ex-boyfriend?" Newman asked.

Trisha snorted. "Not one who'd quote the Bible."

"Ex-girlfriend?" Dorothy asked.

Trisha raised an eyebrow. Dorothy didn't miss much. She could refuse to answer in front of Newman but, hell, Trisha wasn't ashamed.

"There are some women but, again, nobody who'd quote the Bible at me and no relationship of any duration, anyway." She focused on Newman. "I'm very wham-bam-thank-you-ma'am."

Newman flushed. Good, she'd embarrassed him. Petty, but she'd take what little bit of fun she could at his expense.

"I was very short term with, um, people, until Grayson," Trisha added, glancing at Dorothy. "I assume he's not a suspect."

"No, not *him*," Newman drawled.

Now what did that mean?

Dorothy dropped the letters into her overstuffed purse. "Since I'd rather not open the letters and add more fingerprints to them before they're dusted, tell me about them. Do you remember where the Bible quotes were from?"

"The first letter said: 'Say to them that are of a fearful heart, Be strong, fear not: behold, your God will come with vengeance, even God with a recompence; he will come and save you.'" Well, God had certainly not come to save her. "Isiah, though I forget the passage number."

"You memorized that from a letter?" Newman frowned, as if she'd done something wrong. "That's handy."

Again, that weird undertone.

"Nah, I knew the passage already." She pulled out the Celtic cross she wore under her shirt. "Catholic upbringing, though obviously, the letter writer likes the King James version, not the new revised version that most Catholics use."

"Oh, that's bullshit, Trisha," Dorothy drawled. "I know the Bible, and I'd be hard-pressed to quote that passage from memory."

"All right, fine." Trisha held up a hand in surrender. "I went over the letters a few times, looking for clues. Even looked up the quotes."

"Knew it," Newman snapped.

"Knew what?" she asked.

"Enough, partner," Dorothy said. She'd written the quote in her notebook. All business, of course. Hell, Dorothy usually was. Look at how she'd worn one of her impeccable gray blazers to an ER visit on the weekend. "Let's go on to the second letter."

"'But, O Lord of hosts, that judgest righteously, that triest the reins and the heart, let me see thy vengeance on them: for unto thee have I revealed my cause.'" Trisha shook her head. "That passage calls for God to avenge in a more violent way, but then that's Deuteronomy 32, and the Old Testament is full of 'God will avenge' stuff."

"It certainly is." Dorothy turned to Newman. "Give us a minute. Go get the woman a soda, partner."

The big detective grumbled but rose.

"A Coke, Newman," Trisha said, smiling to bug him. "It's the real thing."

Newman ignored the jibe and strode to the soda machine in the corner.

"You like antagonizing him," Dorothy said. "Stop it."

"Life's full of little pleasures. And he's trying to antagonize *me*."

"It would be easier if you'd stay on his good side."

"What's the fun in that? Why?" Trisha asked.

"You trust me? Then take my advice on this one."

Newman returned and held out the Coke can at arm's length. Instead of drinking it, Trisha held the bottle against her forehead to cool the growing headache.

Dorothy grunted. Newman loomed over her. Trisha ignored him but wondered why it was so important to stay on his good side.

"The last letter, the booby-trapped one, contained a passage everyone knows: 'Vengeance is mine; I will repay, saith the Lord,'" Trisha said. "I saw that through the blood splatter. And I knew it all already."

"Romans," Dorothy muttered.

"Yeah, Romans 12:19. I hate it when people quote the short version because they miss the point. The full quote is 'Dearly beloved, avenge not yourselves, but rather give place unto wrath: for it is written, Vengeance is mine; I will repay, saith the Lord.' It's not about you getting revenge, it's about you leaving it up to God." At least, that's what she'd learned in Catechism.

"Maybe you should teach Sunday school," Dorothy said.

Trisha almost dropped the Coke as she choked out a laugh. "Yeah, me at catechism: do as I say and not as I do. That'll go over well." She finally opened the soda and chugged half of it. "Anyway, I'm an ass for opening the last with my finger instead of a letter opener."

"Not the only reason you're an ass," Newman said.

"Christ, Newman," Dorothy said. "You're not helping."

"Hey, it was too good an opening," he replied.

"Gotta give you that." Trisha finished the Coke, pleased as the cool liquid soothed her dry throat.

"You should have reported this after the second letter," Dorothy said. "You knew they were odd and you kept them. What bothered you specifically?"

She had a better glare than Newman. Hell, a better glare than any severe Catholic nun.

"The Bible stuff came from a fanatic. That bugged me, okay?"

"You're saying your instincts perceived a threat?" Dorothy asked.

"My instincts said something was off. So I kept 'em."

"So noted," Dorothy put away her notebook. "Anything else?"

"That's all I got. What about you? What are you doing here? What's the connection of these letters to Major Crimes cases?"

"Wouldn't you like to know?" Newman growled. "Just sit tight. We may need to talk to you soon."

"Now is good," Trisha said.

"None of your business. Yet." Newman shook his finger at her.

"Enough, partner." Dorothy brushed the finger aside. "I'll let you know what I find out, Trisha."

Trisha mirrored her. "Lieutenant, what do you know about this that I don't?"

Dorothy made a show of putting her coat on. "Do you believe *I* have good instincts?"

"You wouldn't be the cop you are without them," Trisha said.

"Then trust me," Dorothy said again. "When I'm certain what I'm dealing with, you'll be the first to know."

"Gee whiz, thanks, Lieutenant," Trisha snapped. "And it's not *you* that I don't trust." She pointed at Newman.

"Trust the truth," Dorothy said, loud enough for the other residents of the waiting room to finally stare at them.

"Meet me outside, Newman," Dorothy said.

A curt nod. "All right," Newman said.

After he left, Dorothy pulled Trisha aside.

"Look, there's a connection between your letter and another crime. It also included a hidden razor blade in a letter. It's possible your case is related, but it's a longshot. You know what police work is like."

Trisha took a deep breath. "Right. A matter of crossing off what's not related to leave what's relevant to the crime. Lots of tedious paperwork and reports."

"Exactly. In the meantime, do something for me."

Trisha zipped up her coat. "What? Be careful?"

"No, you'll never do that. But stay alert and stay on the straight and narrow. This is already a sensitive case."

"Maybe I'd be more alert if I knew what the other case you're working on is…" Trisha prodded.

"Can't comment," Dorothy said. "If it relates to your case, then we'll be in touch." Dorothy picked up her oversize purse. "Tell Edmund about this. He's got the resources to protect you, just in case."

I can protect myself, Trisha wanted to say, but given she was in the ER with stitches, she let it go.

As Dorothy left the ER, for the first time, fear replaced Trisha's anger. Whatever case Newman and Dorothy were working, it had to be serious. Perhaps even murder.

Just how afraid should she be?

* * *

Don't stop now. Keep reading with your copy of BURYING THE LEDE

Don't miss the next book of the *Trisha & Grayson Mysteries*, BURYING THE LEDE, available now, and find more from Corrina Lawson at www.corrina-lawson.com

———

A deadly secret. A relentless killer. Can she survive the truth?

Trisha Connell has it all: a successful freelance career as an award-winning crime reporter, a promising relationship with Edmund Grayson, a former FBI agent turned security expert, and a life she's fought hard to build. But behind her perfect facade, Trisha is hiding a dark secret—one that could destroy everything she's worked for.

Years ago, Trisha made a devastating mistake, and now that haunting past is threatening to shatter her present. When a relentless and twisted serial killer targets her, determined to make her pay, Trisha's carefully constructed world starts to unravel.

As the stakes rise, Trisha faces a terrifying choice: expose the truth and risk losing her career, her love life, and everything she holds dear—or keep the secret buried and risk becoming the killer's next victim. The closer the killer gets, the more Trisha's worst fears come to life. Time is running out, and the line between past and present is blurring.

In a race against time, Trisha must confront her darkest secrets and outsmart a merciless killer before she becomes his final victim. Can she survive long enough to unmask the killer and protect the life she's built, or will the truth destroy her?

———

Please sign up for the City Owl Press newsletter for chances to win special subscriber-only contests and giveaways as well as receiving information on upcoming releases and special excerpts.

All reviews are **welcome** and **appreciated**. Please consider leaving one on your favorite social media and book buying sites.

For books in the world of romance and speculative fiction that embody Innovation, Creativity, and Affordability, check out City Owl Press at www.cityowlpress.com.

ACKNOWLEDGMENTS

Trisha and Grayson were the first characters I created as an adult. Those first attempts at writing showed me how much I had to learn. My teacher, Jennifer Cruise, told me: "You have a fabulous main character but you have no plot." She then proceeded to teach me how to plot and has my undying gratitude for her kindness and writing wisdom Jenny and all the Cherries saw the birth of this book, almost two decades ago, before it was ready, and gave me nothing but encouragement despite its' raw form.

I have so many to thank. I could not have kept writing with my friends Katy and Chris or without the encouragement of Robin. I owe so much to my critique partners: Christine, Liz, Liv, Rebekah, and Beth. I have so many wonderful communities of support: the Cherries, my comic/super-hero people formerly of YABS, and Karen and the GeekMoms.

My husband bought me a desk and my first MacBook Pro. My eldest daughter, Erin, read one of the earlier versions of this story and proceeded then to create fanfic from it. My oldest son, Joe, helped me with submissions and copy edits. My younger son, Kyle, was a second eye on the copy edits and proclaimed "wow, Mom, this is really good." My youngest daughter, Cassandra, gave me the high compliment of saying she wants to be a writer too.

And I would be nowhere without my mom, who always told me I could do anything I set out to do.

Look everyone! It's a book!

ABOUT THE AUTHOR

 CORRINA LAWSON is an award-winning reporter, pop culture blogger, and the author of steampunk mysteries, paranormal and fantasy romance, and erotic romance. (And now, her first mystery!) She lives in rural New England next to a hiking preserve and occasionally bears wander through her yard. She can often be found walking the neighborhood with her young adult twins, chatting about pop culture. She lives with her twins, her husband, the dog, and four cats, including Buster, Lord Floofy Tail.

She is a certified superhero geek and loves attending comic book conventions, especially in New York City and Comic Con in San Diego. And, yes, Lois Lane originally inspired her to become a reporter.

www.corrina-lawson.com

 x.com/CorrinaLawson
 instagram.com/corrinalawson
 facebook.com/corrinalawsonwriter

ABOUT THE PUBLISHER

City Owl Press is a cutting edge indie publishing company, bringing the world of romance and speculative fiction to discerning readers.

Escape Your World. Get Lost in Ours!

www.cityowlpress.com